THE
BLUE
WOODS

THE BLUE WOODS

book 3 of the twin willows trilogy

NICOLE MAGGI

MEDALLION

Medallion Press, Inc.
Printed in USA

DEDICATION

For the teenage me, who needed books like this to
escape into
and
For Irene, without whose support and perseverance
this series would not exist

Published 2016 by Medallion Press, Inc.,
4222 Meridian Pkwy, Suite 110, Aurora, IL 60504

The MEDALLION PRESS LOGO
is a registered trademark of Medallion Press, Inc.

Copyright © 2016 by Nicole Maggi
Cover design by Michal Wlos and James Tampa

Cataloging-in-Publication Data is on file with the Library of Congress

Typeset in Adobe Garamond Pro
Printed in the United States of America
ISBN # 9781605426235

10 9 8 7 6 5 4 3 2 1
First Edition

ACKNOWLEDGMENTS

It has been a long and winding road to the end of this trilogy, and there were many people along the way who lent support, love, encouragement, chocolate, and wine.

To my agent, Irene Goodman, to whom this book is also deservedly dedicated, for her tireless championing of this trilogy and my writing as a whole. Without you I'd be scrawling words on a wall in crayon and chewing my hair.

To my editor, Emily Steele, for her kindness, compassion, and thoughtfulness throughout the four years we've been working together. Whenever I hit a wall, you were there to help me see the doorway.

To the entire Medallion team for nurturing and supporting all three books, especially Brigitte Shepard, Paul Ohlson, and Heather Musick. To Jim Tampa and Michal Wlos for the beautiful covers and design.

To the Los Angeles writing community for cheering me on and holding me up when I wanted to lie down. Special thanks to Mary McCoy for championing my books through the Los Angeles Public Library system, in addition to your wonderful friendship. To Tracy Holczer for your love and constant willingness to drink with me (tater tots and cocktails at the Griffin next week, okay?). To the Los Angeles contingents of the OneFours, Fifteeners, Lucky 13s and Apocalypsies for showing up at all the launch parties and for all the fun we have after the bookstores close . . . I don't know what I would do without you all.

To the Scribblers: we may not meet every other week anymore, but our critique group lives forever. To Anne Van and Will Frank for your invaluable contribution to this trilogy's early days. To Lizzie Andrews for your eternal support, for our weekday writing dates in search of not just inspiration but also great hot chocolate, and for your unabashed love for Heath. To Romina Garber: I just don't think there are words to express how grateful I am for your friendship and your bottomless ability to talk me off any ledge I might be on. You are my soul sister. Wonder Twin Brains, activate!

To Tracy White, for your boundless enthusiasm for my books. You can be my first reviewer anytime. To Jason Polunci, for flying across the country to be at my first-ever book launch and for being a true bosom buddy.

To my sister, Tanya, for your infectious joy at seeing your baby sister finally realize her dream. To my parents, for encouraging my writing from the time I could hold a pencil. A very special thank-you to my stepmom, Dot, who bought me the books that made me want to be a writer: The Song of the Lioness series by Tamora Pierce, which still occupies a prominent place on the shelf reserved for my very favorite books.

And lastly, but most importantly, to Chris and Emilia. With your love, all things are possible.

TABLE OF CONTENTS

PROLOGUE

My mother tells a story of my birth.

There was a freak ice storm, and the closest hospital was forty miles away. The only midwife in the small northern Italian town was called to my mother's bedside. My grandmother bathed her forehead with cool cloths, and my father whispered loving encouragement into her ear.

My grandfather, who thought men did not belong in this world of women's work, was down the street at the bar, drinking Peroni.

The midwife hauled my mother up to a squat and ordered her to push. The pain was so great that my mother thought she would split in two. And for a moment, she lost reality. The room fell silent and frozen as the earth outside. Everything went dark, and all she could hear was the sound of great wings beating hard against the air. "I thought it was Gabriel, come for me," she tells me.

But out of the darkness came a magnificent falcon, its massive wings pumping the air as it flew right for her.

She screamed, and at the same moment the falcon collided with her, the light came back on. The midwife shouted with joy, my grandmother clapped her hands, my father lowered his head in awe, and I slipped out into the world.

My mother looked down at the bundle in the midwife's hand, covered with a slick, shimmering veil of translucent blue. "Born with the caul," the midwife breathed. "A sign of great fortune." She carefully broke open the amniotic sac, and I let out my first cry.

As the midwife placed me in my mother's arms, my mother knew. She knew that I would be a Walker. That the great Falcon she had seen was my soul, coming to join my body. "Walkers are born separate," she says, "and I had the blessing of seeing you become one."

Was it great fortune, or was it a curse? For that, my mother has no answers. "Only you know that," she tells me. "The only thing you can control is your own destiny."

CHAPTER ONE
The Connection

Alessia

The dark Panther stalked toward my cage of light, his emerald-green eyes glowing in the dimness of the underground room. All I could see were those eyes, that gaze fixed on me. I fluttered to the ground. Through the glittering bars of the cage, he and I stared at each other.

Behind me, Heath—the Wolf—growled so deeply that his white fur vibrated. In front of me, the Panther snarled too, and the combined rumble of his and Heath's voices was enough to make an earthquake. Caught in the middle, I thought I would break into pieces.

The bars of light surrounding me, Heath, and Nerina shimmered with tantalizing transparency. Could the magic of my aura be strong enough to break through? Before anyone could tell me it was a bad idea, I gathered myself and flew straight into the light.

It was a bad idea.

Electric shocks fractured across my body, singed my feathers. I cried out and fell hard onto the concrete floor.

For an instant the sickening scent of cooked bird filled the air. Pain coursed through me; I tried to breathe but each inhale was like a stab to my lungs. I closed my eyes. The dark behind my eyes was all-encompassing—no hint of light from my aura. It was going out, like a dying candle. *Like my life source was being pulled out of me.*

Something wet and cold pushed against me. *Alessia!*

I opened my eyes a sliver. Heath's blue eyes bored into me. *Are you all right?*

No, I wanted to say, but I couldn't summon the energy to respond. Nerina bent over me. Tear tracks ran down her usually impeccably made-up face. "Alessia? Can you move?"

I closed my eyes again and concentrated hard on my wings. After a moment, they twitched.

Nerina squatted beside me. She laid a gentle hand on my feathered belly. "The bars have magic from Angel Falls in them. She may have damaged her aura." Nerina moved her palms over me. Warmth emanated from her fingers. "What the hell possessed you to fly into them?"

I thought maybe . . .

Never mind that. Can you help her? Heath interrupted me.

"I hope so. I'm using Redwood magic."

On the other side of the barrier, the Panther growled and scratched the floor. "Shut up," Nerina snapped. "Haven't you done enough?"

He's not . . . He's worried about me . . .

Nerina ignored me and kept gliding her hands over

the length of my Falcon form. My aura began to seal together its cracks, smoothing itself into a whole. The pain ebbed, fizzling into a dull ache.

I opened my eyes wide and turned my head to the barrier, to the Panther on the other side of it. He—the Panther, *Jonah*—lay on his belly, his nose almost pressed against the bars of light, his deep green eyes looking only at me. A low, keening whine came from his throat, setting my feathers on edge. An answering call escaped from my own mouth.

Nerina jerked back. I thought I heard her say something, but my whole mind was focused on Jonah. I could feel Heath trying to break in, trying to warn me, but I pushed him out. I could not tear my gaze away from Jonah. Everything slowed—my heartbeat, my breath, even the world around us. All I could see was the green of Jonah's eyes; all I could hear was the sound of our breath, inhaling and exhaling in unison. It filled my mind, bigger than the ocean, until all the spaces inside me were empty. All I could see or hear or feel was Jonah.

His breath, his gaze, his *being*, filled me with more strength than Nerina's healing had. I lifted away from the floor and came to settle right in front of him, so close that the only thing separating us was the thin sheen of magic keeping me in and him out. A bubble seemed to surround us, shutting out everything beyond us. In that bright, beautiful space, I heard a voice. *Alessia.*

I shuddered with shock. *Jonah?*

Are you okay? That looked like it really hurt.

I feel . . . I blinked. There wasn't any pain, just wonder. *How is this happening? I thought Malandanti and Benandanti—*

—couldn't telecommunicate? I thought so too.

Then how—?

I don't know. It's happened before. I heard Bree at the Waterfall the other night.

We blinked at each other. Somehow it seemed vitally important that we not break eye contact. I could feel his emotions inside my head, his fear just below the surface of his words. I stretched my neck just a fraction of an inch, careful to avoid getting shocked again. I wanted so badly to touch him. We took a breath together and let it out at the same time.

I think it has something to do with connection, Jonah said. *My connection to Bree because she's my twin. My connection to you—*

My connection to you—

Our connection—

We didn't finish. We didn't need to. We let the unspoken words hang there in our minds for a long moment, the size of them covering everything else. I had always assumed that the Benandanti and the Malandanti couldn't talk to each other this way, but it seemed I was wrong. I remembered the few times that we'd been together, transformed, I'd heard a crackle in my mind. That ability had always been there; it was just that Benandanti and Malandanti never needed to speak to each other as Jonah and I did. Why would they want to? Had there ever been as twisted a tale as mine and Jonah's in the history of this war?

I have to get you out of there, Jonah said, breaking the brief reverie that we had fallen into.

If your Concilio *comes back to find us gone, they'll kill you.*

And if they come back and you're still here, they'll kill you. He drew himself up and paced back and forth in front of the barrier. *Do you know anything about this magic?*

No. Bree would know, but . . . no. I fluttered my wings. *Jonah—*

We'll have to make it look like you broke out, Jonah said, cutting me off. *And that I fought you.*

That's all well and good but we still have to find a way out.

Jonah stopped and sniffed the bottom of the bars, as though he could somehow smell an escape route. I followed him along the length of the cage. *Jonah, I'm sorry. For getting Bree involved in this.*

He raised his head, his eyes soft on my face. *It's all right. It wasn't your fault.*

It was. If it wasn't for me, she never would've gotten hurt.

Alessia, if there's one thing I know about Bree, it's that she doesn't do anything she doesn't want to do. He resumed his pacing. *You didn't force her into anything.*

Yes, but I made her feel guilty—about you, about Mr. Foster. When I asked her to be our spy, she couldn't really say no.

Trust me, she could have. He swung his head back to me, his green eyes narrowed. *Wait, did you say your spy? I thought she was just your mage.*

She spied for us first. That's why—

She wanted the internship at my dad's office, he finished for me. *Of course.* He shook himself, his fur bristling. *I wish I didn't know that. It's one more piece of information about her—about you—that they can torture out of me.*

I shuddered, cold fear rippling over my feathers. *I won't let them,* I said, my words fiercer than my conviction. *I don't care if I get hurt, if they find out who I am. I'll protect you—*

Jonah froze in front of me and once again that bubble surrounded us, my mind filled with every thought and emotion tumbling through him. I could tell from the way his whole body shook that it was the same for him, that he could hear everything that was inside of me, too. It was not like this with the other Benandanti—I only heard when and what they wanted me to hear. With Jonah, it was as if a great channel was open between us, as if the depth of our connection was a conduit through which our very souls flowed to each other. *Alessia,* he said. His voice reverberated deep inside me. *That won't happen. Because you are the light, and I am the dark, and I will lay down my life for you if I have to.*

I had never wanted to be human so badly. I wanted to wrap my arms around him, bury my face in his neck, and never let go. *Jonah, we'll get you out. Bree says there's a way—*

"Are you—*talking* to him?"

Nerina's voice jolted me out of the bubble. I spun to

look at her. She stood at the far side of the cage, her face twisted with disgust. "Alessia," she said. Her voice shook with a rage that I had never seen from her before. "Answer me right now. Are you talking to *that Malandante?*"

I didn't know if she could hear me in her mind since she was not transformed, so I nodded at the same time I thought *Yes.* Heath started, his blue eyes wide.

Tell her I want to help, Jonah said.

He wants to help, I echoed to Heath and Nerina.

"Stop it," Nerina muttered. She pressed her hands to the sides of her head, her expression teetering on hysteria. "Stop talking to him. Stop it right now!"

Why didn't you tell me I could talk to him? I demanded. *Why didn't I know Malandanti and Benandanti can communicate?*

They can't, Heath said. *I don't understand this—*
Obviously we can because I'm doing it right now.

"They can, but they must not." An uncontained wave of horror rolled off Nerina, threatening to consume me. I had never seen her this unsettled, she who was always immaculately put together, she who always took charge and knew exactly what to do.

She stalked toward me, her stilettos so sharp on the concrete that I lifted myself into the air, away from her. "It is forbidden. Do you hear me, Alessia? It is unnatural, the ultimate taboo—"

Nerina, you don't understand. He's not like the others.

Nerina stomped her foot hard on the ground. "If you

say one more word to that Malandante I will punish you in the name of the *Concilio!*" Wisps of red smoke spiraled around her shaking fingers, her magic loose and uncontained.

I froze, hovering unsteadily at the top of the cage. I had never seen anyone but a mage with magic like that, had forgotten that Nerina was just as powerful in her own right. *Nerina. Please. We love each other. I thought you knew that.*

"I thought it was over!" Nerina shot her gaze between me and Jonah. "This must stop. You cannot be together. You are enemies. The Malandanti will come back and kill us, and he will be part of it. He has no love for you."

You don't understand—

"I understand better than you think I do." Nerina's voice was like barbed wire. "He is using you to weaken us."

He is not! Do you really think I'm that stupid? That I would do anything to hurt the Clan?

"You are stupid where he is concerned!" Nerina shrieked. "You cannot be trusted around him!"

Please let me explain—

"No!" Her voice made the bars of light jitter and dance. "There is nothing to explain. The only good Malandante is a dead Malandante!"

Jonah roared so loud the world seemed to tilt. I shot toward Nerina, claws out, but Heath reared up onto his hind legs and shielded her from me. I buffeted up to the top of the cage. Heath forced Nerina to the back wall, his head pressed to her hip. I could tell he was speaking to her, but whatever he was saying, he'd blocked me from hearing. Nerina bent her head, her shoulders tense as she listened to Heath. Finally, she raised her gaze to me. "But we cannot trust him," she said hoarsely.

Jonah growled and struck his paw against the light barrier. Though his body shuddered with the jolt, he didn't look away from Nerina. *Tell her*, he said to me. *Tell her that I asked you to help me get out.*

I fluttered a few inches into the air between them. The heat of their anger at one another was thick and stuffy. *He wants out*, I said, making sure Heath could hear me too. *He asked me to help him get out of the Malandanti.*

Heath snapped his gaze to Nerina. She stood as still as ice, her hand pressed to her heart. "It's . . . impossible," she breathed, her lips barely moving.

There is a way. Bree told me—

"An impossible way," Nerina cut me off. She sliced her hand through the air. "That's not important right now. How do we know we can trust him?"

I fought the urge to snap my beak at her. *He wants to help us! You heard what the Harpy said. She said he was wavering. That's why she left him in charge of us: to test his loyalty.*

Alessia, Heath said, *if he lets us go, they'll kill him.*

I looked back at Jonah. *I know. We have to find some way out that makes it look like we overpowered him.*

What's going on? Jonah broke into my mind.

He—the Wolf knows what kind of danger you're in if you let us go.

I don't care. I told you. He keened again, his paw lifted toward me. *I don't care if I die saving you.*

Well, I do. I hopped closer to the barrier, to him. We bent our heads to each other, the only thing separating his thick black fur and my snowy feathers the shimmering wall of light. *Besides, Bree would have my head.*

"Without a mage," Nerina said, making us both look up at her, "we'll have to use what magic we can access."

Our auras, I said. *Like when Bree and I broke into that room here.*

She nodded and raised her hand, her palm less than an inch away from the barrier. "We need that burst of magic that comes when we transform." The bars shivered as she waved her palm over them. "But this is dangerous magic, much more dangerous than that room. The Angel Falls magic contained in these bars makes them deadly." She dropped her hands to her side. "You saw what happened when you collided with them."

So what do we do?

Nerina narrowed her gaze at Jonah and curled her lip. "These bars will only affect a Benandante. But a Malandante . . ."

Jonah pulled himself up tall, his fur bristling. *Whatever she needs me to do, I'll do it,* he told me.

I repeated his words to Nerina.

"Oh, really?" Shadows darkened her face. "I need him to bind himself to the cage, use his aura to bring down the bars. Will he do that?"

Jonah rushed into the barrier. The light exploded around him, sending off long tentacles of electricity. *Stop!*

I screamed as the shock reverberated through him. A cry of agony ripped across my mind and Jonah tumbled backward from the cage. He lay still on the concrete floor, his only movement the heaving of his sides as he panted.

"When I *say*, you idiot," Nerina hissed.

I flew at her and stopped an inch from her face. *How dare you? He's trying to help!*

"He's a Malandante. I don't trust him."

He's our only chance out of here. If you keep treating him like trash he's not going to help any of us.

Heath padded between us, gently nudging me backward. *She's right, Nerina. We have to trust him right now.*

Nerina looked from me to Heath and back again. A little vein at the base of her throat throbbed. "Fine," she said through gritted teeth. She stepped around us. "Get up," she said to Jonah, "and *listen* to the plan before you do anything."

I clicked my beak but held my tongue. At least she hadn't called him an idiot again.

Jonah hauled himself to his feet. *Are you all right?* I asked him.

I'm okay. She's right. I should've listened before I did anything.

Maybe, but she's still being a jerk. I'm sorry.

He shook his head, his black fur glistening in the silvery light of the cage. *Can you blame her?*

"Can you two please stop talking so we can get on with this?" Nerina pushed up the sleeves of her silk jacket and pointed to Jonah. "You."

He has a name, I snapped at her.

She ignored me. "On my count, you will rush the wall."

You saw what just happened. He'll electrify himself, I protested.

"No, he won't." Nerina paced the perimeter of our prison, looking the walls up and down. "The magic will feed into him. It might hurt for a moment"—she waved her hand—"but he'll be fine."

Nerina!

I'll be fine, Jonah said. *Let's just get on with it.*

"As the magic is feeding into him, I'll transform and direct our magic into the barrier. That should be enough to weaken it." She turned in a circle, examining the cube of light that surrounded us. "I should be able to bring it down after that," she murmured. "If only Bree were here . . ."

Cold crept into my feathers. Bree *had* been here, only hours before, trapped and tortured by the Malandante mage. If this didn't work, that was the fate in store for us.

Nerina snapped forward and faced Jonah. "Are you ready?" Without waiting for an answer, she went on. "On my count. One."

Wait, what are we supposed to be doing? I said as she held up a second finger.

"Get out as soon as the bars come down," she said quickly. "And three!"

With a roar, Jonah sprang forward into the barrier. The air reverberated with electricity, fractured lightning bolts raining down on all sides of the cage. I dropped low and back until I was right up against Heath, sparks spewing in every direction. I watched the silvery bars shift into squiggly lines and slowly spiral around Jonah's body. A thin sheet of light shimmered where the bars had been. I fluttered forward, but Heath blocked me. *Not yet . . .*

In one dazzling, brilliant burst of blue light, Nerina transformed into her mythical shape, a Griffin. Her enormous, magnificent wings stretched from one side of the cage to the other, her cerulean aura spilling out between the bars. The atmosphere shivered and danced all around us, making Heath's fur stand on end. I could feel the magic's heat on the tip of my feathers, singeing the air.

The celestial Benandante light crept its way around the dark Malandante magic, turning each bar sheer one by one. When the last bar was gone, all that was left was a translucent bubble of red smoke. The fatal magic of Angel Falls.

Nerina beat her wings against the cage. The red smoke uncoiled itself like a snake and licked at us, deadly tendrils creeping toward me and Heath, reaching to suck out our life source.

No! Nerina shouted. She hovered over us, her wings covering us like a cloak. I could hear Nerina's spell in my mind, strange words that I didn't understand. I peeked out from beneath the shelter of her wings at Jonah. He was still bound into the barrier, its magic undulating around him. His head was bent, his fur bristled, but his gaze locked on me, his fierce green eyes never leaving my face. *Oh, God, Jonah* . . .

He couldn't answer. I heard his struggle in my mind, side by side with Nerina's spell. *Hurry, Nerina,* I thought to myself. *Hurry, hurry* . . .

Bright yellow light crept in from the top of the bubble, its sunny sheen almost cheerful against the murky red smoke. As the yellow magic of the Redwoods spilled down the walls, the tendrils that reached out to me and Heath retracted and slithered upward. And then, in a lightshow worthy of Las Vegas, the red and yellow clashed, breaking the air like shattered glass. They fought each other, the life-sucking Angel Falls against the healing Redwood.

Nerina lifted away from us, her wings spread wide. The yellow light of the Redwoods gave one last dazzling jolt of its magic, and the red smoke of Angel Falls blew away into nothing.

Jonah fell to the floor with a sickening thud. I flew forward just as Nerina dissolved back into her body. I pressed my face to Jonah's throat. *Are you okay?*

Slowly, surely, I felt his pulse against my feathers. *I'm* . . . *Don't talk. Just breathe.*

"Alessia, we have to go." Nerina was already at the door. She pulled a bobby pin from her hair and worked the tumblers until the lock clicked. "Come on!"

We can't just leave him.

Heath galloped to me and nudged me with his nose. *We have to. They could be back any minute.*

It's . . . *okay* . . . Jonah's breath was labored. *It needs* . . . *to look . . . like I fought . . . anyway.*

Nerina backed away from the door and bent over Jonah. "He'll be fine. But we won't be if Fina comes back before we get out of here."

She's . . . right, Jonah said. *Go.*

"Although," Nerina tapped her finger to her mouth. "We should make it look like he fought us." She pointed at me. "Scratch him."

What? No! He looks battered enough.

"He needs to look like he put up a good fight," Nerina said. "Now do it fast and let us get out of here."

But—

Just do it, Alessia. Jonah pushed himself up onto one paw.

I rose above him, my wings wavering. With a heave of effort, he reared up and swiped at me in the air. Out of instinct, I struck out with my talons and caught his ear.

You can do better than that, he taunted as he fell back to the ground. *I've seen you in battle.*

I squared myself against him and charged. My beak sank into the soft black fur at his shoulders, my claws digging into his back. He yowled and rolled onto his back. We tumbled against the floor together in some twisted version of a lover's embrace. I raked my talons across his back once, twice, three times until blood dripped onto the gray concrete. I rocketed off him. *Oh, God, Jonah. I'm so sorry.*

Don't be. Now I . . . don't have to . . . fake it.

"Alessia, let's go!"

I narrowed my gaze at Nerina. *You owe him your life. I'm not leaving until you thank him for that.*

Alessia, this is not the time.

I flew until I was against the back wall. Color flared in Nerina's face. She straightened her shoulders and planted herself in front of Jonah. "I—thank you for helping us. You did well—for a Malandante."

It would have to be good enough. I swooped down and pushed my face into his neck for a moment.

I know, Jonah said, his voice soft in my mind.

You know what?

I love you, too.

"Alessia, out! Now!"

I swept to the door, my eyes still on Jonah. He lay on the floor, panting, his fur glistening with sweat and blood. I felt sick as I dodged out of the room and followed Heath and Nerina through the twisting labyrinth of the Guild up to the surface.

Because no matter what I'd done to him, it was nothing compared to what the Malandanti would do when they found him.

CHAPTER TWO

The Clan Revealed

Alessia

The cold night air was sweet in my lungs when we burst out of the Guild building. We fled up the alley and emerged out onto a quiet side street. It was late enough that the streets were empty, but I still didn't think the sight of a low-flying falcon and an enormous white wolf would go unnoticed for long.

"We have to get back to Twin Willows." Nerina's chest heaved up and down with her breath. "I think we have lost the Waterfall, but we must make sure the rest of the Clan is safe." She looked up the street and began to walk purposefully toward a crimson Fiat parked at the curb. Heath trotted behind her while I flew overhead. "My place is compromised. We'll need to find somewhere safe to stay."

A surge of fear jolted through me. After I'd found Nerina's lair ransacked, I'd been so worried about her that I'd failed to realize something equally scary. Her lair was on my farm, which meant that my mother was in danger. I dodged down to Heath. *My mom . . .*

I know. We need to get her away from the farm.

If they hadn't gotten to her already. But I couldn't think like that, because thinking like that filled my veins with ice and left me paralyzed, unable to help anyone.

Nerina bent over the driver's side door of the Fiat, jimmying the lock. I landed on top of the car. *Hang on— are you stealing this car?*

"*Sí.*"

You can't just steal someone's car! That's so wrong.

The lock clicked. Nerina pulled open the door without looking at me. "I'll give it back."

That's not the point. We're supposed to be the good guys, take the high road.

Nerina banged on the roof of the car, making me jump. "By the time we take the high road back to Twin Willows, everyone we love will be dead." She pointed at Heath. "You, in the backseat. You," she said, pointing at me, "follow us overhead."

I cannot believe *you,* I said, but my moral indignation wasn't enough to stop her. Nerina slammed the door and peeled away from the curb, the tires screeching on the pavement. Wow. Bree was going to be super jealous that she'd missed this. Not only had Nerina stolen a car, but she'd stolen probably the one Fiat in all of Maine. I winged over the car, the little red compact zooming along below me, out of Bangor, back to Twin Willows. Back to the Waterfall.

I didn't want to think about what we would find there.

Nerina ditched the car up the road from our farm and ran to Heath's cabin to transform. She took to the air with me and we skimmed over treetops. Below us, Heath was a white blur against the darkness. Moonlight filtered through the leaves. I glanced at the pale light on the horizon. It would be dawn soon.

The copse of birch trees, their trunks shimmering silver in the dark, loomed ahead. Nerina and I dropped low, joining Heath on the ground. From here, whoever was at the Waterfall would be able to see our auras. I shivered. Would they be friend or foe?

We inched forward until there was a break in the brush big enough for us to see through. My heart thudded in my chest, my feathers rippling with cold and fear. I suddenly thought of the first time I had seen the Waterfall with Heath, how we had hidden in this same brush. The Malandanti had controlled the Waterfall then. Had they reclaimed it?

I peered through the tangled branches. An unearthly silver glow domed from the stream above the Waterfall to the pool below. The water was murky, as though it had been contaminated with something unmentionable. And the Malandante Bobcat paced the edge of the pool, its huge paws imprinting on the soft earth where land met water. I fell back, my heart a hard weight inside me.

We have lost it, Nerina said needlessly, for we could all see for ourselves that the worst had happened. *And we cannot reclaim it until we replace the Lynx.*

Heath walked a few paces back toward the birch trees, his neck bent low. *But,* he said as he turned and raised his head, *we still control three other sites. And last time we regained the Waterfall, we didn't have Bree—or you, Nerina. We're a stronger Clan now. We can win it back.*

I threw gratefulness to him in my mind, unable to put into words how much I needed to hear his optimism. I stared at the silvery magic that encompassed the Waterfall. We would win it back. Good would prevail, and we would turn these woods Benandanti blue once more. There were too many things that were unthinkable right now—what was happening to Jonah at that very moment, where the Stag and the Eagle were, whether Bree was okay, and my mom . . . *my mom*—that this hope was the only thing that kept my wings aloft.

We need to find the Stag and the Eagle, Nerina said. She walked back to the break in the brush and looked through it for a long moment. *I don't see their bodies here, so that's a good sign.*

Oh, my God, *Nerina!*

Well, it is. Look, I'm just being practical.

I spun away from her and faced Heath. *We need to get my mom.*

Yes, but where do we go after that?

I clicked my beak once and swung my gaze between Heath and Nerina. *I know someplace we can go.*

"Mom."

She rolled over, blinked at me, and sat straight up. "Who died?"

"No one. Yet. I think." *I hope*, I added silently. If her dad had died defending the Waterfall, I'd never be able to look Jenny in the eye again. "But it's not safe here. Come on. Get dressed."

"Alessia, what is this about?" She flung the covers aside and grabbed my arm as she stood. "Are you all right?"

"Yes. Just get dressed. Please. I'll tell you everything . . . just . . . we can't stay here." I went to the window and peered out. They could be watching us from anywhere.

To Lidia's credit, she stopped questioning me, got dressed, and followed me outside to Heath's truck. Nerina had gone to the hospital to collect Bree, presumably in her stolen Fiat. It would serve her right if she got pulled over.

I pushed Lidia into the cab of the truck and climbed in beside her. She was muttering under her breath in Italian; not a good sign. I knew a reckoning was coming, that I would have to come clean and tell Lidia everything, but first I needed to make sure the rest of the Clan was safe.

We rumbled up the driveway and turned onto the main road into town. I watched the farmhouse grow smaller in the rearview mirror. Just before it disappeared, a huge black bird swooped over the ruins of the burned-out barn and rose above the house. I gripped the door handle. "They know."

Heath stared into the mirror. I heard his breath catch as he saw the same thing I did: the Raven circling the rooftop of my house. The pig-shaped weather vane turned slowly in the wake of the Raven's huge wings. "I don't think he saw us."

"No." We rounded a bend in the road, and the farm—and the Raven—vanished from view. If the Raven had seen us leave, he would've followed us. "But the farm isn't safe now. We can't go anywhere near it until we've defeated them."

"What is going on?" Lidia demanded, coming out of her Italian-speaking trance. "I can't go back to my own house now?"

I put my hand on her arm, softening my fingers around her wrist. "I'll explain everything, Mom. I promise. But we need to get somewhere safe first."

Heath turned the truck onto Willowbrook Lane. Lidia sat up straight and put her hands on the dashboard. "Why are we going to the Sandses'?"

Neither of us answered her, to her obvious annoyance. She slunk back down and started grumbling in Italian again. This time, I distinctly heard some swears mixed in with the words meaning "disobedient girl."

Heath pulled to a stop in Jenny's driveway. We ran to the front door, the morning air frozen around us. I took a deep breath and rang the bell. A moment later, the curtain over the window next to the door peeked open.

The door swung open. Mr. Sands stood there, bleary-eyed and unshaven, but alive. My knees buckled with relief and I threw my arms around him to keep from collapsing. "You're okay! Thank goodness you're okay!"

"Alessia, what the—?"

I barreled him inside and Heath shut the door behind us. "Is the Eagle okay too?"

Mr. Sands froze and stared at me. I slid my hands into his and squeezed. "It's all right," I said. "I'm the Falcon."

His jaw tightened as he sucked in a sharp, audible breath. "You're the—" He glanced at Heath. "Are you—?"

Heath stepped forward and held out his hand. "The Wolf."

Mr. Sands slid his hand out of mine and took Heath's. "Of course," he said softly. "How could I not have recognized those blue eyes?" He pulled Heath into a brotherly hug and patted his back. Then he slung his arms around each of us and propelled us deeper into the house. Lidia trailed at our heels. She was no longer grousing in Italian. She'd probably been struck speechless.

A tray piled with a steaming pot of coffee, mugs, muffins, and toast sat on the low coffee table in the living room. Jenny sat on the couch, her feet tucked up under her hip, her hands wrapped around a cup of coffee. Her mom, Barb, sat cross-legged next to her, an untouched muffin in front of her. And sitting on the floor was a woman who looked familiar. I stared at her. She was a waitress at our favorite pizza place, Pizza Plus. When she saw us come in with Mr. Sands, she stood, her ginger hair tumbling messily to her tiny waist. "This is Cora," he said. "The Eagle."

Somehow, the four of us found ourselves in a tight circle, crying and laughing at the same time. It was like long-lost twins finding each other in a crowded street. This was my family, as real and connected as Lidia and me. We were bound to each other for life by something stronger than blood. The *Concilio* had gotten it wrong. Knowing each other's true identities made the bond even stronger, unbreakable. It was a stupid rule, I thought as Cora cupped my cheek and touched her forehead to mine. Every Benandante deserved to know who was fighting alongside them.

"Who would've thought the fierce Falcon was a sixteen-year-old girl?" Cora said, pulling back a little to smile at me.

"I'm almost seventeen," I protested. "And who would've thought the huge Eagle was a woman no bigger than my thumb?"

She laughed and hugged me again, until Mr. Sands—Jeff, he now insisted I call him—stole me away from her to hug me himself. I finally broke away from them and collapsed onto the couch next to Jenny. She took one look at me and burst into tears. "Jenny! What—?" But the rest of my sentence was buried in Jenny's shoulder as she flung her arms around me.

"My dad said two Clan members were missing. I thought you were . . ." She pressed her fist to her mouth, unable to say the word. "I'm so glad you're okay," she said instead, and hiccupped.

"We did get into some trouble," I said. I glanced around and realized that Lidia was gone; Barb had taken her into the kitchen, probably to get her out of earshot of the Benandanti's conversation. I exhaled slowly, my chest fluttery. I was off the hook for the moment.

Heath told Jeff and Cora about the Harpy and the Guild. He left out the part about Jonah, for which I threw him a grateful glance that Jenny caught. She kicked my foot. I shook my head at her. "Later," I mouthed.

"Nerina's gone to the hospital to get Bree," Heath finished.

Jenny sat straight up. "Bree?" she asked, her eyebrows raised at me. "As in Bree Wolfe?"

"Jenny," her dad warned in a sharp tone. Jenny slumped back into the couch cushions, her eyes still on me. I nodded once in answer to her unasked question, that I would tell her everything later. "I expect you to treat her with respect and protect her secret like you've protected mine," Jeff went on, his voice still stern. "She's been through a lot."

When her dad had turned back to Heath, Jenny gripped my arm. "It was Bree?" she hissed. "The Clan member who was missing when we were in Massachusetts?"

I leaned in close to her ear so I could whisper without her dad hearing. "Yes. But she's not what you think. She's our mage."

"What the hell is a mage?"

Before I could answer, the doorbell rang. We all fell silent, straining to listen to Barb's footsteps as she crossed to the window. A moment later she called out, "Jeff? I don't recognize these people."

Jeff jumped to his feet. "They're okay," I heard him tell Barb, and the door swooshed open. I stood as Nerina entered the room. Her arm was wrapped around Bree, who still looked like she'd been run over by a steamroller. Nerina deposited Bree onto the couch and stood in front of the fireplace. The cozy, familial atmosphere in the room changed. The official Benandanti Clan had reconvened.

CHAPTER THREE
Worst Idea for a Slumber Party Ever

Bree

I don't know what magic Nerina pulled to get me signed out of the hospital, but somehow I found myself hobbling out the front doors into the gray morning light. I lowered myself onto a bench to wait for Nerina to pull the car around. Just the walk from the elevator to the sidewalk had winded me. My bones protested every movement.

The pain I could live with. It was the uncertainty that was killing me.

A sporty red Fiat whipped around the corner and squealed to a stop in front of me. Nerina bolted out of the driver's side to help me into the passenger seat. "There's a blanket in the back if you're cold," she said and buckled the seatbelt around me.

I reached for the blanket on the backseat. Pain ripped up my arm and across my collarbone. I snatched my hand back, breathing hard in and out through my teeth. Nerina slid into the driver's seat and handed me the blanket. "Thanks," I managed and squeezed my eyes shut. I counted to ten as Nerina put the car in drive and pulled away from the curb. By ten the pain had subsided into a prickly ache up and down my rib cage. I opened my eyes and tucked the blanket around me. "So, where'd you get this ride?"

Nerina glanced at me but didn't answer.

"Seriously? You managed to steal the one Fiat in all of Maine? Impressive."

"I'm going to return it."

"Why bother? The douchebag who owns this is probably too embarrassed to report it."

Nerina snorted. I let her concentrate on driving for a few minutes, but the instant we hit the highway, I put my hands on the dashboard. "Okay. You gotta tell me what's going on. Heath left in a huge rush last night, sent in some redheaded chick who I can only assume is the Eagle to watch me, and then she peeled out of here too. Something big is up."

Nerina glanced in the rearview mirror, changed lanes so she could zoom past an ancient pickup truck rumbling along at forty miles an hour, and sighed. "We lost the Waterfall."

"What?" I sat up as straight as the seatbelt would allow. "How the hell did that happen?"

"The Malandanti found me. They took me to the Guild, the same room where they held you. That's why Heath left you last night. He and Alessia came to get me."

"Jesus . . ." I breathed and slumped down in my seat.

After all our work, after overthrowing the Guild, they'd bested us again. "Well, you're okay, obviously. Are Heath and Alessia okay too?"

"They're fine. They're at the Stag's house. That's where we're going." She glanced at me again. There was something in her face, something shadowy in her eyes, something she wasn't telling me.

"What is it?"

Nerina swallowed. Her hands gripped the steering wheel tight. I squinted at her; she was unsettled in a way that I wasn't used to seeing. "The *Concilio Argento* was there. That's why they were able to retake the Waterfall. Because it was all of them against the Stag and the Eagle."

"Are they all right too?"

"Yes, yes, they're fine."

"Then what is it you're not telling me?"

"When the Malandanti left us, they assigned one of their Clan members to guard us."

She didn't have to say his name. I already knew from the way she could barely look at me. I looked away from her, out the window to the snow-covered farms that rolled past. "Just tell me if he's alive or dead."

"He was alive when we left. But . . ."

"When the Malandanti come back and find you gone, who knows what they'll do to him," I finished for her. I closed my eyes, saw again that horrible basement room in the Guild, saw again Jonah's helpless eyes as the Malandante mage tortured me, hurt me over and over.

But if he were dead, if the Malandanti killed him, surely I would feel it. He was my twin; there was no way he could die without me knowing. I would feel it like a punch to my gut, like a stab to my soul. Nerina was saying something, something that sounded far away. I pulled myself back to her.

". . . helped us escape."

"What?"

"I said, he helped us escape."

I raised an eyebrow. "Wow, Nerina. That must be really hard for you to admit."

"It is not—" She clamped her lips tight. "He surprised me. We would not have gotten out of there without him. Perhaps you and Alessia are right about him."

"Maybe you should pull over before I die of shock."

"Oh really, now."

I grasped the door handle as she zipped around a black SUV. "If the Malandanti find out he helped you . . ."

"We made it look like we overpowered him. I really don't think they will kill him. They'd be down a Clan member, and they can't afford that."

"They could just replace him—"

Nerina shook her head. "It takes time to train a replacement. Time they don't have in this war." She took a deep breath. "However, before Fina—the Harpy—left, she said they were leaving him there because he was wavering. So while I do not think they will kill him, I do think they will keep him under constant watch—probably in the Guild building—and try to reprogram him."

"*Reprogram?* Like, brainwash?" My mind went to an *A Clockwork Orange* place, Jonah strapped in a chair with his eyes pinned open, forced to watch Malandante propaganda for days on end. "We have to get him out."

Nerina swerved the car onto the exit for Twin Willows, nearly colliding with the guardrail. "Absolutely not."

"He's in danger! He—"

"He's a Malandante! We're not risking our necks to save a Malandante."

"Even one who saved your sorry ass?" I slammed my fist against the window, ignoring the shot of pain that bulleted through my ribs. "I thought I was pretty freaking crystal clear about my priorities when I joined the Benandanti, Nerina."

"You need to be patient." The car slowed as we merged onto the country road that led into Twin Willows. "We need to reclaim the Waterfall, defeat the Malandanti. Then we can get him out."

"But he could help us beat the Malandanti. Who's to say he couldn't fight on our side instead?"

Nerina flexed her fingers and resettled them around the steering wheel. "He cannot fight on our side. Not while he's still a Malandante." She took her gaze off the road and looked at me for a long moment, before she had to look back to avoid a crash. "It is physically impossible for a Malandante to fight against his Clan. Their auras prevent them from doing so."

I stared at her. How did I not know this? I'd pored over all of her damn books and not one of them had ever mentioned this. "For real?"

"I've—seen—it happen." Nerina's skin was pale, and not just because she'd been living in an underground lair for the last couple of months. "Bree, I know you found out about turning a Malandante into a Benandante. Alessia told me, and she also told me that Jonah wants out. But what you read about—the way it has to happen—is impossible. You need to get it out of your head."

Her whole body was tense, like she was about to take flight. I narrowed my eyes at her, but she wouldn't turn my way. She was hiding something. I was sure of it. Well, she wouldn't be hiding it for long. I was a freaking mage, after all. I had ways of finding things out.

Jenny Sands's dad was the last person I ever expected to be the Stag, but I had to give him credit for letting the entire Clan descend on his house unannounced. Alessia patted the spot on the couch next to her when I walked in. Jenny sat on her other side, and I saw her eyes widen as I made my way to the couch. I'd checked the mirror before we'd gotten out of the car; I knew what I looked like: purple bruises encircling my eyes, broken blood vessels staining my skin, swollen fingers, medical tape across my chest that peeked out from my shirt's neckline . . . I lifted my chin a hair as I passed her. She could sit on her little popular-girl pedestal all she wanted. I was a god-damn hero.

As soon as I settled next to Alessia, I leaned in close to her ear. "I have to talk to you," I muttered.

"Me too. Later."

"I suppose introductions are not necessary," Nerina said in her I'm-in-charge tone at the front of the room. "Although I guess I should introduce myself. I am Nerina." She paused for a moment, as if she expected applause or something, but everyone just stared at her. I choked back a laugh.

"In any case," Nerina went on, "we should inform the rest of the *Concilio* that we know each other's identities."

"Why?" Alessia asked.

"Because we tell them everything that goes on in the Clans," Nerina said. "They should know that we've been compromised."

"It's a stupid rule," the redheaded Eagle said.

I raised my eyebrow at Alessia. "Her name's Cora," she told me in an undertone.

"Cora's right," I said loudly.

Nerina narrowed her eyes at me. "That 'stupid rule' has saved countless lives," she said. "Even you would have revealed our identities had they tortured you long enough."

"Hey!" I tried to sit up straight, but the overly squishy couch cushions wouldn't let me. "I resent that. I would've held out." I pointed my finger at her. "And actually, by your reasoning, if the *Concilio* knows we all know each other's identities, then *they* could be tortured for that information too."

"She's right," Jeff said.

Nerina looked thoroughly annoyed that we'd out-reasoned her. She threw her arms up in the air. "Fine. I won't tell them. Let's get past this. We need to figure out our next move."

"We should go in tonight," Mr. Sands—Jeff—said. "With a complete Clan, I'm sure we could retake it."

"But we are not a complete Clan," Nerina said. "We are missing the Lynx."

"We have you," Jeff replied.

"Yes, but technically I am not a member of the Twin Willows Clan. The spell will not work," Nerina said. "Besides, we will be even stronger if we can find the Lynx's replacement and go in with six of us." She ran her hand through her hair, making the ends twitch with static. "It may even take more than that."

"What do you mean?" Cora asked.

Nerina and Heath exchanged looks. "You saw the Harpy at the battle the other night," Heath said.

"Their entire *Concilio Argento* is here," Nerina added. "We cannot go up against that many Malandanti, even as a complete Clan."

"But why is their entire *Concilio* here?" Cora asked. "The Waterfall isn't the only site they've lost. Why haven't they spread out to the other sites we control?"

"Presumably, they will," Nerina said. "The only way we will know if they have left is if one of our *Concilio* members tells us they've been spotted at one of the other sites. So until that happens—"

"We wait," Jeff said.

"We wait, and we train the Lynx's replacement as soon as he—or she—is Called." Nerina paced in front of the fireplace against the wall. "We heal," she said, nodding at me, "and we plan. The Malandanti will be out for blood in the wake of the Guild's downfall. We cannot underestimate what they might do."

"Um, I have a question," I said, raising my hand slightly. "Where the hell am I supposed to stay? I can't go home. They know where I live."

"Neither can I," Alessia said. "Or Heath, or Nerina, or my mom. When they found Nerina's place, the whole farmhouse became compromised."

"Someone can stay with me," Cora piped up. "I think my place is still safe."

"But it's in Willow Heights," Jeff said, naming the next town over. "I'd feel a helluva lot better if everyone were close by." He scrunched his face up, looking around the room. "You can all stay here."

"That's going to call attention to you," Heath said.

Jeff shrugged. "The farmhouse has mold," he said. "Black mold, deep in the walls. You're all staying here until they get rid of it."

"My mother would eat canned tomato sauce before

she'd admit to black mold in her house," Alessia said.

"Well, then she's going to eat canned tomato sauce, because that's all we have in this house anyway," Jenny said.

"Nerina and Cora can share the upstairs guest room. Lidia can take the pullout in the den. Heath can sleep on the couch. And Bree and Alessia can bunk with Jenny." Jeff winked at the three of us on the couch. "You girls will be up all night giggling anyway."

I tightened my jaw. I did *not* giggle. I glanced over at Jenny, who had folded her arms across her chest and was shooting her dad a daggered look. Between us, Alessia slumped deep into the cushions. I was sure she was thinking the same thing I was. Eight people crammed into a three-bedroom house. She, Jenny, and I sleeping in the same room. Nerina without her fancy espresso machine, forced to drink drip coffee. If the Malandanti didn't do us in, that certainly would.

"I'll let Barb know the arrangements," Jeff said. He pressed his lips together. "And I guess we oughta call the school to tell them you three will be out today. That might raise some eyebrows."

I stared into the cold, ash-swept fireplace. The school probably cared more about me being absent than my parents did. They hadn't reported me missing in the two days I'd spent in the Guild, or come to the hospital. Dad was probably holed up in his office, trying to figure out his next move to cover his ass now that the Guild was in shambles. And Mom . . . She was probably totally obliterated. Both their kids were gone. What the hell was wrong with them? I hardened my jaw. I could take care of myself. I'd proven that in the basement of the Guild, holding out against that bastard Malandante mage.

"You'll probably be out of school for a while." Alessia broke into my thoughts. "You can't go looking like that."

Jenny leaned across her. "If you're going to be rattling around here all day long, you'd better not get into my stuff."

I smirked at her. "Don't worry, Sands, I wouldn't dream of borrowing your cherry-flavored Bonne Bell lip gloss."

"I don't wear *Bonne Bell*, thank you very much. I *have* seen the inside of a Sephora."

"Coulda fooled me."

"Oh, my God, you guys!" Alessia threw her hands up. "Look, it sucks, okay, but we all have to deal with it. So can we please just get along?"

Jenny slumped back into the couch and folded her arms. I would've done the same if I didn't know it would cause a riptide of agony. Instead I took a deep, dramatic breath and held my hand out to her. "Truce. I won't play with your toys."

Jenny rolled her eyes, but she sat up and took my hand. "Deal." When we let go, she tilted her head at me. "Those bruises do look really bad. My mom has some like super-hippie homemade ointment that actually works pretty well. Want some?"

"That would be great. Thanks." When she got up, I

turned to Alessia. "But I want to at least go back to my house to get some stuff. You do too, right?"

"Well yeah, but I don't know if we should risk it." Alessia chewed her lip. "Pratt—the Raven—showed up there right after we left."

"I was thinking maybe I could use a masking spell," I said. "I could probably pull one off long enough for each of us to pack a bag."

"You need to be healing, like Nerina said. I don't want you to overexert yourself."

"Well, I am not borrowing Jenny's underwear," I said. I glanced around to make sure no one was listening, but Cora, Heath, and Nerina were deep in conversation and Jeff had left to get Barb. I lowered my voice anyway. "Nerina told me what happened in the basement. About Jonah."

Alessia looked down at her hands in her lap. "Did she tell you everything?"

I cocked my head. "I don't know. What's everything?"

She knotted her fingers together. "We could talk to each other, Bree. Even though we were transformed."

My heart did a little spin inside my chest. I'd suspected. "Did he say if he heard me? At the Waterfall, during the battle?"

"Yes." Alessia raised her gaze to my face. "He heard you."

I breathed in deep, the corners of my mouth turning up. "I knew it. I knew it was possible."

"He thinks it has to do with connection. Your connection because you're twins . . . our connection . . ." She looked down at her fingers again.

"Ugh, stop." I held my hand up. "I don't need to hear about your, ahem, *connection*." I reached out and nudged her shoulder lightly. "But this is *huge*. It means that we can communicate with him during a battle. Even if he can't fight against the Malandanti while he's still one of them, he can still tell us what they're going to do before they do it. This could be super helpful, Alessia."

She scrunched her forehead. "What do you mean, he can't fight against the Malandanti?"

Before I could answer, a glass smashed to the floor. Alessia's mother stood at the edge of the living room, her arm stretched out, her finger pointing straight at Nerina. Her whole body shook, and her face was contorted with disbelief and white-hot anger. The only other person I'd ever seen in a full Italian rage was Nerina, and Lidia definitely looked like she could give her a run for her money.

She took one trembling step toward Nerina, her lips pale. "*You!*"

CHAPTER FOUR
The Truth at Last

Alessia

I jumped off the couch. "Mom! What's wrong?"

But Lidia didn't answer me. She stalked toward Nerina, her face white as moonlight. Nerina stood, her back straight and her expression haughty, but I could see something in her eyes, something like regret. "Lidia," she said, "after so many years, we meet again."

She had switched to Italian. She didn't want the rest of the Clan to hear. But she had to know that I would.

"Is this your fault?" Lidia asked, answering in Italian. "Did you bring my daughter into all this?"

"You had to have known," Nerina said. "You knew what she would become the moment she was born. It was destined."

"Destiny is nothing," Lidia said. "We choose our own destiny."

Nerina stared at my mother so hard that Lidia flinched. "Like you chose yours?" she said, very softly but with an edge that could kill.

Lidia raised her chin. "Yes. As I chose mine. And I stand by that choice."

Nerina's lips twisted. Before she could speak, I stepped between them. "Enough," I said, also in Italian to make sure they knew I'd understood what had just been said. I didn't know what the hell was going on, but I was going to find out. I grabbed Lidia's arm and dragged her out of the living room and into the den.

Barb had gone a little overboard with the manly Daniel Boone theme in the den, which was ironic considering she and Jeff were vegetarians. All four walls were padded with faux leather, including the back of the door. When I closed it, all sound from the living room was shut out. Lidia collapsed onto the plaid couch and buried her face in her hands. I came around and knelt on the braided rug in front of her. "Mom? What was that all about? Do you know Nerina?"

Lidia raised her head. Although her face was streaked with sorrow, her eyes were clear. She cupped my face, her calloused palms warm on my skin. "I'm so sorry, *cara*. I never wanted this life for you. I never wanted you to be a Benandante."

I jerked away from her. I'd long suspected that Lidia knew about the Benandanti, but to hear the word tumble from her lips with such ease was still startling. I took a few long breaths. "You knew."

"Yes," she whispered. "I knew." She tried to touch my face again, but I moved back far enough that she couldn't reach me.

"You've known about the Benandanti all this time, haven't you? How?"

Lidia dropped her hands and turned her head so that I could see only her profile. She stared at the singing bass that hung on the wall that she'd always called tacky but that Jenny and I thought was funny. She was seeing something far beyond that silly little fish—something in her past. "She came to me," Lidia said. I didn't need to ask who the *she* was. "When you were born."

"Why?"

Lidia swung her gaze back to me. Her dark hair, which she had messily put up into a bun when we'd rushed from the farmhouse, tumbled in front of her eyes. "Because she'd come to me once before. When I was sixteen, like you."

My breath caught. I couldn't move.

"Nerina came to me," Lidia said. "Called me, told me I was destined to be a Benandante. Gave me the choice that all Benandanti get." She brushed a lock of hair behind her ear and peered deep into my eyes. "I refused."

Breath crept back into my body as my mind curved itself around the truth. "You're a Refuser." It all made sense. "I bet Nerina didn't like being told no."

Lidia's mouth pinched. "No. No, she did not." Her gaze narrowed and shifted to the door, as though she could see her on the other side of it. "And she had her revenge. Seven years later, when you were a year old, she came back to me. She told me that you would be chosen to fulfill the destiny that I had denied. I fought with her," Lidia said, her voice raspy and low. "I said I would not allow my child to be put in that kind of danger. And she replied that the Benandanti would come back for you when you were old enough to make the decision for yourself. That night, I told your father that I wanted to move to America."

I pressed my hands to the sides of my head, trying to wrestle this knowledge in with all the other secrets I'd been keeping. "Did Dad know?" I asked, finally saying aloud the question that had haunted me for months. "Did he know about the Benandanti?"

Lidia nodded. My chest squeezed tight, and I couldn't say the thing I feared most. Had he been a Benandante too?

"He knew about them because both of his parents were Benandanti."

I came off my knees and eased away from her. I had no memory of my paternal grandparents; I had always been told that they died when I was a baby. That was why my dad had returned to Twin Willows with his new wife and child: to run the farm that they had left behind. "Did they . . . die in battle?"

Lidia swallowed hard. Her eyes were shiny with tears threatening to spill over. "Yes. It happened about six months after we came to Twin Willows."

Six months. So I *had* met my grandparents. Or rather, they had met me. Try as I might, the only image of them I could conjure in my head was the picture of them, kind-faced and surrounded by goats, that we had on the mantel at home. My brain spun as all the pieces of the puzzle finally began clicking into place. That was why Nerina had built her lair on our farm, why she'd placed the amulet in the basement of the farmhouse. Bree didn't know how right she'd been when she once called my home Benandanti Central.

"But Dad had to have known that they would find me here, too. The Waterfall in the woods behind our house—that's the site of magic we're protecting. He knew about it; he used to take me there. Why did you come back here to Twin Willows if you knew they were here, too?"

Lidia closed her eyes. Now the tears did spill over, staining her cheeks. "Because he didn't agree with me," she said, so low that I had to lean in to hear her. "Because he knew that you would be a great Walker. That you would be a hero. He did not believe that you could escape that destiny, no matter where we were."

God, that word, *destiny*. I could never escape it, no matter how hard I tried. "So I've just been fulfilling some master plan all along?" I pushed myself up to my feet and paced the length of the couch. "You all knew that I was going to be a Benandante someday, didn't you?"

"Alessia, I never wanted this for you. I had hoped it would never come to this, or if it did, that you would make the same choice I did. That you would refuse."

I whirled to a stop in front of Lidia. "The *coward's* choice?"

She winced. A stab of guilt pierced my gut, but I was

too angry to really feel its pain. "How long have you suspected that I was a Benandante?"

"I . . . I don't know . . . maybe a couple of months . . ."

"A couple of *months*?" I tore my hands through my hair. "And you didn't say anything to me?"

"I knew that you would not be allowed to talk—"

"But I could've talked to you!" I flung my arm in the direction of the living room. "Jenny's known her dad was a Benandante since she was twelve. Barb knows. Dad obviously knew about his parents. It seems like I was the only one in the Clan following the rules, and I was the one who most needed to break them." I couldn't breathe; the anger and frustration were like bands across my ribs.

"*Cara* . . ."

"Don't *cara* me! I *needed* you and I was so afraid to say anything, afraid for your safety. And now I find out you knew all along." I was surprised to taste salted tears in my mouth; I hadn't realized I'd started crying. "If you had come to me, I would've told you everything."

Lidia looked up at me, her face a bottomless pit of grief. "I didn't want to believe it was true. It was easier to think it wasn't . . ."

"Yeah, easier for you." My legs felt so rubbery, I was in danger of collapsing on the rug. "My whole life, you've overprotected me. God, you wouldn't even let me go to Paris on a school trip. And the one time when it would've been really great to have you be overly involved, you stepped back."

Lidia hunched over and buried her face in her hands. Her shoulders shook with the force of her crying. I stood in the center of the rug, my chest heaving with every emotion that coursed through me. The only other time I'd seen her cry like this was when my dad had died. That time, we had curled up together, comforting each other's grief. This time, I couldn't stand the thought of touching her. "Did Dad really die of a heart attack?" I asked. My words landed like barbs, and she flinched. "Or was he killed by the Malandanti?"

She raised her face from her hands, her eyes a swollen red mess. "No. I swear, Alessia. He really did die of a heart attack."

I breathed in sharp through my nose. "How do I know you're telling the truth? You've been lying to me *my whole life.*"

"Alessia, everything I have done, I did to protect you. To keep you safe." She rubbed her face. "And every step of the way, I have been blocked by *that woman,*" she said, jabbing her finger in the direction of the living room.

"Oh, don't blame Nerina, Mom! You know it's not her fault." I shook my head. "The only person you have to blame is yourself. For refusing the Call in the first place. Because if you hadn't, I never would have been Called."

"If I hadn't, you never would have been born," Lidia shot back. She stiffened her shoulders. "We choose our own destiny, yes, but there are some things that just can't be stopped . . ."

"Stop saying 'destiny'!" I balled my hands into fists and dug my nails deep into my palms. "Destiny doesn't matter. What matters is that you knew what was going on and you did nothing to help me. What matters is that at the moment I needed my mom the most, you refused to be there."

"Alessia . . ." Lidia stretched her arms out, reaching for me, but I backed up all the way to the door.

"Don't, Mom. Just don't." I collided with the soft padding on the door and felt for the handle. "Dad would've been there for me. The minute he suspected I'd been Called, he would've been there."

"That's not fair." Lidia stood up. A flush crept up her neck. "I did what I thought was right."

I flung open the door so hard it slammed against the wall. My existence in this town, *my entire life*, had been built on a lie. "The problem is," I told her, my voice shaking, "that you couldn't have been more wrong."

CHAPTER FIVE

I'd Give Anything for a Ritz-Carlton Right about Now

Bree

When Alessia came back into the living room, she looked like she'd been punched in the soul. Lidia trailed behind, her hair and face looking like something a cat coughed up. Without looking at anyone, she veered off into the kitchen. Alessia collapsed onto the couch so hard it made my ribs ache. "Jesus," I said. "What the hell happened to you?"

"I don't want to talk about it," Alessia muttered, shooting a death-ray glance at Nerina. "What did I miss?"

"Nothing," Nerina said quickly. Whatever Shakespearean plot twist had happened between Alessia and her mom, I guessed that Nerina had more than a supporting role. "We were just about to break up and get settled in here."

I stretched my arms overhead, my chest prickling with pain. "Well, I need a cigarette," I announced. "Alessia, will you help me outside?"

"You are not allowed in my room smelling like smoke," Jenny said. "I'm not going to die from second-hand smoke because of you."

I rolled my head to the side to glare at her. "Oh, for Chrissake," I hissed. "I need to talk to Alessia alone and I was trying not to be obvious. Happy?"

That, at least, put a shadow of a smile on Alessia's face. I leaned into her as we hobbled to the front door. "This is going to be the most not-fun slumber party in the history of slumber parties," I muttered. I glanced into the kitchen as we passed. Lidia was at the stove, stirring something in a big pot over a low flame. It smelled like tomato sauce. Really delicious, homemade tomato sauce. Lidia looked up, her eyes big as a doll's, but Alessia squared her shoulders and pulled open the front door.

Outside, the cold slapped me across the face. Should've grabbed my coat on the way out. I propped myself up against the side of the house. "So what the hell was that all about?"

Alessia sighed and dropped to sit on the steps. "Apparently my mother has been lying to me my entire life."

"Join the club," I said. "I can't remember a time when I didn't feel like my parents were keeping something from me."

"Yeah, well, some of us aren't used to that." Alessia looked at the patch of bare trees that filled the space between the house and the street. "My grandparents were Benandanti. They didn't die in an accident like I thought. They died in battle when I was a baby. Oh, and that wasn't the reason my parents moved back here from Italy. They moved back here before that because my mom wanted to get me away from Nerina."

"How did your mom know Nerina? Italy isn't that small."

"I guess Friuli is," Alessia said. She blew out a breath, making a loose strand of hair dance across her face. "Nerina Called my mom when she was my age. My mom's a Refuser."

"Really?" I gazed at the sky. "It's nice to know I'm not the only one."

"Well, I'm glad you're happy to hear it." Alessia shook her head. "She says she's known for months that I'm a Benandante. But she never said anything. What the hell kind of parenting is that?"

"The crappy kind," I said. "I can't believe Nerina didn't tell you this."

"Well, it wasn't her place to tell me," Alessia said. "And actually, that doesn't surprise me at all. I mean, Nerina keeps a lot of stuff from us. I think she truly enjoys knowing things the rest of us don't."

If Nerina was a nail, Alessia had just hit her on the head. "That's for damn sure," I said. I moved to sit next to Alessia, every joint and muscle creaking. "In the car on the way over here, she told me that the Malandanti can't fight each other. Their auras prevent it. I'd never read that in any of the books—and I went *deep* into those books. If it had been in there, I would've known."

"So do you think she's lying?"

"No." I flexed my fingers. All my nails were chipped and broken. The Rabbit owed me a manicure, among many other things. "I think it's probably true, but for some reason she didn't want that to be common knowledge. After all," I cocked my head, "who do you think wrote those books to begin with?"

"The *Concilio*," Alessia answered. "Maybe not her specifically . . ."

". . . but her people at least." The cold concrete made me feel like I was sitting on a block of ice. I shifted so that I was on the doormat, leaving enough space for Alessia to settle next to me. "I definitely think she's hiding something, though. Something else. Something big that maybe she *really* doesn't want us to know."

"She *freaked* out when Jonah and I were talking to each other," Alessia said. Her eyes looked far away, like she was seeing that room again, that room that I hoped neither of us would ever go back to. "And it wasn't just a Benandanti versus Malandanti thing. It went . . . deeper than that."

"She told me that I had to get the whole idea of turning a Malandante into a Benandante out of my head," I said slowly, bringing the conversation back into my mind. "She said it was impossible and that I had to forget it."

"Well . . ." Alessia watched a lone bird spiraling in the sky. "In order to do it, someone from my Clan has to die. I'd like to think that's impossible, too."

"I know, I know." I pressed my palms to my thighs. "But he's my brother. I have to keep looking."

Alessia nodded. "Oh—something else. It was pretty

obvious that she and the Harpy knew each other. It didn't hit me at the time, because I figured that they've both been around for so long it would be odd if they *didn't* know each other."

A memory slammed back into me. When I was trapped in that room, the Harpy had stood in the corner and laughed while the Rabbit tortured me. I didn't remember most of what she'd said in those long hours; it was gone in the haze of pain and horrifying hallucinations the Rabbit had made me see. But one thing I did remember. *She'll pay for what she did to us,* the Harpy had cackled. *The little Lioness will pay.*

"She's made such a big deal about us knowing each other's identities," Alessia went on, interrupting my thoughts. "Something doesn't add up."

I shoved the memories aside and knocked my knee against Alessia's. "I'm gonna get to the bottom of this. With all of us living under one roof, someone is bound to let something slip. And I am nothing if not sneaky." I put my hand out. "Now help me up. I'm fricking freezing out here."

Jenny's room had an actual bunk bed in it. Apparently her parents thought they'd have another kid someday but either nature or someone's nerve had failed. Alessia climbed to the top bunk. "Jenny hates heights," she explained. "Obviously I don't mind them." She dumped the contents of her bag out onto the bed. We'd gone back to her house and I'd done a masking spell while she and her mom ran all over the place, throwing crap into bags to bring back to Jenny's. And the whole time, they hadn't spoken to each other. I'd sat between them in the truck on the way over, collateral damage in their battle of icy glares. That was a barrel of laughs, let me tell you.

I'd managed to get back to my own house too. I'd done the masking spell, but the house had been empty. Dad was still in Boston, being interviewed by the feds. And shockingly, my mom hadn't been laid up in bed with a bottle of prescription drugs next to her. She hadn't been there at all. I had no idea where she was, but considering how concerned she'd been when I was missing, I decided not to lose sleep over it.

I flopped onto the air mattress that Jeff had set up. "I guess it'll have to do," I said and eyed the bottom bunk. "Although maybe I should take the bed. You know, since I'm injured and all."

Jenny rolled her eyes and leaned against the wall beneath her Taylor Swift poster. "Trust me, the bunk is not that comfortable. I've been begging for a new bed since I was ten."

"Is that when you put that poster up?" I asked, narrowing my gaze at Taylor's signature red-lipsticked smile.

"Hey!" Jenny pointed at me. "Do not mock Taylor. That girl knows how to spin her shit into gold, man."

"Man? *Man?* I saw the shag carpeting downstairs, but I didn't realize I'd time-tripped back to the seventies."

"You're lucky to even *be* here, Bree, so don't make fun of my house."

"Oh, my God, you two, let it go." Alessia dangled her feet over the edge of the bunk. "Seriously, if you two can't get along, I'm going to lose it. There are things bigger than all of us going on."

I grabbed an elastic from the makeup bag I'd brought from home and pulled my hair up into a ponytail. "Alessia, it's *because* of all those big things that I'm just trying to lighten the mood. Jeez."

"Well, don't do it at my best friend's expense."

Jenny grinned, then glanced at the clock. "God, it's not even noon. Staying home from school is boring." She launched away from the wall. "Wanna watch bad reality TV with me in the den?"

"Guess there's nothing better to do." I stood up and stretched. "Ow. You don't happen to have any Percocet, do you?"

"Please. I had to beg my mom to vaccinate me. I think the best I can offer you is willowbark."

Our path to bad reality television was blocked in the hallway by Nerina. "Alessia, I need to talk to you."

With a loud sigh, Alessia waved us on. "I'll meet you downstairs." But as soon as Jenny and I had turned the corner to the steps, I stopped and leaned against the wall. Funny how spying on people had become second nature to me.

"You know, I've had a really rough couple of days," Alessia said. "Can't I just hang out with my friends and

57

relax for a couple of hours?"

"For a couple of hours, yes." Nerina's voice was low. Whatever she said next, I couldn't hear. I did, however, hear Alessia's response. Probably the whole house did.

"I don't really care how sorry you are." Alessia's anger echoed off the walls down the hallway. "I'm sick of being lied to. You know, Jonah told me how much the Malandanti lied to him. I'm starting to think you're no better than they are."

Whoa. Low blow, Alessia. But I couldn't blame her. I was so used to familial lying that it didn't really faze me, but if you'd been raised to be as guileless as Alessia, you'd probably be pretty offended.

"All I can do right now is apologize," Nerina said. Her voice was stronger. She'd taken charge again, stepped back into her *Concilio* persona. "But whatever differences you and I or you and Lidia have, what matters is the Clan. Can we at least agree on that?"

I guessed Alessia nodded, because Nerina said, "Good. You have a job to do tonight."

I leaned forward, using the wall for support.

"What job?" Curiosity and suspicion rounded Alessia's voice. But Nerina's next words made my jaw drop.

"I have found our replacement for the Lynx." I could almost hear the self-satisfied smile that was surely plastered on Nerina's face. "And you will be his Guide."

It looked like Alessia's already complicated life was about to get even more interesting.

CHAPTER SIX
The New Guide

Alessia

It felt odd to be driving rather than flying to my new charge's house. I shifted gears in the ancient truck, chugging up the hill as I crossed the border from Twin Willows into Willow Heights.

Whereas everything in Twin Willows looked slightly rundown, Willow Heights was shiny, sparkly, and clean. The houses there were newer and bigger, the streets lined with trendy shops, and there was even a fancy wine bar on one corner. As I passed the dark alleyway next to the bar, I spied a couple leaning against the building's brick wall, their bodies melding together, and thought of Jonah. Where was he now? Still in that deep underground room at the Guild? What were they doing to him? My breath hitched and I wrenched my attention back to the road in front of me. Tomorrow I would think about Jonah. Tonight I had to deal with our new Clan member.

"It's pretty convenient that there are so many potential Benandanti near here," I had remarked to Nerina as she instructed me on where to go and what to do before I'd left Jenny's house.

"It's not convenience," she'd retorted. "There are always clusters of potential Benandanti around each site. It has been that way since the beginning."

I wondered about the ancient Benandanti who'd protected the Twin Willows site. Had the Native Americans guarded the Waterfall long before Europeans had landed here? I shivered. Who would protect the site after I was gone?

The truck sputtered at the next intersection and I turned left into a residential neighborhood. The wealth of Willow Heights was even more evident on this street. Wide, sweeping lawns graced big, important-looking houses. I turned right at a house that had a fountain at the head of the driveway. It was covered in icicles.

Halfway down the block, I jerked the truck to a stop. My heart convulsed, shuddering with the force of transformation. Not my own . . . the new Benandante's. He was nearby.

I pulled over, threw the truck into park, and jumped out. My skin tingled, the back of my neck on fire. I could feel the new Clan member trying to break his soul free from his body, could feel the struggle inside me as if it were my own. And beneath the pain there was something else . . . a stitching together . . . a mending of the hole that the Lynx had left in our Clan.

Standing very still, I closed my eyes and listened. *There.* One house down, a moan, a whimper, coming from the second-story window. I felt the new Benandante's pain in my own chest, the ache of being torn apart. Even though I was so used to the transformation now, that first one still felt fresh.

I ran to the house and examined my options. I could break in through the front door, but that might wake the entire household. The snow crunched under my boots as I raced around to the backyard. A wooden staircase led to a second-story porch. Jeez, rich people really liked their outdoor space.

The steps and porch above were slicked with ice and snow. Cold crept up through my feet, chilling me as I tried the back door. Unlocked. Nerina had given me her lock-picking kit in case I needed to break in, but apparently crime wasn't a problem in Willow Heights.

Inside, the house was wrapped in a warm middle-of-the-night hush. I tiptoed along the hallway, the tug in my heart growing stronger as I neared the front of the house. The door at the end of the hall was cracked, dim light spilling into the darkness. When I reached it, I took a deep, full breath. *You're ready for this,* Nerina had assured me. Whether I was or not, I pushed the door open.

Our new Clan member lay on the other side of the bed, twisting on the floor. I crept around the bed, spying bare feet, then golden-haired legs, navy blue boxers with the word *Yale* all over them, a bare chest, muscled and tanned, and then finally a face. His face. Our new Clan member. He was barely older than me. Rage shot through me like a sudden burn. *Really, Nerina?* Another kid whose life I had to ruin?

I dropped to my knees beside him. "It's okay," I murmured, grasping his shoulders as a shudder ripped through his body. His skin was sticky with sweat. "Don't fight the shift. Just let it happen."

He opened his eyes, dark blue beneath his mop of sandy hair. "You've . . . come," he gasped. "At . . . last." His hand covered mine, squeezing hard.

I stared at him. Tension tightened his body again. "I'm Alessia," I said. "I know it sounds crazy, but what's happening to you—"

"I know . . . what's happening . . . to me," he muttered in a strangled voice. Blue light gathered at his heart, swirling faster and faster. He was going to shift, any second now. "I've been . . . waiting . . . my whole life . . . for this."

And before I could respond, the light flared out in all directions, shattering the room in a million pieces. I fell back, shielding my eyes from its brightness. When it cleared, the boy lay motionless on the floor, and next to him stood a huge, fierce-looking feline. He wasn't a Lynx; our Lynx, Sam, had been sleek and silvery, the kind of animal that could disappear into a snowdrift. This animal was a Catamount, rugged and tawny, with dark spots markings his face and flank. His oceanic eyes stared out from beneath the ridged fur of his brow.

He let out a low growl and pawed the floor, making the wooden floorboard tremble beneath me. "Shh,"

I hissed, but it was too late. The door to the bedroom
swung wide open, and a tiny firecracker of a woman
stepped into the room. Her dark eyes flashed, taking in
the scene before her. "I—I—he's okay," I managed to get
out, trying to figure out what the hell I could say to this
poor woman whose son was lying as though dead on her
Persian rug.

She looked from me to the boy on the floor to the
Catamount next to him. "Ah," she breathed. "It's finally
happening. I knew it would. I saw it long ago." Her voice
had a slight lilt to it. Not Italian; maybe eastern European.
She marched over to me. I scrambled to my feet just as
she threw her arms around me. "Take good care of him,"
she said. "I know he will serve the Benandanti well."

I jerked away and backed up until I hit the wall. She
gave me one final smile and disappeared out of the room.
What the hell?

Narrowing my gaze at the Catamount, I tore my soul
free. Here I was, prepared to answer a million questions
about what was happening to him, and it seemed I was
the one who needed answers. My body dropped to the
floor beside the boy's and I flew to the ceiling. *You know I
had a whole spiel about who the Benandanti are,* I said. *But
it sounds like I might be wasting my breath.*

If it was possible for Catamounts to grin, he was grinning. *I've known what the Benandanti are since I was little,*
he said.

I blinked. *Doesn't it interest you that we're talking*

telepathically right now?

He leapt lightly from the floor to the window seat that was nestled into the large bay window at the front of the room. *Not really.*

Okay, seriously. I winged down to him. *What the hell is going on?*

Why don't we start with names? You're Alessia. I'm Calvin, only no one but my mother calls me that. Everyone else calls me Cal.

Okay, Cal. How do you know about the Benandanti?

He padded in a small circle around himself. *This is the coolest thing ever! I'm a freaking lion!*

Catamount, I corrected, ruffling my feathers. *And you didn't answer my question.*

You're a Falcon, right? You are so lucky you're a bird. I was kinda hoping I'd be one too so I'd get to fly. But a lion is cool too. Are you going to take me to the magical site? I know there are seven of them. I also know that—

Just—hang on a minute, okay? Jeez! I soared back and forth across the room. How the hell did he know all this? That Benandanti web page I'd found all those months ago didn't have anything about the seven sites on it. And why wasn't he upset that he'd just had his life ruined? The room felt too small suddenly, like my wings would break apart the walls if I were trapped here any longer. *Fine. Let's get out of here.*

Cal led me down the hall to the back door that I'd come through. With a swipe of one of his huge paws, he pushed it open. I swept out into the night, the cold air an elixir for my rumpled soul. I curved around the house, waited for Cal to appear beneath me, and continued up the street. *Follow me. Hope you're up for some exercise.*

Are you kidding? I feel like I could run all night.

The wine bar was shut up and dark now, the kissing couple long since gone as we raced up Willow Heights' quiet Main Street. *Okay, no more dodging. Tell me how you know about the Benandanti.*

I'm not dodging, Cal answered. He jumped over a bench on the sidewalk next to a bus stop. *I'm just excited. This is the best night of my life.*

What? Why?

My mother's a psychic, Cal began. *Not one of those crackpots you see on TV. A real, honest-to-God psychic. When I was born, she had a vision that I would be a Benandante.*

I soared higher, away from him for a moment, my gaze fixed on the stars. *And she told you about it? She didn't hide it from you?*

No, Cal said. *She's been preparing me for this for as long as I can remember. I've studied everything I could find on the Benandanti. We even took a trip to Friuli a few years ago.*

I pinched my mind closed to him. What if Lidia hadn't hidden the Benandanti from me? What if she'd agreed with my dad, that I had a great destiny to fulfill? Would I have been bowled over with excitement the day Heath had Called me? I opened up again. *What about your dad? What does he think about all this?*

He died when I was a baby.

Oh, Cal. I dropped, skimming down over rooftops. *I'm so sorry.* The ache of my own dad's loss uncoiled inside me.

Thanks . . . but I never knew him. My mom really makes up for me not having a dad.

Still, that's really hard . . . being a single mom. I knew the stress, the loneliness that sometimes Lidia couldn't hide.

We do okay. My dad ran a tech company that went public right before he died, so he left her a lot of money. We moved here because we knew it was close to one of the sites.

The great willow tree that marked the boundary between Willow Heights and Twin Willows loomed into view, its sweeping branches crystalline with tiny icicles. I veered around it, the blood pulsing in my head. There wasn't a day, an hour, a minute when I didn't miss my dad. Would it be better to have never known my dad, so I couldn't miss him? So I didn't have that constant pain in my heart where he should be? I soared right through the tree's branches, breaking icicles off in the wake of my beating wings. No. Cal should be pitied for never knowing his father. I was a better person for having known mine. But the other things—the mother who'd been honest with him from day one, the easy money they had to live on without having to struggle. A hot-white bolt of an emotion I didn't like shot through me. Stop it, I told myself. After all, I was the Guide. I had to rise above.

You know, you get a choice, I said. *You can refuse the*

Call. So if you have any major life plans . . .

Well, I did get early admission to Yale, with a soccer scholarship, Cal said. *But I'm going to defer.*

What? Are you nuts? If I'd gotten into an Ivy League school when Heath had come to me, I would've told him to take his Call and shove it.

Who cares about Yale? Cal exclaimed, his enthusiasm bounding around my head like a toddler on sugar overload. *What the Benandanti do is infinitely more important than studying literature written by dead white men.*

Twin Willows' shabby Main Street blurred beneath me. We passed Joe's, Mr. Salter's hardware store, and the high school, all quiet and dark. When he put it like that, the Benandanti's work was more important than anything school could teach, but it still would've been nice to have had the choice. A voice niggled inside me, reminding me that I'd *had* a choice. I wanted to argue with it, but I couldn't. I had made my choice, and I had to stand by it. And deep down I knew that if I could go back and do it all over again, I'd make the same choice.

So I guess I don't need to give you twenty-four hours to decide, huh?

Nope. I'm accepting right here and now.

Snowcapped roofs dotted the world below me. Cal's figure moved in and out of view like a shadow, backlit in cerulean light. *You need to be sure. You need to understand what you're giving up. Your life is going to change drastically. You'll have to lie to your friends. The Benandanti expect you to give up everything in service to them.*

Oh, I know, Cal said. *Yale was actually just a backup in case I didn't get Called. But I knew I would. It's fate.*

Fate, destiny—those words kept chasing me, like a hunter I couldn't outrun. *Seriously?* I asked Cal. *Wouldn't you rather be in the safety of Yale's walls than out here, risking your neck for a future you'll never have?*

I can go to Yale anytime, Cal said. *This is what I need to do right now.*

His certainty made me want to slap him. He had no clue what he was getting into, how his spirit would falter after weeks of no sleep and not even one small victory over the Malandanti, how his heart would break the first time he saw one of his fellow Benandanti fall.

I flew higher, closing my mind to him again. This boy, he would regret this someday.

The air sharpened around me. I circled above rooftops, my feathers knife-edged against the cold night wind. Maybe he wouldn't regret this. Maybe he was sure that this was all he was meant to do in life, that there wasn't anything else out there as important as this. Maybe he really *did* know.

Maybe I wasn't worried for him. Maybe I was jealous.

Which way now?

I didn't answer; I just veered to the left toward my farm. The farmhouse was gilded with moonlight. The weather vane spun as I flew past, its old familiar creak sending a streak of longing through me. I wished I could go home again. I missed my room, the well-worn living room couch, and Lidia's kitchen. Another twinge of longing stabbed me, and I realized what I really wanted was to go back—back to the time when this house was a refuge, when I could trust everyone in it.

Beyond the house, the gloomy ruins of the barn stood shadowed against the night. *Whoa,* Cal said. *What happened here?*

This is my farm. The Malandanti burned down the barn. As a warning.

Crikey, Cal said. *That sucks, Alessia. But we'll get them back, won't we?*

Well, we had gotten them back—by retaking the Waterfall. And then they'd killed the Lynx. And then we'd destroyed the Guild. And then they'd tortured Bree and captured Nerina and reclaimed the Waterfall again. It was a never-ending cycle of destruction. I wanted to believe, like Cal did, that we would get them back, that we would end this, but it was just so hard to keep hope alive anymore.

We passed the empty hen trailers at the edge of the pasture; when we'd claimed the house had mold, we'd moved the hens to the same farm where we were boarding the goats. Cal sprang over the stone wall that marked the edge of the farm, and the gateway to Nerina's old lair, before the Malandanti had discovered it. Branches broke as he barreled through the forest beyond. *We're getting closer,* I told him. *I suppose you already know what this site is.*

Actually, I don't. You guys keep that information really secret. I don't know what any of them do, just where they are.

Well, at least we'd kept one thing out of public knowledge. Like I was reciting a prayer, I listed the sites. *Twin Willows is the site of the Waterfall. One drink of the water will give you a vision of the future. But you cannot choose what you will see. And you may not like what you do see. The Redwood site contains the power of healing. The Congo site has the power to control minds. The Tibetan site is the source of all our power, the power to separate our souls from our bodies. The site in Pakistan has the power to manipulate time and space. The magic of Angel Falls can suck out a life force. And the power of Friuli, the Olive Grove, is the power that binds all these together. Immortality.*

Finally! I've been dying to know all this for years! Cal charged through brush and trees. *So what happens when you accidentally touch the water?*

Slow down, I told him as twigs snapped beneath his paws. *We're almost there.*

Have you ever touched the water? What did you see?

The silvery bark of the birch trees shone in the darkness, and the rumble of the Waterfall echoed back to us. *I mean it, Cal—slow down—*

Was it like a hallucination or was it like a dream that you had to decipher?

Slow down! I screeched.

Too late. Cal's powerful body burst through the trees before he could stop himself. He skidded to a halt at the frozen bank of the stream above the Waterfall and missed colliding with the magical barrier by inches. At the pool down below, the Bobcat and the Boar looked up.

I dove in front of Cal. *Get back,* I ordered.

But—

I swiped one of my talons a breath away from his nose. *Do NOT question me! GET BACK!*

He stumbled into the brush at the same moment that the Boar reached the top of the Waterfall. From the other side of the stream, Cora burst into view. She'd be in hiding, on patrol. In an instant, she was by my side. We dove, claws outstretched. The Boar feinted away from me, but Cora caught it on the other side. It squealed, blood pouring from its nose, and tripped backward. I clipped its flank with my beak, and it rounded on me, its long, pale tusks aimed right at my heart. I buffeted up out of its reach as Cora struck it again, this time at its neck.

Breathing hard, the Boar made one last attempt to gore us, but we were too fast for him. He knew better than to waste his energy trying to catch two winged creatures who could endlessly fly out of his reach with every attack. It stumbled back inside the barrier and joined the Bobcat at the bottom of the Waterfall. During the entire fight, the Bobcat hadn't moved at all, keeping the Malandanti's hold on the Waterfall secure by remaining inside the barrier.

Cora and I flew back into the birch trees and found Cal pacing back and forth. *I could've helped,* he said.

You're not trained, Cora said. *You could've been hurt.*

It was just one Malandante—

The only way we will regain the site is if we have a complete Clan, I said. *We can't risk any threat to that. Until you are fully trained, you will stay out of battle and listen to everything I say.*

Cora cocked her head at me. *I don't think your own Guide could've said it any better.*

Pride and reluctance warred inside me. I still didn't think I was ready to be a Guide. But I couldn't go against the *Concilio,* and I had to trust that Nerina knew what she was doing. It was vital that our Clan be complete, and there was no way Nerina would allow me to be Cal's Guide just for kicks or just to teach me a lesson. *Are you going back on patrol?* I asked Cora.

No sense now that they know I'm here, she said. *I'm going to head back to Jeff's.*

See you back there. Cal and I headed back into town while Cora swooped away toward Jenny's house. *So what happens now?* Cal asked.

Now we train. Every night. I told him that the Sands house was our home base for now and why we were all staying there. *You should just plan to be there every day after school. There's a lot going on right now, with all the Clans.*

When we got back to his house, Cal paced around his body for a minute. I remembered what Heath had told me, so long ago. *Think of something that ties you to your human form.*

He stilled, and a moment later the Catamount disappeared. While Cal gulped down big breaths of air, I dissolved into my own body. I kept my eyes closed for a moment before I sat up, trying to calm the beating wings of the Falcon that still lived inside me. When I opened my eyes, Cal sat on the edge of the bed, his hand pressed to his heart.

"Are you okay?" I asked, getting to my feet.

"I think so. It's just a . . . new sensation."

"Understatement of the year." We stared at each other for a moment and then both started laughing.

"Guess so." Cal grabbed a T-shirt from the floor and pulled it over his head. "Come on, I'll show you out."

The edges of the sky were just beginning to lighten as Cal walked me to my truck. I breathed in the dawn and turned to him. "I think you'll be a good addition to the Clan, Cal." I stuck out my hand for him to shake.

But instead of taking it, he pulled me into a tight hug. I buried my face in his shoulder for a second, breathing in the sleepy, spicy scent of him. He smelled different from Jonah. Softer. Not as complicated. I pushed him away.

"Thanks for being my Guide," he said, his mouth widening into a smile.

"Oh. It wasn't really my choice." His smiled faltered. I put my hands up. "Only because I didn't think I was ready. But, um, now I'm glad."

"Good." He shivered. "I'm gonna go in before I freeze to death. See you tomorrow," he tossed over his shoulder as he jogged back to his house.

"Today," I called after him. He waved to show he'd heard me. I climbed into the truck, started the engine, and turned the heat up to full blast.

A thin line of pink illuminated the horizon as I drove through Willow Heights back to my own town. Maybe I'd underestimated Nerina's cleverness. Because I couldn't help but think that she'd known about Cal, that he'd been Benandanti-obsessed since he was a kid, that he was the eager opposite to my reticence, and that he was the golden sun to the darkened moon that was Jonah. I turned the truck onto Willowbrook Lane. Oh, yeah. She'd known exactly what she was doing when she paired me with Cal.

CHAPTER SEVEN
Like Daughter, Like Mother . . . Finally

Bree

The problem with being beaten within an inch of your life was that it took a really long time to recover. I wanted to punch the movie producers that showed ordinary guys running around like heroes the day after getting pummeled. It was so not realistic.

I lay on the air mattress, cataloging all the things I should have been doing instead of staring at the ceiling: Finding Jonah. Researching another way to get him out of the Malandanti. Spying on my dad to see if I could figure out the Guild's next move. Finding Jonah, finding Jonah, finding Jonah.

Instead, all I could do was watch the shadows move across the walls. I tried to roll over, but every muscle screamed, every bone creaked.

"Hey, Bree. You asleep?"

I turned just my head to the bottom bunk where Jenny lay on her side, watching me. "I wish."

Jenny sighed. "I'm worried about Alessia."

I lifted my gaze to the empty top bunk. She'd gone out to find our new Clan member. Even if she hadn't told me where she was going, I could still sense it deep down, that another Benandante had been Called. Ever since the spell we'd performed at the Waterfall, the one that had brought down the Guild, my mind felt even more attuned to the Clan. Like somehow that spell had woven me deeper into the fabric of the Benandanti. I only wish it attuned me closer to Jonah. I had never felt so far away from him before, and it was making me crazy.

"I'm sure she's fine," I said, pulling my focus back to Jenny. "It's not like they're going into battle or anything."

Jenny flopped onto her back. "Sometimes I wish I was a Benandante."

"Why? 'Cause you see how much fun it is?"

"No, I know, it's stupid." She reached her hand up and ran her fingers along the wooden bars of the bunk above her. "But sometimes I feel like I'm part of it already, because of my dad, but without the superpowers. And that kind of sucks, being on the fringe like that."

"Oh, I don't know. There's a lot to be said for the fringe." I should know. I'd been living on the fringe ever since we started moving around. "You can watch everything that's happening without risking your own neck. And sometimes you can see things more clearly than everyone on the inside."

"Well, that's true." She dropped her hand and looked at me. "For instance, I see that even though you like to keep yourself separate, you really want to be part of the big picture."

I pressed my lips together. "Wow, Jenny. Psychoanalyze much?"

"Why else would you get involved with the Benandanti?"

"Um, *to save my brother*?"

She squinted at me in the dark. "What does your brother have to do with this?"

Holy crap, she didn't know. I had to hand it to Alessia for not spilling that secret. With a grunt, I hoisted myself up on my elbow. "Jonah is a Malandante. I figured Alessia told you."

"Shit." Jenny whistled long and low. "So *that's* why they broke up."

"Yep. Nothing like finding out your boyfriend is actually your archenemy."

"I warned her," Jenny said in a disgustingly smug voice. "I warned her that he was a bad boy."

"Yeah, yeah, you're smarter than the rest of us," I said, then added, "He's not evil. He wants out of the Malandanti. Alessia and I are trying to figure out a way to do that."

Jenny brushed her hair away from her face. "You can't just resign your post from the Malandanti. Or the Benandanti. My dad tried when I was born, but they wouldn't let him."

"In it for life, baby." I slid back down under my blanket. In some ways, there was not much separating the Malandanti from the Benandanti. Both sides required absolute dedication from their members. Both sides made you sign a contract for life. No exceptions.

Except . . .

There was an exception. I squirmed a little, trying to get comfortable. That thing I'd found, buried deep in the Angel Falls book, that thing that no one wanted to talk about. A Benandante could die and willingly gift his or her essence to a Malandante, turning one side into the other.

The bedroom door creaked open and Alessia's shadow stretched across the floor and the wall opposite. She shucked off her boots and tiptoed past me, obviously under the mistaken impression that I could possibly sleep.

"How's the new guy?" I asked when she'd put her foot on the bottom rung of the ladder up to her bunk.

"Jesus!" She stumbled off the ladder, her hand pressed to her chest. "You scared the crap out of me." Taking a deep breath, she looked from me to Jenny and back again. "How'd you know it was a guy?"

I shrugged. "Just assumed, since Mr. Foster was." Actually, that wasn't true. I'd sensed his maleness, just like I'd sensed his Calling. But I wanted to keep my sharpened senses to myself for a little longer.

"Yeah well, I'd be a lot happier if he was a girl." Alessia pulled her sweatshirt off, padded out of the room, and returned a moment later with a glass of water. "This guy, *Cal*—he's been obsessed with the Benandanti since he was like a toddler. His mother had a vision that he'd be Called. A *vision*." She gulped down the water so hard that some splashed onto the front of her tank top. "He's all like, 'I've been to Friuli! I'm going to defer my acceptance to Yale because nothing's more important than the Benandanti! Don't you think nothing's more important than the Benandanti, Alessia?' *God!*"

Jenny started laughing. I leveled my gaze at Alessia and asked, "Does my brother need to be worried?"

Alessia stared at me. "What? No. Absolutely not. Cal is the most annoying person I've ever met."

"And so starts every great romantic comedy ever made," Jenny said.

"Oh, my God! Not even a little bit. Will you guys stop it?" She stomped over to the bed and hoisted herself up the ladder. "He's actually happy he got Called. He has no clue how much it's going to ruin his life."

"The lady doth protest too much, methinks," I said.

"Seriously, Alessia." Jenny knocked on the bars of the bottom bunk, making Alessia jump a little. "You act like being a Benandante is the worst thing in the world. It's not."

"Um, I think I know better—"

"No, you don't." Jenny jumped out of bed and stood in the middle of the room, her hands on her hips. "Look at my dad. He's been in the Clan since he was twenty-six. I was still a baby. He was going to go back to grad school. Instead he settled here to protect the Waterfall. He made a different life for himself than what he thought he wanted, but that doesn't mean he's not happy." She jabbed a finger in Alessia's direction. "There isn't a day that goes by when he doesn't tell my mom and me how blessed he is. You should be so lucky." She blew a long, hard breath out. "So quit your bitching."

I dragged myself up to sitting and clapped, whistling loudly. Alessia glared at me. Jenny turned slightly pink and slid back into her bunk. "Shut up," she told me. "You'll wake the house."

"I have to find Jonah," I told Alessia the next morning while Jenny was in the shower and we had the room to ourselves. "I can't stand lying around here without knowing what's going on with him."

"I know," Alessia said. "Every minute that I don't hear from him is a minute that he could be . . ."

"Don't say it."

"I wasn't going to. He's okay. I have to believe that." Alessia tugged a thick blue sweater over her head. "Maybe I'll see him at school today . . ."

"He's not going to be there. I don't think the Malandanti will let him out of their sight."

"Unless the Malandanti have a Clan member at the school watching him." Alessia pulled on her beat-up UGGs and sat in the swivel chair at Jenny's desk. "I mean, if he doesn't show up at school, that's going to raise suspicion, isn't it?"

"Maybe." I stretched my arms overhead, testing to see how far I could go before the pain kicked in. Stabbing pain arced across my ribs. Not far, it seemed. "Look, I know you and your perfect GPA are dying to get back to school, but do you think you could skip today? I need to get out of this house and do some snooping, but I can't do it alone."

Alessia grinned at me. "Wow, Bree. I think that's the first time I've ever heard you ask for help."

I pointed at her. "You'd better not screw up and make me regret it."

She chewed her lip. "The thing is, I'm not really talking to Lidia right now, so I can't ask her to call in for me."

"Get Nerina to call. She has an Italian accent. No one in the office will know the difference."

Once half the house went out either to school or work, and Nerina had made the call, Alessia and I slipped out the front door. "We'll go to my house first," I said. "No use trekking all the way to Bangor if Jonah's just around the corner."

Alessia shot me a look. "Do you think he is?"

I shook my head. "But it's worth a shot."

"What if your dad is there?"

"That's why I needed you to come with me." We took another residential side street to get to my house, rather than take Main Street and risk being seen by all our classmates on their way to school. "We'll have to sneak in through the second-story bathroom in order to avoid being seen."

"Wait, *what*?"

I didn't say anything else until we reached my block.

Sure enough, both my parents' cars sat in the driveway. I tried not to think about the last time I was in that driveway, when the Harpy dumped me into her trunk and hauled me away. My bruises ached with the effort of not thinking about it.

"This way." I led Alessia around the side of the house, careful to skirt the outside of my dad's office. "I just need a boost up this tree," I said, pointing to the long, sturdy branch that stretched out beneath the bathroom window.

"Are you kidding me?"

I raised my eyebrows. "What's the problem?"

"Don't think I didn't notice how much you huffed and puffed on the way over here. You winced with every step, Bree. You can't go climbing up that tree."

"Well, every other way into the house is way too obvious. The back door opens about four feet from my dad's office. So what do you suggest?" I moved to the tree and reached up toward the lowest branch, careful to keep from scrunching up my face in pain.

"Oh, fine. Here." Alessia knelt down and cupped her hands for me to step into. I hoisted myself onto the branch with a grunt, gritting my teeth as my ornery ribs protested. But from the lowest branch, it was an easy climb to the window ledge. I waited at the top for Alessia to clamber up behind me. "Hope it's not locked," she said when she reached me, a little breathless.

I knew it wouldn't be; Jonah and I never locked it, in case something just like this happened, and Mom and

Dad didn't use this bathroom. I slid the window up and eased into the bathroom. I spied my tube of mascara on the sink and stashed it in my pocket. In the mirror, I caught Alessia rolling her eyes at me. "What? I need long eyelashes to distract from the bruises."

We tiptoed out into the hall and straight down to Jonah's room. It was cold and empty, the bed neat and unslept in for who knew how many days. His messenger bag sat filled with his schoolbooks on the floor next to his desk. Alessia pointed to it at the same moment I spotted it. "He hasn't been here in a while," she whispered. I tried not to notice how pale her face had become. Sometimes I forgot that I wasn't the only one affected by Jonah's absence.

"He probably hasn't been back since he was at the Guild with you guys," I murmured back. "They must still be keeping him there."

Alessia ran her hand over a sweatshirt that hung on the back of the desk chair. "We can't go back there to look for him. There's no way we'll get out alive this time."

"I know." I hugged myself and turned in a slow circle, taking in the room like one of Jonah's uber-pretentious posters was going to help us. I glanced back at Alessia, who had brought the sweatshirt to her face, breathing in deep. *Oh, for Chrissakes.* "He's not dead, Alessia. Stop wallowing."

She looked at me. Her eyes were shiny. "I'm sorry. I just . . ." She trailed off and sniffled.

I crossed the room and pulled the sweatshirt out of her grasp. "I know I make a big show about being the older twin and looking out for Jonah and all, but the truth is he's not helpless. He can take care of himself, you know. Whatever it is the Malandanti are doing to him, he's figuring out a way to get out of it."

She dried her wet cheeks on the sleeve of the sweatshirt. "You're right. He's stronger than you give him credit for."

"Gee, thanks." I tugged her arm, nudging her out of the room. Without Jonah, it was too gloomy in here. "Come on. Let's not have this trip be a total waste."

We headed back into the hall. I popped into my room to grab a few things I'd forgotten the last time we were here, other than the mascara, and shoved them into my backpack. On our way toward the stairs down to the kitchen, I stopped. The sound of a morning talk show drifted from the crack beneath my parents' closed bedroom door. "Wait here," I told Alessia.

Gently, I pushed the door open.

The lights were off inside the bedroom, giving the impression of dusk when it was actually nine in the morning. The light from the television flickered across the bed, where my mother lay, staring at the screen without seeing.

"Mom?" I whispered.

She didn't answer. I crept closer. An empty bottle of pills lay on its side on the nightstand, next to a half-full glass of amber liquid that I was certain wasn't iced tea.

"Mom?" I asked again.

The covers surrounding her rustled a tiny bit. She blinked, moving her gaze from the television, across the bedspread, and onto the sheepskin rug on which I stood. Her eyes widened when they saw me. "Bree?" she croaked. Then, like she used to do when I was little and had had a nightmare, she held up the covers as an invitation for me to climb in.

A tiny sob escaped me. I crossed to the bed in two aching strides and slid into bed with her. Beneath the covers, I felt her frail arms come around me. I buried my head in her pillow, hiding from her the tears that spilled down my face. "What happened to you, baby?" she murmured, stroking my hair. I sniffled and looked up. Despite the pills, her eyes were surprisingly clear. "Where's Jonah?" she asked.

I stared at her. The sound of the television fed into my consciousness, and I became aware of what it was playing. MSNBC was running a special program about the fallout from the revelations about the Guild. Mom followed my gaze to the television and tightened her arm around me. "It's finally happening. All your dad's chickens are coming home to roost."

I could swear there was a note of glee in her voice. I turned away from her and watched the television for a few minutes. A news ticker scrolled along the bottom: *Mysterious illness grows worse in Asia . . . Doctors are stymied as the death toll climbs . . .* God, the world really was fucked up. I shifted away from all the bad news on the screen and faced Mom fully. "Mom, I can't explain, but Jonah and I are involved too. I have to stay out of the house for a while. It's not safe for me to be here, so I'm staying someplace where I can be protected. Okay?"

She took my face into her hands. "I'm so sorry, Bree. I should've put a stop to all this a long time ago. I should've run away with you two before your dad could drag you into all this."

"Yes, you should have." She jerked back at the baldness of my truth. It was true. But it also didn't matter now. I sighed. "Mom, we've all made a lot of mistakes. And hopefully we'll all have a lot of time to make it up to each other. But right now, I can't be here to make you feel better about yourself."

Mom studied my face. "I don't blame you for being mad, Bree. I know I haven't been around enough, but right now, whatever you need, I'm here to help." With her thumbs, she stroked my brows, her eyes soft on mine. "I got a phone your dad doesn't know about. I'll text you the number. You can reach me on that." Her jaw clenched. "As soon as all this is over, I'm getting us out of here. Just the three of us—you, me, and Jonah. I'm done being the punching bag in this family."

And suddenly I realized, the pills and the whiskey on the nightstand . . . They were an act. She wanted my dad to think she was helpless and catatonic, completely unthreatening. She was like the lioness that crouches in the brush, ready to defend her cubs at the slightest hint of danger.

Well. Score one for Mom.

I glanced toward the door. "I have to go. Is Dad here?"

She nodded. "He's downstairs in the office with that awful assistant of his."

I gave her a tight, quick hug and slid from the bed. "I'll call you later so you know I'm okay."

"All right, baby." When I reached the door, her voice stopped me again. "Bree?"

I turned.

"Whatever you're doing, I know it's the good fight. I'm proud of you."

And just like that, the mom I'd had when I was nine years old was back again.

Alessia and I didn't speak as we snuck downstairs. I pseudo-signed that my dad was in the office and somehow she understood. We held our breath until we reached the back of the house where my dad's office was and saw that the door was closed. I turned to her.

"There's a window in his office," I whispered. "He usually keeps it cracked because that room overheats. We might be able to hear better from outside than through the door."

"Let's go."

We went out through the kitchen and edged along the house until we got to the office window. Sure enough, it was open a few inches, and angry male voices spiraled out of it. Alessia and I dropped to the ground and crawled until we were directly beneath it. We sat with our backs up against the house, the cold snow that dappled the earth seeping in through our jeans.

"We have control of the Waterfall again. We can start building the plant any day now—"

"How dense are you, Wolfe?" Pratt said, cutting my dad off. "The federal government has ordered a halt on all projects until the investigation is over. That will be years. And we know it won't end well."

"I don't understand. What happened to the magic? Why is this all coming out now?"

The sound of a hand thudding against wood made the wall shake. Pratt had obviously pounded the desk, and he kept hitting it on every other word while he spoke. I hoped his freaking hand broke. "They had a mage, Wolfe. And you want to know who it was?"

I cringed.

"Your fucking daughter."

The silence that stretched across the room and through the crack in the window toward us was horror-movie thick. Alessia grappled for my gloved hand and squeezed it with her own.

"Are you—are you sure?" My father's voice was laden with some emotion I couldn't read. Not without seeing his face. I wanted to peer in through the window so bad, but Alessia kept me still.

"Oh, I'm sure. The *Concilio* took her into custody, but she managed to escape." There was a creak, like Pratt had just leaned back in Dad's old leather desk chair. "Do you know where she is?"

Dad cleared his throat. "Ah, no. No I don't."

Another creak. "Are you certain of that?"

"Just what are you accusing me of, Pratt?"

"Well, let's see, Wolfe. Your daughter is a member of the rival faction and performs a spell that dismantles all the magic the Guild was using, throwing us into complete chaos and effectively rendering us useless. Now, I know kids can be smart, but I have a hard time believing she got there on her own."

Dad barked a short, sharp laugh. "You obviously don't know Bree."

Despite myself, I smiled.

"I'm not joking around here, Wolfe."

"Do you honestly think that I had anything to do with Bree joining the Benandanti?" Now it was Dad's hand pounding the desk. "After all the years of loyalty I've given the Guild? After I sacrificed my own son to the Malandanti?"

"You know, it doesn't matter what I think. It matters what the *Concilio* thinks, and I can guarantee they're not happy with you. That's not a good place to be right now, when they're looking for a scapegoat."

"I am not going to take the fall for this!"

"Well, someone has to, and it's not going to be me." The chair creaked again, and I heard Pratt's expensive shoes click across the floor. "But if you're lucky, it won't come to that."

"What do you mean?"

"We have a failsafe in place, of course. Give the *Concilio* some credit. They are always prepared."

Alessia tensed at the same instant I did. We both tilted our heads up, listening hard. A failsafe? What the hell did that mean?

"Just tell me what I have to do. You know I'll do it." Dad's tone was soft and low, defeated. Despite everything, despite the absolute disgust I felt for him, my heart squeezed just a little. I knew he'd gotten himself into this mess, that he'd made his bed a long time ago and now he had to lie in it, but still. He was my dad.

"I haven't been given instructions yet, but when I get them, you'll know." Pratt's footsteps crossed the room away from us, and I heard the door open. "I'm on patrol in fifteen minutes. Oh, and Wolfe?"

"Yes?"

"If you see your daughter, if she comes back here, you know what you have to do."

A bone-deep chill swept through me. My father didn't answer, but he must have acquiesced, because I heard the door close behind Pratt as he left. I tugged away from Alessia and raised myself up so that I could just peek into the window. Dad sat slumped at the desk, his head in his hands, his fingers pulling hard at his hair.

Alessia hauled me to my feet and together we stumbled through the woods at the back of my house, cutting through backyards on our way to Jenny's. I felt like I'd just survived a house of horrors, that I'd escaped the chainsaw-wielding serial killer and come out on the other side, bruised and battered but alive. I became slowly aware that Alessia was talking, talking, talking next to me. I stopped, squeezed my eyes shut, and shook my head a little to clear out my thoughts. When I opened my eyes, I faced her. "What did you say?"

"I said, we need to know what that failsafe is."

"Well, I think I can rule out going back there to eavesdrop again. You heard what they said. I don't think I can even go to school safely."

"No, you definitely can't," Alessia agreed.

Above us, the bare branches rattled in the wind. I watched the clouds shift between light and dark, dark and light. My phone buzzed in my pocket. When I pulled it out, I had one new message from a number I didn't recognize. It just read *Mama Wolf.*

It was what I used to call her when I was little. I punched in a reply.

> I need you to call the school and excuse me for a while. Not safe for me to go there.

> OK.

I held the phone tight. I might not be able to step foot out of the Sands house without risking my neck, but at least I still had a lifeline to home.

CHAPTER EIGHT
The Date with the Panther

Alessia

When we got back to Jenny's house, Cal was sitting on the living room couch, flanked by Heath and Nerina like an Egyptian Pharaoh perched on a dais with his loyal subjects surrounding him. "Who's that tasty dish?" Bree asked as we took off our coats and hung them by the door.

"That's Cal." I watched Bree give him the once-over. She made an appreciative noise, and I bit back a grin. I could see it now: the golden boy and the bad girl. They were a perfect match. *Take that, Nerina.* "Come on, I need some coffee."

Bree followed me into the kitchen and dropped into a chair at the table. The rings around her eyes seemed to have darkened since we left her house. I reached for the full and thankfully fresh pot of coffee on the counter and offered it up to her. "You want?" She nodded. I poured her a cup and set it on the table in front of her. "You should get some rest this afternoon."

She snorted. "I don't think I'll ever sleep again."

"Yeah." I sat next to her, wrapping my hands around my mug. Heat seeped slowly back into my fingers. "I know what you mean."

We drank our coffee in silence for a while, listening to the bits and pieces of the conversation that drifted back to us from the living room. Nerina and Heath were schooling Cal on the finer points of what it meant to be a Benandante. He was probably taking notes. With a glitter pen in his sparkly Benandanti notebook. And doodling *I <3 the Benandanti* in the margins. I rubbed my temples. I didn't know how I was going to focus on his training when I had so many other things crowding into my mind. Like where was Jonah?

"I'm sure he's still alive," Bree said, somehow reading my thoughts. "If he was dead, my dad would've been told. Pratt would've been out finding his replacement."

"I'm on patrol at the Waterfall tonight," I said, suddenly remembering. "Maybe he will be too."

"Let's hope," Bree said. She stared down into her coffee. "They must be keeping him at the Guild, and we sure as hell aren't getting back in there anytime soon." Her phone buzzed and she pulled it out of her pocket. "My mom says she'll snoop in Dad's office as soon as he leaves the house."

"So our trip wasn't a complete waste." I pressed my lips together. "Was she, you know, okay when you saw her?"

"Surprisingly, yes. But she's been a mess for a long time and I don't want to push it." Bree ran her finger around the rim of her mug. "It's so weird—it's like the minute my dad starts to shrink, she starts to grow."

"Your dad kept her down for a long time," I said, remembering all the things Jonah had told me about how his mom used to be the breadwinner of the Wolfe house, and then his dad made her quit her job and stay at home after he was hired by the Guild. "Maybe she's finally getting her chance to step up again."

Bree looked out the kitchen window. A gust of wind rattled the pane. "Maybe. I hope so. But I don't want to get ahead of myself."

"I won't say anything," I promised.

"Thanks." She looked back at me. "You know, we make a good team, Jacobs. Who would've thought?"

I grinned at her.

Nerina appeared in the doorway to the kitchen, her phone pressed to her ear. "How many did you say there were?" She was speaking in Italian, so I assumed it was a *Concilio* member on the other end of the line. "But that's impossible."

A voice crackled through the phone, not quite loud enough for me to hear. "Yes, perhaps they did transfer them from another site," Nerina continued. "That would be the best explanation. I don't even want to think what the worst might be."

Bree nudged me. "Translation, please?"

I translated Nerina's side of the conversation for Bree while Nerina said good-bye and hung up. "What was all that about?"

Nerina tapped the phone against her mouth. "That

was our *Concilio* member who is stationed at the Angel Falls site. Last night they attempted to retake the site and were met by a horde of Malandanti."

"Did we retake it?" I asked at the same time that Bree said, "What do you mean, *a horde*?"

"No, they failed. There were over two dozen Malandanti. They were lucky to get out alive," Nerina said.

"But that's impossible," I said, echoing what Nerina had said moments earlier.

"Yes, I know." Nerina gazed out the window for a long moment, her eyes fixed on the gray sky. "But there are possibilities, things we don't even want to imagine."

"You said not to underestimate the Malandanti," I said, "so we have to imagine them."

"*Sí,* you are right." Nerina snapped her attention back to me. "By the way, I want you to take Cal out on patrol with you tonight."

"What? Why? I wasn't allowed on patrol for, like, weeks after I was Called," I said, following her back into the living room where Heath and Cal sat on the couch. If Jonah was there tonight, having Cal around was going to be a major hindrance.

"We don't have time for that," Heath said. "He needs to get the lay of the land around the Waterfall."

"I don't want to get into another confrontation with the Malandanti," I said, giving Cal a pointed look.

"I'm really sorry about that," Cal said, a look of contrition painted across his features. On most other people it would seem phony, but you could tell it was genuine on him. He had a good heart—the *Concilio* wouldn't have Called him if he didn't—and that radiated out through his face. "I was rash and dumb, and it won't happen again."

"Don't go past the birch trees," Nerina suggested. "They won't consider us a threat unless we get too close to the barrier."

I looked at Heath with pleading in my eyes. "Can't you come? I don't know the first thing about Guiding someone."

Heath stumbled backward with his hand over his heart, like I'd shot him with an arrow. "That hurts, Alessia. That really hurts."

"Oh, come on." I rolled my eyes. "You just barely finished training me. I don't know why everyone thinks I'm ready to be a Guide."

"You are a lot more ready than you think, *cara*," Nerina said.

"I have faith in you," Cal piped up from the couch. I half-laughed, half-snorted. Okay, maybe there *was* something kind of refreshing about his enthusiasm. I'd only been in the Clan for like four months, and I was already jaded. Maybe if I'd been Called at a time when the Guild hadn't been breathing down our necks, if my boyfriend hadn't turned out to be a Malandante, I would be just as gung ho about the Benandanti as Cal was. But there were too many ifs and maybes now, and my heart had been broken one too many times.

But if Jonah *was* at the Waterfall tonight, I'd have to figure out a way to keep Cal and his enthusiasm out of the way.

Bree sauntered into the room, her hands wrapped around her refilled mug of coffee. Cal took one look at her, sat up straighter, and smoothed his hair down. I'd become so used to Bree's presence that I'd forgotten the effect she had when you saw her for the first time, with that long raven hair and crystal-green eyes. Her usually luminous skin was still mottled with bruises and cuts, which made its own impression. She looked like a porcelain doll that could take you down with a single blow.

Cal cleared his throat and got to his feet. "Hi, I'm Cal. I don't think we've met yet."

Bree leveled her gaze at him. "Bree. I'm the mage."

Cal glanced from her to Nerina. "What's a mage?"

"A mage is the person who's going to save your ass in battle," Bree said. She took Cal's offered hand, a slow grin stretching her mouth wide. As they stood staring at each other, their hands still clasped, I saw Nerina roll her eyes and shake her head. I bit my lip to keep from laughing out loud. So much for her plan to distract me from Jonah.

Bree pulled her hand free from Cal's and turned to the rest of us. "Alessia and I were just at my house," she announced.

Nerina rounded on her. "What? Without any kind of protection?"

"That was really risky, Bree," Heath said.

"We're here, aren't we?" Bree shrugged. "So it all worked out okay."

"Why on earth did you go back there? You know the Harpy is looking for you."

Bree's gaze flickered to me. I gave a tiny shake of my head, so small that Heath and Nerina missed it. But I could've sworn Cal saw it. His eyes narrowed at me. I ignored him.

"I needed to check on my mom. She's not doing great, obviously," Bree said. "We eavesdropped outside my dad's office. He was in there with Pratt—"

"—the Raven," I supplied to Cal.

"—and they were talking about the Guild, about them having a failsafe in place in case something like this happened."

Nerina clenched her jaw. "Did they say what it was?"

"No." Bree leaned against the mantel over the fireplace. "Could it have something to do with the telephone call you just had?"

"Yes. Or no. It could be anything." Nerina ran her red-nailed fingertip over her bottom lip. How she had time to keep her hands perfectly manicured, I had no idea. "There are so many pieces flying around. It is hard to see how they fit together, *sí*? But at least we know they are planning something. And I would bet it involves one of the sites they still control."

"I'll hit the books we salvaged from your lair," Bree said.

"I'll help you," Heath offered.

"And I'll see if I can find out anything at the Waterfall

tonight." I crossed the room until I stood right in front of Cal. "Listen. Tonight, on patrol, if I tell you to do something, you do it. No matter what. No questions asked. Okay?"

Cal nodded. "Absolutely. No problem." He shifted his weight from one foot to the other. "Should I—stay here? Help with the research?" He shot a look at Bree, who tossed her hair back and ignored him. Wow, she really had that hard-to-get thing down.

"No, you should get some rest before patrol tonight," Nerina said before I could answer. "Sleep now while you can."

Cal looked a little crestfallen, but he obeyed Nerina and left. "He could've helped," I said to her. "Three pairs of eyes are better than two."

"The last thing we need right now is for our mage to get distracted," Nerina said.

"I resent that," Bree snapped. "I'm not Alessia."

"Hey, *I* resent *that*," I said.

"Stop it, you two," Nerina said, heading for the den. "There's enough teenage angst in this house as it is."

"I don't do angst," Bree said, and the two of them bickered all the way into the den, their voices carrying back into the living room.

I ran my hands through my hair and looked at Heath. "Please come with me tonight. Please."

He slung his arm around my shoulder. "You really are ready to be a Guide. I wouldn't have let Nerina choose you if I didn't think so." I avoided his eyes. Better to let him think that was the reason I wanted him to come. But

Heath was smarter than that. He pulled his arm away. "You want to talk to Jonah tonight, don't you?"

"If he's on patrol, yes." I swallowed hard. "If he knows something about this failsafe, he'll tell me."

"And if the Malandanti find out what he's doing . . ."

"I know." I gripped Heath's hand. "But I need to talk to him. And it will be harder with Cal there. This way you can keep Cal occupied and I can . . ."

Heath closed his eyes and inhaled deep. "Fine. Fine." He jabbed a finger at me. "But I hope your Padawan will someday cause you as much stress as you've caused me."

My heart pounded loud as I flew away from Jenny's house that night. Heath and Cal streaked across the ground below, their auras shimmering like beacons in the dark. We headed for my farm and led Cal down my driveway and over the hill behind the house.

Will you rebuild it? Cal asked when we passed the ruins of the burned barn.

I hope so. I flew over the stone wall that marked the edge of our property, while Cal and Heath leapt over it. *And Nerina's underground hideout too. But not until it's safe to come back here.*

Not until we destroy them, right?

It's a lot easier said than done, Heath said. *The war between the Benandanti and Malandanti has been raging for centuries.*

But there's something about now, isn't there? asked Cal. *Somehow it feels like it's all coming to a head, doesn't it?*

I swerved around the tops of tall pine trees, the wind whistling through my feathers. Cal was right. It *did* feel like the war was coming to a head. I wondered if it felt like that just because I was part of it now, if every generation of Benandanti had felt the same as me. Was I just one small part of the longer story, or was I appearing in the final chapters?

We can only hope you're right, Heath said, interrupting my solitary thoughts, *and that we are the ones who prevail.*

Up ahead, the birch trees came into view. I dropped low, darting through and around bare branches until I reached the birches. *This is as far as you go,* I told Cal.

True to his word, Cal didn't protest. He belly-crawled into the thickest part of the copse and hunkered down. Heath picked his way into the brush just beyond the birches. *You go ahead,* he said to me.

I almost didn't want to crest the trees. If Jonah wasn't there . . . I'd gotten my hopes so high that even the idea was crushing. I had to remind myself there was a good chance he wouldn't be there, that he was still trapped inside the Guild. With heavy wings, I rose up and over the back side of the stream, peering into the magical bubble below.

Almost immediately, the Raven's hateful black shape loomed just inside the barrier at the top of the Waterfall. He beat his wings, so fast and so mocking that I wanted to punch through the barrier and slice his throat open with my talons. *I know who you are,* I thought at him, my body humming with anger. *I know what you're doing. Alessia?*

I tumbled backward in the air, the sound of Jonah's voice in my head a shot of sweet pain. Tearing myself away from the Raven, I rounded the barrier and flew down to the pool at the base of the Waterfall. Jonah stood on its banks, his paws sinking deep into the snowy ground there. *I felt you,* he said to me. *I heard what you said to the Raven.*

Jonah! My body shook with relief and gratitude that he was there, that he was alive, that he seemed to be okay. I flew close to the barrier, remembering just in time how much it would hurt if I actually hit it. *Are you all right? What did they do to you?*

Wait. He leapt lightly up the rocks at the side of the Waterfall. The Raven fluttered down to meet him. After a moment, Jonah wheeled around and burst through the barrier. *Go. Fly like I'm chasing you.*

I took off like an arrow through the trees, over the brush, and past the birches. Jonah rushed after me. I heard Cal howl as he ran past, but Heath muffled his cry with one of his own. I had no idea what Heath would say to explain this to Cal, but I couldn't worry about that now. I drew Jonah far away from the Waterfall, back over the stone wall, all the way to the shadowy ruins of our barn. There was no moon tonight, and the crumbling structure would hide us from anyone or anything that happened past.

Jonah crouched beside the remnants of the milking

pens, the blackness of his form blending into the dark so that only his green eyes showed. I fluttered down to him and pressed my face into his neck. *Are you okay? Where have you been?*

They've been keeping me at the Guild in Bangor, he said.

What did they do to you after they came back and found us gone?

I felt him shudder against me. He shifted so that I could settle between his front paws, almost like an embrace. It wasn't close enough, but it would have to do. *They weren't happy. But I think they believed me, that you guys overpowered me and escaped. I mean, they must have, because they didn't kill me. But they were definitely suspicious.*

And they've been keeping you locked up since then?

Yes. It's been a regular reeducation camp.

A sick feeling dropped in my gut. *What do you mean? Have they been . . .*

I didn't need to say the word; Jonah felt it in my mind. *No, they haven't been torturing me. Not physically, anyway.*

Then . . . what? I didn't want to know, but I needed to.

They never leave me alone. There's always a Malandanti—or a member of the Concilio—*with me.* His aura crackled, the anger from his words fueling it with energy. *If there's one thing the Malandanti are experts in, it's mind games.*

Oh, Jonah.

His eyes met mine and in their jeweled depths I saw a twinkle, the spark of the Jonah I knew and loved. *Luckily,*

I am even more skilled at mind games than they are. After all, I learned from the master.

Bree?

Bree, he confirmed, a note of laughter in his voice. *Is she okay?*

She's healing. She's worried about you. I nestled my head right against his throat, feeling the thrum of his pulse there. *We went to your house today and overheard your dad and Pratt talking. Something about a failsafe.*

I've heard them mention it too. Before I could ask, he answered. *I don't know what it is. No way are they trusting me with that information.*

Damn. I arced my head back and forth, stroking the curve of his neck with my face.

But it might have something to do with the Tibetan site.

Why do you think that?

Because half the Concilio *left for Tibet last night.*

I pulled away from him. *Really? That's huge. Thanks. I'll tell my Clan to start looking there.*

Don't thank me. I'm just doing what's right. His paw scratched the ground. *Come back here.* I snuggled back into him. We were silent for a long moment. I listened to his heartbeat, deep and strong.

Do you think they'll let you come back to school soon?

I hope so. Maybe tomorrow. He lowered his head so that it rested on my feathery back. *I'm definitely gaining back their trust. That's why they let me out on patrol tonight. Plus . . .*

I held my breath. *What is it?*

I think . . . I don't know . . . it feels like they're desperate.

What do you mean?

Well, look what happened at the Guild. Why didn't they just kill me for letting you get away?

Because they can't lose a Clan member.

Yes . . . because it would take too long to find a replacement and train him, right? But why? They've done it before, killed someone for stepping out of line, I know they have. So why take the time then and not now?

Because the war is coming to a head, I answered, echoing Cal's words. *Because they don't have the time to spare.*

Exactly. Jonah tilted his head upward, his gaze fixed on the stars above us. *They're in a precarious position and they know it. I think they used to believe that a Malandanti victory was a given, and it's not anymore.*

No, I said, *it's not. At least I hope it's not.*

Jonah brought his head back down, pressed his face to mine. *And I hope I'm on the right side when it does end.*

I didn't answer. I couldn't. Not when wishing for such a thing meant the death of one of my Clan. Cold wind swept through the ruins, rustling my feathers and Jonah's fur. He brought his hind legs in closer, curling tighter around me. *Who was that Catamount?*

Our Lynx replacement. We just Called him last night. Oh, and I've been chosen as his Guide. So not my decision.

Ugh, that sucks. Like you need one more thing on your plate. He paused. *Him?*

Yeah, it's a guy from Willow Heights High. He's all like, "Being a Benandante is the best thing ever!" Makes me want to vomit.

Uh-huh. Jonah moved slightly away from me. *So he's a, uh, kid . . . like us?*

Yeah. He's a senior.

Do you like him?

He's okay, I guess.

Jonah backed away even more, and I looked up at him.

Oh, my God, no! Not like that at all. Come on. I can't deal with your jealousy on top of everything else.

Sorry. He resettled next to me. *It's just, you get to spend all this time with him and we have to lie to everyone in order to meet.*

I know. I hate it too.

The wind swept through the barn, rattling the loose fragments of burned wood. Clouds shifted over the moonless sky, turning everything smoky gray. *I should get back,* Jonah said. I could feel the tug of sorrow in his words, the same tug I felt in my heart. *I'm going to tell him I injured you, so don't follow me.*

I pulled myself away from him, already cold from his absence. *Stay safe.*

I will. Mind-game master, remember?

I know, but . . .

Alessia, it's going to be okay. Maybe I'll even be at school tomorrow.

For a long moment, we stood inches apart, our eyes

devouring each other in the same way I knew our arms and lips and bodies would be if we were human. *I love you,* I said.

I know, he said. *It's the only thing keeping me alive.* And then he was gone, sinking into the night as deeply as the pain sank into my heart.

CHAPTER NINE
The Old Guide

Alessia

So, Cal said when I got back to the birch grove. *You and the Panther, huh?*

I snapped my beak at Heath. *You told him?*

I didn't, I swear. I told him you didn't need help, and he got suspicious.

I was accepted for early admission to Yale, Cal said. *I'm not an idiot.*

I didn't know he was a Malandante when I fell—met him. Obviously.

Obviously. Cal winked one of his huge, amber eyes at me. *That must really suck.*

Yeah, it's not ideal.

But you know . . . I could tell that Cal had blocked Heath out, that he was speaking only to me now. *Okay, I hope this comes out the way I want it to. But, you're lucky, too.*

What do you mean?

To love someone like that. Even if you can't be with him. To feel that deeply. I know it might seem like cold comfort, but that's something, Alessia. I've never been in love like that. Not yet, he added, and I wondered if he was thinking about Bree.

I guess . . . I never thought about it like that.

It's probably hard to when you're right in the middle of it. He breathed out hard through his nostrils, making little white clouds in the air. *Anyway, that's what I think. I'm a bit of a romantic.*

That's not a bad thing. I clawed at the birch branch I was perched on. *I hope you love someone like that someday. And I hope it's someone you can actually be with.*

Hey, if you two are done having a secret conversation, can we get back to work? Heath broke into both our minds, like a door banging open in a quiet library.

We took Cal all around the perimeter of the site, keeping beneath the brush so the Malandanti couldn't see us. Heath showed him all the good vantage points, where he could watch the Waterfall without being seen. He'd already been told our whole history at the site, so by the time we started back to Jenny's, we had moved on to battle tactics for retaking the Waterfall.

So the entire Clan needs to be inside the barrier in order for the spell to work? Cal asked.

Yes, I said. *And all the Malandanti need to be outside of it. You can see how that will be a challenge with half their Concilio here. We'll be outnumbered.*

Half? Heath asked. *Where are the rest of them?*

Jonah told me they've gone to Tibet. He thinks that's

where the failsafe is. I'll tell Nerina as soon as we get back.

Why doesn't our Concilio *come here to help out?* Cal asked.

That's a good question, I said pointedly.

They're a little preoccupied elsewhere, Heath answered. *Their priority is regaining control of as many sites as we can, especially Friuli. This is the first time that site has ever been out of our hands in the entire history of the Benandanti.*

Well, why don't we go there to help them out?

Because our priority is the Waterfall, both Heath and I answered at the same time.

I shot up toward the stars. I'd become such a company man that I was echoing Heath now. But it was true. I understood why we needed to stay put. The Benandanti had divided into seven Clans so that each Clan would be able to protect their own site and not have to worry about any of the others. As frustrating as it was, I understood why it had to be so.

The moon was just starting to sink below the tree line when we returned to Jenny's. Cal and Heath raced through the back door while I soared in through the upstairs bedroom window and dissolved into my body. Air filled my lungs and I breathed deep. I rolled over and slid out of the bed onto the floor. "Bree," I whispered, shaking her shoulder lightly. She grunted and swatted my hand away. "Bree," I said again, shaking a little harder.

Her eyes opened. "Who died?"

I rolled my eyes. "No one. Jeez, you're just like my

mom." I waited for her to wake up a little bit more before I spoke again. "I saw Jonah. He was at the Waterfall."

Bree sat up, her blankets pooling at her waist. Her black tank top had the words *Mother of Dragons* emblazoned in fiery orange across the chest. "Is he okay? Did you get to talk to him?"

Glancing at the sleeping Jenny, I motioned for Bree to follow me out of the room. When we got out into the hall, I heard the murmur of low voices coming from downstairs. Heath had probably woken Nerina to give her an update. "He's fine," I said. "They've been keeping him at the Guild, but he's trying to earn back their trust. It must be working, because tonight is the first night they've let him out."

"But he wasn't hurt or anything?"

"No."

Bree sagged a little against the wall, just below Jenny's fourth grade picture. "Come on," I said and headed for the stairs. "There's more."

"Good, there you are," Heath said when Bree and I hit the bottom of the stairs. Cora sat on the couch, her long red hair a jumble around her sleepy face. Heath must've woken her up too when he went to get Nerina. Cal was stretched out on the floor, doing leg lifts. "Do you ever sleep?" I asked him. "How do you have so much energy?"

He switched legs. "I'm all riled up after transforming. Don't you get that way?"

"I guess I used to when I was first Called," I said. "Now I just want to sleep." But that wasn't quite true.

I did still feel the pull of my Falcon inside me, long after I transformed back. I glanced around. "Should we get Jeff?"

"I'm already here," he said. I whirled around. He was a few steps above me and Bree, pulling a sweatshirt over his plaid flannel pajamas. "Clan meeting?"

"I have some news," I said. Nerina yielded me the floor, and I took center stage in front of the fireplace. I looked around at my Clan, who were all looking back at me. Heat rose from my neck into my cheeks. I twisted my fingers together in front of me. "I guess you all know about Jonah," I said softly.

Jeff cleared his throat. Cora glanced from him to me. "Nerina may have mentioned it," she said.

I pulled in a shaky breath. I was glad Nerina had spilled the truth so that I didn't have to get into it. "He was at the Waterfall tonight. We were able to talk."

Cora shook her head. "I still don't get how you two can communicate. I always thought it was impossible."

"It has to do with connection," Bree said. She shifted her position against the pillows on the couch. I noticed her wince and touch her rib cage. Too bad we couldn't send her to the Redwood site to heal. "I was able to do it at the battle last week. Because we're twins."

Jeff held his hand up. "Look, I get that whole teenage Romeo-and-Juliet thing. I do. But," he went on, ignoring my protest, "we can't trust him. Period. He's a Malandante."

"He wants out—"

"I know. Nerina told us." Jeff rubbed his face. "And

maybe he's telling the truth. But as far as I know, there's no way out for him. He's a Malandante for life."

Bree and I exchanged a look. She gave an almost invisible shake of her head. I pressed my lips together. Now wasn't the time to bring up the spell. Not when it meant the sacrifice of someone in this very room.

"Well, I trust him," I said loudly, shutting up everyone who had started to mutter in the wake of Jeff's little speech. "I don't expect you all to trust him too, but I think you can at least give him the benefit of the doubt."

"Can we all get past this and move on to the important stuff?" Bree asked, snapping her fingers at me. "What did he tell you?"

"The failsafe," I said. "I asked him about the failsafe."

"And?"

"He doesn't know what it is, but he said he thinks it's happening in Tibet. Half their *Concilio* was dispatched there last night."

Nerina leaned against the mantel, running her finger across her bottom lip. "This opens up a whole range of bad possibilities."

I tried to think what those could be. What was worse than what the Malandanti were already doing? Than what the Guild had done under the pretense of helping people? Maybe I was just too naïve to think that dark.

Cal raised his hand. "Just to refresh, the Tibetan site holds the magic to separate the soul from the body, right?"

"Glad you were paying attention the other night," I said.

"Yes," Nerina said, raising her voice above mine. "It is the magic from which we all derive our powers. The Tibetan magic is older than the Benandanti. The monks in those mountains used it to shadow-walk."

"I thought you couldn't use the magic without causing damage," Cal said, "to yourself, and to the earth."

"Shadow-walking is different," Bree said. Everyone looked at her. She straightened a little, lifting her chin in that haughty way, as if to remind everyone that she was, after all, our mage. "You don't transform. Your soul just, you know, takes a walk. You're still in your human form. Besides, it's not like Buddhist monks are using the magic for their own selfish gains. It's probably like taking ayahuasca or peyote for them. They do it to expand their consciousness."

"In addition," Nerina said, drawing our attention back to her, "the Tibetan site is the only site that has always—*always*—been under Malandanti control."

Cal drew his legs in. "That just seems so at odds. I mean, Buddhist monks and the Malandanti? They seem like very strange bedfellows."

The corner of Nerina's mouth twisted. "It isn't the Buddhist monks who are in bed with the Malandanti. The Mongols and the Chinese have been fighting over it for centuries. And do you know what year the People's Republic of China invaded Tibet?"

"Nineteen fifty," Cal supplied as if he was reciting an answer to an SAT question.

"Correct," Nerina said. "One year after the Guild incorporated itself."

"They took advantage of a precarious political situation," Jeff added. "Installed a government that is under Malandanti control."

"And it's the people who suffer," said Heath. "The Tibetans are some of the most oppressed people in the world." He looked out the window, where the sky was beginning to lighten. "I've been there. It *is* at odds with itself. So beautiful and yet so sad."

I stared at Heath. He'd never told me he'd been to Tibet. Had he gone on a Benandanti mission? Or during his wanderlust days?

"In any case, it makes sense that the failsafe is originating there," Nerina said. "Seeing as it's a Malandanti stronghold. We still have the book of the Tibetan magic," she continued, nodding at Bree, "so we'll start our research there."

"I want to help," said Cal.

"You can," Nerina said, "by training with Alessia. That is your job right now."

"But . . ." Cal glanced at Bree. It was so obvious, I almost laughed. "Part of my training is learning about the different sites, right? Plus, we just got back from the Waterfall. We won't be going back out until tomorrow."

"Don't you have school?" Bree asked.

Cal shrugged. "I'm already accepted to—"

"Yale." Bree rolled her eyes. "*We know.*"

"So what are they going to do to me if I don't show up?"

"Call your mom. Give you detention. Expel you. Failure to graduate will cancel that early acceptance to Yale right out." Bree got to her feet. "But, sure, if you're willing to risk all that, I could use the help." She stalked out of the room, heading for the den where I knew Nerina had all the books stored.

Cal looked and sighed, his face an open book of emotions. He had a crush on Bree, probably as bad as mine on Jonah had been when I'd first met him. I couldn't blame him. I, of all people, knew the charms the Wolfe twins could work on a person.

"She'll come around," I said. "Just ignore her until she does."

"I can't," he muttered, running his hand through his sun-colored hair, his eyes dark on the door to the den where Bree had disappeared.

Something hot and uncomfortable shot through me. I squeezed my eyes shut. I wasn't jealous that Cal wanted Bree. But I was jealous that he could have her, if he wanted to.

"Are we done?" I asked Nerina, my throat suddenly so tight. She nodded at me as she headed for the den, too.

I bolted from the room, up the stairs as fast as I could, and clambered into my bunk. Jenny was still fast asleep below me, her breathing slow and steady. I curled into a ball, my shoulders shaking. I tried to breathe, but my lungs were squished together. I hiccupped and gasped, hugging myself smaller and smaller. My mind was blank except for the memory of Jonah, the scent of him, the feel of his arms around me, the press of his lips on mine, and then tonight. Being with him without really being with him. It was so screwed up. My heart twisted, wanting so much more than I could have.

I rolled onto my side and stared at the wall. I wished I could talk to my mother. And I could; she was just down the hall. But that white-hot resentment remained and stopped me from getting out of bed and going to her. I could wake up Jenny. She would definitely listen and be sympathetic. But she wouldn't really understand. There wasn't anyone who could.

Except maybe Heath.

My lungs loosened, and my breathing slowed. I slipped out of bed and tiptoed to the top of the stairs.

Heath sat alone on the couch, staring into the fire. At the sound of my footsteps, he looked up and gave me a weary smile. "Can't sleep either, huh?"

I shook my head.

He patted the cushion next to him.

I settled into the pillows and pulled a throw blanket over my knees. I nudged Heath with my elbow. "I didn't know you'd been to Tibet."

"Yeah." Heath stretched his arms behind his head and leaned back. "The *Concilio* sent me there a few years ago. The Clan there was down one member and needed a loaner, I guess. We tried to overtake the site." He sighed. "We failed, obviously."

"Was anyone—?"

"No. Thankfully. But it was rough." He pulled his legs up into a crisscross. "I was there for a couple of weeks and got to spend time with the locals. It really is beautiful."

"You're so lucky you've gotten to travel," I said. The firelight flickered on the brick hearth. "I'm never going to get out of this town."

"You might," Heath said. "If we defeat the Malandanti—"

"You said it yourself tonight—this war has been raging for centuries." I swallowed hard, that hot lump threatening to appear in my throat again. "I'll probably never get out."

"There's nothing wrong with spending your whole life in a place where you are loved," Heath said softly.

I turned my head to stare at him. He wouldn't look back at me, so I studied his profile. The shadows on his face somehow made him look sadder than I'd ever seen him. "What do you mean?" I finally asked.

The fire crackled and spit. A log broke in half, tumbling deeper into the flames. "Have I ever told you how I ended up in Friuli?" Heath said.

It wasn't really a question because he knew damn well that he'd never told me. I didn't know anything about Heath's past, no matter how many times I'd asked him about it. I held my breath, scared that if I made a sound he would change his mind and not tell me.

"I grew up in Iowa," Heath said, and I did start at that. Although he had that whole blond-haired, blue-eyed, corn-fed look to him, I'd always thought of Heath as cosmopolitan. "My dad died before I was born. My mom raised me. She was very religious."

"Kinda like me," I murmured.

Heath's gaze snapped to me. "No," he said, sharp as a jagged rock. "Not like you at all. My mom didn't pray to a Virgin Mary statue on Sundays. *My* mom didn't let me read anything except the Bible. Because all books except the Bible were written by the devil."

I sucked in air so fast it whistled in my teeth.

Heath started to talk fast, as though the story wouldn't come out any other way. "When I was fourteen, I started to spontaneously transform. It's very rare, but sometimes it happens to potential Benandanti. I didn't know what was happening to me, and I couldn't control it."

"What—what did your mother do?" I kept my voice low, like I was talking to a frightened animal.

"She thought I was possessed by demons," he said. "First she tried to beat it out of me. That didn't work, so she locked me in the basement." He met my eyes. "For eight months."

My insides froze.

"Finally she called her minister to come over and perform an exorcism. I knew him well; we'd been going to his church for years. I also knew that he'd put at least two children in the hospital 'performing exorcisms.'" Heath's whole body was rigid. I could see how much this story was costing him to tell, and I imagined he'd probably only told it one other time in his life. "So the moment she opened the basement door, I was ready. He stepped onto the top stair, and I was there. I pushed him down the stairs, I knocked her to the floor, and I ran.

"I ran all the way to New York City, and I got a job as a cook's assistant on a cargo ship across the Atlantic. We docked in France, and I worked my way to Provence, where I got a job on a dairy farm." A small smile played across his lips. "They were nice to me there. I learned French and all about cheese." The smile dropped away. "But eventually they caught me transforming too, and they chased me off the farm. With a shotgun." Heath exhaled slowly. "By then I'd learned about the Benandanti, so I made my way to Friuli."

Heath tilted his head back and closed his eyes. I could tell he was seeing something in his mind's eye, something precious and sacred. "I will never forget . . . I got off the train and stood in the town square, turning in a circle to take everything in. And when the circle was complete and I was back in the place I'd started, Nerina was there, standing right in front of me. 'So,' she said, 'you have finally come.' She took me back to the seat of the *Concilio*, and they Called me, and I was home." He opened his eyes and looked at me. "Nerina and I fell in love, but the *Concilio* forbade it because she's immortal and I'm not. It made no sense. We both knew the risks, but we were willing to take them. And still they said no."

"And she chose them," I whispered. "And then they

sent you here."

Heath nodded. His eyes were wide and bright, dappled with firelight. "Out of all the places I've been, even Friuli, this place, this town, has been the most *home* to me. Because I've been loved. By you, by your mother, by the Clan. I've been accepted. I will go wherever the *Concilio* asks me to go, but I hope they never ask me to leave Twin Willows." His gaze narrowed, as though he could see right into my heart. "Don't ever take this place for granted, Alessia. No matter how much pain you feel right now—from Jonah, from your mom, from the Malandanti—there are people here who love you no matter what." He turned back to the fire, his face in shadow again. "Everyone should be so lucky."

CHAPTER TEN
Walking to Tibet

Bree

Cal followed me into the den like a freaking puppy dog. Part of me wanted to order him to *sit stay good boy*, but the other part of me . . . well, okay. Cal was cute and smart— *Yale,* for God's sake—and there were worse boys to have following me around. In fact, I usually did have worse boys following me around. Maybe it was time I let a good one come calling.

"Here, take this." I thrust one of the ancient texts into his hands and gestured to the couch. "You can start looking in there."

Cal examined the pages. "Latin?"

"Yeah. There's a translation codex in the back."

"Don't need it." He flopped onto the plaid-covered cushions and grinned at me. The smile sparkled all the way up into his blue eyes. "I read Latin."

"*Of course* you do." I snatched the book away and handed him another. Time to show him who was boss. "How's your Sanskrit?"

"Um . . ."

"You don't know Sanskrit? Jeez. And they let you into Yale?" I clucked my tongue.

"*I'll* take the Sanskrit," Nerina said, plucking the book away from Cal and handing him back the Latin one. "You don't read it either, Bree."

I rolled my eyes and picked up another Latin text. It was the most common language in the books and texts we'd stolen from the Guild, and I could read it now without having to check the codex in the back too much. I glanced around the room. Nerina sat in the huge lounge chair in the corner, her silk-pajama-clad legs tucked up beneath her and her manicured finger running along the words on the page as she read. Jeff and Cora sat with their heads bent together at the desk against the wall, studying one of the texts in Middle English. The only seat left for me was on the couch, next to Cal.

I went to sit, but just before my butt hit the cushion, a wave of pain crashed through me. I froze, my teeth gritted, breathing in and out hard. A gentle hand on my elbow guided me down, and I sank into the pillows. I closed my eyes for a moment until I could breathe normally again.

"Are you okay?" Cal asked, keeping his voice low so that the others didn't come rushing over, which I appreciated.

"I'm fine." I tossed my hair back and smiled at him. "I just got tortured, that's all."

He grimaced. "Yeah, I heard something about that. That sounds . . ." His eyes squinted.

I laughed. "There's not really an appropriate word, is there? It's not like Hallmark makes a Sorry You Got Tortured card."

Cal leaned in closer to me. The scent of the forest still lingered on him, pine and bark and snow, and something about it eased the pain in my ribs. "The new Sorry You Got Tortured line is in stores now! Featuring the Hey, At Least You Didn't Lose Any Fingers and the You Still Have Your Kneecaps designs."

I choked, trying not to draw Nerina's attention by laughing too hard. "Nice," I said to Cal, fumbling for a snappier comeback, but for once I felt like I didn't even need it.

A Cheshire-cat grin spread across his face. He was obviously pleased with himself for making me laugh, but somehow instead of rolling my eyes in annoyance, I smiled back. Okay. I'd let him have that one.

I turned one of the thick, weathered pages of my book. The sun crested into the room through the cutesy wooden shutters on all the windows. "I just don't see how the Tibetan magic could be used as a failsafe," I said, rubbing my eyes. After not sleeping all night, they felt all itchy and swollen. "The magic only works for the Benandanti and the Malandanti—those who've already been Called and potentials. How would they use it to get their power back?"

"I thought you said monks could use it to shadow-walk," Cal said.

"Yeah, but they're not dipping into the actual magic," I explained. "They're using its essence to reinforce their own ability."

"There *is* a way." At the sound of Nerina's voice, we both looked up. Her face was pale. "But it is too horrible, even for the Malandanti."

"Nothing's too horrible for the Malandanti," I snapped. "We all know that."

"Yes, but this has real consequences—consequences that would be difficult to hide from the rest of the world. Even with magic." She shook her head. "I just don't think they'd risk it. They're not that desperate yet. Keep looking."

Before I could answer, the door to the den opened and Alessia poked her head in. "I'm heading to school," Alessia said. Even from the couch, I could see the gray circles under her eyes and the invisible weight that dragged at her shoulders. "I'll let you know if I hear or see anything in town."

I hauled myself up, waving Cal's hand away when he tried to help me. "I'll walk you out, Alessia."

"How's it going in there?" she asked as we crossed the living room where the TV was blaring even though no one was in the room.

"Such a waste. We're not finding anything." I skirted around the pullout in the middle of the room that Heath hadn't folded up yet. "We need something more concrete to go on." I stopped in front of the TV, captured by the image of a young girl weeping at the foot of a bed where a body lay draped in a sheet. It was a report on the news ticker alert I'd seen at my house.

"At least four hundred people have died," the voice-over said as the camera panned out from the girl to a hallway filled with sheet-draped beds, "and the number continues to grow every day. Researchers are baffled as to how the disease is spread, and there is no cure or treatment. Doctors Without Borders is overwhelmed and asking for more volunteers . . ."

"I know, it's awful," Alessia said, following my gaze to the screen. "We've been talking about that in Clemens's class. He's making us all come up with epidemic response scenarios. You are *so* lucky you're missing out."

The report switched to an interview with a nurse, but the image of that young girl stuck with me. "Yeah, that sucks," I replied shakily as we left the room. There was something about it other than just the sheer humanity of it that struck me deep. It raised my hackles—the hackles that were reserved just for the Malandanti. But was it a real, true feeling or remnants of the spells the Rabbit had done to me? I couldn't be sure.

We passed the kitchen. I peeked inside. For some reason, Mr. Salter from the hardware store was in there with Lidia. They stood hip to hip at the sink, doing dishes. I narrowed my eyes at them. What the hell was he doing here? A non-Benandante hanging around here was surely on Nerina's no-no list. Mr. Salter leaned in to murmur something in Lidia's ear. She laughed, her eyes bright and her cheeks spotted with color. Beside me, Alessia sucked in a breath. I glanced sidelong at her, and the look on her face told me this was one more item to add to the list of why she wasn't speaking to Lidia.

Alessia grabbed my arm and hustled me to the door. But before we could get outside, Lidia looked up and saw us. "Alessia, wait," she called out. She grabbed a brown paper bag off the counter and headed toward us. "I made your favorite," she said. "The prosciutto isn't ours, of course, but it's still good."

Alessia stared at her mother. I shifted my feet. The last thing I wanted at the moment was to be caught up in Alessia's mama drama. But she had a death grip on my arm. "Enough with the food, Mom, okay? You're not going to bribe your way out of this with prosciutto."

"*Cara . . .*" Lidia glanced at me and sidled in front of me in an obvious attempt to block me out of their conversation. "I want to talk to you about all of this."

"Yeah, well, I'm not really ready to listen just yet." Alessia pulled open the front door with a hard tug. Cold blasted in—the kind of wet cold that meant it would snow soon. Great. More snow. Just what Maine needed. I heard Lidia call after her daughter in a sort of sad, thin voice as Alessia dragged me outside with her and slammed the door shut behind us.

"What the hell was that about?" I asked her, wrenching my arm away from her so I could hug myself against the cold. I hadn't really prepared to be standing outside in the freezing morning.

"Her and Mr. Salter? Are you kidding me? As if she hasn't been lying to me enough!" Alessia jammed her hat onto her head and looked at me. Her eyes widened as my teeth chattered. "Go inside! You're so lucky you don't have to go to school."

"I'd almost rather be in school than stuck inside all day with Nerina and her books." I reached for the door handle, realizing I wasn't dreading it as much as I claimed. Because Cal was there too? I wasn't ready to think about *that* yet. "Hope something interesting does happen at school today. Like a certain raven-haired someone shows up."

"Me too."

"And hey," I said, trying to sound casual, "I want to hear more about that project Clemens has you working on when you get home." It couldn't hurt to dig deeper and find out if my hackles were right. I pulled the door open and almost collided with Jenny. "Watch it!"

"Bitch, please. You're in my house." Jenny pranced around me.

I laughed; I kinda liked her after all.

She linked arms with Alessia. "What's wrong with you?"

"Ugh." Alessia shook her head. "Tell you on the way."

"Have fun storming the castle!" I called after them as

they headed up the driveway.

When I got back to the den, I found Cal, Nerina, Jeff, and Cora all sitting in a circle on the floor, the site books spread out in the middle of them. "What's up?"

"Oh, good, you're back. Where'd you go?" Cal asked, his eagerness spilling off him like water.

I planted my hand on my hip. "What, did Nerina promote you to be my keeper now?"

"Bree," Nerina said, shaking her head. But beneath her long snaky locks, I could see her smiling. "I want you to try something."

"What?"

Nerina laid her hand on one of the books. It was the Tibetan book, its cover an inky gray with a silver medallion in the center. The medallion showed a snake shedding its skin and then joining back with it again. For some reason, the image gave me the heebie-jeebies.

"I want you to shadow-walk to Tibet."

I cocked my head. "Bitch, you crazy."

"Bree!" Cora put her hands over her face, her shock dissolving into laughter.

"Why is that crazy?" Cal asked, his face innocent as he looked from me to Nerina.

"That's, like, several thousand miles away. Your soul can't walk that far," I told him.

"Yes, it can," Nerina said.

"But I've never—"

"Just because you've never done it doesn't mean it

can't be done." Nerina got to her feet and guided me to the couch. "We'll all be here with you. We'll monitor your physical form so if anything happens, we can pull you back."

When I'd learned to shadow-walk with Nerina, weeks ago, she'd had to pull me back several times. It was an icky, squelchy feeling, kind of like how I imagined a leech felt when you pulled it off your skin. And the furthest I'd gone was Boston. It seemed like there should be an in-between place before I tried to go all the way to Tibet. "Why don't I visit the Redwood site instead?"

"Why? We already have control of that site, so we know the failsafe isn't happening there."

"Friuli?" I suggested hopefully.

Nerina looked heavenward. "Bree, you're the strongest mage I've ever seen, and I've seen a lot."

"Yeah, and they all died horrible deaths in battle."

Cal bit his lip, his eyes clouded with worry. "She has a point. She's still recovering. Maybe this is too much to ask."

Oh, really? Little Mr. Early Admission to Yale thought it was too much to ask? I stretched out long, my feet knocking one of the pillows onto the floor. "Let's do this." Show the new kid just what a mage was capable of.

There was a moment when everyone scrambled around the couch, asking if I needed anything, putting pillows behind my head, propping my legs up, bringing me a glass of water. "Everybody, shut up and stop." I flung my forearm over my eyes. "I need you all to be quiet.

Nerina, put on that sound machine app."

I heard her clicking through her phone for a few seconds and then the calm, constant sound of ocean waves. Whenever I heard them, my heartbeat steadied and slowed. I loved the ocean, but I feared it as well. The ocean had almost taken my brother from me. I remembered that day so well, the cloudless Mexican sky over my head, the hot white sand beneath my toes, my dad's obnoxious chatter on his cell phone behind me, Jonah disappearing suddenly from my view, and watching, waiting, watching to see him come up again. Somewhere far away someone was screaming his name . . . No, no, they were screaming *my* name. . .

With a force that practically tore me in two, I broke the surface and sat up. "Breathe, breathe," Nerina urged, her hands tight on my shoulders. I gulped in air. It felt like my ribs were going to crack from the effort of trying to get enough air into my lungs. "Steady," Nerina murmured.

Cal pushed in next to her. "Are you okay?" His oceanic eyes had darkened with concern, like a storm over the sea. Aw, how sweet. But I wasn't about to get swept away, not when I had a job to do.

I shook him and Nerina off. "Just kidding," I said and waited a moment for my breathing to calm down. "I'll try it for real now." I lay back on the pillows again. Okay, so maybe Mexico wasn't the best place to think of when I was trying to get to Tibet. *What should I think about?* Of course. I was an idiot. The little Tudor house that was always my refuge. I closed my eyes, and I was there. Selling lemonade in the front yard. Jonah painting the sign to put up on the fence. *Fresh Lemonade 50¢.* My dad putting out a plate of chocolate-chip cookies and then eating half of them himself. Warmth spread through me. I stared up at the sky through the leafy trees. The sky was the same everywhere . . . in Charlottesville, in Twin Willows, in Friuli, in Tibet . . .

I blinked, and the scene around me changed.

A huge expanse of dark green grass stretched out before me. I turned. I was in the shadow of a great mountain, the greatest mountain, its summit so high that it couldn't be seen from where I was. It could only be seen from the clouds.

Something jingled nearby. I followed the sound and saw a cluster of yaks, their collars clinking with little brass bells. A colorful row of prayer flags stretched from the fence posts that surrounded them, flapping in the constant wind that hushed over the land. I breathed in deep, the air cold and clear in my lungs. It tasted different than any air I'd ever breathed. I looked again at the mountain, its white peak jagged against a mottled blue sky.

Holy shit. I was in Tibet.

The most important thing I'd learned about shadow-walking was that you had to lose your head. You couldn't let your mind guide you; you had to turn inward and listen to your instincts. As I gazed out over the foreign landscape, I waited for my gut to tell me where to go. I had no idea where—or what—the magical site was here, and it wasn't like I had a map.

A map of all the sites. That was a good idea. *I should come up with one,* I thought. *Sell them at all the Benandanti conventions.*

A whisper of wind fluttered my hair. I listened hard. I could just hear the fragment of something, a voice maybe, coming from the east. I turned in that direction and strode away from the yaks. They watched me placidly as I went, and I could hear their bells for a long time in the distance.

After a little while, I lost the soft voice on the wind. I stopped, listening inside again. I tried to keep my breath slow and even, because I knew that if I lost that thread, I'd wake back up on the couch at Jenny's. That was the other important thing I'd learned from shadow-walking: be patient. Not exactly my strength. So I had to fight for it.

A feeling tugged at my gut, telling me where to go. I was now in the deep shadow of the mountain, snow dappling the air. It was freezing, but I didn't feel the cold. My body was safe and warm in Maine.

I know what you want to see, said a voice behind me. I spun around. Standing just a foot away from me was a leopard. But not just any leopard. A snow leopard. One night when I was really bored and there was nothing on television, I'd watched a show on PBS about snow leopards. They were one of the most endangered species on the planet. But here was one standing in front of me. Talking to me.

And it was haloed in blue light.

Do you know who I am? I asked it.

Of course, the Snow Leopard replied. Its voice was definitely male, deep and warm. *You are our mage. We've heard about you.*

I'm not really here, you know, I said.

I know that, he replied. *I'm not an idiot.*

I laughed. I got the feeling if I met him in real life, I'd like him.

Follow me, he said.

And we climbed. For the Snow Leopard, it was a piece of cake. But for me, even though I wasn't truly corporeal, it was freaking hard. Shards of rock slid all around us. The air thinned the higher we went, and my breath worked harder and harder. It just seemed wrong that my soul, even without my physical form, still needed to breathe. Shouldn't I have been exempt or something? Apparently not.

Turn around, the Snow Leopard said after a while. I did as he asked, expecting to see the magical site at last.

Oh, I gasped.

The world spread out beneath us, mountains and valleys, cliffs and ridges, green and brown and white. Right above our heads sat fat puffy clouds, so close that I only had to reach my little finger up to touch them. Now I knew why this mountain was called The Roof of the World.

Can we see the site from here? I asked.

No, the Snow Leopard said. *I just think that everyone should see this view at least once in their lifetime.*

Yes, I said. *I agree.* We stood for another long moment before the Snow Leopard started walking again. This time we didn't continue up, but rounded a ridge in the mountain's face. The ground here was thick with hard-packed snow. I wondered how far we were from Base Camp, and whether I could legitimately claim I'd climbed Everest.

In Tibet, we call this mountain Chomolungma. Goddess Mother of the World, the Snow Leopard said. *The womb from which all life flows.*

That was a little gross, but okay.

You know, of course, the magic contained here, yes? the Snow Leopard said.

It's where the power to separate your soul from your body comes from.

Yes. You're drawing on that power right now, to be here and there at the same time.

But I'm not draining the site or anything, right?

No, you're not. There's only one way to drain the site, and the Malandanti have been doing it for years. We came over a small crest, the ground jagged beneath our feet. The Snow Leopard stopped. *We are here.*

I gazed down. Just below us, built into the mountainside, was an ornate temple. Its tiered roof shone gold in the bright sunshine. Bright white walls made a square just at the edge of a cliff. Prayer flags crisscrossed the inner courtyard, their multicolored triangles fluttering in the wind. And I could hear the faint jangling of bells, like I'd heard on the yaks at the foot of the mountain.

That's the site? But . . . where's the magic?

Look closer.

I squinted. Now I could see a cluster of yaks in the courtyard, their black bodies decorated with colorful yokes, the bells hanging from furry balls on their horns. *The yaks? They're the magic?*

The magic is contained in their blood. The Snow Leopard padded a little way up the ridge. I followed. *If the Benandanti controlled this site, those Yaks would be untouched. But the Malandanti have been slaughtering them for centuries, spilling their blood into basins to make their Clan here stronger.* He hunkered down, his belly resting on the ground. *These Yaks are many times descended from the original herd, who were murdered by the Malandanti. The magic has been diluted through breeding, and so the Malandanti must kill more of them, more frequently, to get what they want.*

I watched the animals mill about the courtyard, totally unaware of the horrible fate that awaited them. They weren't exactly pretty, but there was something sort of beautiful in their functionality, in the slow way their bodies shifted amongst each other. After a few minutes, I turned to the Snow Leopard. *Have you noticed anything unusual lately? Because we have reason to believe that the Guild had a failsafe in place in case we took them down like we did, and that whatever it is, it's happening here.*

Yes, we have. Watch.

I settled next to him. It felt like forever that I waited

for something to happen, then someone emerged from the Temple. He wore the long red caftan of a Buddhist monk, with a thick swath of orange fabric draped from shoulder to hip. *That's no monk,* the Snow Leopard said, his voice heavy with pain and disgust.

The figure was too far away for me to see clearly. I stood to move closer, but the Snow Leopard stopped me. *Any nearer and he'll see you,* he warned.

I'll risk it.

I picked my way across the rocky snow, keeping low. Several feet down the ridge, I stopped and straightened. The faux-monk had led one of the yaks to the edge of the courtyard. The rest of the herd shuffled restlessly, sensing something bad was about to happen. I held my breath, my shadow-heart beating fast. Faux-monk pulled a machete from beneath his robes. In one swift movement, he slit the Yak's throat and let the blood pour into the trough below.

The rest of the Yaks—the lucky ones—brayed and stomped their feet, those incessant little bells jingle-jangling their outrage. It was enough to make me a vegetarian for life. Wait until Barb heard about this.

When the poor Yak had been drained, Faux-monk let go of its yoke. The animal fell to the ground. The other Yaks backed away, their dead comrade a warning that they would be next.

Faux-monk walked around the trough of blood, his hands hovering over its surface. When he got to the side facing me, he looked up. I edged a few feet closer—near enough that I could finally see that he wore glasses. He froze, and in that instant I knew he'd seen me too. He could wear monk's robes all he wanted, but I knew who he was no matter what disguise he put on.

The Rabbit.

CHAPTER ELEVEN
The Dark before the Dawn

Alessia

There was something comforting about walking up Main Street with Jenny and going to school, as though life was completely normal. I leaned into her. "Did you see my mom and Mr. Salter this morning?"

Jenny grimaced. "I was hoping you didn't." She tightened her arm around mine. "What do you think about all that?"

I didn't want to think about it, at all, ever. "Why is he hanging around your house now, too? He has nothing to do with the Benandanti." But that wasn't what was bugging me and I knew it. I couldn't get the image of Lidia and Ed, hip to hip and laughing over the sink, out of my head. "My dad *just* died," I whispered. "It's like she's forgotten."

"Oh, Alessia." Jenny stopped and hugged me close. I breathed in her almond-scented shampoo. "She hasn't forgotten. No one could ever forget your dad, least of all your mom."

"Then why—?"

Jenny pulled away and held her hands up. "Look, I'm just going to tell you what I see, as a total outsider who loves you *and* your mom. Can you handle that?"

I sighed. "Yeah, I can handle it."

"Your dad died a year ago. And I know that seems like a minute ago, but a lot has happened in the past year." Jenny looked off toward the woods. "You got Called, and you and your mom grew apart. She—"

"That's her fault," I cut in. "If she'd told me she knew, there wouldn't be this rift."

"I know, and I totally agree with you," Jenny said, putting her hand on my wrist. "She should've said something. But for whatever reason, she didn't, and she probably felt really alone, and Ed was there and he was grieving too, and they bonded. It makes *total* sense." She hunched one shoulder. "For what it's worth, my mother called this like six months ago."

I stared at the ground. "It just feels like she's leaving me more alone than ever."

Jenny snorted. "Isn't that what you've wanted forever? For your mom to stop being so overprotective?"

I put my gloved fingers to my temples. Jenny was right; I'd been complaining about Lidia not leaving me alone for years, and now that she finally was, I wanted her meddling back. "Guess you never know how much you need something until it's gone," I said, trying to make my voice sound light even though my insides were heavy.

"Guess not." Jenny linked her arm through mine again, and we continued to school. "Besides, Lidia deserves to be happy. Doesn't she?"

Yeah, she did. But it didn't seem fair that she got to be happy when I was so miserable.

The school loomed into view. "You think he'll be there?" Jenny asked me in a low voice.

If there was one thing that could distract me from Lidia's love life, it was Jonah. I glanced at Jenny and shrugged one shoulder. "He said he was working on it, but I think he'd have to do a pretty fancy song and dance to get the Malandanti's permission to come to school," I said. But still my heart hoped. Maybe he'd proved himself on last night's patrol. Maybe Pratt had believed that he'd injured me, and coming to school would be his reward for that. I almost laughed. It was insane that the Malandanti had put Jonah into a position where *school* was a reward.

A handful of kids dotted the snowy lawn in their colorful coats, but most were inside with the overheated radiators. Jenny and I dashed up the front steps. As we made our way across the foyer toward the main office, one of the auditorium doors squeaked open. And, unbelievably, there he was. He'd done it. He'd played the Malandanti's mind games and won. He beckoned to me and closed the door before anyone else could see him.

I turned to Jenny. "Cover for me in the office, okay?"

"Okay, but you'd better be in second-period French."

She squeezed my arm. "You *and* Jonah."

"We will," I promised and dashed across to the auditorium before anyone stopped me. The door whooshed closed behind me, shutting out the hubbub of the hallway.

Jonah was half-hidden in the shadows in one of the alcoves against the wall. I ran to him, my footsteps muffled on the well-worn carpet. I couldn't reach him fast enough—it seemed like so many minutes ticked by until he was three feet, two feet, one foot away from me . . . and then at last my arms were around him.

In the last several days, the only times I'd seen him were when I was a Falcon and he was a Panther, two animals that were not exactly made to embrace each other. Feeling the human curves of him was like drinking water in a desert. He pulled me tight against him, one hand on the small of my back, the other buried deep in my hair, and turned us so that I was up against the wall. His lips crashed against mine and took my breath away. I faded into him, forgetting everything outside the sanctuary of his arms: Lidia and Mr. Salter, Bree and Cal, Heath and Nerina, the Benandanti and the Malandanti.

The first-period warning bell buzzed over the loudspeaker, causing a cruel jolt. We shuddered apart, our breath short and ragged. I leaned my forehead against his shoulder. "You're okay," I murmured, more to reassure myself. "They let you out."

Jonah stroked my spine. "I got them to move me to Pratt's house here in town, and I convinced them that my absence from school would raise suspicions," he said. "But there's a Clan member here at the school who's keeping an eye on me."

"Who is it?"

He shook his head. "I wish I knew. The only one whose identity I know is Pratt." He cradled my face in his hands, his gaze burrowing deep into mine. "God, it's good to see you. Like, for real see you."

"You too," I whispered.

"You're very pretty as a Falcon, but I can't kiss you like that." He drew my mouth to his, the kiss this time soft as a rosebud. "We can't be seen together," he said, his words tumbling onto my tongue and down my throat. "If they know I care about you, they'll know they can use you against me."

I pressed the back of his head with my hand, pressed his lips, his breath, his being harder into me so that I wouldn't have to deal with reality, just for a moment longer. The second bell sounded, and with a groan we pulled away from each other, the heat of unfulfilled promises thick between us. "I should go," he said. "If I'm not in class . . ."

"Go." I put my hand on his chest and gave a little push. Jonah pushed back and leaned in for a last kiss.

"Figure out some way for us to meet. Tonight. Not on patrol," he said, a little breathless. "The town hall basement?"

"No, it's too well known. I'll think of something better." I bit my bottom lip, which still tingled from Jonah's love. Jenny would know a good place. She'd been sneaking out to meet boys since middle school. Jonah took my hand and backed away, up the aisle toward the auditorium door. He held my hand until both our arms stretched out long. His fingers grazed my palm, my knuckles, my fingertips . . . and then he was gone.

"What about just meeting back at your house?" Jenny suggested as we walked to second-period French. "It's empty now."

"It's also being watched," I said, keeping my voice low as kids jostled past us. "Don't you have some super-secret make-out spot or something?"

Jenny grimaced. "Unfortunately, all my super-secret spots are not so secret anymore." She stopped and snapped her fingers. "Hang on—why don't you ask Cal? I bet he knows someplace good in Willow Heights that's way out of the way."

"I'm not asking *Cal* advice about make-out spots. *I'm* the one who's supposed to be the Guide," I said. "Besides, he probably doesn't know any. He's probably been too busy stalking the Benandanti to ever have a girlfriend." But Jenny was already pulling her phone out and sending a text, presumably to Cal. I gritted my teeth. "Why do you even have his number?"

"Dad thought it would be a good idea, in case he needed to contact one of us and you guys were transformed or something."

"Who's transformed?"

We whirled around. Carly had snuck up behind us just outside the French classroom door. "Uh . . . Gillian," Jenny said. She hit the Send button on her phone and looked up, a lopsided grin on her face. "Gillian Carson. She just got a new haircut and looks totally, you know, transformed."

Carly raised her eyebrows. "I didn't even know you were friends with Gillian."

"I'm friends with everyone!" Jenny tossed her long blonde hair. "Jeez, Carly, step outside your box once in a while," she added and sashayed into the room.

I went to follow her, but Carly put her hand on my elbow. "How's it going at her house? You about ready to kill her yet?"

"A little bit," I said with a forced laugh. "But it's fine. Like a big sleepover." Except without the fun, I added silently.

"Well, you know you can always take a break and stay at my house if you need to. Your mom, too." We walked into class together and headed for our assigned desks. Jonah wasn't there yet.

"Thanks, Carly. I just might take you up on that." I knew I wouldn't, but I gave her a grateful smile for offering.

Just before the bell rang, Jonah ducked into the room and walked to his seat behind me, keeping his head down and his face turned away from me. Carly gave me a look, but I ignored her. I swallowed hard, trying to force down the heat that rose up the back of my neck.

Halfway through class, when Madam Dubois was writing on the blackboard, Jenny checked her phone. A minute later, a note landed on my desk.

Cal says there's a prop storage room at WHH. He'll give you the key this afternoon.

I scribbled *Midnight?* at the bottom of Jenny's note and passed it back to Jonah. At that moment, Madam Dubois faced the class again, and it wasn't until the end of the period when we were all gathering our books to leave that I felt Jonah press the note into my hand.

I'll be there.

When we got back to Jenny's house after school, we found her bedroom in complete disarray and Bree shoving things into a duffel bag. "Do you have any travel-size moisturizer?" she asked the minute we walked into the room. "Mine is way too big to fit into my makeup bag."

"Where are you going?" I asked.

Bree looked up from the turtleneck sweater she was rolling into a tight ball. "Tibet. First thing in the morning."

"What?" Jenny and I yelled at the same time.

"Half the *Concilio* is going," Bree said. She slid the rolled sweater into the bag and started counting out pairs of socks. "We're going to take the site."

"Holy crap." I sat on the edge of the bottom bunk.

"So the failsafe is definitely happening there."

"We still don't know for sure." She stuffed the socks into a side pocket. "But I shadow-walked there this morning and saw the Rabbit. So shit is definitely going down there." She looked up at me. "Did you find out anything more about that epidemic in Asia?"

"What? Why?"

"Because I think it has something to do with the failsafe."

I stared at her. "You think the failsafe and the epidemic are connected? How?"

"I don't know. I was kinda hoping you'd give me something I could use to figure it out."

"We didn't work on it today," Jenny said. "Clemens was super distracted and made us watch a video about the Supreme Court instead. Who knew Ruth Bader Ginsberg was such a badass?"

"Damn." Bree zipped up the side pockets. "Guess we'll find out when we get there."

"Is anyone else from our Clan going?" I asked.

"Just me and Nerina." She grimaced at me. "Sorry."

I flopped back onto the bed. "You are so lucky! I never get to go anywhere."

"Oh yeah, I'm lucky." She tossed a couple of discarded sweaters into the corner of the room. "I'm so lucky I get to go to Tibet and fight the Malandanti, who are definitely doing something super evil over there. I'm so lucky I'll probably get killed in battle." She sat down on the air mattress with a heavy sigh.

I pushed myself back up. "Bree, you're going to be fine. We all know you can hold your own. And the *Concilio* will be there to protect you."

"I guess—"

The door opened wider. "Oh, hey, guys," Cal said, leaning against the door frame. "Guess you heard the news."

"Bet you wish you were going to Tibet instead of stuck here with me, right?" *And without Bree,* I added silently. A little spot of red had appeared in his cheeks as he watched Bree tuck underwear into her bag. I was dying to tease him about this little crush he'd developed the next time we trained. Maybe we could bond over our fascination with the Wolfe twins.

"I definitely don't think I'm ready for that yet," he said, tearing his eyes away from the pair of black lace panties Bree had just packed.

Bree muttered something about the weather as she held up another sweater.

"Alessia, I have those keys," Cal said, crossing the room to me. He pulled a ring of keys from his pocket and slid two of them off. "This one opens the side door of the school," he said, holding up a shiny gold key first, then a small silver one. "And this opens the storage room. Just make sure you lock both doors when you leave."

"Does the school have an alarm system?"

"Nah." He pressed both the keys into my hand. "There shouldn't be anyone around, but if someone stops you, just tell them you're a friend of mine."

"How do you have these?"

"I design all the sets for the school plays. I'm there late at night a lot."

"Is there anything you *don't* do at that school?"

"Apparently, I don't attend classes anymore, since I got Called," he said with a laugh.

"What's that for?" Bree asked. She nodded at the keys and tossed something into the growing pile of clothes in the corner. Jenny growled and began to clean all of the messes Bree had made around the room.

"Oh. I'm—" I toyed with the keys. "I'm meeting Jonah tonight. He was at school today."

"He was?" She lowered the makeup bag she'd picked up and stared at me. "Is he okay?"

I nodded. "He's staying at Pratt's house. And apparently there's a Malandante at school keeping an eye on him."

"Bet it's Principal Morrissey." Bree ran her hand through her hair. "Maybe I should come tonight to check in with Jonah too. Since I'm leaving tomorrow."

"It's not Principal Morrissey," I said. "And, um, don't come." I looked away from her.

"But what if I don't—?"

"You will," I said, still avoiding her eyes. "I just, um, need to see him on my own." Heat flared in my cheeks.

"Gross," Bree said, a wicked grin widening her mouth. "At least try to get some information out of him before you do the nasty."

"Oh, my God!" I buried my face in my hands. "Why is everyone obsessed with sex?"

"I'm not," Bree said and returned to packing her makeup.

"I'm not," Jenny said. I rolled my eyes at her. "Okay, yeah, that's a lie."

Cal wisely said nothing; he just cleared his throat and backed out of the room. I shook my head and got my backpack. It was hours and hours until midnight; I thought I might as well fill the time with homework so my GPA didn't go down the tubes along with everything else.

Jenny turned to Bree. "Hey, there's a bunch of travel-size stuff in the bathroom. Top drawer of the cabinet. Help yourself."

"Awesome, thanks." Bree grabbed her makeup bag and dodged out of the room.

The instant she was gone, Jenny sat down next to me. "Okay, listen. The best way out of the house is through the back door. Watch out for the third step on the back stairs; it creaks. You'll have to go around the living room, but hopefully Heath will be asleep. Don't use the front door. It makes a racket when it opens."

"Thanks."

"And Lessi?" She pointed at the bottom drawer of her nightstand. "Take a condom."

"We are not going to have sex!" I yelled, throwing my hands up.

She laughed. "The lady doth protest too much, methinks."

"You sound just like Bree," I told her.

I had no intention of having sex with Jonah that night, no matter what Jenny or Bree said. But my heart thudded against my ribs as the minutes ticked with agonizing slowness toward midnight. At last the clock read 11:30. I slid out of my bunk, tiptoed over Bree's sleeping form, and reached for the doorknob. "Have fun," Jenny whispered from her bunk. "Don't do anything I wouldn't do."

"Which pretty much gives me free rein," I whispered back.

Carrying my boots in my hand, I crept down the hall to the back stairs. I kept to the right on the third step and it stayed silent. When I reached the first floor, I hugged the wall as I skirted the living room.

Firelight flickered from the hearth in the living room. Shadows moved across the wall opposite me. I froze. Two silhouettes danced in rhythm, arching and bending. Voices whispered across the room. My curiosity got the better of me. I stepped away from the wall just enough so that I could see the floor in front of the fireplace.

Heath and Nerina lay on the rug, their naked bodies wrapped around each other. I clapped my hand to my mouth and backed away fast. They were in too deep to even know I was there, to know anything was going on around them at all. I squeezed my eyes shut, trying to unsee what I'd just seen, but their embrace blazed on the back of my eyelids. The way he held her, like she was the most precious, beautiful creature on earth.

And to him, she was.

I turned and fled to the back door, not caring if anyone heard me. Once outside, the cold slapped me like an angry lover. I pulled my boots on and barreled to my mom's truck, thrust the key into the ignition, and turned it on. I hugged the steering wheel and bent forward until my forehead touched the cool leather.

I breathed hard in and out, the cold freezing like icicles inside my nose. Well, fine. If Heath could spend the night with his forbidden love, then so could I.

I blasted the heat and backed out the driveway without even checking the rearview mirror. At this hour, the streets of Twin Willows were empty, and I ran right through the one red light in the middle of town. The road curved and bent until I got to Willow Heights and then I drove seventy miles an hour to the high school.

A dark figure stood next to the side door. I parked the car at the curb and bolted out, didn't stop moving until I was with him. "Come on," I breathed, twisting in his arms to get the door open.

Inside, the air was close. We'd come in the back of the dark auditorium, and a short walk led us to the storage room. My fingers trembled as I unlocked it. Jonah flicked on the light when I opened the door.

Harsh fluorescents flooded the room with bright white light. Backdrops from various shows were stacked upright against the walls: a fancy restaurant with a chandelier, a Renaissance villa, a red-roofed barn. Random pieces of furniture populated the rest of the room: tables, high-backed dining chairs, overstuffed sofas, and a day-bed draped in red velvet. I turned away from Jonah, breathing hard, and turned off the fluorescents. "Too much light," I whispered. As soon as my eyes adjusted and I could see the outline of his face, I went to him.

The space between us closed into nothing. He dug his fingers into my hair and covered my mouth with his. I peeled my coat off and then his, feeling the hardness of his shoulders with the palms of my hands. I stroked down his back, down, down. He groaned and with one swift motion lifted me into his arms. I wrapped my legs around his waist and let him carry me backwards until we fell with a crash onto the velvet-covered daybed.

Jonah pressed the length of his body against mine, the heat of him burning through every layer of my winter clothing. It wasn't close enough. The distance of wool and denim was going to kill me. I trailed my lips from his ear to the base of his throat, feeling the pulse of him there. I pushed him up off me slightly, reached for the hem of his sweater, and pulled it over his head.

Clothing came off with breakneck speed, shoes and belts unbuckled, skin kissed the instant it was bared. We stretched long on the daybed, him in just his boxers, me in my bra and panties, and curled into each other. He was so warm, it could've been ten degrees below zero in that room and still I would've been on fire. He kissed in a line down my neck, my collarbone, my stomach, and pulled my underwear off, growling a little like the Panther inside him. I squirmed, wanting at once to shy away from the exquisite torture that flooded my body and to dive in headfirst. God, they were right . . . I was going to have sex with Jonah Wolfe tonight.

My spine arched as his mouth loved every inch of my skin. I struggled to breathe as he rose to lie next to me, his eyes so soft on my face that I wanted to die and be buried in them. "I love you," I managed to say.

His arms came tight around me. "I love you too," he murmured into my hair. I twined my legs through his, bringing him closer, close enough that I could feel how much he wanted me. I tilted upward and kissed him long and slow.

"Do you have something?" I asked into his mouth.

He pulled away and kissed my forehead, the arch of my brow, my cheek. "No," he said softly, "but that's not why we're not going to make love tonight."

I jerked back, but he cradled me closer. Now I was the one being held like I was the most precious creature on earth. As I looked into his eyes, their green glow so warm on my face, I realized that to him, I was. Everything squeezed tight inside me, my veins overflowing with love. "It's okay," I said. "I want to."

"I do, too," he said, his voice strangled. "God, I do." He dipped his head and smothered my face and neck with kisses. His hands gripped me tight and I could feel him tremble, like there was an earthquake inside him that he couldn't contain.

"Then why not?"

He held my gaze for a long minute. "Because I don't deserve you. Not yet."

I laid my hand on his cheek. "I'm not a saint either, Jonah. We're both human. We've both made mistakes."

Jonah reached up and took my hand, weaving our fingers together. "I've made significantly more mistakes than you have, Alessia." Still, always, the way he said my name sent ripples through me. "When I've done enough good things to make up for those, then I'll be worthy of you."

I breathed in deep, the smell of sawdust mingled with Jonah's scent of pine and spice. "Okay," I whispered, and drew him down so that we lay tangled together, his head on my chest. My heart cracked beneath his cheek, like a tiny fracture in a blown-glass ball. "Okay," I said again, and waited for the dawn—both outside and within—to come.

CHAPTER TWELVE

A Trip to the Other Side of the World

Bree

I had to hand it to the *Concilio Celeste*; they'd invested their money wisely. So wisely, in fact, that Nerina was able to charter a private jet to take us to Tibet.

I'd been on my fair share of private jets. The Guild had flown us on their company jet many times. It really was true that once you go first class—or private—you never go back. I secretly thanked the *Concilio*'s accountant that we weren't flying coach to Lhasa.

"Adamo, Magdalena, and Cecilia are meeting us there," Nerina said as the plane lifted into the air.

"Sounds like the cast of *Mob Wives*," I said.

Nerina pointed sharply at my face. "I don't want to hear any of your sarcasm when we are with the *Concilio*."

"But I can't help it," I said. "It's just who I am."

"Well, you'd better hope they're so impressed with your abilities that they overlook it." Nerina pulled a bag stuffed with files onto the seat next to her and rifled through it.

"Are they all as old as you?"

"No. Magdalena is the youngest. She's a little over two hundred years old. Cecilia is about a hundred years younger than me. Adamo is older than me—he's over five hundred."

"Tell me again why the rest of the *Concilio* isn't showing up to take a site we've never had control of."

Nerina peered out the window into the black night. "It's too risky to leave the sites we do control without *Concilio* backup. With only half of *Concilio Argento* in Tibet, we should be evenly matched."

"And then there's me against the Rabbit," I muttered. I guessed everyone was counting on me to be able to deal with him on my own. But I'd gone up against the Rabbit twice and won only once.

Nerina opened one of the files she'd pulled from her bag and tilted her seat back. "Try to get some sleep, Bree. Once we get to Lhasa, things will move very fast."

One thing I'd learned in the last several years of criss-crossing the globe was how to sleep anytime, anywhere. I reclined my seat until it was nearly flat and pulled one of the soft, fluffy blankets over me. The whoosh and hum of the engine beneath me was like an old familiar lullaby. I fell asleep quickly, but my overactive mind kept me only barely below the surface, jumbled images twisting themselves into vivid dreams.

It felt like only a moment had passed when a jolt and a long shudder woke me. I rose up on one elbow. Artificial orange light flooded into the plane. "We're in Vancouver to refuel," Nerina said, glancing up from the file she was reading. It was a different file than the one she'd been looking at when we'd left Bangor; there was a small stack of them next to her. "We still have a long way to go."

"Shouldn't you get some sleep too?"

Nerina ran her hand through her long, snaky hair. "I couldn't sleep if I wanted to."

"Well, we have no idea what we're up against in Tibet," I said. "That's enough to keep anyone awake."

The cabin door opened, and the pilot walked in. "We'll be taking off in just a few minutes, ma'am," he said and headed into the cockpit.

Nerina narrowed her gaze in the direction the pilot had gone. "Did he just call me *ma'am*? That hurts."

I laughed and snuggled down into my blanket. I tried to close my eyes as we taxied then sped down the runway and lifted back into the air. But there wouldn't be any more sleep for me on this flight. At last I sighed and sat back up.

"It's not just Tibet," Nerina said. I looked over at her. She stared out the window, watching the dark clouds shift over the wings of the plane. "That's not the only thing that's keeping me awake."

It didn't take a genius to know what—or whom—she was talking about. "Heath."

She nodded, still not looking at me. "We, ah, *reconnected* last night."

"Oh, please," I said. "You don't need to use euphemisms with me." I sat forward in my seat. "So while we were all blissfully asleep, you two were doing it in the living room?"

"Must you be so crass, Bree?" Nerina rubbed her temples. "It was wrong. We can't go down that path again. It will only end in heartbreak. The *Concilio* . . ."

"Screw the *Concilio*." I pounded my fist against the side of my seat. "This is totally unfair of them."

"No, it is not. They are trying to save me from the consequences. As they have saved me so many times before." She spoke the last sentence almost to herself. I raised my eyebrows. She faced me. "I would do anything for the *Concilio,* Bree. You have no idea what I owe them. *No idea.*"

I would've gone another round with the Rabbit to find out exactly what she owed them, but I stayed silent.

"And yet . . . how can they ask me to live for the rest of eternity without love? Even if it is only for a brief moment in my long immortal life, don't I deserve to have the kind of soul-shattering love that we all dream of?" She turned her head to the window again. A tiny tear glinted in the corner of her eye. "I am made from two halves. One that would do anything for her family. And one that only wants to love Heath. I have become so used to these two sides of me that I cannot imagine living one without the other."

I understood her better than she knew, maybe even

better than she understood herself. It wasn't just the *Concilio* that kept her from Heath. It was the fear of what came after. After that one moment was over and Heath was long gone and she was still alive forever. I knew that because, minus the immortality, it was the same thing that kept me from making friends at any of the schools we'd gone to over the last seven years, from having a real boyfriend. The same reason I knew I'd never do more than flirt with Cal. Sooner or later, everyone leaves. Especially me.

Still, if it were me, I'd tell the *Concilio* to go screw themselves and have fun while it lasted with Heath.

The descent into Lhasa was rocky. I tried not to look at the jagged mountaintops just outside the window or notice how ridiculously tiny the airstrip looked. At last we hit the ground with a bump that nearly knocked me out of my seat. I followed Nerina off the plane and through the throng of tourists in the airport. A group of Patagonia-clad Everest wannabes clustered near the entrance. I wondered how many of them would actually summit, and how many would die trying.

Once out of the airport, Nerina headed straight for two wrinkled old men who stood next to a couple of rickety mopeds. "Ah, Nerina!" they cried, greeting her first with little bows and then big hugs.

"This is Jintao and Quinglin," Nerina told me.

"They'll be our Sherpas up to the temple. Their two families have been friends of the Clan here for generations. Climb on."

I eyed the moped she gestured to with trepidation. I was all for thrill-seeking, but the thing looked like it was going to fall apart two miles up the road. "Isn't the Temple at the site controlled by the Malandanti?"

"The Benandanti Clan has another temple not far from the Temple site that they use as their home base." Nerina secured her bag in the little luggage compartment on the back of the moped and settled herself on the seat behind Quinglin. I stored my own bag away and, taking a deep breath, swung my leg over the moped. If I'd been Alessia, I probably would've crossed myself.

"You ready?" Jintao asked me. I nodded and tightened my arms around his waist. He stepped on the throttle and the moped roared to life. We zipped away from the airport and into the mountains.

After a little while, I began to forget that I was on the back of a deathmobile and take in the sheer magnificence of my surroundings. Mountains rose up on either side of the twisty road, their peaks so high I had to crane my neck back to see the top. Fat clouds drifted across the blue sky, which seemed so close I had only to stretch my arm up to touch it. And the air . . . I hadn't really gotten to enjoy how fresh it was when I'd shadow-walked here. The taste of copper and water, of all the elements mixed into one, was strong medicine on my tongue. "The air here is amazing!" I shouted into Jintao's ear.

"For now!" he shouted back. "It will not be long before the Chinese pollute this part of the world, too."

I watched a herd of yaks graze on the bright green grass in the valley below us and could totally imagine a cluster of stinking, Malandanti-constructed smokestacks billowing filth into the clear air. Well, that was what we were here to stop.

The road narrowed into barely more than a hiking trail and wound its way up into the mountains. The moped tires kicked up clods of dirt and pebbles, and Jintao gunned the engine to get us up the mountainside. As we rounded a steep ridge, a little cluster of gray buildings loomed into view. They were built right into the cliff, almost as if nature, and not man, had put them there. "Is that it?" I yelled over the whine of the moped's engine.

Jintao nodded. Now we began to descend toward the compound, the backside of the moped swinging back and forth on the steep path. I clung to Jintao and whooped as he floored it for the last few hundred yards and skidded to a stop at the entrance.

Nerina popped off the moped in front of us. Somehow, her hair still looked perfect. I could only imagine what mine looked like. I grabbed my bag and followed Jintao in through the wide wooden doors.

We emerged into a small courtyard with a well in the center of it. Prayer flags of every color crisscrossed the courtyard and danced in the constant wind. The walls surrounding us were carved with images of animals: yaks, snow leopards, and then more fantastical ones like a phoenix, a dragon, and a griffin. Quinglin whistled and people poured out from every doorway leading off the courtyard. Tibetan men, women, and children, their hands filled with flowers and bowls of fruit, chattered in Tibetan as they approached. They were all dressed simply, but they looked happy and well fed. Like somehow these walls had kept the Chinese oppression out.

"These are the families of the Tibetan Clan," Nerina said to me as we were handed flowers and fruit and embraced like long-lost relatives. "They live here together."

"So that whole secret-identity thing doesn't exist here?" I asked, bowing to a smiling woman as she pressed apples into my already loaded hands.

"The rules here have always been a little different," Nerina admitted, "because this site has never been under our control. Just as Friuli is different."

A fact I'm sure everyone just forgot to share with the rest of the Clans. Wait until Alessia heard about this.

Three decidedly non-Tibetan people came out into the courtyard from the main entrance. "Ah!" Nerina cried. She shoved her offerings into the arms of the closest person and galloped over to them. I watched her embrace each one. "Bree, come!" she called to me.

Jintao took my gifts, and I walked over to meet the *Concilio*. A squiggle of nerves shot through me. Sure, they were immortal, but I was the most powerful mage they'd had in centuries. That was worth something too. I raised my chin.

Magdalena, the youngest at two hundred years old, looked like the baby sister of the bunch. She had a round face and a sweet smile, but I could see sharp wit behind her eyes. Cecilia was tall and gray-haired, with a ramrod back and a serious expression. But after she'd kissed both my cheeks, she pulled back and smiled. It lit up her whole face, and I couldn't help but smile back. Adamo towered over all of us, his broad shoulders and chest the width of a barrel. He looked like the type of older brother who would beat up anyone who messed with his sisters.

All three of them embraced me and kissed me on both cheeks. I hung back as we walked into the closest building, listening to them chatter with each other in rapid-fire Italian. So . . . this was the *Concilio.* Or half of it, at least.

I barely had time to unpack before Nerina popped her head into my room. "Come on. We're going in."

"Right now?" I followed her out of the room and across the courtyard. Dusk had fallen, lengthening pink and gray shadows over the compound. Torches had been lit along the walls, flickering orange light against the darkness. We entered a wide circular room dominated by a giant golden Buddha statue at its center. A bowl at his feet overflowed with fruit and flowers. Silken pillows of all different colors encircled the statue. Nerina squeezed onto a pillow between Magdalena and Cecilia. Five other people—the Tibetan Clan, I assumed—lay on the other pillows. One of them, a middle-aged man with a kind face, sat up and gestured to me. I tiptoed through the crowd of the Clan's families and went over to him.

"It is nice to see you again, Bree," he said, bowing his head slightly. "I am Shen."

I looked from him to the other members of the Clan. "Have we met?"

He laughed. "Yes. But I looked somewhat different."

"Oh!" I sat down next to him. "You're the Snow Leopard." I gestured to the packed room. "So, what's all this about?"

"Every time the Clan goes into battle, the families come to pray. They will sit here all night, keeping vigil over our bodies, until we return."

I swept my gaze over the throngs of men, women, and children, all here in service to the Benandanti. This was the way to do it. I didn't know what the rest of the Clans were fooling around with, but I didn't think there was anything more comforting than knowing an entire village of people was praying for your safe return while you were out fighting the bad guys.

A low hum of chanting rang around the room, growing as more people joined in. Jintao held up a singing bowl, its bright round tones echoing off the walls in harmony with the chanting. Even though I couldn't understand the words of the chant, I felt them in my bones, the intent behind them: the prayer for a good fight, a victorious battle, a safe return. As the music reached its climax, my heart swelled. The Benandanti fell back on their lush pillows, and a blaze of sky-colored light filled the room.

When it cleared, I was the only Benandante left. The others had shifted themselves right out of the compound. I rose to join them. As I passed Jintao and Quinglin, they both murmured, *"In bocca al lupo."*

I knew I'd need that blessing tonight. We'd done no reconnaissance, no planning; I had no idea what we were going into, and I knew a lot of what happened tonight would rest on me. My heart skipped a beat. And in that space where a heartbeat should've been, something else crept in. I gritted my teeth. Fear. That goddamn Rabbit had made me afraid where once I'd been fearless.

Reckless, said a voice inside me. *Foolhardy.*

I closed my eyes and punched that little voice, hard. Fuck the fear. It wasn't going to help me. In fact, I'd bet my college fund that the moment they let the fear in was the moment the other mages had met their deaths.

I ran through the courtyard to join the others. When I came through the doors, I slid to a halt. The Benandanti Clan fanned out on the mountainside, all five of them Snow Leopards. I squinted, trying to figure out which one was my Snow Leopard, the one I'd shadow-walked with. They all looked so much alike . . . but their markings . . . yes, their markings were different. The one with the black smudges beneath his eyes—that was Shen. *The rest of you are Snow Leopard One, Two, Three, and Four,* I told them. *Where are the Concilio?*

Look up, Shen said. *They are coming in from overhead.*

I'd gotten used to Nerina in her Griffin form, but the other three mythical beings took my breath away. Adamo, the Phoenix, lit up the sky with his tail of fire. The Pegasus, Cecilia, glowed ethereally against the stars. And Magdalena took the form of an enormous gray She-Wolf. I felt a swell of pride at seeing this vision of sheer magnificence. We were going to win. We had the greatest army on earth.

I followed the Snow Leopards, the cold ground crackling beneath our feet, to the top of the next ridge. The Temple spread out just below us. The swell of pride vanished, replaced with that sick, cold fear.

At least a hundred silver-haloed Malandanti swarmed the site, their forms shifting in and around the compound like locusts. *What the hell?* I said, moving closer, my eyes fixed on the impossible sight. *How can there be so many? This is more than all the Malandanti Clans combined . . .*

It is as I feared, Nerina said. *They are using the magic on ordinary people.*

Oh, God. A pit of nausea lodged in my gut. The magic at any of the seven sites was never meant to be used on regular people who didn't possess the power of the Benandanti and Malandanti inside them. To use it on someone who wasn't born with the caul, who didn't have that potential . . . *How are they doing this? Why are people falling for it?*

They must be recruiting them with empty promises, Nerina said.

Which is not hard, given the suffering of so many people on my side of the world, Shen finished for her. *So many of us are desperate for any way to help our families.*

And I can only assume that the Malandanti are failing to tell them the consequences, Magdalena said. The feathers in her huge white wings ruffled in the wind. *Thousands must be dying in this way.*

But wouldn't that be noticeable to the rest of the world?

And as soon as I thought the words, the wheels in my brain spun into place, connecting all the pieces at last. The mysterious plague sweeping Asia, the incurable disease that had doctors stumped . . . because they didn't know what they were truly seeing. They were trying to fight magic with medicine, and you cannot. You have to fight magic with even stronger magic.

This is evil beyond anything we have ever seen the Malandanti do, Adamo said. *They have killed innocents in the past, like on the bridge when the Twin Willows Falcon was Called. But the magnitude of this is a million times worse.*

What—what happens to these people? We were still at the top of the ridge, far enough away that the Malandanti below—if that's what they were—hadn't yet spotted the blue Benandante glow.

The soul is freed from the body, but it cannot return. Shen's voice shook with rage just below the surface. *It will wander the earth until the body finally dies. Meanwhile, the body is experiencing a horrible death.*

The image from the news report, of the little girl weeping at the foot of the bed where a sheet-draped body lay, flashed in my mind. I swallowed hard and tasted bile.

We must take this site tonight, before any more inno-cent people fall victim to their evil, Nerina said. *We are outnumbered, yes, but we have more power than them. The fake Malandanti do not have full strength—you can see how their auras flicker.*

She made it sound so simple, like it was no big deal at all. But the enormity of it punched me in the gut. Tonight's battle really did rest on my shoulders. The Tibetan Clan might be able to take the Temple, but the only thing that could stop this spell from killing more innocent people was me.

CHAPTER THIRTEEN

My Tudor House in Ruins

Bree

I peered over the ridgeline. The silver glow from the horde of quasi-Malandanti did look fractured, like a patchwork quilt of light instead of the smooth halo of the real Clan. I took in a deep breath. *So what do I need to do?*

Magdalena and Cecilia, you two go straight for the Yaks, Nerina said. *Herd them into a safe place, away from the fighting. Once you have the Yaks secure, come back to help us.*

Got it, Magdalena said.

Adamo and I will focus on any Concilio *who are here. The rest of you, take on the Malandanti Clan.*

Um, and me?

Nerina swung her great head to me, her eyes fierce in the darkness. *Bree, I want you to focus on the fake Malandanti. I believe that if you use the magic of Angel Falls, you can magnify the magic to take several of them down at once.*

But . . . I took a deep breath. *I'd be killing innocent people.*

They are already dead. This came from Shen. He padded into the circle and faced me. *Right now, their bodies are suffering a horrible fate. I have seen it in the villages at the base of the mountain. If you destroy the soul, the body will die right away. You will be granting them a great mercy.* He walked to stand directly in front of Nerina. *I would consider it a great honor if you would allow me to be the mage's protector in battle tonight. I will keep her safe while she uses the magic.*

So be it, Nerina said. The animals flared out, their bodies tense and ready to fight. So was mine. My skin itched with the need to do magic, to stand in front of the Rabbit and take him down.

You know what we are up against. But that is nothing compared to our power. They are the dark, and we are the light. In bocca al lupo, Nerina said.

The Clan echoed the blessing back. "*In bocca al lupo,*" I whispered. And in one breath, we charged down the hill.

There was no stealth attack here. This wasn't like the Waterfall, surrounded by trees and brush that you could hide in for days on end. The snowy mountainside hid nothing, and the day-bright glow of the *Concilio*'s auras was impossible to conceal. The Malandanti flooded out of the compound to meet us, the Harpy sweeping above them. *Follow me,* Shen called and swerved in a huge curve to the side of the compound. *I know a back way in.*

I dashed behind him, close on his heels, and risked looking back over my shoulder just before we disappeared behind the walls. Magdalena and Cecilia had broken through the line of Malandanti and raced to the main entrance of the compound, heading for the courtyard where the Yaks were kept. Adamo rose several feet in the air. With one flick of his fiery tail, he incinerated at least ten of the fake Malandanti. But just behind him, half a dozen of them were on Nerina's back, dragging her beneath them, and the Harpy was diving in. I made a motion to return to the hillside, but the Snow Leopard blocked me. *No,* he said. *You have your orders. You will be more help inside than out here.*

I knew he was right, but God, I hoped the Benandanti could fend off the Malandanti until I was able to work the spell. Now that we were at the compound, I could see just how outnumbered we were. Lynxes, Tigers, Leopards, Hawks . . . fake Malandanti in every kind of form poured out of the gates, saturating the snow with their glittering silver auras. There were so many of them that it was impossible to spot the five real Malandanti in their midst.

And then I realized that the real Malandanti weren't out there. They had to be inside the magical barrier protecting the Temple, where they would stay for the whole battle. We would have to kill every single fake Malandante in order to draw them out, and we had to draw them out of the barrier in order to take the site.

I steeled my shoulders and followed the Snow Leopard in through a small door hidden in the wall. Inside, it was eerily quiet, the only sound the faint jingling of the Yaks' bells in the distance. I hoped Magdalena and Cecilia had gotten to them.

Shen led me through a twisting maze of stone walls until we came to a small chamber nestled in the far corner of the compound. A fire pit took up most of the room. A brazier swung above the flames, pitch-black smoke pouring out of it. I took a breath and gagged. The stench blackened the inside of my nostrils—it was worse than the Twin Willows High cafeteria on meatloaf day. I started to back out of the room, but Shen blocked me. *That's it.*

What is that disgusting smell?

Yak flesh. They're cremating them in here and harnessing the blood's magic.

Gross. Seriously, why couldn't this site have had, like, magical flowers or something? At least at home the Waterfall was just, you know, water. Clean and simple. I pushed my sleeves up and moved toward the fire pit. Nerina owed me a spa day when we got back to the States.

Shen positioned himself in the doorway, his fur bristling as he kept watch. I leaned over the fire, bathing my face in smoke. Gripping the sides of the pit, I closed my eyes. Yes, I could feel the magic spilling out from the brazier—whatever was inside it was keeping the spell going. I hovered my hand just above the top of the brazier. Could it really be so easy? I brought my hand down hard onto the little metal contraption, knocking it off the chains that held it above the fire.

Jets of silver light shot out from the pit. I ducked just in time and missed being fried to death by about a millimeter. The silver bolts tangled together, wove themselves into something that began to take shape . . . an animal, two animals . . . no, three animals . . .

Watch out! I yelled to Shen. He whirled just as the fake Malandanti leapt at him. In a jumble of blue and silver light, he crushed one against the wall. The fake Malandante's aura shattered into a million shards that shimmered like a broken mirror. I shot the red magic of Angel Falls at the second Malandante, pulling the bands tight around its middle until it popped and disintegrated into the air with a puff of silvery smoke. But the third Malandante raced away, pulled by some unseen force to the battleground outside.

"Shit," I muttered, bending over the fire pit again. "Of course it couldn't be that easy." I peered deep into the embers. Okay, so whatever had been in the brazier was what pulled the poor souls out of the people the Malandanti had condemned to this ugly fate. The little metal ball dangled over the flames, and one of the three chains that had held it up was broken. It swung hypnotically, taunting me with its hidden power. I guessed that if the fire hit it in such a way again, another three Malandanti would burst forth. "Let's shut you down before that happens."

Nerina had said the magic of Angel Falls would work on it. Probably what I should've done in the first place. Dammit, I really hated it when she was right. I reached deep inside me, down the halls of that Tudor house, and summoned the dark red magic. It seeped out from my pores. I let it spill into the fire pit, holding my breath, waiting . . . waiting . . .

With an angry burst of will, the Malandanti magic fought back from beneath the flames, twisting and writhing. I struggled to keep hold of my magic, to keep myself from being pulled under into the abyss. The two forces met and broke apart, met again and meshed together into one.

My eyes flew open. The magic burst up from the pit and crashed into me like an unstoppable wave. It should've drowned me, but instead an incredible strength reached into every corner of my being. I expanded outward, my soul growing bigger and bigger . . .

The fire went out. The brazier tumbled to the floor, whatever had been inside it gone cold. I dropped my arms to my sides, feeling huger and taller and broader than any human being had the right to feel. I hadn't just destroyed the spell. I'd absorbed the magic and made it my own, turned dark into light. *Wow,* I thought. *I really am Obi-freaking-Wan Kenobi.* I knew something extraordinary had just happened, something beyond just destroying the Malandanti's spell, but what it was I couldn't begin to comprehend.

Shen spun to face me. *It's done,* he said. *The fake Malandanti have all disappeared. We can take the site now.*

Wait. I walked out into the hall and stood still, listening. The Tibetan magic pounded both inside and outside of me. There was more of it, somewhere deep in this compound. I had to find it . . .

Stay with me, I said. *Just for a little longer. There's something else here . . . something I need to find . . .*

Shen didn't ask any questions, he just followed me. I didn't know where I was going, I only knew there was something else I had to do here, one other piece of the puzzle I needed to solve. I ran through the maze, blood pounding in my ears, my footsteps echoing off the stone walls. Somewhere deep inside the compound, a fire burned, its orange glow scattering shadows all around me. I followed its blaze, searching, searching, searching for the heart of this maze, the beating, bleeding heart of this monster whose head I needed to chop off.

I skittered around a corner, scraping my shoulder against the jagged rock wall. "Mothereffer," I muttered and ran on, toward the light, toward the fiery ball of hell I'd have to leap into . . .

The glow brightened. Warmth flooded into the cold hallways, heat pulsing through me, making sweat drip behind my ears and into my eyes. "Where the hell is it?" I shouted to Shen, but his only answer was the soft padding of his racing feet beside me. Damn the Benandanti and their freaking figure-it-out-for-yourself philosophy. Sometimes I didn't want to figure it out for myself. Sometimes I just wanted to be told the goddamn answer so I could then get on with more important things, like, you know, killing our freaking enemy.

And then suddenly the hall ended. I almost ran right into the wall, which would've been beyond ridiculous. I jerked to the left and skidded to a stop in a large open-air chamber. In the center burned a huge bonfire, sparks dancing up into the night sky. The smell of burning wood filled my nose, with something underneath it, something dirtier, older, earthier. Two figures stepped around the other side of the flames. The Rabbit grinned at me from beneath his hood. I gritted my teeth. He wouldn't be grinning for long. I'd see to that. But the other figure . . . my gaze darted to him, my mind not quite grasping, my heart not wanting to believe.

"Dad?"

Half his face was in shadow, black and unreadable, while the other shone red with the firelight, so that he looked like half a devil and half a ghost. He stepped forward, the red light shimmering all around him. "Why, Bree? Why did you have to get involved in this?"

"Are you kidding?" It was hard to breathe, like I was wearing a corset someone had laced too tight. "How could I not get involved? This war is a regular Wolfe family reunion." I fought to get air—any air, just one little tiny sip of air—into my lungs. "You sacrificed Jonah to this war. I had to get involved to save him." *And maybe even you*, I added silently, thinking the thought that lay so deep and dormant inside me—that if I saved Jonah, if I ended this war, maybe we could all go back to how it used to be. But standing before my dad, him on one side and me on the other, I finally realized that was never going to happen.

A movement fluttered in the corner of my eye. I whirled, the magic ready at my fingertips. "Don't even think about it," I said as the Rabbit raised his arms. Red smoke poured out of him, but I just cocked my head. "Really, dude? You think I'm an idiot, don't you?" I shot Pakistani magic at him with a wave of my hand, and he disappeared with a pop, banished to another time and place.

It wouldn't be for long, so I closed the space between me and my dad in a few strides. "Dad, come on. Let's go. The Benandanti can hide you. Just come over to our side and let's have done with this."

Shen growled. *The* Concilio Celeste *would love to have him in their custody. Imagine the secrets we could get out of him.*

"Just shut up, okay?" I yelled at him over my shoulder. "This is between me and him. Stay out of it." And to my relief, he didn't argue. He simply backed up to the chamber's entrance to keep a lookout.

Dad reached out and grasped my shoulder, forcing me to look into his eyes. There used to be laughter in those eyes, but that had long ago been replaced with darkness. And now that I peered into them, I could see a lonely sadness beneath that dark. "I can't leave, Bree."

"Just come with—"

"Bree. Honey. Bree-girl." I stilled at the use of the nickname he used to call me when I was little. *Bree-girl and Jonah-boy.* We'd chase him around the living room and make him our pony. He cupped my face in his hands. His fingers were so cold that my cheeks felt encased in ice. "I can't come with you. I signed a contract."

I didn't need to ask what kind of contract. I could only imagine what the Guild had made him agree to when he'd taken the job with them. Something more than binding, something longer than life. Something like what the devil gives you when you sign away your soul. And I knew better than to think there might be a way out.

"Then, what? You stay here and help them kill me?"

"No. I promise I won't hurt—"

"Actually, yes, that is what he is sworn to do."

I spun around and came nose-to-nose with the Rabbit. The grin was back on his face, and before I had time to wipe it off, he rammed into me. Damn, that little four-eyed geek must have spent his free time at the gym, because he was freaking strong. I pushed back, but I was no match. He punched me in the stomach, knocking the wind out of me, and shoved me back into the opposite wall.

I crumpled to the floor and lay still, trying to summon breath back into my body. Pain arced across my middle. Bastard probably rebroke my ribs. I squinted across the chamber to see what the Rabbit was doing to my dad, but my vision blurred and twisted.

Bree. It was Shen. *Use the Redwood magic.*

Oh. Right. I really hated it when someone came up with a good idea before me. I squeezed my eyes shut and entered that little Tudor house filled with all my knowledge of the magic. I entered the door to the Redwood magic, let its soft yellow light envelop me. It wouldn't heal any major internal injuries—I'd have to actually visit the Redwood site to get that benefit—but it filled my spirit with energy. Kind of like a jolt of magical coffee. I could have bottled it and become a millionaire . . . but I guessed that fell under the heading of Using the Magic for Selfish Purposes.

The pain in my ribs dissolved. I pulled myself up to all fours. My dad and the Rabbit were on the other side of the fire, out of my view. I crawled around the back side of the bonfire, keeping low and quiet so the Rabbit wouldn't catch on that I was up and about. I saw their shadows before I saw them, huge black figures etched against the back wall. The Rabbit held a bowl high above his head. I heard him shout something in a language that was as old as the mountains themselves. He tipped the bowl toward my dad, and in the dim glow of the firelight, I saw the stream of red.

"No!" I scrambled to my feet, screaming the word over and over, trying to get to him before the blood touched his lips. But the Rabbit never turned, probably didn't even hear me coming, so deep in the ritual he was. By the time I reached them, my father's face was streaked with the ancient, magical blood of the Yaks. I grabbed his sweater and dragged him down to the ground. "Dad. Daddy. It's okay, I'll undo it—"

"You can't undo what's already been done, Bree-girl." His voice was shredding as the magic took him apart, undid his being cell by cell. "This was done a long, long time ago."

His gaze flickered to something behind me, a warning. I spun just as the Rabbit shot red smoke at me. It snaked around me, squeezing tight, trying to force the life out of me. For a moment I considered just letting it happen, letting myself die here next to Dad. I looked at him at the moment his body crumpled to the ground and an enormous Bengal tiger stood next to him. "No," I gasped.

Bree. Don't let him win.

It was not Shen. It was not Nerina or any of the other Benandanti, fighting their battle outside the compound. It was Dad. The great taboo was not enough to block our thoughts from each other. It seemed we did have a connection, that I was a daddy's girl after all.

You have to survive so you can fight. For Jonah, for your mom, for this whole damn crazy war. Please. Come on, Bree-girl. Don't let me die in vain.

I met the Rabbit's soulless coal eyes glowing from beneath his hood. Using every bit of strength I possessed, I dug deep inside and pulled out the Redwood magic. I built a wall of yellow light around me, bursting the red smoke into wisps. The Rabbit stumbled back and I went after him, throwing ball after ball of yellow light at him. The Redwood magic was more powerful than most people gave it credit for; while it could be used to heal, it could also be used to weaken your enemies.

He tried to hit me with Pakistani magic, but I dodged easily to the side. *You made this so fucking personal, you asshole,* I thought, *you deserve whatever's coming to you.* God, I wanted to kill him. And I had never been more justified.

I summoned the red smoke, and this time I wasn't afraid of it. I welcomed its dark power, let it flood through me. It poured out of me as I stalked toward the Rabbit. He shot one last blast of Pakistani magic at me, but I knocked it aside and kept coming. He was backed against the wall. I slammed the red smoke into him and tightened it around him. I would pop him like a grape, watch him die like he was forcing me to watch my own father die, like he'd forced my brother to watch me being tortured.

Somewhere in the back of my mind, I heard Dad and Shen telling me not to, telling me to let go, but I couldn't. I held my palm up and pushed the magic deeper into the Rabbit. He met my eyes and had the nerve to wink at me. And then, with a sickening whoosh, he was gone. Disappeared.

I shrieked my anger and frustration into the night, pounded my fists against my thighs. He'd used his last bit of power to send himself to another time and space. *Fucking coward. I would've stayed and fought to the death . . .*

And sometimes you need to know when to let go, the Snow Leopard broke in. I turned to face him. He padded over to Dad's dying body and lay beside it.

The Tiger that was Dad's soul paced the chamber. *I*

have to go out there, he said. *They're summoning me, telling me to come out and fight.*

"Well, you gotta do what you gotta do," I said. Every inch of my insides felt defeated. I'd had the Rabbit in my grasp and I'd lost him. And now I was going to lose Dad.

He swung his magnificent orange, black, and white head to me. His eyes bored into me. *That's right, Bree-girl. And you know what you gotta do.*

I stared at him. The only sound in the chamber was the crackling of the fire. Shen keened into the silence, a long low howl filled with all the pain that I felt. *No,* I said. *No, don't make me do that.*

Bree, you have to. Shen moved to Dad's body and laid his head on his chest. *Otherwise who knows how much damage he'll do before his body dies out.*

I held my hand up, trying to silence him, trying not to believe what I knew to be true. I crept toward the Tiger. I could feel the anxiety coming off him, the need to be with his Clan. *Daddy?*

His eyes never left me. *Yes,* he said. *Yes, do it.* I was right in front of him now. I came down to my knees. *It's okay, Bree-girl. Look at my body. I'm already dead.*

I glanced over. In the flickering firelight I saw the decay spreading across his face and neck. I knew it could take days, that his body would just suffer and suffer. Even if he couldn't feel it, the thought of it made me sick. I threw my arms around the Tiger's neck and buried my face in his soft fur. As I did, a powerful déjà vu swept through me. I had seen this before . . . done this before. This moment was the one true vision the Waterfall had given me the night we'd brought down the Guild, the night the Rabbit had put so many false visions in my mind.

I clung to the Tiger, my tears matting down his fur.

I love you, Bree-girl. I know I wasn't the best father, but I always loved you.

I wasn't exactly the best daughter, I murmured into his fur. *But I loved you too.*

Take care of your brother and your mom, okay? Tell them I died a good death.

I will. I promise.

A guttural sound of longing ripped out of his throat. *You have to do it now. I can't stay here much longer . . .*

Somehow, I managed to tear myself away from him and stand up. Somehow, I managed to turn inward and enter that Tudor house. Somehow, I managed to find the door to the magic of Angel Falls and summon the red smoke.

But I don't remember anything after that. In that moment, my mind flooded with memories. The real Tudor house on that quiet street in Charlottesville with the white picket fence out front, jumping into the piles of leaves that Dad had just raked, the lemonade stand he'd built, the swing in the backyard that he'd push me on. *"Higher, Daddy, higher!"* And he'd push me so high I'd touch the sky.

When I came back down to earth, I lay on my back, the stars bright above me. I felt Dad's lifeless body next to me. We were alone. Shen had left me, gone to join his Clan so they could claim the site. So Dad and I lay there, side by side, counting the stars like we used to in our Charlottesville backyard until the dawn faded them from view.

CHAPTER FOURTEEN
The Awful, Terrible Truth

Alessia

It was odd to not have to step over Bree and her air mattress when I got up in the morning. I washed my face and went down to the kitchen, hoping that Lidia wouldn't be up yet.

No such luck. She and Mr. Salter sat at the kitchen table, their fingers just barely touching across the wooden surface. What the hell was he doing here? Was he *sleeping* here now? The second she saw me, Lidia snatched her hand back and jumped to her feet. "*Buongiorno, cara.* There's coffee and muffins, or I can make some eggs if you want."

"No, thank you," I said, my spine stiff as I sidestepped her and went to the counter. I poured two cups of coffee and turned around. I headed toward the living room, but Lidia blocked my path. "What?"

"Alessia, this is silly. Please let's talk after school, *bene*?"

"Won't you be busy?" I jerked my chin toward Mr. Salter.

"Alessia, your mother and I—" he began.

"I really don't want to hear it," I said, a little too loud. I shot a glare at Lidia. "You know he shouldn't be here. You're putting him in danger."

Mr. Salter stepped in front of Lidia. "It's okay, Alessia. I know about the Benandanti."

That word, coming from his mouth, punched me in the gut. "What?" I said, looking between them. "Is there anyone in this town who *doesn't* know about the Benandanti?"

"I was as surprised as you," said Heath, coming up behind me from the living room. He plucked one of the mugs of coffee out of my hand and took a sip. "I sat him down last night to tell him everything, but he already knew."

"Did Nerina okay this?"

Heath shrugged. "Not really, but I told her if he was going to be hanging around he should know what's going on."

"I can help," Mr. Salter offered.

"How? How can you possibly help? Can you dismantle the magical barrier surrounding the Waterfall? No? Didn't think so."

"Alessia!" Heath elbowed me.

"And how the hell does he know, anyway?" I narrowed my eyes at Mr. Salter. "You said you didn't know about the Waterfall that night you were over for dinner."

"I *didn't* know about the Waterfall. Not until Heath told me." Mr. Salter's voice was calm, which infuriated me.

"Then how do you know about the Benandanti?"

"Because . . ." He swallowed and his face softened.

"Because Dolly was one."

"Dolly was a Benandante?" My hand shook, sloshing coffee onto my wrist. Heath took the cup from me and set it on the table. "Did she—did she die in battle?"

Mr. Salter shook his head. "No. It was the cancer, just as everybody thought. Even Benandanti can get sick." A sad smile twisted his mouth. "She never told me about the Waterfall. She told me only the barest minimum, to keep me safe."

I tried to wrap my brain around the image of sweet Dolly, kicking Malandanti ass at the Waterfall. Actually, I could see it, because along with that sweetness had come a heavy dollop of sass. I wondered if my dad had known, if he'd suspected that his neighbor was in the same Clan with his parents. And who had replaced her when she died? Had it been Cora?

The answer hit me like a smack across the face.

I put my hand to my mouth, my words escaping between my fingers. "It was me, wasn't it?" I whispered. "I replaced her."

No one spoke for a moment; no one needed to. I knew I was right. God, how twisted was this? How many families across Twin Willows had been drawn into the Benandanti's legacy? How many generations backward did it stretch?

Mr. Salter opened his mouth to say something, but before he could get a word out, Jeff ran in from the living room, Cora on his heels. "They've done it!" he yelled, waving a sheet of paper in the air.

I whirled, grateful for the distraction, and snatched the paper out of his hand. It was a printed email, sparsely written. "'Tibetan site claimed,'" I read out loud.

Cora crushed into me, whooping in my ear. Heath and Jeff threw their arms around both of us so that we were a tight circle of hugs and tears and laughter. I buried my face in their nearness and let the joy of victory wash away the shock of what I'd just learned about Dolly. Even though I hadn't been there in Tibet, I could taste the success in my mouth. I pictured the scene in my mind, the brilliant blue barrier of Benandanti magic surrounding the site, blasting out the silvery gray of the Malandanti. They had done it. Nerina and Bree—they'd won us a site we'd never before possessed.

"I didn't even read the rest of the email," Jeff said after we'd all calmed down. "What does it say?"

I pulled away from the circle and held up the paper to read the rest. "'No casualties on the Benandanti side,'" I said.

"Thank God," Jeff murmured.

"'Will return in two days,'" I continued. My eyes scanned the next line, and the words died on my lips.

"What is it?" Heath asked.

I looked up at him. My breath froze in my lungs, my insides like icicles.

Heath took the paper from me. "'Travis Wolfe dead. Bree not doing well.'" He met my eyes. "Oh."

My mind crumpled, too many thoughts for it to

contain. What had happened? Did he die in battle? He must have. And if that was the case, he must've died at the hands of one of our own . . . or—*God*—even Bree herself. Did Mrs. Wolfe know? *Did Jonah?*

Without a word, I turned and ran to the front door. Everything else that had happened this morning was wiped away. I had only one coherent thought: get to Jonah. I wasn't even sure where he was but I knew I had to try. Halfway up the driveway I heard footsteps behind me. "Alessia, wait. Wait!" Heath caught up to me and grabbed my arm from behind, pulling me to a stop. "You can't just go over there. It's too dangerous."

"I don't care. I have to see him." My vision blurred with tears, and I swiped them away. "I know a back way in. Mrs. Wolfe is on our side—she's been helping Bree. It'll be okay." I tugged my arm, but Heath held me fast. "Please. Heath, you have to let me. He *needs* me now."

Heath looked skyward, as though the clouds might help him control his unruly charge. "Okay. One hour. If you're not back in sixty minutes, I'm coming after you."

"Thank you." He let go of me and I ran, faster and faster until I got to Jonah's house. I didn't know if he was there or not, but it was the first place I could think of to look for him. What if he didn't know yet? What if I was the one who had to tell him? I grasped the lowest branch of the tree outside the bathroom and heaved myself up. I didn't want to be the one to tell him, but better the news come from me than from Pratt, who I imagined had all the sympathy of an anaconda.

The bark scraped my gloveless hands, but I propelled myself up as fast as I could until I reached the bathroom window. It was unlocked; Mrs. Wolfe had said she'd leave it open for Bree to come in if she needed to. I landed with a soft thud on the bathmat and tiptoed to the hallway. The instant I poked my head out, Mrs. Wolfe's bedroom door creaked open.

"Alessia!" she hissed and gestured frantically for me to come to her.

When I reached her side, she shoved me behind her into the room, hard. I was about to protest when I heard the sound of a door opening farther down the hallway. "Miriam?"

I froze. It was Pratt.

"I was just coming to check on Jonah," she said, her voice shaky.

"I'm handling it. If I need you, I will fetch you." He slammed the door with such force it shook the wall I was pressed against.

Mrs. Wolfe backed up into the bedroom, shut the door, and locked it. "I'm so sorry about that," she whispered. "But I heard you come in through the bathroom and I was afraid he had, too." She picked up a towel that lay draped on the chair by the door and stuffed it into the crack beneath the door. "That'll help a little, but we have to be quiet. They're just next door in Jonah's room."

"So he's here, then? Is it just Pratt with him?"

She nodded. "Pratt brought him over . . . to be with me." Taking my elbow, she propelled me to the bed to sit. Her laptop bounced a little on the mattress, and she moved it to the nightstand before settling next to me. She swallowed hard. "Jonah's father died yesterday."

"At the Tibetan site. I know. I'm so sorry." I touched her arm, and she leaned into me. I suddenly realized I was probably the only friendly support she had at the moment, surrounded as she was by the enemy.

"It's an odd feeling," Mrs. Wolfe said. She sounded as though she was thinking hard about her words. "I always knew this would end badly. The moment he took that job, I knew." She looked out the window at the bare branches of the tree just on the other side of the glass. "Once upon a time, we had a lovely life together. And when I think about that, I'm sad." Her gaze flicked back to me. "But I lost that life, that Travis, a long time ago. And so, in a way, I've already mourned."

I looked at her face. It was almost serene with the understanding that she was now a widow. I thought of how my mother's face had permanent tearstains beneath the black lace veil she had worn for days after my father had died. My throat tightened. I had to get to Jonah in the next room. My heart, my mind, my bones ached to be with him. What were they saying to him? What could they possibly say to him that would make anything better for him? If I could get to him, I would know what to say. Or what not to say. He would want silence now, not the cruel, empty words of Pratt and his cohorts. I knew how complicated Jonah's relationship with his dad was. I knew he would try to brush off his death as if he didn't care but that an ache would start deep down and wouldn't go away. Not for a long, long time. Maybe not ever.

"I have to go to him." I slid off the bed. "He needs me more than those jerks."

"Alessia, no." Mrs. Wolfe hurried across the room and blocked me at the door. "It's too dangerous."

"They don't know that I'm a Benandante," I said. "They only know I'm his girlfriend."

"*Ex*-girlfriend."

"Even so. Wouldn't I come over if I heard his dad had died?"

"But how would you know? They told me to not tell anyone. They're not making this knowledge public. The Guild wants the federal government to think that Travis skipped town to avoid the investigation, and they want to distract the feds by making them search for him."

"Damn." I stepped back. It was just like the Guild—sneaky but smart. "I just wish I knew what they were saying to him. Because it's probably causing more harm than good."

Mrs. Wolfe chewed her lip. "The attic," she said suddenly. "There's a vent in his room. You'll be able to hear them." I followed her into the walk-in closet at the corner of the bedroom. She pulled the string that dangled down in the center of the closet, and a ladder unfolded. "Keep to the beams," she said. "Try not to step too heavily or they might hear you."

"Aren't you coming up?"

"They'll definitely hear both of us," she said. "I trust you to report back what you hear."

The attic was a maze of luggage, empty television and computer boxes, and rubber bins labeled with things like CHRISTMAS and BABY CLOTHES. I crawled along the center beam in the direction I knew Jonah's room to be. Voices floated up as I neared the vent, soft and unintelligible at first, then louder as I got closer. When I reached it, I lay down along the beam with my ear against the cold metal.

"Your father knew what he was getting into." Pratt sounded like he was trying to come off as sympathetic, but it was impossible for him to sound anything other than annoyed and superior. "Just as you did when you joined the Clan."

"Are you fucking kidding me?"

I jerked upward. The anger and pain in Jonah's voice blasted through the vent like something solid. I gripped the sides of the beam, my knuckles white.

"I had *no idea* what I was signing up for. You have lied to me over and over. Everything that comes out of your mouth is a fucking lie!"

There was rustling, a grunt, and then a sickening smack like the back of a hand against flesh. "Listen to me, you little brat. You have been warned time and again, and you are on very thin ice. In fact, it was probably only your father who stood between you and the full wrath of the *Concilio*. Now that he's gone, I'd think long and hard before acting out."

A long silence stretched below me in which all I could hear was sharp, ragged breathing. Heat blocked my throat. I could feel Jonah's pain radiating up through the vent. I wished I could tell him I was there and I would take care of him and everything would be okay.

"You cannot tell anyone." Pratt broke the silence. "The federal government needs to believe your father has gone on the run. If they know he's dead, they'll turn the investigation on us, and that would be very inconvenient at the moment."

"No." The single word carried so much hate as it came from Jonah's mouth. "You cannot come in here, tell me my father is dead, and expect me to carry on like nothing has changed. *Everything* has changed."

"Oh, come on, Jonah, you didn't even like him."

"That doesn't matter! He was still my father—"

"I repeat, you cannot tell anyone."

"And I repeat, I need to talk to someone about this—"

"Talk to your mother. Talk to me."

"You are the last person I would talk to! You are the crappiest Guide in the history of Guides—"

Wood knocked against wood and footsteps quickened across the room, as though Jonah had dodged out of Pratt's way to avoid being smacked again. "You can't stop me from telling someone. You can't stop me from talking."

"If you tell anyone, especially that girlfriend of yours, the next death I'll be reporting will be hers."

My hands tightened around the beam, the wood digging into my palms. In the room below, a cold silence descended. Did they know about me?

"She's not my girlfriend. We broke up."

"Oh, please. Anyone at that school can see you two making moony eyes at each other."

"You stay away from her, Pratt. She has done nothing wrong." I could feel the tension in his voice, the barely restrained rage vying with fear.

"Well, that has yet to be proven, doesn't it? Her mother probably knows something. Her father definitely did."

I flattened myself even harder against the beam. The file we'd taken from the Guild. What exactly had my dad known that they found out about? I strained to hear Pratt and Jonah over the pounding of my heart.

"What did he know?"

"He knew about the Waterfall. His parents were always suspected of being Benandanti, but that was before my time. He was seen at the Waterfall numerous times. Sometimes he brought that daughter of his."

"So? He probably just thought it was a waterfall, plain and simple." It was like Jonah knew I was listening, knew I needed to hear this. *He needs to hear it so he can tell me later*, I thought. And in that moment, I loved him even more, for putting aside his own pain so he could spy for me.

"No. He never touched the water, for one thing. And the last time he was seen there, he was with the Stag. They obviously knew each other."

All the breath left my body. I wasn't sure what I was surviving on. My dad and Jeff had been best friends since high school, as close as Jenny and me. The whirling tick of knowledge clicked in my brain. *He was Called when I was really little*, Jenny had told me. Probably exactly a year and a half old. Why had I never realized it before? Jeff had been Called to replace one of my grandparents. And of course my dad would've figured it out.

"Oh, come on. It's not like they could talk to each other."

"It was obvious they were communicating somehow. And we couldn't have an outside person working with them."

"Are you saying . . ."

My whole body tensed as I mouthed the words along with Jonah. *Are you saying . . . what I think you're saying?*

"We took care of it. I saw them together at the Waterfall, I made a call, and the Rabbit paid him a visit. Did a great job, too. No one suspected it was anything other than a heart attack."

A sound bubbled up from inside me, a strangled cry that would've turned into a scream if I hadn't shoved my fist into my mouth. I bit into my fingers, shrieking into my flesh. Lidia had been wrong. Heath and Nerina had been wrong. It wasn't a heart attack. It was the Rabbit, that horrible, evil excuse for a human being, wielding the magic of Angel Falls like he'd tried to wield it on me.

"So you see, she's the last person you can talk to about this. Because inevitably she will have questions, and those questions could lead back to us, and then, well, you'd have two people to mourn."

I grappled at the vent, trying to tear the screws out with my bare hands. I was going to drop into the room, right on top of Pratt. I was going to kill him. I was going to watch him die.

"It's time for patrol."

"But—"

"Jonah, I've taught you how to compartmentalize. You need to do that now. I'll meet you at the Waterfall."

There was the sound of the window opening and a gust of wind so strong it blew through the vent. I pulled myself up and scrambled backward so fast that I was at the ladder before I knew it. On the floor below, Mrs. Wolfe gripped my arm. "What happened? You're white as a sheet—"

"Open the window," I demanded.

"What?"

"Open the window, open the goddamned window!"

She let go of me and threw open the bathroom window. I spotted the Raven, a black dot in the distance, winging to the Waterfall. "Don't touch my body," I told Mrs. Wolfe, and in an instant, I was flying after him, chasing down my revenge.

CHAPTER FIFTEEN
The Failure

Alessia

I had never moved so fast in my life. Wind whipped through my feathers and tore across my face. My vision was fixed on the Raven, just ahead of me, growing and growing as I gained on him. Somewhere far below, Jonah raced along the earth, but for once he was on the periphery of my thoughts. All I cared about was the Raven, that fucking monster who had killed my father. When I was done with him, I'd find the Rabbit. I'd pierce his eyes with my claws.

We flew over my farm, over the ruins of our barn. The sight of it spurred me faster, and I caught up to the Raven as we crossed into the forest.

He must've felt me coming, because at the instant I stretched my talons out toward him, he disappeared. That damn trick of popping in and out of time and space—Bree had never had the time to teach it to me. I swerved in a circle, every nerve in my body on fire. I was hyperaware, ready for him to reappear at any time, in any direction.

There was a loud *pop*. A black shadow loomed over me. I dodged to the side just as he dove for me. I danced in the air, taunting him, just out of his reach as he swiped at me again and again. But I was too fast. Falcons are quicker, lighter, more agile than ravens, and I had a fire in my belly that he couldn't possibly understand.

I dropped past him in the air, the wind in my tail feathers like a slap to his face. He took the bait and chased me, trying in vain to catch up. I could hear the Waterfall now, just ahead. I swerved as I flew, slowing him down as he tracked me. He was doing exactly what I wanted. I was going to drown him in the stream above the Waterfall while the Malandante who was stuck inside the barrier watched.

We zoomed over the birch trees, so fast I just barely caught a glimpse of tawny fur on the ground below. My wings fumbled at the same instant that Cal burst into my head. *What the hell, Alessia?*

Stay out of this! He's mine!

What is going on?

I didn't answer; I shut him out. He wasn't going to distract me, not now, when the Raven was within my grasp.

We reached the stream. I turned with an abrupt jerk. The Raven couldn't stop fast enough and collided into me, but I was ready for it. The moment his black feathers touched mine, I sank my talons into him.

The Raven's scream shattered the wintry stillness of

the forest. In the barrier below, the Bobcat leapt up the rocks that lined the Waterfall, but he stopped at the top. He was stuck there until another Malandante showed up, which probably wouldn't be long. I had to work fast.

I dragged the Raven down, down, down toward the water. His bones felt light and brittle beneath my talons. He thrashed in my grip, but I held him strong. *I broke your wings once,* I thought. *I'll do it again.*

Alessia! I'm Calling Heath!

Do it, I fired at Cal. *I don't fucking care.* My insides were filled with the color red, the taste of blood on my tongue. We hit the water, the Raven and I, with a powerful smack. I rose above the surface almost immediately, my wings outstretched to keep me balanced as I held the Raven. The water flowed over him. He tried to raise his head, and I plunged it back under with one hard shove. He fought beneath me, trying to throw me off. I shook with the effort to keep him under. His motions were growing slower, the life flowing out of him, like the life had flowed out of my father . . . It wouldn't be long now.

A gigantic black figure barreled into me, knocking me so hard that I tumbled through the air and landed on the opposite bank of the stream. I righted myself just as Jonah loomed in front of me.

I heard him at your house! He killed my dad! Without waiting for an answer, I flew above Jonah's head, aiming for the dazed Raven, who was winging toward the barrier. But before I could get to the stream, Jonah jumped in the air and caught me in his mouth, dragged me down to the earth. He'd done this once before without hurting me. This time his teeth were not so gentle.

Jonah! Get off!

He dropped me to the ground, but before I could get up, his paw was at my throat. He leaned down, his lips pulled back, his fangs bared in a way that sent a shiver through me. And for one horrible sickening moment, I thought the boy I loved was going to kill me.

Jonah brought his head right down to mine. His breath ruffled my feathers. *I am not going to let you become a killer,* he growled. *Not for him. Not for any of them. You are better than that.*

The world around me froze like a snow globe trapped in time. Something inside me broke, something that maybe had been straining to stay together since the day my dad died. I could feel the pieces of my heart, jagged and splintered, impossible to mend. And I saw what Jonah saw: killing the Raven wouldn't put me back together. It would only break me more.

I'm sorry, I gasped. *I'm so sorry.*

You don't have to be sorry. You just can't lower yourself to their level—

Jonah, your dad. I'm—

I know.

An orange blur streaked from the other bank of the stream and slammed into Jonah. He rolled away as Cal went after him, his golden fur standing on end. *Cal! He wasn't hurting me—*

That's not what it looked like! He snarled at Jonah, who sprang to his feet and snarled right back at him. They circled each other like boxers in a ring, black against gold, shadow and light. I flew back and forth above them, my thoughts ricocheting between them.

Cal, just leave it and let's get out of here.

Nerina was right! You're blind when it comes to him— he had his teeth at your throat! Cal snapped his jaw and Jonah snapped right back.

Jonah, he doesn't know what he's doing. We're leaving.

It doesn't look like he's leaving. It looks like he wants to stay and fight me.

Oh, my God! I couldn't believe the pigheaded maleness going on five feet below me. *You two just stop!*

I soared away from them, but before I could reach the opposite bank, the Raven blocked my path. We rushed at each other like two knights on a joust field, but at the last possible second I twisted away. He fell, righted himself, and came at me again. I was suddenly so tired, so weary of this ridiculous game we were playing. *Go away,* I thought even though he couldn't hear. *Just go away, or let me kill you.*

But the Raven would never give up, never stop coming at me, even if I tried to call a truce. I had to fight, and I had to win. He went for me and I feinted; I went for him and he dodged. Over and over we moved back and forth. I knew what he was doing, knew that he was trying to tire me so that he could go in for the kill. He thought I was an idiot. I might have been about some things, but not about him.

I drew him farther and farther away from the barrier that kept the Waterfall under Malandante control. Below us the Panther and the Catamount played the same game, danced the same dance. How long would this go on? We were too evenly matched, and at least two of us didn't truly have it in our souls to kill.

A commotion rustled the brush and the White Wolf and the Stag bounded into the stream. *Alessia! What the hell do you think you're doing?*

I didn't answer Heath; if I looked away for a second, if I even blinked, the Raven would take me down. I careened through the trees with him on my tail. The Waterfall was out of our view now; I could only hear the sound of the rushing water and imagine the fight happening there.

The Raven performed his little disappearing trick, leaving me alone amongst the pine trees. I stopped in midair, my wings beating so heavily that pine needles showered to the ground. *Face me and fight, you coward,* I screamed in my head.

And with that infuriating little pop, he reappeared right in front of me. *That doesn't work on me anymore,* I thought and craned my neck forward. My beak met his throat. He screeched and fell through the tree branches, spiraling down fast to the ground. My heart stopped.

Had I killed him after all?

Far below, just above the ground, the Raven pulled up. He winged away, his flight jerky as he vanished into the forest. Disappointment and relief fought for space inside me. I wanted him dead, but Jonah was right. I was better than that.

As I swooped down low, I spotted bright red blood staining the snow beneath the tree. At least I'd wounded him enough to put him out of commission . . . for now.

Alessia! Where the hell are you? Meet us at the birch trees now.

Crap. I could only hope that Heath would understand after I told him about Pratt and my dad. But when I burst into the copse of birches, my stomach bottomed out. The Stag knelt on the ground while Heath tried to heave Cal's limp Catamount body onto the Stag's back. *What happened? Is he—is he—?*

No. But it's bad. Come on, help me.

I gripped Cal's front shoulders, trying not to let my talons sink in too deep, and pulled as Heath pushed Cal's backside with his head. When he was safely perched on the Stag's back, we took off toward town. Halfway there, I remembered where I'd left my body.

I'll meet you back at the house.

Hurry.

Mrs. Wolfe had thankfully left the bathroom window open. I shot through it and dissolved into my body in one breath. When I sat up, she appeared in the doorway.

"What happened? Is Jonah—?"

"He's okay," I said and then realized I didn't know if that was true. My gut turned over with a sickening thud. Had Jonah attacked Cal? I scrambled to my feet. "But I have to go. Thanks for everything, Mrs. Wolfe."

She let me out the back door, and I took off. My feet pounded over hard earth and pavement until I reached Jenny's house. When I burst through the front door, Jenny met me on the threshold. "They're in the den," she said. I looked down at her hands. She was carrying a pile of blood-soaked towels.

"Oh, my God," I moaned and pushed past her.

Inside the den, Cal lay on the couch, his eyes closed, his skin ashen. One arm was fully bandaged. His shirt lay open, and bandages crisscrossed his chest. I watched the stain of blood grow larger and larger across his rib cage. "We need to change that bandage again," Jeff said.

Cora peeled the dirty gauze away from Cal's skin. Six deep gouges ran from his collarbone to his belly button. My head swam, and I grasped the back of the desk chair to keep upright. "We have to take him to the hospital," I whispered.

"No," Jeff said. "It will compromise his identity. The Malandanti will be looking for someone with his injuries."

"His mother is on her way here," Cora said as she laid down fresh gauze. "Apparently she was a nurse before she got married." She pressed down hard on Cal's chest.

He groaned and turned his head.

"I'm so sorry," Cora murmured. "I just have to stop the bleeding."

"I didn't think wounds like this showed up in your human form," Jenny said from the doorway. She held a stack of clean towels.

"They can if they're deep enough," Jeff said. "It's also possible the Bobcat was using some sort of magic to make sure they did."

My breath caught in my throat. "The—the Bobcat?"

Heath turned and narrowed his eyes at me. "Yes. It was the Bobcat."

"So it wasn't—it wasn't Jonah?"

"No, Alessia. It wasn't Jonah. They switched places right after Jeff and I got there." He pressed his mouth into a thin line. "Not that it matters; they're all still Malandanti."

I sagged into the chair and lowered my head to my knees. *It wasn't Jonah. It wasn't Jonah. It wasn't Jonah.* It did matter.

The doorbell rang. Barb, who had been hovering over Cora as she applied the bandages, dashed off to answer it. A moment later she returned with Cal's tiny, dark-haired mother. "This is Dika," Barb said, but before she could make any more introductions, Dika marched over to the couch.

"Move," she ordered Cora, who took one look at the set of Dika's jaw and got out of the way.

Dika slid her hand into Cal's and held it up to her cheek. "*Mily chlapec*, I'm here. You're going to be just fine."

She opened the heavy-duty plastic box she'd brought with her. "Bring one of those towels," she said, pointing at Jenny. "Spread it down on the floor here."

She laid out her tools on the towel: needle and surgical thread, tape, more gauze, an Ace bandage. "It would be better if everyone left," she said as she threaded the needle. "Except you," she barked at Cora. "You can stay to help."

"Oh, can I?" Cora muttered, but as the rest of us filed out, she knelt beside Dika without further protest.

I went to follow Jenny up the stairs, but Heath grabbed my elbow. "Oh no you don't," he growled and propelled me into the laundry room at the back of the house.

"What the hell were you thinking?" Heath snapped as soon as the door was shut. "Cal Called me and told me you'd gone after the Raven on your own. What on earth would possess you to do such a thing?"

"What was Cal doing at the Waterfall by himself?" I countered. "He's not ready to be patrolling alone."

"I know that," Heath said. "And he wasn't supposed to be. *You* were supposed to be there with him. But you ran off to see your boyfriend and completely forgot, didn't you?"

I picked at a rust spot on the washing machine. Yes, I'd completely forgotten. The news about Jonah's dad had wiped it all from my mind . . . and then the revelation about my dad had wiped all *that* out. "I'm sorry," I murmured. "But I found out something while I was at Jonah's house."

The door to the laundry room creaked open. "You

guys okay?" Jeff asked.

"Fine," Heath said. "I'm just lecturing her about the importance of responsibility."

Jeff grimaced. "I'll leave you to it, then."

"No, wait," I said. Jeff opened the door wider and stepped inside. "*I* was just telling Heath that I found something out when I was at the Wolfes' house. Pratt—the Raven—was there talking to Jonah."

"And?" Heath asked.

I swallowed hard, hearing again the words that changed everything in my mind. "He told Jonah about my dad. That he'd seen my dad at the Waterfall with—with you," I said, looking at Jeff. "And he called the Rabbit. And the Rabbit killed—killed my dad."

Jeff's face, normally full of life and color, drained empty. He shut the door and slid down the length of it until he hit the floor. I knelt in front of him. "He knew about you, didn't he?" I asked. "He knew because you were Called to replace one of my grandparents."

He nodded and ran his shaking fingers through his hair. Behind me Heath leaned down and put his hand on my shoulder. "I never wanted to believe it," Jeff said after a long moment. His voice quavered with every word. "I thought the timing was suspicious, but people die of natural causes all the time, right? Dolly had just died of cancer, so it was easy to think that . . . I didn't want to believe the Malandanti had killed my best friend."

I twisted around to look up at Heath. "Do you see?

Why I went after him? *He killed my father.* My father, who wasn't a Benandante, who wasn't involved in this at all. Just for being there. That's why he died."

"Well—" Jeff said, and I turned back to him.

He took a deep breath. "He wasn't *not* involved. He knew a lot. His parents had always kept him in the loop, and then I did, too. We had all heard rumors that the Guild was planning to set up shop in Twin Willows. Your father was fighting it . . . quietly, through back channels. But the Guild must've found out somehow."

"He still shouldn't have had to give his life!" I slammed my palm into the side of the washer, the metal ringing like a bell with the blow. The force of it shuddered up my arm, but the pain felt good. It was something tangible, not like the heart-twisting pain of everything else that had happened this afternoon. "He died for a cause that wasn't even his."

Jeff touched my arm. "Protecting the Waterfall was always his cause," he said softly. "His parents had taught him that it was a sacred place when he was very young. He may not have been a Benandante, but he would've died to keep it safe all the same." Jeff squeezed my wrist. "And he would be so proud of you," he whispered.

The tightness that had been holding me together burst. I let out a sob and bent forward until I was a little ball, my shoulders shaking. I felt Heath come down next to me and gather me up, like I was a little girl who'd fallen off the swings. "You are the best kind of Benandante,"

Heath spoke into my ear. "Full of fire and passion, fiercely loyal, and deeply loving. But sometimes you have to set that aside. There are other people in this war, and one of them got hurt today because of your personal vendetta."

I sniffled. "I'm so sorry. It was so stupid . . ."

"Yes, it was," Heath said. "Cal could've been killed." He shook me a little so that I sat up. "Being a Benandante isn't about revenge," he added. "It's about the greater good, no matter what personal stake we may have in it."

Personal stake. My stakes in this were beyond personal. I'd been Called to replace someone I'd known and loved. And was there anything more personal or any stake higher than my dad? I nodded at Heath—what I'd done today *was* stupid, rash, not thought out at all. But I also knew that the next chance I had for revenge on the Raven, I wouldn't waste it.

Chapter Sixteen

Even Mages Get the Blues

Bree

There was a whole block of my memory that was just gone, like someone had gone in with a sharp little tool and chiseled it out. I don't remember who found me with Dad, how we got back to the compound, or how long we were there. Maybe my subconscious had roofied me, because all I remember after that was being on the jet with Nerina, winging our way back to Maine.

I lay in my reclined seat, blankets pulled up to my chin. My head felt like I'd gone on a bender. I could almost feel the dark circles under my eyes, their weight dragging at my face. "How long till we get home?" I croaked.

Nerina started, nearly spilling the cup of coffee in her hand. She set the cup down. "We just took off from Vancouver. So another five hours or so."

I turned my head, stared out the window at the black night.

"Bree." Nerina rose and came over to me, laid her hand on my arm. "Shen told me what happened inside the Temple. You did your father a mercy."

I couldn't look at her. My throat had closed up. The effort of not crying made it hard to breathe.

"This war is so unfair. It asks too much of us." Her fingers tightened around my wrist. "We've all made sacrifices."

I spun so fast away from the window that Nerina jerked backward. "Did you have to kill your own father? Did you?" I shook her hand off me. "Don't try to justify it with words like *mercy* and *sacrifice*."

Nerina stood over me, her face a perfect mask of compassion. I wanted to slap her. "The Malandanti killed your father, Bree. Not you."

"I doubt my mother and brother will see it that way." The tightness stole back into my throat, threatening to cut off all my oxygen. I tried to imagine telling Mom and Jonah what had happened. My whole body clenched up, fighting off the grief, battling against the horror . . . if I let go for just one instant it would destroy me.

"They will. They will forgive you." Nerina dropped back into her seat. She stared at me, but she was seeing something else, something only she could see. "But you have to forgive yourself."

My hands trembled. I dug them deep into the blankets, trying to warm them even though I knew nothing could. "I will never forgive myself," I whispered.

Nerina nodded, still that faraway look in her eyes. "I understand," she murmured. "But one day you will do something good, and you'll know you've finally been redeemed."

Well, *that* was an odd thing to say. Curiosity cracked through the veneer of grief. "What did you do that you had to be redeemed for?"

Her eyes shifted back into focus. "I've had a very long time to make a lot of mistakes, Bree."

I wasn't in the mood for her vague crap. I stared at her wordlessly.

"What?" Nerina said.

"You've been lying to me for weeks. You know something about that spell that turns a Malandante into a Benandante, but you refuse to tell me."

She rubbed her hands over her face. For once she wasn't perfectly made up, and I could see dark circles of her own painting her skin. "Why would I give you details on a spell that I hope you never have to use?"

"Because it could help Jonah!" I flung the blankets off me and stomped to my feet. "You tell me to wait for redemption . . . Well, this is it! There is no better way to redeem myself for killing my father than restoring my brother's soul to the light." As soon as the words were out of my mouth, I knew they were true. I *needed* the spell . . . maybe even more than Jonah did . . .

"You seem to conveniently forget the other part of the spell, Bree." Nerina, too, got to her feet and faced me, her hands on her hips. "A Benandante must die in order to complete it. Which one of our Clan would you choose?

Me? Cal? Alessia?" She flung her arms wide. "Take your pick, Bree. Choose which Benandante you'd like to sentence to death. Do you think that's your redemption?"

I stayed silent. How could I answer her? I knew she was right. I couldn't willingly choose which Clan member I wanted to die. Slowly, I sank back into my seat and pulled the blankets up.

After a few minutes, Nerina sighed. She sat down and turned away from me, staring out the window.

But I did know this: If all the elements of that spell aligned, I wouldn't hesitate one damn second to perform it. For Jonah . . . and for me.

The instant we were on the tarmac in Bangor and my cell phone had rebooted, I called a cab to take me back to Twin Willows. I couldn't stand to ride in more silence with Nerina, and I didn't want her to tell me where to go or where not to go. Because if she did, I didn't think I'd be able to restrain myself from telling *her* where to go.

I was going to see my mom, and no one could stop me.

As the cab turned onto our street, my chest squeezed and wouldn't let go. But no matter what, I wasn't going to let myself off the hook. I wasn't going to try to justify what I'd done. Maybe it was okay in the eyes of the Benandanti, but those weren't the eyes that really mattered to me right now.

I paid the cabbie and walked down the path to the

front door. Before I reached it, the door flew open. "Bree!" Mom gestured wildly to me. "Get inside. They're watching the house." The instant I was inside, Mom pulled me in tight against her. "Thank God you're okay. We hadn't heard anything since . . . since . . ." She held me a little away from her and touched my cheek. "I'm so sorry, sweetie. Your father died."

I stared into her eyes, clear and open and loving. She didn't know. I could lie right now, make her think I had nothing to do with it . . . *no*. Redemption started today. "I know, Mom. I was there."

"Oh, sweetie." She pulled me deeper into the house, into the kitchen, which for once wasn't covered with remnants of her cooking experiments. "You were in Tibet? How long? When did you get back?"

"Just now. I came straight here." I perched on one of the kitchen stools. Mom set a glass of water in front of me, but I didn't touch it. "How do you know they're watching the house?"

She grimaced. "Please. The same black town car drives by every half hour. If they think I'm not going to notice that, they're idiots." She laid a plate of sliced apples and peanut butter next to the water. "Eat."

"I'm not hungry." I wrapped my arms around myself. "Do you know what happened in Tibet?"

Mom shook her head. "They haven't been very forthcoming with details." She bit her lip, her eyes searching my face. "Do you want to talk about it?"

"No," I whispered, "but I think I'd better." I swallowed. "Is Jonah here?"

Mom nodded. "Upstairs in his room. They let him come home after your dad . . ."

I hopped off the stool and headed up the stairs, Mom on my heels. I didn't even knock on Jonah's door, just pushed it open to find him lying on his bed, staring at the ceiling, headphones stuck in his ears. When he saw me, he sat up, pulled off the headphones, and opened his mouth to say something.

I held my hand up. "I need to tell you what happened in Tibet," I said. "And then I don't want to talk about it ever again." I looked from Mom to Jonah and walked over to the window. Sure enough, a black town car drove slowly by the house, its dark windows shielding whatever coward was inside. I jerked the curtain shut so that I wasn't visible, but I stayed by the window. I didn't turn around the whole time I was talking. I could feel the heat of their gazes on me, burning into me, crackling my skin like they were burning me in hell for the sinner I was. When I was done, I still couldn't turn around. I couldn't face them.

Silence swept the room for a long time, the only sound the soft whir of the heating system. There was a rustle, the tap of footsteps, and then I felt Mom's arms come around me from behind. "Oh, baby," she murmured into my hair before she turned me to face her and then hugged me tight. "Come lay your head, Bree-girl." She tried to draw me down to sit on Jonah's bed, to comfort me, but I pulled away so hard that she stumbled backward.

"No," I said, my voice sharp. "I don't deserve it."

"Bree." Jonah spoke from where he sat on the bed, his legs drawn up to his chest. "You showed him a lot more mercy than I would've."

"And that's supposed to make me feel better?" Angry tears squeezed out of the corners of my eyes, and I slapped them away. "Whatever he did, however much of an ass-hole he was, he was still our father, Jonah. And I killed him. *I killed him.*"

"Yes, you did." We both looked at Mom. "You killed him, and Jonah killed him, and I killed him. All of us in this room had a part in his death."

"Mom—"

"It's true." She thrust her hands into her hair and pulled. "I knew something was wrong with the Guild. I knew he shouldn't have taken that job. I should've put my foot down about it, threatened to leave him . . ."

"I should've taken responsibility for Emily," Jonah said. His green eyes—my green eyes—were bright against his pale face. "If I'd just owned up to what I'd done, he wouldn't have been in so much debt to the Guild."

"But I was the one who actually killed him," I yelled. Why were they being so nice? Why weren't they throwing me out of the house, telling me they never wanted to see me again? That I could deal with. This kindness . . . it made me want to stab something. "I delivered the actual death blow. Not you. Me. Me. Me." I punched my heart hard with each syllable until Mom grabbed my arm.

"No, you didn't, Bree." The softness in her voice struck me more than any blow I could give myself. "The Guild . . . the Malandanti . . . that *mage* . . . They did that. You saved him. In the end, you were the one who saved his soul."

A little chink appeared in my armor, a tiny hole through which a thin beam of sunlight poked its way through. Mom hugged me again. I gave her a feeble push and then sank into her. Maybe . . . just maybe . . . *no*. Just because they forgave me didn't mean I was forgiven.

CHAPTER SEVENTEEN
The House Call

Alessia

A chill settled over Twin Willows for the next few days, dipping below zero. It was too frigid to even walk the half-mile to school, so Jeff drove me and Jenny. We jumped out of the car and hurried indoors, unwrapping our scarves as soon as the heat blasted through us. "I thought spring was just around the corner," Jenny complained as she plucked her gloves off. "Isn't that what that stupid groundhog said?"

I pulled my hat off my head. "That groundhog is obviously a Malandante."

"What's a Malandante?"

We both whirled. Carly had come in behind us, her face half hidden beneath a thick woven scarf. "Uh, it's a bad word in Italian," I said.

Carly unzipped her parka. "Really? I've never heard you use it before."

"I just learned it." I forced myself to shrug, even though my whole body shook. "Lidia is getting a little lazy about hiding the swears from me lately."

"I guess it must be tough, being holed up at Jenny's house."

"Hey, I resent that." Jenny punched Carly lightly in the arm. "My house is a barrel of laughs, thank you very much."

The front door to the school opened, sending in a gust of icy wind and Melissa. "Oh, my God, I am so over this cold," she said as she joined our little circle. "Can it just be summer already?"

I tried to imagine summer, the trees green and lush, the hillside behind our farm dotted with goats again. Would we be able to live there again? Would the barn be rebuilt by then? Would the Waterfall be under Benandanti control? Would the woods be Benandanti blue again, instead of Malandanti silver? I shook my head. It was impossible to see that far ahead.

Melissa nudged me. "Alessia? Are you okay?"

I squinted at her. "What? Oh, yeah. I'm fine."

"We should totally have a sleepover at my house this weekend," Carly said. "What do you think?"

"Uh . . ." I exchanged glances with Jenny. "I don't know if I can."

"Why not? You're sleeping at Jenny's anyway, so what's the big deal?"

"There's just . . . a lot going on."

Now it was Carly and Melissa exchanging a look. I caught it and tilted my head. "What?"

"Yeah, that's kinda what we'd like to know," Melissa said. "You two have been thick as thieves since Alessia moved in and, well, we . . ."

"We feel left out," Carly finished for her.

"Oh, for Pete's sake," Jenny said. "We are not thick as thieves. You're just jealous because you think it's like one happy-go-lucky sleepover. Trust me, *it's not.*"

"It's not like I asked for my house to get black mold," I said. "Lidia is totally mortified about it."

"Speaking of Lidia," Carly said, and I could tell by her tone that she wasn't quite ready to let us off the hook yet, "did you know that she and Mr. Salter are a thing?"

"Carly!" Jenny rounded on her. "You're being a real bitch, you know that?"

"You two started it—"

"Oh, my God, *grow up!*"

"Stop it!" I shoved myself between them. "Look, it's not my fault we're holed up at Jenny's house. It just made sense because the Sands are Lidia's closest friends. The fact that you're jealous is idiotic," I said, shooting a hard look first at Melissa and then at Carly. My gaze lingered on her face. "And, yes, I did know about Lidia and Mr. Salter. And to be honest, it hurts a ton and she and I aren't really speaking right now. And if you were a good friend, you'd be supporting me instead of trying to make me feel even worse." I turned on my heel and stalked off to the office. I felt bad about leaving Jenny to deal with them, but the anger was hot inside me and I thought if I said anything else, it would be something mean that I'd regret.

Jenny met me in the hall on the way to second period.

"She's being such a twat," she said.

"Jenny! That is not a nice word."

"Well, fine, but that's what she's being." Jenny linked her arm through mine. "And the problem is, I feel really bad. We *do* have something going on behind their back, and we can't tell them. It *sucks*."

"Now you know how I felt all that time before you found out about me," I said. "The biggest thing going on in your life, and you can't even share it with your closest friends."

Carly ignored us as she took her seat in French. Jenny huffed as she pulled her textbook out of her bag and dropped it on her desk with a loud bang. Carly flinched but didn't turn around. I sighed and took out my own book. Carly *was* being an idiot, but I couldn't blame her for feeling left out of the secret club that Jenny and I had going on.

Madam Dubois called the class to order and took attendance. When she got to the bottom of the list, she paused after Jonah's name. "Has anyone seen Monsieur Wolfe? This is his fifth straight absence."

I could feel every eye in the classroom straining to *not* look at me. Even though we were supposed to be broken up, I was still the person closest to Jonah. I put my hand into the air. "*Oui*, Mademoiselle Jacobs?"

Screw the Malandanti. "Um . . ." They didn't want Jonah and his mom to tell the world, but I wasn't under their orders. "His dad died."

There was a collective intake of breath. Everyone swiveled in their seats to look at me. Madam Dubois lowered her attendance book, her face pale. "What?" She was so shocked she'd forgotten to ask it in French. "How—when—did it happen?"

"Last week," I said, squirming in my seat with so many people staring at me. I hadn't really thought this through. Of course everyone would want to know how he'd died, and I couldn't really tell them he'd been killed by a mage in Tibet. "I, uh, think it had something to do with all the stuff that's going on with the Guild."

"They killed him?" asked Susan Turner from the front row.

"Don't be stupid," Jason Freeman hissed from the desk behind her. "I bet he committed suicide so he wouldn't have to face prison."

I rubbed my temples. "Um, I really don't know exactly what happened." That wasn't a lie. I hadn't seen Bree since she and Nerina had returned from Tibet, so I only had Nerina's secondhand account. "I just know he's dead and that's why the Wolfes aren't in school."

A low hum of murmurs echoed around the room. Carly twisted in her chair and met my eyes. *I'm sorry,* she mouthed. I nodded to show I accepted her apology and looked down at my lap. I wasn't sure if I'd done the right thing by telling the world about Mr. Wolfe, but there was no going back now.

Up at the front of the room, Madam Dubois clapped

her hands. "All right, all right, everyone. Calm down. Let's move on. Mademoiselle Jacobs?"

I looked up.

"Please give Monsieur Wolfe and his family our sincerest condolences."

"I will. Thanks." I laid my hands flat on my desk, rested my chin on top of them, and didn't hear anything Madam Dubois said for the rest of the period.

I texted Bree the minute school let out.

> I'm coming over.

The reply came soon after.

> The house is being watched. There's a car that drives by every half hour. I'll let you know when it's clear.

I waited outside the school, my phone in my hand so I would hear it the moment it went off. Jenny offered to wait with me, but I sent her off to Joe's with Carly and Melissa to make peace. Several minutes after they left, my phone buzzed.

> Coast is clear. But hurry. Back door.

When I was within a few yards of the door, it cracked open. "Get in, get in." Mrs. Wolfe waved me in, and I ran full tilt until I was inside. She peered for a moment across the backyard and down the street before she shut the door behind me. "Did you pass anyone up the street?"

"No."

"Good." She gave me a quick hug. "It's good of you to come, Alessia. I think the kids could really use a friendly face—besides mine." She tucked my arm into hers, and we walked slowly toward the front of the house. "Listen, don't press Bree for too many details. She doesn't want to talk about it."

"Did she tell you what happened?"

Mrs. Wolfe nodded. Before we reached the part of the house that opened into the kitchen and living room, she pulled me to a stop. "Travis was killed by the magic of the site," she said. This I knew; Nerina had said the Rabbit had forced the magic on him before Bree could stop it. "But before he could do any damage to the Benandanti, he asked Bree to . . . end his suffering," Mrs. Wolfe went on. "Which she did."

I sucked in a cold whistle of breath. My heart thudded against my ribs, so hard the force reverberated into my throat. That, Nerina had left out. Maybe she didn't know.

I closed my eyes. Of course Nerina knew. She knew everything. But I could see why she hadn't told us. I almost wish Mrs. Wolfe hadn't told *me*. It was bad enough to lose your dad—even one as crappy as Mr. Wolfe—but to lose him at your own hand was the stuff of nightmares. "No wonder she's a mess."

"She needs to forgive herself," Mrs. Wolfe said. "What

she did was an act of mercy."

Not to mention an act of enormous courage on behalf of the Benandanti. But I highly doubted Bree saw it that way.

In the living room, Bree and Jonah sat on the couch, a party-size bag of Cheetos between them. "Welcome to Depression Manor," Bree said. "Wallowing required."

Mrs. Wolfe patted my arm. "I'll get you a soda," she said and whirled into the kitchen.

For a moment I just stared at the Wolfe twins, side by side on the couch. I tried to remember the last time I'd seen them together; it had been weeks ago, before Bree had become a mage. They looked like a matched set of porcelain dolls, perfectly mirroring each other in every detail right down to the hollow look in their emerald eyes. I forced myself to go to Bree first and leaned down to give her a hug that she barely returned. "I'm so sorry, Bree."

"For what? For my dad dying? Or for the fact that I killed him?"

I drew away from her, trying to keep the shock off my face. "For . . . all of it." I grabbed her hand and squeezed. "I'm not going to pretend I know what you're going through. Losing a parent is different for everyone." I'd learned that in the days and weeks after my dad had died: how much I hated when people told me they understood what I was feeling. No one did. Grief looked different on everyone, inside and out. "But I'm here. If you want to talk. Or not talk."

To my surprise, Bree squeezed my hand and raised

her eyes to mine. "I know you are, Alessia. Thanks." She cleared her throat and pulled her hand away to reach into the bag of Cheetos. "What's going on over at Benandanti Central? Is Nerina about to lose her shit?"

"Nerina is always about to lose her shit," I said. I glanced at Jonah. I knew he was on our side, but I didn't know how much information we should share. Whatever he knew could be tortured out of him. "I think the *Concilio* is regrouping after Tibet, trying to figure out the next move."

"They should go after Friuli," Jonah said. "Our *Concilio* isn't there at the moment."

"Really? I'll tell her." I crossed to Jonah's side of the couch. He patted the space next to him, and I squeezed in between him and a plush throw pillow with a pheasant on it. "Thanks."

He snaked his arm around me and drew me in close to his side. I snuggled in tight and turned my face up to him. He bent over and kissed me, his mouth warm and sweet. I put my hand on the back of his head, tangling my fingers in his hair. "Thanks for coming over," he murmured against my lips. "It's been lonely and sad around here."

"I missed you too," I whispered back. I pressed my face into the side of his neck, breathing in deep the scent of spice and pine.

"If you guys are going to act out *Fifty Shades of Grey*, please go upstairs," Bree said from her end of the couch.

"Actually, I'd prefer if you *didn't* do that and stayed down here," Mrs. Wolfe said as she came into the room with a cup of soda and a plate of cookies.

"Mom," Jonah groaned, drawing out the syllable. "Don't be gross."

I took the soda that Mrs. Wolfe offered me and snagged a cookie from the plate as she put it on the coffee table in front of us. For a brief, beautiful moment I could see how life would be if we were all normal, if Jonah was just some boy I was dating and we were just two regular teenagers hanging out at his house after school, if there wasn't a car that drove by doing surveillance on the house every half hour, if there wasn't a life-and-death war tugging us apart. I bit into the cookie, let the chocolate chips dissolve on my tongue. I wanted that life, to be that girl.

Jonah sucked in a hard breath, his body trembling against my side. I stared at him for a moment, but when he drew his arm away from my waist and pressed his hand to his chest, I knew. I knew that there would never be one minute when we could just be normal, never one second to be just us.

He stumbled off the couch. "I don't want you to see this," he muttered and ran up the stairs, taking the steps two at a time. I rose to go after him, but my phone buzzed in my backpack at my feet.

An instant later, Bree's phone went off too. We picked them up at the same time.

> We have the Congo. We're going to retake the Waterfall tonight.

CHAPTER EIGHTEEN

The Wild Dogs of Africa

Alessia

"Why the Waterfall? Why tonight?" I asked Nerina the second I was back in Jenny's living room. The Clan was gathered, clustered on the couch and comfy chairs, listening to orders before we all transformed.

"We regained the Congo three days ago—"

"And we're just hearing about it now?" asked Cal.

"That's actually like a freaking miracle," Bree said from behind me. "Their communication system is—shall we say—antiquated. We barely had electricity when I lived there."

"As I was saying," Nerina said, raising her voice, "we still do not possess the Twin Willows and Angel Falls sites. The *Concilio* feels that once we possess all the 'lesser' sites, the Grove will be easier to reclaim."

"No, they should go after Friuli," I said. "Jonah just told me their *Concilio* isn't there at the moment."

"Yes, because they were just in the Congo," Nerina said. "So they aren't here either."

"They *do* have airplanes there," Bree said. "They could've gotten back here by now."

"Unlikely." Nerina waved her hand. "Our orders are to go in now, while they are still licking their wounds."

"Which is exactly what they're expecting!"

Nerina spun to face me. "Did you not hear me when I said *our orders*? This is what the *Concilio* has ordered us to do, and I agree with them. We go in tonight. End of discussion."

I backed up until I was in the only empty chair in the room. This didn't feel right. There was a reason Jonah had been Called tonight, and not because he was on patrol, which he wasn't. I gripped the arms of the chair.

"It's okay," Heath murmured to me. He leaned over the edge of the couch toward me. "If their *Concilio* is there, we'll retreat. You just make sure you look after Cal. This will be his first big battle."

I swallowed, my stomach a mess of tangles.

In front of the fireplace, Nerina was talking to Bree, their heads bent close together so that none of us could hear what she was saying. I looked over at Cal, whose eyes were fixed on Bree like he was in a desert and she was a mirage. Like the way Jonah had looked at me just a few minutes ago. I forced air into my constricted throat, trying to dispel the heat and fear and nerves that gathered there.

When Nerina was done talking to Bree, I vaulted out of my chair and grabbed Bree's elbow. "Are you up for this?" I asked softly.

Bree met my eyes. "My dad told me to not let his death be in vain. I might be a basket case outside of work, but trust me . . . when I'm on the job I am *more* than up for this."

"We're all here for you," Cal said. He'd come up behind me, and I backed away so that he and Bree could face each other. He took one of her hands into both of his, and to my surprise, Bree let him. "Whatever you need."

Bree cocked her head, and for a moment I saw her trademark spark return to her eyes. "What I need is for you not to get killed. Think you can do that?"

"I'll try." Cal winked and let go of her hand.

"*Andiamo,*" Nerina said. Everyone arranged themselves in comfortable positions, ready to transform. "*In bocca al lupo.*"

"Wait."

We all watched Bree pull a small golden Buddha statue out of her backpack and place it on the mantel. "Shen—one of the Tibetan Clan—gave it to me. It'll watch over us while we're gone."

Nerina nodded impatiently, but Heath got to his feet and walked over to the statue. "That's lovely, Bree. Thank you." He took her hands in his. "I remember how all the families at the Tibetan site would watch over their bodies while the Clan was out fighting. It was . . . comforting."

"I sorta thought maybe we could do the same thing here," Bree said. She looked across the room at Barb and Jenny, who stood in the doorway to the kitchen. "Like, the American version or something."

"It would be our honor," Barb said, curving her arm around Jenny. With a start, I realized Lidia was standing just behind them. I met her gaze and gave her a small smile. Things were still a mess with us, but I didn't want to go into battle so angry on the inside. From the shadows of the kitchen, Mr. Salter materialized next to Lidia. My goodwill plummeted. Why did he always have to be here? Why couldn't he leave Lidia alone with me for once?

Lidia pushed past Barb and came across the room to me. "*In bocca al lupo, cara,*" she whispered, her hand on my cheek. Her palm was warm and for an instant I let myself lean into it. "I will watch over you while you are away."

The Call tugged at my heart, pulled me apart. For one moment, I hovered in the air as Lidia stared up at the magnificent Falcon her daughter had become. I flew across the room and let the very tips of my wings brush her awestruck face as I passed. Barb threw the front door open for us, and I followed my Clan into the night.

If anyone in Twin Willows had actually been out, they would have freaked out at the sight of a wolf, a catamount, an eagle, a falcon, and a stag carrying Bree on its back racing across Main Street. Not to mention a griffin, which wasn't supposed to exist. But it was too cold for anyone to be outdoors. I felt the wind deep in my bones, felt the ice in my feathers as I winged toward my farm. The pasture lay dark and dormant, the burned-out barn like a nightmare shadow against the moonlight. We raced over the stone wall and into the woods, closing in on the birch trees that marked our place of attack.

But as the pale gleam of the birches loomed into sight, I knew at once something was wrong. Their bark was too silver, too brilliant, too much like the glow of the Malandanti's aura.

I opened my mind to find Jonah. The instant I did, his voice ricocheted in my head. *Get out of here! You're outnumbered!*

Nerina! Jonah says—

But before I could finish the thought, an unholy sound ripped through the forest. Out of the copse rose a silver figure, its huge scaly wings beating so hard that one of the trees was flattened. I stopped in midair, my heart plummeting as the thing shot upward, high enough that we could all see its form, black and silver against the night sky. A Dragon, its scales shimmering like multicolored fractals, its jaws opening wide.

Get back! Nerina screamed.

A stream of fire roared out from the Dragon's mouth, scorching the trees just beneath, just missing Cal, who in typical fashion had raced ahead of the rest of the Clan. He stumbled out of sight into some brush. *Cal! Are you okay?* I called to him.

Yes. Just a little singed—

Retreat. RETREAT! Nerina ordered. We all fell back on her command just as the Dragon let loose another jet of fire. I dodged up and away, following the Clan as we raced back to the farm.

A freaking Dragon? Bree gasped. *Are you kidding me?* Far below me, she clung to the Stag's neck as he rocketed over a fallen log.

He's the head of the Concilio Argento, Heath said. *Their* Concilio *turn into mythical creatures just like ours.*

We have one too—Dario turns into a Dragon—

Who the hell cares? What are we going to do? The Dragon was still chasing us over the treetops. Cora kept pace with me as we swerved this way and that, trying to shake it off. *I told you they'd be here—*

Nerina ignored my dig at her. *We have to retreat until we know it's gone—*

It'll track us right back to my house, Jeff said. *We need to throw it off.*

But as we crossed over the stone wall that marked the edge of my farm, an unearthly glow came over the pasture. Hundreds of Malandanti in all shapes crested the hill, swarming the ground like a plague of locusts. *Jesus,* Heath breathed.

I thought I destroyed all of them! Bree said.

These must be the last ones left—

But what the hell are they doing here?

Nerina didn't answer, probably because she didn't know the answer. It didn't matter what the hell they were doing here—the fact was that they were here and we had to deal with them. We couldn't retreat; there were too many of them, spread out across the whole length of the farm. I whirled to look back at the forest. The Dragon hovered over the treetops, daring us to face him. And out of the woods below, another figure shot up to join the Dragon: the Harpy's ebony wings beat in rhythm with the Dragon's.

An army of Malandanti in one direction. The *Concilio* in the other.

We were trapped.

Nerina faced us. *Bree, you deal with the fake Malandanti. Jeff, Cal, and Heath, get to the Waterfall and see what we're up against there. Alessia and Cora, you're with me.* She didn't have to say what she wanted us to do. We were the winged creatures of the Clan. The only ones who could take on the Dragon and the Harpy.

No one had to be given their orders twice. Cal, Heath, and Jeff raced back over the stone wall, their bright blue auras disappearing into the woods. Bree cloaked herself in shadows, swallowed up by the night. Cora, Nerina, and I soared toward the Dragon and the Harpy. *Watch out for the fire,* Nerina warned.

No shit! Cora said.

He has a tell, Nerina said. The Dragon rose higher. He sliced his huge serpentine head to the left, then to the right. *There. Did you see it? He shakes his head once. Then—*

A wall of fire lit up the sky, blasting us backward. *Look for that,* Nerina said. *You two go low. I'll go high.*

Cora and I dipped low, bursting through the fire just as it fizzled out into the air. As we wove in and out of the trees, little balls of silvery auras appeared all around us. The winged fake Malandanti surrounded us on every side. My heart stuck in my throat as the silver auras multiplied. This was not good. This was not going to end well . . .

Come on, Bree . . .

We veered up behind the Dragon and the Harpy as Nerina dove toward them. A dozen Malandanti shot up after us, nipping at my feathers. I struck my talons out, catching one across the nose. It tumbled away toward the earth, its aura fracturing like shards of lightning. Two more took its place, trying to catch me. I swerved back and forth, flying blind, my eyes fixed on their beaks and claws . . .

Alessia, watch out!

They just keep coming! I can't shake them off!

No, above you!

I swiveled my gaze away from the Malandanti and met the cold black eyes of the Dragon. I'd flown too close to it in my attempt to get away from the fake Malandanti. The Dragon shook its head left, right . . . I dove just as it opened its huge mouth and exhaled a stream of fire that caught my tail feathers. I plummeted to the ground, my body a ball of fire and smoke, excruciating heat climbing up up up as I went down down down.

I hit a patch of snow, and the coolness washed over me like a baptism. *Alessia!* Cora yelled in my head. *Answer me!*

I'm okay, I'm okay.

They're right above you.

Got it. I zoomed up, bits of snow raining from my feathers. Just above the trees, the Harpy met me. She stretched out a talon, but I dove beneath her and then shot back up, right into her underside. She screeched as my beak bit into her belly. I slashed her again and again before diving out of her reach.

The Harpy fell back, tumbling down into the forest below. Cora and Nerina faced off with the Dragon. I soared over to help them, but Nerina stopped me. *We'll hold him off. Fly around the perimeter. Tell me what's happening.*

I climbed in the air to get a better view of the scene, high enough so that I could see the entire Waterfall site and the surrounding woods. It was beyond anything I ever could have imagined. There were just too many of them. I scanned the circle of the Waterfall. Cal, Heath, and Jeff were holding their own against the Malandanti Clan. Inside the barrier, Jonah stood rigid, watching the fight. I forced myself not to open my mind to him. I could not be distracted right now.

As I worked my way out into the forest, an itchy feeling started in my gut. Why weren't the fake Malandanti at the Waterfall, fighting with the real Clan? Why were they staying just outside, in the woods?

I spiraled outward, my eyes sharp on the ground below. Deep in the brush, I spotted seven dog-like shapes, slinking low and quiet along the ground in a close-knit pack. I would've missed them, so stealthy were they, save for the telltale silvery glow that encircled each of them. *You guys,* I said, *there's a bunch of Malandanti Dogs in the woods.*

Are they real or fake? asked Jeff.

Dropping a foot to get a closer look, I peered at their auras. *They look real. Not fractured like the other ones.*

One of the Dogs raised its head and sniffed. I dodged behind a thick pine tree, hoping its scent was enough to cover my own. The Dog put its nose back down. A moment later, the seven Dogs broke apart from each other and fanned out. *They're surrounding the entire perimeter,* I told the Clan.

Holy shit, Jeff said. *It's the Wild Dogs from the Congo Clan.*

What? Why aren't they in Africa? Cal asked.

They don't need to be, Nerina said, *not since we retook the site.* I looked back at her. She and Cora zoomed around the Dragon in circles, disorienting it. *Alessia, stay up there and track their movements. They are extremely cunning hunters, so stay alert.*

I fluttered from treetop to treetop, using branches and pine to cover me. Though the Wild Dogs were now several feet apart from each other, they moved in absolute unison, closing in on their prey with an almost beautiful precision. If Cal, Heath, or Jeff were to leave the Waterfall now, they would be pounced upon by one of the Dogs.

I couldn't just sit there, perched on a branch that towered above everything. I launched myself into a dive, right at the Dog near the birch trees. My talons were deep in its haunches before it even knew I was coming. The Dog yelped and snapped its jaws at me, but I twisted every which way to inflict as much damage as I could. With a powerful push, I shot several feet in the air. The Dog leapt up after me just as I dove again. There was no way on earth or anywhere else that Dog could ever hope to catch me. When it landed back on the ground, I heard one of its hind legs snap.

Whimpering, the Dog dragged itself into the brush, its aura sizzling from the injury. I rose back into the air. The other Dogs were still in place; they hadn't even moved an inch to help their fellow Clan member. They obviously had their orders. But now there was a hole in their ranks, a window through which one of my Clan could pass.

A cry of fear and triumph, of inhuman effort and sorrow, tore through my mind. With a force that shook the trees, a blast of light exploded over the Waterfall, rippling out all the way to my farm. One by one, the fake Malandanti disappeared, each of their artificial auras dissolving into the ether. I paused in midair to watch it, saying a prayer as each light went out. Far away across the world, people were mourning over the bodies of their fathers and mothers, sisters and brothers, sons and daughters and friends. It was disgusting what the Malandanti had done, and I was glad to see those souls finally at rest.

A figure tumbled out of the window I'd created in the forest and came to rest against one of the birch trees. I floated down. When I got close enough, Bree raised her head. Tear tracks ran down her cheeks. I landed on her shoulder. She buried her face in my feathers and sobbed.

You did the right thing, Bree. You brought those people peace.

I still killed them. Just like I killed—

I pushed against her. *No. You didn't kill them. The Malandanti did that. What you did was . . . extraordinary.*

Bree snorted in that totally Bree-like way. *I have to go help Nerina,* I said and lifted off her. *You stay here and rest until we need you again.*

I soared upward, wind whistling through my feathers. I still didn't think we would reclaim the site tonight, but now with the elimination of all those Malandanti, we would at least get out of there alive. I set my sights on the Dragon above me, climbing the air toward Nerina and Cora. Just before I reached them, the Dragon spotted me. He flicked his long spiky tail, nearly catching me. My wings faltered, and I tumbled down several feet before I could right myself. As I did, something on the ground below stopped my blood in my veins.

Cal had drawn the Malandante Coyote out toward the birch trees. But before he could get back to the Waterfall, the Wild Dogs closed in, and Cal's golden fur disappeared from my view.

I plunged down and down, but suddenly the Dragon was there, blocking me, hurling fiery blasts at me. I dodged over and under each breath, trying to see what was happening on the ground below. *Cal! Cal!*

He didn't answer. I could hear his panting in my mind as he fought the Dogs off. God, he wasn't ready for this kind of battle . . . I hadn't trained him well enough. And now he was going to get hurt—or worse—again because I'd failed him.

With a burst of angry speed, I shot around the Dragon and zoomed down. I latched my talons into the back of one of the Dogs. It yelped and twisted away, revealing Cal's battered form beneath its paws. He bucked off one of the other Dogs. His head rose above the fray, and he gasped for air. I dove in to claw at the Dog closest to Cal's throat. At the last moment, the Dog turned its head. With one snap of its sharp, saliva-dripping jaws, it caught me in its mouth.

Pain sliced through me. I screeched, thrashing in the Dog's mouth, but its teeth bit into my flesh. Warm blood spilled over my feathers. My heartbeat filled my ears, fast, shallow, and desperate. I tried to scream, tried to cry for help, but the pain clouded everything. I fought for each breath, every tiny bit of air that would give me just one more second to cling to life . . .

In a last feeble attempt, I reached out across the Clans . . . *Jonah?* . . . but it was nothing more than a whisper. Dimly I heard Cal yelling for help . . . a glimpse of white fur flashed by me . . . Heath, always Heath to my rescue . . . I opened my eyes and saw myself surrounded by blue light . . . *At least the last thing I'll ever see is Benandante blue,* I thought. Then silver streaked across the blue . . . there was a yowl, a crash like lightning. The world shut down around me, and all I saw was black.

CHAPTER NINETEEN
One Step onto the Path of Redemption

Bree

If someone had told me six months ago that in half a year I'd be battling a Dragon and shooting magic at it that I'd learned from ancient books written on bark, I would've asked them what they were smoking and could I please have some. Because you'd obviously have had to be really high to predict that.

Yet somehow that was what my life had become. I twisted cords of red smoke around the Dragon, trying to weaken him enough to shoot him out of time and space. He breathed a long lick of fire at me. I blocked the fire and turned it into smoke, shot it back at him to cloud his vision. He screamed in frustration. Oh, sure, I got it. Some little bitch who was no bigger than his tail comes along and thinks she can take on a Dragon. I'd want to fry me to a crisp too, if I were him.

But I wasn't him. My power unfurled inside me, filling me from the top of my head down to my red-polished toes. I tugged at the cords of smoke and the

Dragon lowered down and down, unable to fight against the binds that held him fast. I raised my hand, ready to blast him out of this sphere.

Bree! Where are you?

My head rang with the force of Jonah's voice. *Fighting off your goddamn Dragon!*

Alessia! Those Dogs are going to kill her!

My hold on the cords slackened and the Dragon buoyed up. I yanked him back down. *I'm a little busy right now—*

Just get to her! Near the birch trees.

I flung my hand, almost like an afterthought, and the Dragon vanished. He wouldn't be gone for long; his own magic was too powerful for that, but we'd have enough time to get the hell out of here. We should never have come to the Waterfall tonight.

Alessia! Answer me!

Help . . . But it was not Alessia who answered; it was Cal. *By* . . . *the birch* . . . *trees* . . .

His voice sounded far away in my mind—too far away. I ran through the woods, flinging branches out of my way, kicking up bits of hardened snow and dead leaves. The instant I saw the glow of silver, I shot Pakistani magic at it and the silver disappeared. In its absence I saw only the faintest of blue light, the telltale sign of a weakening Benandante.

I burst through the birch trees. Cal lay on his side, his body a mass of cuts and bites. He hauled himself to his feet when he saw me, and relief spread through me.

Good; at least he was standing. But Alessia . . .

She lay on the ground, her aura dim and crackling, its light going in and out, in and out. I knelt beside her and hovered my hands above her broken body. The yellow smoke of the Redwoods spiraled out of my fingertips. Alessia shivered as the magic seeped into her. I closed my eyes and listened. Her heartbeat was quick—too quick—but the thread of life in her was still strong. *We have to get her back to her body.*

I picked Alessia up, my hands trying to find a decent way to hold her that wasn't going to hurt her more. *Jonah.* I felt the spark of connection in my mind. *I've got her. But she's bad.* I closed my mind to him before he could answer. I couldn't deal with comforting him on top of everything else.

Holding Alessia against my chest like she was a ticking bomb, I ran back through the forest, Cal limping along by my side. I could hear his pain in my mind, but he was pushing through it, staying strong for the Clan, for Alessia, for me. *You did good,* I told him. *You definitely earned your stripes tonight.* To the rest of the Clan I said, *Alessia is really hurt. I'm heading back to Jeff's with her.*

Right behind you, Heath replied. As we reached the stone wall, he and Jeff caught up to us. I balanced Alessia in my arms as I clambered over the wall. In the sky above the hillside, Nerina and the Harpy waged war with each other, their auras sizzling as they clashed again and again. Cora dodged right and left, trying to get a jab in, but it was obvious that Nerina wanted the Harpy all to herself. Her movements were fueled by fury; I could see it in every slash and bite she threw at the Harpy. If there was anyone who recognized revenge, it was me.

Let's go, Cora said as she plummeted toward us. *She doesn't want our help.* And once again I wondered what it was between Nerina and the Harpy, how they were connected in some long-ago story.

Bree, get on my back, Jeff said. He bent his two front legs so that I could climb on. I cradled Alessia in one arm and clung to his neck with the other, and we raced across the pasture, up the driveway, and down the road back to his house.

The minute we got back into the living room, the Italian histrionics started. Lidia wailed, and not even Mr. Salter could get her to stop. Barb ran to the bathroom to get the first-aid kit, and Jenny danced from one foot to the other, covering her mouth with her hands and asking between sniffles, "What should we do?" I ignored them and laid Alessia the Falcon on top of Alessia the Human. She was too weak to even transform back.

I stood and pressed my palms to my temples. "Everybody, shut up! If you can't be helpful, then leave the goddamn room!" I pointed at Lidia. "Stop crying. She's not dead yet, and she's not going to be if I can help it."

To her credit, the woman pulled herself together. Mr. Salter kept an arm around her as she ran her shaking fingers through her hair. "What do you need us to do?" he asked.

At least someone was thinking clearly. I gestured toward Cal. He had shifted back into his body and looked like he'd gotten the short end of the stick in a bar fight. "Help Cal. He's pretty banged up."

I bent over Alessia, tuning out the noise around me.

Heath crouched beside me and laid his hand on Alessia's head. "Maybe we should take her to the hospital."

"How are we going to explain her injuries? 'Oh, yeah, Doctor, she got into a fight with a bunch of wild hunting dogs and, by the way, her wounds are magical'? That'll go over real well. You know we can't do that. Don't be an idiot." I glanced at Heath, whose jaw tightened. "Sorry."

"It's okay. We all get a bad attitude when our loved ones are hurt."

I pressed my lips together. I wouldn't exactly classify Alessia as a loved one. I was saving her for Jonah, because I could only imagine the shit-show that would result if his girlfriend died at the hands of his fellow Malandanti. But as I laid my palm on Alessia's forehead, I knew that wasn't the whole story. Despite my best intentions, Alessia had become my friend.

"Where's Nerina?" Jenny asked. She was curled into the deepest corner of the couch, her knees drawn up to her chest.

"Hell-bent on revenge back at the woods," I muttered as I drifted my hands back and forth over Alessia's two halves.

Heath shot me a look.

I met his eyes. "You can't tell me I'm wrong.

Something's going on there that she's not telling us."

"Just focus on Alessia for now."

I couldn't exactly argue with him on that. I turned my attention deep inside, listening for Alessia's heartbeat, searching for that thread of life inside her. It was fraying, fiber by fiber, and it would be whittled down to nothing unless I did something fast.

I did the first thing I could think of. I touched the Tibetan magic inside me, opened that door in my little Tudor house. It popped right open, the magic blossoming at the lightest prick of my mind's finger. I shoved aside the memory of the last time I'd used this magic and poured it into Alessia. A moment later, her Falcon form dissolved back into her body, leaving a handful of shimmering particles dancing in the air above her. I sat back on my haunches. Okay, I'd crossed that bridge. Now what?

Bruises and cuts formed on Alessia's skin, and two angry puncture marks appeared across her collarbone. I knew these wounds went more than skin deep; they were soul deep. No hospital could cure these injuries. You had to fight magic with magic, and that rule applied to healing as well.

But I had never used the Redwoods magic to heal a person besides myself. And the Redwoods magic was tricky. Its main use was for good, not like the other sites whose magic was used most often to hurt people. And if you pushed it too hard, it went off the rails.

"There's a first time for everything," I whispered.

The front door banged open and Nerina burst in, her celestial aura blinding the rest of us. The light faded bit by bit as she shifted back into her body. "How's Alessia?"

"Not good." I felt her approach behind me, her shadow darkening Alessia's form. "Do you mind?" I looked back. "I'm trying to work here."

She tensed, but before she could say anything, Cora grabbed her arm. "What the hell was that back there?"

"I don't know what you—"

"Oh, yes, you do. You practically knocked me out trying to take down the Harpy by yourself."

"I wanted you to help Alessia."

"Don't even. You didn't know Alessia was hurt until we were fleeing the scene."

Nerina shook Cora off and stomped to the other side of the room. "The Harpy and I have a history. She is always going to come after me."

"Yeah, and we can help! Don't try to take her on all by yourself."

"I can handle it."

"Obviously you can't, or the Harpy would be dead!"

"Can you guys *please shut up*," I yelled. Alessia hadn't moved or made a sound during their entire fight, and that worried me more than anything else. "We have bigger fish to fry right now."

Cora tossed her ginger hair back and bit her lip. "You're right. I'm sorry." She raised an eyebrow at Nerina, obviously expecting an apology. Before Nerina could give it—which I didn't think she would do unless hell froze over—loud pounding echoed through the house from the front door.

Whatever tension stretched across the room ratcheted up about a thousand notches. Jeff held his hand up. No one breathed. My hands shook as I brought them back up to Alessia. If the Harpy or the Dragon was on the other side of that door, Alessia was as good as dead unless I healed her in the next twenty seconds.

Whoever it was pounded again. The house shook with the force of it, rattling us all. "Jeff," Barb whispered, "get the shotgun." I turned and stared at her. What the hell was with Maine? What were a bunch of hippie vegetarians doing with a gun in the house?

But before Jeff could move, a muffled voice accompanied the next round of knocking. "Bree? Bree, let me in."

"Jesus," I breathed, letting out all the air I'd been holding in. "It's Jonah."

The room came back to life. Heath got to his feet and Nerina rounded on me. "What have you done? Why is he here?"

"He knew she was hurt! She tried to reach out to him—"

"And how convenient that he failed to help."

"Actually—" Heath began.

Nerina cut him off and pointed at Jeff. "Do not let him in."

"Are you kidding me?" I scrambled to my feet. "He could help!" I waved my hand at Alessia's inert form.

"They have a connection. Having him here could help her come back from—from wherever she is."

"He's a Malandante!" Nerina shrieked. I jerked back. Seriously, I'd never heard her voice go that high. She spun to face the rest of the Clan. "We cannot allow a Malandante into our safe house."

"I think he already proved himself in the Guild basement," I shot back. Out of the corner of my eye, I spotted Jenny uncurling herself from the couch.

Jeff stepped forward. No one but me noticed Jenny tiptoeing across the room. "I'm inclined to agree with Nerina. Even if we can trust him, who's to say what he would tell the Malandanti under duress?" He folded his arms. "It's my house and my decision."

"It's my house too," Jenny said from the entryway. Everyone turned to look at her, but before anyone could stop her, she flung open the door.

And just like that, Jenny Sands became my new best friend.

I sent everyone out of the room except Jonah. Partly because I really needed to concentrate on working the Redwoods magic but mainly because I couldn't deal with the tension in the room. Forget cutting it with a knife; nothing short of a chainsaw was getting through that.

Jonah scooped Alessia up in his arms, holding her like she was the most cherished and endangered creature on earth. He moved her to the couch and laid her out, settling her head in his lap. "Just stay there," I told him. "I don't know if having you here will help, but it definitely can't hurt."

He nodded. His face was pale, his gaze traveling the length of Alessia's body. He buried his hands in her hair. "You can heal her, right?"

"I—I don't know."

"Come on, Bree. I've seen your magic. You can do this." He swallowed hard. His hand moved from her hair and cupped her face. "You *have* to do this."

Okay, maybe I had come to love Alessia, and sure, I was doing this for her. But watching him, I could see what it would cost to fail. It wouldn't be just the loss of a Benandanti Clan member. It would be the loss of my brother, because losing Alessia was something he would never come back from.

I knelt beside the couch and closed my eyes. All the doors of my Tudor house sprang open, but I moved past them, shutting each one until I found the one I needed. The yellow magic spilled out of the doorway, flooding my hallways until the house was just a ball of golden light. I opened my eyes. Jonah was staring at me, his jaw unhinged. "Christ, Bree. You're *glowing*."

You should see what you look like when you're a Panther, I wanted to say, but I didn't need to. He'd heard me in his mind without my even meaning for him to. The magic had taken me over. I was completely undone; only the mage was left now. With a shiver, I recognized the same feeling I'd had in Tibet. Something *had* happened when I destroyed that brazier . . .

Whatever . . . I couldn't worry about it now. Sunshiny light poured out of me. I focused it on Alessia, let it seep into her, through her skin, into her bones, down to her soul. The world, the room, even Jonah dimmed around me until all I could see was Alessia. One by one, I dropped the Redwoods magic on each of her wounds. The magic bent to my will with the lightest touch. There wasn't one site that eluded me now. The power of all seven sites was inside me, part of me . . .

I wasn't just controlling the magic anymore. I *was* the magic.

Beneath the light, Alessia stirred. My vision broadened as the magic began to fade, its work done. The bruises on her face and arms faded, the puncture wounds on her collarbone healed themselves over. Jonah stroked her face and kissed her forehead. Alessia sighed, and at last she opened her eyes.

Jonah drew in a long, shuddering breath. "Are you okay?" he asked, his voice shaky.

She stretched a little, licked her lips. "Water," she said hoarsely.

I jumped up. "I'll get it." As I backed away from the couch, Jonah bent over and kissed her.

Gross. But also . . . she was going to be okay. *I had made her okay.*

I smiled and turned toward the kitchen.

Cal stood in the doorway, watching me. The corners of his lips curved up, making them seem fuller and redder than normal.

I tried to glance away but couldn't. "I think she'll be fine."

He nodded, the heat of his gaze never leaving me. "You are magnificent, Bree."

The force of his words touched something deep inside me. I met his eyes, blaze for blaze, a fiery ball spinning in the pit of my stomach. And then, because even though we'd lost the Waterfall, I'd still won something deeper that night, because the magic was still radiating through me, and because he was just so damn cute, I put my hand on the back of his neck and pulled his mouth down to mine.

CHAPTER TWENTY
The Light in the Dark

Alessia

The world was a mess of pain and darkness. Somewhere below me, an infinite number of souls pulsed and writhed, reaching for me, calling me down to them. But I didn't want to go down. I wanted to go up, but there was nothing for me to grasp onto.

And then, from a great height above me, a golden rope dropped. I grabbed it with every ounce of strength left in my broken body. I'd never been able to climb those stupid ropes in gym class, but I hauled myself up this one, every muscle screaming, every upward inch agony. But still I climbed.

Halfway up, whoever was at the top of the rope gave a tug and pulled me the rest of the way.

Sunshine-yellow light spilled over my face, warming away the cold that had seeped into me from that deep, dark place. The pain disappeared bit by bit, and I could breathe again. I gulped in air, filling up my lungs. Someone's hands lay on my collarbones. Close by, the fire crackled. I opened my eyes slowly. Everything was blurry. I blinked several times and Jonah's face came into focus, just above me.

His green eyes peered into mine. In the forest of his irises I saw everything that I felt: fear, pain, relief. I swallowed; my mouth and throat felt full of gravel. I wanted to say something meaningful, reassuring, loving . . . but all that came out was "Water."

"I'll get it." Bree's voice was close to my ear. When she moved, I felt the hands on my chest slip away; they were hers. I turned my head to watch her retreat to the kitchen.

Jonah bent over, blocking my view. With the gentleness of a butterfly, he brushed his lips against mine. A tingle ran down my spine, lessening the pain that still ached through me. "How are you feeling?"

I coughed and stretched a little, testing my muscles. Everything felt tight and slightly off, like my skin didn't quite cover all my insides. "You should see . . . the other guy."

Jonah winced. "I'd like to kill the other guy."

"Yeah, those Wild Dogs are not . . . my favorite." I tried to sit up, but a sharp pain arched across my chest. Jonah caught me as I gasped and laid me back down in his lap. "Ow."

"Maybe moving isn't the best idea right now." He brushed his hand across my cheek, tucking loose strands of hair behind my ear. "Alessia, I'm so sorry. I tried to get them off you, but I—I couldn't." His gaze was locked on mine, but he was seeing something else. The words tumbled out of his mouth like a confession. "That Dog had you in its mouth and I tried to attack it, but . . . something happened. My aura clashed with the Dog's, like it was solid or something. And the Dog's aura blew me backward. It almost knocked me out."

I closed my eyes. The streak of silver and the yelp of pain just before I'd blacked out . . . that was Jonah. Jonah, trying to help me. Jonah, trying to fight his own side in order to save me. I reached up and touched his face, opened my eyes and looked into his. I had never loved him more than at this moment. "A Malandante cannot fight another Malandante," I whispered. "It's physically impossible. Didn't you know?"

Jonah shook his head. "How did *you* know?"

"Nerina told me."

"Actually . . ." Bree came over to the couch and handed me a glass of water. "Nerina told *me*, and I told Alessia."

I propped myself up a little on my elbow so I could drink the water. It tasted delicious in my sandpapery mouth.

Jonah looked from me to his sister. "And how does Nerina know that?"

Bree planted herself in front of the couch and folded her arms. "If I had a nickel for every time I wondered the same thing, I'd be a freaking millionaire. And she knows way more even than she's ever let on."

"That's not really what we should be worried about

right now." I set the glass on the floor. Holding tight to Jonah's hand, I pulled myself up to a sitting position with a groan. Jonah kept his arm around me, his hand stroking up and down my side. Every inch of my body ached from the fight, but Jonah's touch eased it away. "Even though you couldn't attack the Dogs, you tried. And they saw you try." His arm tightened behind me. I leaned my head on his shoulder. "They know, Jonah. They know you're actively working against them."

A thick silence descended over the three of us. Only the crackling of the fire stretched between us. Finally, Bree said, "I used the Pakistani magic on them. It's possible they got displaced enough that they weren't able to report it to the *Concilio* or Jonah's Clan."

"Do we really want to take that chance?"

"But what can we do? He'll have to risk it and talk his way out of it if they confront him—"

"Hey, if you guys are done arguing over what *I* should do, can I say something?" Jonah glared at Bree, who had that petulant look on her face that I bet she'd perfected when she was three. "Bree, give me a few minutes alone with Alessia. Please."

Her jaw tightened, but she nodded and left the room. I turned to Jonah, but before I could say anything, he cupped my face in his hands and kissed me. My soul blossomed beneath his touch and any pain left from the attack became a distant memory. He kissed me like it was the last moment on earth. I held him to me; I wanted it to go on forever.

"Alessia," he murmured into my mouth, "come away with me."

I pulled back. "What?"

His fingers pressed into my skin, his gaze fierce. "If the Malandanti know, then I'm as good as dead. So I'm going to leave. I'm going to get out of Twin Willows, go far away where they can't find me." He searched my face as though it was the answer to the only question he ever had. "Come with me."

I leaned into him so that first our foreheads touched and then our lips met again. Heat spiraled between us. A desperate longing overwhelmed me. I lay back, pulling him down with me. He buried his face in my neck, searing my skin with kisses. I held him to me for that moment, that one beautiful, flawless moment, because I knew when it was over, the pain would be twice as bad as anything one of those Wild Dogs could do to me.

He brought his mouth back to mine, catching my bottom lip between his teeth. "So you'll go with me?"

I kept his mouth against mine as I answered. "I can't."

A groan shuddered through him as he sat up, dragging me up with him. I curled into his lap and laid my head against his chest. Beneath the layers of clothes I could hear his heartbeat, fast and hard. I put my hand at the side of his neck. "You know I can't, Jonah. I can't leave my Clan incomplete."

"But if I leave mine," he said, "your Clan could win."

"The Call . . ." I began. "The Call reaches everywhere, Jonah. You can't outrun it."

He rubbed his hands over his face and through his hair. "I hate this so much. I just want to get out of here . . . leave it all behind me. But I can't, can I?" His voice broke, and he looked away. My heart twisted. I could see it all over him, the pain and stress cracking him like a fractured aura. If the Malandanti didn't kill him, the pressure would.

I threaded my arms around his neck. "We'll find a way, Jonah. Somehow . . . there has to be a way." I kissed him hard, as though somehow that would make up for the fact that I was probably lying.

The door to the den banged open. We broke apart as Nerina click-clacked her way over to us. The look on her face told me she knew exactly what was going on before she came into the room. "Still here, Mr. Wolfe?"

Jonah stood. "I had to make sure Alessia was okay."

"Well, you've done that." Nerina folded her arms. If her gaze could shoot ice, the whole room would be frozen. "So now you can go on back to your little Malandanti Clan."

I groaned and dropped my head into my hands. What the hell was her problem?

"For your information"—Bree had come in from the kitchen and met Nerina's icy glare with one of her own—"Jonah tried to save Alessia. His aura clashed with one of the Dogs'. So now his 'little Malandanti Clan' knows he's fighting against them and he *can't* go back."

Nerina's nostrils flared. "If you're suggesting we keep him here, that is never going to happen."

"Why the hell not?" Bree yelled. I dug my fingers into my temples. The aches from the attack were coming back.

"If the Malandanti track him here, we are all dead."

"I'll reinforce the protection spell on the house—"

"And the Rabbit could easily undo that."

I drew my knees up to my chest, trying to make myself small. In front of me, Jonah dropped to a crouch and put his hands on my arms. "Bree's being her usual pain-in-the-ass self," he whispered. Somehow, in spite of everything, he grinned. "You know I can't stay here, right? No way am I putting you in that kind of danger."

"I know." I leaned forward until our foreheads touched again. It was just me and him, our connection blocking out the shouted argument that raged just feet away. His breath was warm on my nose. I closed my eyes and breathed in his scent. Spice and pine. "But where are you gonna go?"

"I have some friends I could go to. Far from here."

"Why don't you two stop fighting and ask Jonah what he wants?" Heath's voice broke into our bubble. With a start, I realized the entire household was now crowded into the living room. A ray of heated anger stretched between Nerina and Bree, their eyes blazing at each other. Heath crossed through them and came over to the couch. He put his hand on Jonah's shoulder. "What's your plan?"

Jonah swallowed and rose so that he and Heath stood eye to eye. "I thought . . . I'd go to New York. I have friends there and I figure that's a big enough city for me to disappear into."

"I have a better idea."

Everyone turned.

Mr. Salter stood at the foot of the stairs.

I gritted my teeth. I still couldn't get used to him being here all the time. What was going to happen when we got to go home to the farm? Would he just move in? I didn't say anything as he stepped forward.

"He can stay at my cabin. It's way the hell out in the middle of nowhere. That way we know where he is if we need him."

We? There was no *we* here. He wasn't a Benandante; he didn't get a say.

But before I could open my mouth, Bree softened her stance and cocked her head at Mr. Salter. "I could do a protection spell around the cabin. No one would think to look for him there." She turned to Jonah. "But if they Call you . . . I can't do anything about that."

"I don't think there's anything anyone can do about that," Jonah said. My chest squeezed tight for him. The thought of him all alone in the middle of the woods, fighting the Call. Hot tears gathered at the corners of my eyes and I tried to blink them away.

Mr. Salter crossed to the couch. "We've only got an hour or so before dawn." He clapped his hand on Jonah's shoulder. "We should leave now."

"I'm going with you." I held Jonah's hand as I got to my feet, but as soon as I was upright, a wave of pain and dizziness crashed over me. I gasped and fell back to the couch.

Jonah leaned over me, cradling my face in his hands. "You need to rest," he whispered. "I'll be okay."

"But . . ." My shoulders hunched. There were too many people watching. I wanted them all to leave. But they weren't going to, so I couldn't care what they said. I put my hand on the back of his neck and pulled Jonah's mouth to mine. We were back in our bubble, the world belonging just to us, for as long as the kiss lasted. I wanted his lips to brand mine, leave a mark there forever.

He pulled away a fraction of an inch, enough that I could memorize the flecks of gold inside his jeweled irises. "I love you, Alessia. Always."

"I love you, too."

A minute later, he was out the door, Mr. Salter, Heath, and Bree following. I sank into the couch, my arm across my eyes, trying to block out the light from the dawn and the pain in my heart.

CHAPTER TWENTY-ONE
The Blue Book

Alessia

The next morning when I went down to breakfast, Lidia took one look at the backpack slung over my shoulder and pursed her lips. "You're not going to school today."

"Why not?" I dropped my bag on the floor and slid into a chair next to Bree, who was already at the table, eating bacon. "I feel fine."

"Thanks to me," Bree said.

I rolled my eyes. "Bree, I already thanked you like a million times for saving my life."

"Hey, a girl can never hear too much of that kind of appreciation." She pointed a second piece of bacon at me. "Why do you want to go to school anyway? You know *he's* not going to be there."

"I know." I toyed with a frayed edge of the table-cloth. A fresh knife of pain stabbed through me. Missing Jonah—knowing he was someplace where I couldn't go—was like a tangible monster who had taken up residence in my chest. I cleared my throat. "But it seems stupid to stay home when there's not really anything going on here right now." It was true. Nerina had been locked in the den all night, making all sorts of long-distance phone calls to the rest of the *Concilio*. Without cluing in any of us, of course. And the thought of sitting around here all day with nothing to do but worry seemed like madness.

"God, you really are a Goody Two-shoes." Bree shoved the rest of her bacon in her mouth and pushed away from the table. "Take a day off for once in your life."

The moment she was gone, Lidia slid into her empty chair. I tensed, keenly aware of all the things that were still unsaid between us. She put her hand over mine, but I didn't soften. "*Cara,* when Bree came in with you last night, I . . . I . . ."

I could picture the scene in my mind, and for a sliver of a moment I imagined the chaos and fear she must've felt at seeing me so hurt. I swallowed. "I'm okay, Mom. Really."

She shook her head. "This is exactly what I didn't want for you. What I tried to protect you from."

"Well, you can't." I drew my hand out from under hers. "You can't keep me in a bubble, no matter how many lies you tell or how many trips to Paris you don't allow me to take."

"Alessia." The sharp tone in her voice stilled me. "I did what I thought was right. I made a mistake. You have to forgive me."

I stared into her eyes, their soft brown depths pleading

with me. When had my relationship with her become so complicated? How had it gone from being the one thing that I could count on to the thing I was most unsure of? "Tell me exactly what's going on with Mr. Salter."

She blinked. "Alessia . . ."

"You want me to forgive you? Then you have to be honest with me about *everything* from here on out."

The only sound in the kitchen was the drip-drip of the coffee machine. We sat staring at each other, finally recognizing each other for what we were: a mother who was as human as I was, and a daughter who was capable of much more than her mother realized. "Okay, Alessia." She touched my hand again. "You are right. You deserve to know the truth."

"Which is?"

She hitched one shoulder up. "We are . . . dating, if you want to put a common label on it."

"Oh, come on. He's here all the time. There's more to it than that." I tightened my jaw. "Are you in love with him?"

"I . . ." Lidia looked out the kitchen window for a moment before turning back to me. "I am very fond of him. He makes me laugh. I could see myself being happy with him for a long time. So, yes, in that way I guess I do love him." Her fingers tightened on mine. "But do I love him the same way I loved your father? No. I will never love anyone the way I loved your father. Just as Ed will never love anyone the way he loved Dolly. We have been very honest with each other about that." The corner of her mouth turned up. "But that does not lessen our affection for each other."

"Are you sleeping with him?"

Lidia pulled her hand away. "That, young lady, is none of your business." But I could tell from the two bright spots that appeared on her cheeks what the answer was. And I kinda wished I hadn't asked that question.

I picked at a chip in the table. "It was nice of him to let Jonah use his cabin," I said finally. "Bree said he stocked up on all sorts of supplies on their way up there."

"Ed is nothing if not resourceful." Lidia glanced past me, toward the living room, and leaned in close. "And speaking of resources . . . there is something I need. Back at the farmhouse."

"What?" I pinched my brows together.

"I know everyone thinks it's dangerous, but I thought that you . . ."

My eyes widened. "Oh, my God, this is the real reason you didn't want me to go to school today, isn't it? Wow, Mom. You've got more in common with Nerina than you know."

"I do not have anything in common with that woman." Lidia stood up. "Get your coat."

The air outside bit into my skin. Spring was still weeks away, and winter sure was having a hell of a last party. "What do you need from the house?" I asked, my voice muffled by my thick scarf. "And why do you need me to come with you?" When Lidia didn't answer, I threw my arms up. "Come on, Mom, I thought we were being honest with each other."

"I can't answer you because I'm not sure what I'm looking for." She clung to my arm as we braved the wind. We crossed Main Street and turned down the road. The farmhouse was in sight now, the weather vane spinning madly in the wind.

"What's that supposed to mean?"

"Many years ago, your father told me that he had hidden something in the house, something that might help the Benandanti should they ever need it." Lidia glanced up and down the street. "But he never told me exactly where or what it was. And I thought, with your magic . . ."

"You think I'll be able to find it faster," I finished for her. "You would've been better off with Bree. I bet she could find something like that in about five seconds."

"Well, I do not want Bree. I want my daughter."

Behind my scarf, I half-snorted and half-smiled. It didn't matter if whatever was at the house was useful; she wanted something we could bond over. Although I was pretty sure this was the strangest mother-daughter outing I'd ever been on.

We reached the top of the driveway. I pulled away from her and swept my gaze up and down the street. A bus lumbered past, on its way to Bangor. I looked beyond the house, past the barn ruins, and over the hillside. Patches of brown grass poked up through the crusty old snow. Heath's cabin lay dormant at the edge of the pasture. The hen trailers were quiet. And the forest beyond appeared empty and barren beneath the gray sky. It all seemed normal. Still . . . "Let's get inside fast," I said, and we practically ran down the driveway.

"Any idea where we should start?" I said when we'd closed the front door and shrugged out of our coats.

Lidia unwound her scarf from her throat and hung it over her coat on the rack. "He would've hidden it someplace he thought was safe. Someplace he thought no one would be able to find it."

"But if he told you about it, he would've wanted *you* to be able to find it." I tapped my finger on my lips. "The safest place probably would've been Nerina's bunker, but if it was there, then the Malandanti definitely have it." Everything had been overturned, torn apart, and undone in the underground lair when I'd last been there, the day Nerina had been taken, the day Heath and I had gone after her and been trapped in the Guild with Jonah as our guard . . . I squeezed my eyes shut. That day seemed like forever ago. I opened my eyes. If I let myself stand here in the living room and think about Jonah, I'd be lost. I had to keep moving, or I'd be stuck still forever.

"I thought perhaps . . ." Lidia took a few tentative steps toward the kitchen. "Maybe it was hidden near the amulet. The one you found in the basement."

"It's as good a place to start as any." I followed her into the kitchen and down the basement stairs. It was freezing, the brick walls seeping with a bone-chilling cold. I went right over to the loose brick where I'd found the amulet.

None of the other bricks around it seemed to be loose as well, but I felt my way along the wall, testing each brick to see if it would give.

Lidia stood in the middle of the basement, her eyes fixed on the shelves filled with jars of *mostarda* and jams, dried meats from last season, and canned fruits. "I should really take some of these back for Barb," she murmured.

"*Mother.*"

She glanced at me crouched on the ground, digging my fingers around each brick. "Sorry." She went to the corner opposite me and began her own search.

We worked in silence for several minutes. My fingers were red and sore from scratching along the bricks, and more than one of my nails cracked with the pressure. I finished the length of the first wall—the one where I'd found the amulet—and turned the corner.

The sound of loud knocking on the front door above us froze my hands.

Across the room, Lidia slowly rose to her feet, her gaze fixed on the basement door. "It could be anybody," she whispered. "Maybe just one of the neighbors."

If it was one of the neighbors, then I was a Malandante Dragon. I bit the inside of my cheek. We were stupid to come here, in the bright light of day . . .

Another round of knocking echoed through the house, making my insides shake.

Lidia squared her shoulders and marched to the stairs. "Mom, no!"

"I'm allowed to be in my own house," she said, her jaw set. "Stay down here."

"Mom!"

But she ignored me and disappeared up the stairs, shutting the basement door with a snap.

My breath shallow, I moved to the next set of bricks, my ears fine-tuned to the floor above me as my fingers worked. The front door creaked open and I heard Lidia say, "*Buon giorno*. May I help you?" in her best imperious Italian accent.

"Good morning, Mrs. Jacobs."

At the sound of Pratt Webster's voice, my blood turned to ice in my veins. And at the same time, my fingers hit a snag, a place in the wall where the mortar had been scraped clean.

"My name is Pratt Web—"

"Yes, I remember you, Mr. Webster. What is it you want?"

I bent my head, my hair dangling around my face, and slid my fingers into the space where the mortar should have been. With a little tug, first one brick came out and then another. Dust clouded the air, and I pinched my mouth shut to keep from coughing.

"I'm surprised to see you here. I heard the house was being treated for black mold."

"Well, Mr. Webster, I'm surprised to see *you* here. I thought I made it perfectly clear the last time you set foot in my house that you are not welcome."

"You can understand my concern when I saw you

enter a house that is supposed to be toxic."

"I don't really see how that's *any* of your concern."

My hands grappled inside the wall. I couldn't breathe, couldn't make air come through my mouth into my lungs. Bile rose in the back of my throat. God, she was up there with the man who'd killed my father. But I hadn't told her. I'd been so preoccupied with how she'd betrayed me that I hadn't told her about Dad . . . and she had no idea how dangerous Pratt Webster truly was.

Mortar crumbled away, and my fingers hit something smooth and solid. I got a good grip on it and pulled hard. With a shower of powdered brick, a leather-bound book came tumbling out of the wall with such force that I fell back on my bottom. The book fell against my knee with a painful smack. It was a kind of old-fashioned journal, large and square with thick leather binding.

"Perhaps it's my concern because there really isn't black mold in this house."

"Just what are you suggesting?"

I grabbed the book and bolted up the stairs. "Mom, I found it. I was such an idiot to leave it behind." I slid to a stop in the living room, looking at Pratt like he was the last person I expected to see. "Um, hi." I walked to the coat rack, holding the book behind my back. "We really shouldn't be in here for too long. They told us the treatment is super toxic." I held Lidia's coat out to her, hoping Pratt couldn't see how my arm shook.

"Then why were you here?"

"I left one of my textbooks in the basement." I pulled my own coat off the rack, keeping my face turned away from him. *Just breathe,* I told myself. *Don't think about stabbing his eyes out.*

"Really." I felt Pratt's gaze on me.

Don't look at him, don't look at him . . .

"Don't you dare talk to my daughter like that, Mr. Webster. In fact, don't you dare talk to my daughter at all." Lidia stormed to the door and flung it open. "Please leave."

An angry breath of wind gusted through the door. "So sorry to have bothered you," Pratt said, his voice so honeyed that it made my stomach turn. He took a step toward the door. "Though I do find it interesting that your daughter's textbook is *glowing blue.*"

I gasped and brought the book around to my front. It was enveloped in a halo of the telltale Benandanti blue. But it hadn't been glowing in the basement. I backed away, the book held in front of me, my hands bathed in its celestial aura. My traitorous hands . . . the book must have unlocked only for a Benandante, the light only have shone when a Benandante held it.

"Get out!" Lidia screeched, and I didn't know if she was screaming at me or at Pratt. I stumbled backward into the kitchen, heading for the back door, but Pratt crossed the length of the house in a microsecond. The instant I reached for the knob, he slammed his palm flat on the door above my head, trapping me in.

"So it's you," he breathed, his words hot on my face, in my hair, down my neck. "I thought it was your mother, but it's you. Jonah's sweet little girl is a Benandante. No wonder he won't kill you."

I raised my gaze and finally looked into Pratt Webster's eyes. As I searched their soulless depths, tendrils of rage uncurled in every corner of my body and spiraled outward. "Yes, it's me," I spat, thrilled to see a healthy drop of my saliva land on his nose. "I'm the Falcon. The one who broke your wings." Breath came hard and fast, making my insides burn. "I'm also the one whose barn you burned down. And the one whose father you had killed. But you already knew that."

He reared back, his free hand ready to strike . . . I went low and drove the book hard into his gut. He sputtered and hunched over. I thrust the book right into his throat and his Adam's apple smashed with a sickening shudder. He fell back against the door, but as I went in for one more strike, he kicked his foot out. My legs flew out from under me, and I hit the floor with a bone-crunching thud that made me cry out. I scrambled backward on my butt as he came at me, his hands grabbing. The book . . . he wanted the book . . . I shoved it behind me, half sitting on it. He'd have to kill me to get to it. And when I looked up into his face, I realized that was exactly what he planned to do.

His hands closed over my neck. He dragged me up, his grip so strong that my feet left the floor. I clawed at his fingers, kicked at his shins, but he held me fast. I fought for air, trying to get in one tiny sip. Lines crisscrossed before my eyes, my vision blurring at the edges. I scratched his face, but he barely flinched. The edges were closing in . . . getting darker and darker.

"Get your hands off my daughter."

He let me go.

I fell in a boneless heap on the floor, gasping, filling my lungs again and again. I never knew how much I loved breathing. It took me a minute to realize Pratt had backed up all the way to the wall, his hands held above him. My hand on my throat, I turned around.

Lidia stood in the doorway to the kitchen with my father's shotgun clutched in her white-knuckled hands. I grabbed the book and clambered to my feet. The butt of the gun was jammed into her shoulder, the barrel was pointed straight at Pratt's head, and the safety was off. I'd been taught to fear and respect guns since I was a child, and I knew the safety didn't come off unless you meant business. I got behind Lidia and put my hand on the small of her back.

"Is what she says true? Did you kill my husband?"

Pratt didn't answer. In the dim light that filtered in from the window, I saw him swallow, his throat bruised where I'd hit him with the book. Good. I could only imagine what my own neck looked like.

"It's true," I said, my voice coarse and dry. "I heard him tell Jonah."

Lidia stalked toward him, her steps measured, like she was hunting prey she had absolutely no doubt she'd capture. Pratt looked around, his eyes wild, but he was against the wall with nowhere to go. When Lidia stopped, the shotgun was less than an inch from the bridge of his nose.

"Open the door," she said.

He fumbled with the knob behind him. Cold air rushed in, along with the faint acrid smell from the burnt-out barn. "Walk," Lidia ordered.

I followed her out, closing the door behind me. Pratt half-walked, half-jogged around the side of the house, glancing over his shoulder at the barrel of the gun. If I hadn't been filled with such blinding-white rage, I would've laughed at how swiftly his arrogance had abandoned him.

We came to the front of the house. Pratt's sleek silver Mercedes was parked in our driveway. Lidia nudged him with the gun until he was backed up against the driver's side door. "Get in," she said. "Drive away. If you set foot on this property again, you will be shot. If you come within one hundred feet of my daughter anywhere in this town, this state, this *world*, you will be shot."

Pratt's gaze shifted from Lidia to me. His face darkened as he looked at the book, his lips snarling. "You cannot win," he said.

"You Malandanti keep saying that," I said, "and yet there are four sites under our control and three under yours." Our eyes met and there was almost an

understanding there, like we knew we'd just keep on trying to kill each other until one of us succeeded.

"Get off my farm," Lidia said.

Pratt ducked into his car, gunned the engine, and
fired out of the driveway like a rocket. Only when the
last curl of smoke had disappeared from the road did my
mother lower the gun. And begin to shake.

I grabbed her arm. "Don't, Mom. Keep it together.
We have to go."

She nodded once, and we bolted up the driveway,
down Main Street, and onto Willowbrook Lane. I burst
into Jenny's house, ran to the den, and flung open the
door. Nerina, Heath, and Bree sat clustered around
the desk, an ancient book made out of what looked like
bark open on the surface in front of them. I skidded to a
stop and dropped the blue-haloed book on top of it. "He
knows," I panted. "Pratt Webster knows I'm the Falcon."

Heath leapt to his feet and grabbed my arms. "How?
How did he find out?"

"He came to the house. He saw me with that book . . ."
The words tumbled over themselves, loose and confused
in my mouth.

"What the hell *is* this book?" Bree asked, touching
her finger to it.

"Something my father hid."

"Your father?" Heath said. "Why would he—?"

"I don't know, but now Pratt knows about me and he
wants the book."

"We have to hide you," Heath said.

"We can hide her in the cabin with Jonah," Bree said, and for a crazy tortured moment my heart leapt at that thought.

"No." Nerina rose to her feet and we all fell silent. She laid her palm flat on the book. The blue light wove around her fingers like shimmering thread. "I have just been telling Heath and Bree our next orders. The *Concilio* believes we should've gone after the Olive Grove instead of the Waterfall—"

"Duh," Bree muttered.

Nerina ignored her. "So Bree and I are flying to Italy to assist them." She reached out with her other hand and touched my cheek. "And to remove you from danger here at home, you must come with us."

CHAPTER TWENTY-TWO

Nerina's Big-Ass Secret

Bree

We flew another private jet to Cividale, the seat of Friuli and the home of the *Concilio*. I could tell Alessia was super impressed but trying to play it cool, like she took trips on a private jet every weekend. "When was the last time you were on a plane?" I asked her as we taxied down the runway.

"Um, we went to Florida when I was seven."

I smirked. "Should we get you a barf bag just in case?"

Alessia rolled her eyes. "I think I'll be just fine, thank you." She pulled a trashy-looking novel out of her bag and sat back to read. I'd never seen Alessia read anything other than school assignments, and this book was definitely not on any extra-credit reading lists. So she'd decided to take my advice and take a day off. Good for her. Not that I blamed her after what had happened at the farmhouse.

"Tell me again how Lidia pointed a gun at Pratt's face."

Alessia lowered the book a few inches. "You've already heard it like three times."

"I don't think I'm ever going to get tired of it."

One corner of her mouth turned up. "It *was* pretty awesome." The half-smile disappeared. "If it hadn't been so terrifying." She touched her fingers to her neck, where the shadow of Pratt's handprint still lingered.

I leaned forward. "We're going to get him, Alessia. Him and every other goddamn Malandanti out there."

Alessia didn't answer. Instead she lay her book on the arm of her seat. "Change of subject," she said and gave me a wicked grin. "What's up with you and Cal?"

I gritted my teeth together. "Um, nothing."

"Really."

I puffed out a loud sigh. "We kissed. Once. No big deal."

A super-smug, super-annoying look spread across her face. "Uh-huh. No big deal. Right." Her eyes had turned so gleeful that I wanted to smack her. "For what it's worth, I approve."

"Um, your approval of my love life is worth zero." I glared at her, which made her smile wider. "Oh, just shut up."

She did shut up, but that infuriating grin didn't leave her face as she picked up her book again. I leaned back in my cushy leather seat and stared out the window. The plane sped up and lifted off the ground, and the comfortable whoosh-whir sound of airplanes filled the cabin. Nerina sat across from us, turning the pages of the *Vogue Italia* she'd picked up at the airport. It was actually kind of impressive that the newsstand in the Bangor airport even carried *Vogue Italia*.

I looked from her to Alessia, their noses buried in their respective reading choices. "Seriously?"

They both looked up.

"We have like a million things to talk about and you guys are just going to *read*?"

"Actually, we should all be sleeping," Nerina said, her face calm as she flipped another page in her magazine. "We probably won't get much rest while we're in Cividale."

"Oh, my God." I flopped my arms out wide and slumped down, tapping my foot against the bottom of my seat, rat-a-tat-tat like a really annoying tune you can't get out of your head. "We should've put you below with your Louis Vuitton suitcase."

"That's uncalled for, Bree," Nerina said.

Alessia tossed her trashy novel aside and folded her arms. "I think Bree has a point. I think there are a lot of things we should be talking about. Things we've been dancing around for far too long."

Nerina raised an eyebrow. "Such as?"

"Like why the hell you won't talk about the spell to change a Malandante into a Benandante."

I almost whistled, but I stopped myself. Apparently it took a near-death experience for Alessia to finally stop trying to be nice to everyone. "Yeah, that seems like a good place to start," I said.

Nerina snapped her *Vogue* shut and tossed it onto the seat next to her. "You two have no right to question me on that. You have been members of the Benandanti for less than half a year. I have been a Benandante for *four centuries*."

"Oh, come off it, Nerina." I crossed my arms. "We've proven ourselves over and over."

"I am so tired of everyone else deciding what I should and shouldn't know," Alessia said. "First my mother and then you. I am not a child. I can handle the truth."

"It's not about handling the truth," Nerina said. "It's about the fact that a Benandante has to die in order to do the spell. Is that what you want?"

"Of course we don't want that," I said. "But we should at least talk about it, because if—God forbid—that happens, we should be prepared."

"I would rather not test the Fates by preparing for such things." Nerina reached for her *Vogue* again, the tone in her voice final.

Oh, no. Girlfriend was not getting off that easy. "Don't even think about picking up that goddamn magazine. You can't write us off this time. We're trapped in a metal tube ten thousand feet in the air, and we're going to get some answers before we land."

"Why won't you even talk about it?" Alessia asked. "At least tell us if it happened in your lifetime."

I could see the look in Nerina's eyes, like an animal caught between two larger predators. I'd been kidding about being trapped at ten thousand feet, but it had obviously been a barb that stung. Maybe if we backed her up far enough . . . "Nerina, as the Benandanti mage, I deserve to know. It's part of my training."

"It is not part of your training to learn a spell you are never going to use." Her words were clipped and cold.

"Fine." I kicked my feet out in front of me. "I'll just ask Dario when we get to Cividale. Let's see what he says."

A flush crept up from beneath her cashmere sweater and spread across her throat. "He won't tell you."

"But maybe he'll be interested in why *you* haven't told Bree," Alessia said.

"There are six other *Concilio* members I can ask—"

"Don't you dare go behind my back about this!"

"Then stop lying to me!" I leapt to my feet and jabbed my finger at her, which I wished wasn't shaking as much as it was. "You were in Tibet. You were there when Shen practically had to drag me out of the Temple, after *I killed my own father.*"

"You didn't—" Alessia began, and I wanted to strangle the gentleness out of her voice.

"*I did.* I did, and I would do it again, for the Benandanti. Because everything I've done has been to save my brother." There were tears in my eyes and I stomped my foot so hard the floor trembled, as if that would make the grief and anger and shame inside me go away. "You know what I've sacrificed for this gig, what it's cost me—"

"And you think I haven't paid a high price as well?" Nerina was on her feet now too, her eyes blazing at me, like the cornered animal inside her was gonna go down swinging or die trying. "You know the sacrifices I've made . . ."

"Oh, big frigging deal, the *Concilio* won't let you be with Heath." I was so sick of hearing this excuse. "News flash, Nerina: you are the *Concilio*. You have a say in that too. In fact"—I couldn't believe this idea hadn't occurred to me before—"I think the *Concilio* should know about you two. About the fact that you've been screwing each other since Tibet. Maybe they'll reconsider . . ."

"Bree." Nerina's gaze was so dark that I almost took a step back, but I held my ground. Her jaw worked up and down. "That is between me and Heath and the *Concilio*. It is none of your business."

"It is if I think it's interfering with your ability to run the Twin Willows Clan," I said. I could feel Alessia's gaze on me, like she was wondering how low was I going to sink, but I didn't care. I'd been in places much lower, and I wasn't afraid to revisit them. "And that's exactly what I'm going to tell them."

"You wouldn't dare—"

"Oh, I will dare." My breath came hard and fast. "Unless you tell me about that spell."

A cold, hard silence thickened the cabin. *Your move, Nerina,* I thought. She stared at me for so long that I could practically see the wheels spinning inside her head, calculating exactly how much truth she could get away with to satisfy me. But then her shoulders hunched and she dropped back to her seat, her head in her hands. White heat shot through my gut. God, I'd broken her. Like an overused Barbie doll, I'd snapped her in two. I didn't feel quite as triumphant as I'd thought I would.

Her face still covered by her hands, Nerina spoke in a dry, deadened voice. "What do you want to know?"

"Were you there?"

"Yes. I was there."

"Who performed the spell?"

"The Benandanti mage at the time, Rosalina."

The name didn't ring a bell amongst all the other mages Nerina had told me about. I pinched my brow together. "When was this? How old were you?"

Nerina raised her head. Her eyes were weary, like the last few minutes had stripped away the façade she held up to hide just how old she was. Like she was so tired of the world and everything in it. "Oh, Bree," she said, "have you not guessed? Have you not, in all your cleverness, figured it out?" She folded her hands just beneath her chin, as though praying. "The Malandante who became a Benandante was me."

CHAPTER TWENTY-THREE

The Curse to the Blessing

Alessia

It all made sense. Why she hated Jonah, how horrified she was about us communicating with each other. Why she refused to speak about the spell. Because a Benandante had had to die in order for her to switch sides, and she was still carrying that guilt more than four hundred years later.

Bree stumbled back a step and fell into the seat beside me. She had not, in all her cleverness, figured it out. I could tell by the white shock on her face that she had definitely not expected it. And I hadn't either, but now that I began to piece it all together, I couldn't believe we *hadn't* figured it out.

"That's why you and the Harpy know each other," I said, remembering the barely contained rage between them in the basement of the Guild. "You were in the same Clan."

"She was my Guide," Nerina whispered. "You cannot imagine her hatred for me."

Bree was still in stunned silence; it looked like I'd be the one asking the questions.

"How old were you?" I asked.

"I was fourteen when I was Called by the Malandanti." She looked past us, through the little round windows into the black night, her expression full of memory. "I knew nothing. They were so charismatic, so convincing. It wasn't like today, when you can find every opinion on something with the click of a mouse. Back then we knew only what our elders told us."

"How did you even know about the spell?" The pieces were coming together now, starting to form a picture. "Who knew to bring you in?"

Nerina hugged herself. "It was Dario. He was the local priest. I used to go to confession nearly every day, begging God to forgive me for the sins I committed in the name of the Malandanti." A hint of a smile brushed her lips. "You know, when you confess to a priest, it's supposed to be confidential. Little did I know that I was confessing to the head of the *Concilio Celeste*."

"So he knew that you were remorseful," I murmured. I could imagine the fourteen-year-old Nerina, her head bowed in penitence in the little confessional booth, Dario listening with his mind already whirling with plans.

Nerina nodded. "It happened about two years after I had been with the Malandanti. One of the Friuli Clan was mortally wounded in battle. By Fina . . . the Harpy."

"And she knew your human identity," I said. "So it wasn't safe for you."

"*Sì.*" Nerina stroked the armrest. "After the spell, I was immediately moved into the home of the *Concilio Celeste*.

The home that was concealed from the *Concilio Argento* for so many centuries, until they destroyed it last year. That was where they kept me hidden away."

"But you were just a regular Benandante at this point, right? When did you become part of the *Concilio*?"

"Two years after I joined the Clan, one of the *Concilio* died. I'd spent so much time in seclusion with them that they chose to promote me. Plus, it gave me extra power against the Harpy." Nerina touched her temple. "Always, she has hunted me. When she became a member of her own *Concilio*, it became an all-out war between us. Sometimes Dario had to remind me that I had an entire Clan to fight, not just her."

"Which explains why you were more intent on fighting her than making sure I was okay in our last battle," I said, my gaze laser-focused on her. I hadn't forgotten that. I didn't think her relationship with Heath interfered with her ability to lead, as Bree had threatened to say, but her revenge trip with the Harpy did.

"This is what you meant."

Nerina and I jumped at the sound of Bree's voice at last. I turned to her, but she kept her eyes on Nerina like it was just the two of them in that cabin. I couldn't blame her. How many hours had they spent together in training, while Nerina kept this gigantic secret from her? I'd be pretty pissed too.

"When you said you'd made mistakes you were still atoning for," Bree finished.

"When you are a Malandante," Nerina whispered,

"there are things you do that, if you have a conscience, if you have humanity in your soul . . . No matter how many deeds of justice I perform as a Benandante, I will never be clean." She looked from Bree to me and back again. "So you see? Why I cannot go against them? I owe Dario everything. If it hadn't been for him, I would still be trapped in that hell of shame."

"But they're wrong," I said, bringing my hands down hard on the armrests. "Sorry, but I totally disagree with them about Heath."

"It doesn't matter, Alessia." Nerina's eyes were bright; she was coming back to life. "They could ask me to wear my shoes on the wrong feet for the rest of my life, and I would do it. I owe them everything."

"I don't think you owe them this," Bree said. "You should ask them again. Press your case."

"If I did that, they would remove me from Twin Willows." Nerina ran her shaking fingers through her hair. "I swore to Dario when I saw him at the Redwoods site that I had not renewed my relationship with Heath."

"And you think it's better to lie than be honest about it? Better to lie than tell the truth to the person you say you owe everything to?"

Bree made a pretty good point. For someone who claimed she had sins to atone for, Nerina seemed rather okay with lying to the people she had to atone for.

Nerina glared at Bree, turning the cozy cabin icy. The façade was building again, the wall between the *Concilio* and two teenage members of the Benandanti rising once more. "Yes," she said, "in this case I believe it is better to lie. I have told *you* the truth, so you can drop it now." She picked up her magazine. "Do not ask me about that spell again."

I felt Italy in my blood even before the plane touched down. The heartbeat of my birthplace echoed in my own chest, like there was an invisible thread between me and the land. I breathed in deep when we stepped onto the tarmac, and the fifteen years of my absence seemed to disappear.

Nerina walked several steps ahead of me and Bree through the tiny airport. "You weren't expecting that, were you?" I muttered to Bree.

She shook her head. "But now that I look back, I'm kind of an idiot for not figuring it out."

"She didn't tell us anything about the actual spell."

Bree looked sideways at me. "Don't worry your pretty little head. If I'm ever called upon to perform that spell, I'll be able to do it." We followed Nerina out of the airport to the curb, where a black sports car sat. A man standing beside the car handed Nerina the keys and loaded our bags into the trunk. He tipped his hat to us and disappeared into the airport.

Despite the sunny blue sky and the fact that I was actually hot in my winter coat, the air inside the car was icy. Nerina ignored us as she drove the car away from the airport and onto the roadway that would take us into Cividale.

In the backseat next to me, Bree glanced at the back of Nerina's head and rolled her eyes at me. "So, Alessia," she said in a falsely bright voice, "are you happy to be visiting your grandparents?"

I smirked. "Why, yes, Bree, I am. I haven't seen them in fifteen years."

"Wow, fifteen years. What do you remember about them?"

"Oh, stop it, you two."

Bree snorted and sat back with a huff. I settled into my seat and stared out the window. Spring had already touched this part of the world. Early buds poked through the branches, and the hillsides were green and brown instead of endlessly snowy white. The town of Cividale appeared in the distance, a cluster of buildings with sharply slanted, tiled rooftops. We drove across a high stone bridge to reach it.

Nerina wound us through medieval streets lined with narrow, red-roofed houses. I pressed my face to the glass, catching the names of the streets. Via Monastero Maggiore, Via Adelaide Ristori . . . They all sounded somewhat familiar even though there was no way I could've remembered them from when I was a baby.

We emerged into a large town square, the main part of it closed to traffic. The car slowed as people walked across the road. A beautiful Renaissance church loomed over the square, the copper roof of its bell tower gleaming in the sunlight.

"Wait," I said. "Can you pull over?"

As soon as Nerina rolled the car to a stop, I leapt out. The square was crowded; it was just past noon, and everyone was on their way home for lunch, or dining out in one of the restaurants that ringed the square. I stood in the midst of the hustle and bustle, staring up at the church.

"What is it?"

I started; I hadn't realized that Bree had followed me. "I remember this," I said, pointing up at the church. "I remember this from when I was a baby."

"Wow," Bree said, and for once I didn't think she was being sarcastic. "That's pretty cool that you remember something from so long ago."

"It's amazing what the mind holds on to," I said. My heart stopped. I pressed my hand to my mouth. Jonah had said the exact same thing to me, all those months ago, in the alley beside Pizza Plus the night of Carly's party. My insides flooded with longing. I had barely been able to get him a message before I'd left Maine, and that had just been a warning that Pratt knew who I was. I winced. I hadn't even told him I loved him.

Standing there on the other side of the world from Jonah, he felt so lost to me, like a dream I'd been trying to hold on to long after I'd already woken up. Tears blurred my vision as I gazed up at the church, its tall stone bell tower blocking out the sun. "It's never going to end, is it?" I asked, not quite sure who I was talking to. "Jonah is stuck in that cabin in the middle of nowhere, I'm here, and the Malandanti will always be between us."

"Out of everyone, you're the person I least expect to lose faith," Bree said. "Don't fail me now."

"But how can I keep it when everything seems so hopeless?" I dug the heels of my hands into my eyes. My palms came away wet with tears. "I can't protect Jonah, he can't protect me, and no one will help us figure out a way to get him out." I shook my head. "I just feel like I'm caught in this endless cycle. We got Tibet, and then we lost at the Waterfall. Maybe we'll win here but the Malandanti will win somewhere else . . . We'll never get ahead of them." My throat closed up, and I stopped talking.

"Don't think ahead."

I looked away from the church and at Bree. I had to shield my eyes so I could see her face clearly.

"That's what I do. I just think only to the end of each minute. Once that one is over, then I get through the next one." She shrugged, but I could tell she was fighting off tears, too. "Thinking any further than that will only drive you crazy."

I swallowed the lump in my throat. I had always thought ahead. My whole life, I'd been thinking ahead to the day I would get out of Twin Willows and live my real life. But maybe that day would never come.

This was my real life. And it was time to wake up.

My grandparents lived on a narrow side street that wound up a hillside. Their house was at the very end of the lane, two tall willow trees marking their driveway. I stared up as we drove beneath the bending boughs. Was it coincidence that made my mother move from a house with two willow trees to a town named Twin Willows? Or was it destiny?

Nonna and Papa stood on the front step outside the house. I burst out of the car and ran to them. "Ah, *cara mia*, my beautiful Alessia, at last," Nonna cried as I flung my arms around her. She smelled of fresh-baked bread and Chanel No. 5. I remembered that scent, too, as clearly as I'd remembered the church.

"Welcome home," Papa said as I gave him a hug too. "Come in, come in."

Introductions were made as they ushered us inside. Conversation flew in a mixture of Italian and English. The house was bigger than I remembered—what I did remember of it—with two levels and lots of sunlit rooms filled with tastefully old furniture and lots of books. Maybe it was here that my love of writing had been born.

They showed Nerina to a room upstairs. "You and Bree will have to share," Nonna said to me. "*Bene?*"

"*Bene.*" We followed them back downstairs and across the living room. Nonna opened the door to a large, light-filled room with two daybeds against opposite walls. A thick medallion-patterned rug covered most of the terra-cotta floor, and a little table with two chairs sat beneath the huge half-moon window. "This room has its own bathroom," Nonna said. "I thought you girls would like that."

"It's beautiful," I said. "Have a bed preference, Bree?"

She shrugged and plunked her bag onto the bed nearest her. I moved to the window and looked out. The countryside spread out before us, rolling hills covered in green and brown.

Nonna came next to me and slid her arm around my waist. "You know, this is the room you were born in."

"It is?" I turned and surveyed the room with fresh attention.

Bree jumped up from the daybed. "Oh, gross," she said, her lip curling.

Nonna laughed. "Don't worry. We've gotten new furniture since then."

"Thank *God*." Bree sat back down and started to pull her boots off. "Do you mind if I take a shower before we meet the *Concilio*?"

"Be my guest," I said with a glance at Nonna, hoping she'd missed this exchange or at least not thought anything of it.

Bree padded into the bathroom and shut the door.

Nonna, her arm still around my waist, steered me back out through the living room and into the kitchen.

I could tell the instant we walked in that, just like at my home, this room was the heart of the household.

Sauce bubbled on the stove, and the long wooden table in the center of the room was covered with food in various states of preparation. Papa sat at the head, drinking a Peroni.

Nonna laid out a plate of antipasto. "Sit. Eat."

When an Italian grandmother tells you to sit and eat, you obey. I picked up a slice of cheese and a slice of pepperoni from the antipasto plate. They were a thousand times fresher and more delicious than anything we got in Twin Willows, except for what we made on our own farm. Nonna sat at the table next to me, a pile of vegetables waiting to be chopped in front of her. "Your mother told us why you were coming," Nonna said.

My eyes widened. I looked from her to Papa and back again. "She did? She told you about . . . about . . ."

"The Benandanti? *Sì.*" Nonna put her hand over mine, but that didn't stop the skittering of my heart. "We all know about the Benandanti here in Cividale. It is the fabric of our town."

Seriously? After all the secrecy I'd been sworn to? It should be the fabric of Twin Willows, but no, we weren't allowed to speak of it there. "That's just . . ." I clenched my jaw. "That's very different from how things are done in my town."

Nonna laughed. "Your town did not have the Inquisition pounding on its doors. When that happens, everyone—" She bit her lip. "What is the saying about the wagons?"

"Circling the wagons?"

"Ah, *sí.* When the Inquisition came, Cividale circled the wagons."

"They say the townspeople changed the signs on the road to head the Inquisitors away from the Olive Grove," Papa said.

"Do you know where it is?"

Nonna shook her head. "We mere mortals do not have access to such things." She smiled and sliced neatly through a red pepper. "Who needs eternal life? Whatever years God chooses to give me are good enough for me."

I gazed over her head at the painting of the Virgin Mary that hung on the wall, looking down at the kitchen in benevolent beauty. Her blue robes—celestial blue, the blue of the Benandanti—shone in the lamplight, her tempera crown bright as the sun. *Whatever years God chooses to give me are good enough for me.* Did I have the wisdom to hold such a belief? The serenity to be content with whatever life handed me?

"Your mother also said that she is seeing someone," Nonna said. I turned my attention back to her. "A man." She winked at me.

I curled my lip.

"What? You do not like him?"

"No, it's not that." I sighed. "He's great. We've known him forever. Maybe that's what makes it so weird."

"Perhaps it would be weird with anyone," Papa said, "besides your father."

I rolled my eyes. "I know, I know."

"Alessia, no one blames you for being upset," Nonna said. "But be patient with your mother. Being a widow is lonely."

As angry as I'd been at Lidia, the instant I'd seen her holding that gun at Pratt, I'd known just exactly how far she'd go to protect me. How far her love for me expanded—into infinity. Mr. Salter wasn't going to steal her away from me, and he wasn't going to replace my dad. No one could. "Okay," I said. "I'll try."

Nerina strode into the kitchen, her high heels heavy on the terra-cotta floor. "It's time to go."

I got to my feet and bent over to hug Nonna. "Thank you," I whispered in her ear. "For having us here, for everything."

"Nonsense." Nonna planted a kiss just above my ear. "This is your home."

Tears stung my eyes as I pulled away from her. She was right. I may not have been here in fifteen years, but this house, this town, felt as much my home as Twin Willows. And more than that, it felt like a refuge. As I moved to leave, Nonna called after me. "Be safe, *cara. In bocca al lupo.*"

I smiled at her and Papa, sitting so calmly at the kitchen table, their hands entwined as if they were teen-age lovers. "*Grazie. In bocca al lupo.*" May the wolf hold you in its mouth.

"*Crepi il lupo,*" Nonna said.

I froze. My blood went cold in my veins. I turned. "What did you say?"

"*Crepi il lupo*," Nonna repeated. "It's the traditional response when someone says *in bocca al lupo*. Didn't you know?"

No, I had never known that. I had never heard the entire exchange; my mother had never taught it to me. Finding my feet again, I followed Nerina out into the chilly night. I mouthed the phrase as we passed under dim streetlights. *Crepi il lupo.*

May the wolf die.

CHAPTER TWENTY-FOUR

Did Anyone Order an Abbess?

Bree

I barely had time to get out of the shower when Nerina poked her head into the room. "Are you ready to go?"

"Do I look ready?" I spread my arms wide, showing off my towel-wrapped body. "Give me five minutes."

"Meet us outside."

The night was pitch-black, no moon, just a smattering of stars, and no city lights to soften the darkness. It was like Twin Willows, but the air here was warmer and gentler. Spring would arrive here a hell of a lot sooner than it would be in Maine.

Nerina and Alessia were already transformed, their auras lighting up the dark like lanterns. I followed them over the hill behind the house. We crested a small ridge, and my breath left my body.

The five members of the Benandanti Clan fanned out in the shallow valley below, and the six other members of the *Concilio Celeste* surrounded them. Nerina lifted into the air and flew down to join them. Alessia kept pace with me, hovering just above my head. *This is a little nerve-racking,* she said. *Meeting them for the first time.*

They won't bite, I said. *They're probably pretty happy you're here to help.*

Or mad I had to come because I got found out.

That would be a little hypocritical of them, considering everyone in this town knows about the Benandanti.

I know, right? Alessia did a fancy loop-the-loop. *It's just like the Italians to make up rules for everyone else that they themselves break.*

We reached the valley basin. Adamo the Phoenix and Cecilia the Pegasus circled in the air with Nerina. On the land were Magdalena the She-Wolf and two huge White Tigers that Nerina introduced as the brothers Gio and Sal. And there, hovering over them all, was . . .

"Jesus," I breathed.

No, just Dario, he answered.

Well, hey . . . the head of the *Concilio* had a sense of humor. I had thought the Malandante Dragon was impressive (and scary as all hell), but Dario blew him out of the water. His scales shimmered red and gold in the darkness, so that he looked like he was on fire. His wings stretched out at least fifteen feet across. He turned his massive head and breathed out a lick of fire. It burst into a ball as bright as the sun, spun for a moment, then extinguished.

Yeah. Good luck to the Malandanti who came up against *that.*

There will be no element of surprise tonight, Dario said. *I am sure they know we are coming. We can only hope that you*—he flicked his tail in my direction—*are all the surprise we need.*

Watch where you point that thing, I said.

I am itching for the Concilio Argento *to be on the other end of it,* he retorted.

I grinned. A Benandante who wasn't afraid to show a little bloodlust. I think I liked him.

Welcome to our visiting Falcon from Twin Willows. Dario dropped lower. *We are honored to have you join us.* He swished his tale, leaving a stream of blue light in its wake. *Let us delay no longer. In bocca al lupo!* In his voice, the words were a battle cry instead of a blessing.

As one unit, we flooded the valley. I was dying to see this Olive Grove that was the "source of all things," as Nerina was so fond of calling it. Dario circled back and hovered over me as I ran alongside the Clan.

Now that I was so close to the site, I could feel my magic opening inside me, and I could feel the Rabbit was there. I could feel that little weasel's presence. My skin itched to meet him in battle again. He was going to pay for what he'd done to my father. I wasn't going to lower myself to his level, but somehow, in some horrible, unspeakable way, he'd pay.

Don't. You are better than that.

I jerked my head up. Dario pumped his wings to climb the air. I was pretty sure I'd had my mind closed . . . but maybe Dario was so anciently powerful that there weren't any barriers he couldn't get through.

I will tell you a secret, Bree, maybe something that Nerina has never told you during your training. What brought down all the previous mages—what proved to be their ruin—was revenge. Dario swished his tail. *Their need for that became greater than their need to protect the seven sites. Do not fall into the same trap.* He flew ahead, catching up with Nerina, their two brilliant halos meshing together as one.

He was right, Nerina hadn't told me that in my training. And it might've been handy to know. Yet another thing to put on the list of Things Nerina Should've Shared.

The Benandanti auras in front of me brightened as the night deepened around us. It was like the freaking circus coming to town. There was no way the Malandanti wouldn't see us coming. I jogged to keep up, my breath coming in little white puffs just beyond my nose. Dario's words swam in my head. I could see his point, but it was also really hard to not want revenge on the asshole who made me kill my dad.

Silver lightning fractured the sky, searing the ground in front of us. The Malandanti burst into view, surrounding us. Up close, their *Concilio* was a scary-ass army of demonic creatures, a mix of Hellhounds that was like a comic book nerd's worst nightmare. I pulled myself out of time and space, popped from inside the circle of Malandanti to outside, and found myself in the shadow of olive trees. These weren't the sacred ones—that site was deeper into the grove—but these at least provided some cover while I assessed what to do.

Dario and the Malandante Dragon screamed at each other, their fire meeting in the air like swords. I whirled out of the way just before a jet of flames blew past me. My eyes watered. I dodged behind a tree, trying to get a good vantage point. There were twelve of them plus the Rabbit, wherever he was, and there were fourteen of us. Plus me. No way were we losing this today. Not on my watch.

As the Benandanti fanned out on the offensive, the Malandanti broke ranks and their circle collapsed. The Harpy tore through the air, heading straight for Nerina. I raised my hands to blast her away, but out of thin air, with the faintest pop, Alessia appeared right in her path. *Ha!* I congratulated myself on finally teaching Alessia that trick.

Before the Harpy could even turn, Alessia latched onto her haunches with her talons. The Harpy yelled, trying to pull away, but Alessia held fast. The Harpy snapped her long beak at Alessia, so close I thought she'd get bitten in half.

Bree! What are you doing? Nerina flashed by me, her claws outstretched as she galloped right for the Harpy. *This isn't a show!*

Oh, right. I was here to do a job, not watch everyone else do theirs.

Making sure I was cloaked in shadows, I stepped out

from behind the tree. I couldn't see the Rabbit, but I knew he was there; I could sense him like a bloodhound senses a fox. He and I were locked by some weird, twisted connection, and it would only break when one of us was dead.

I moved through the battle, unseen by the warriors. Something inside me had risen above the fray, and the magic moved through me by instinct. I had come to the place where I no longer had to work at it. The magic was just there, always inside me, always ready.

With one wave of my hand, I blasted two of the Malandanti out of time and space. The Dragon shot fire at me as I passed beneath him, but I turned it to water with a flick of my fingers. The water poured down on another Malandante with enough force to knock it out. The Dragon chased me down but Dario blocked his path, beating the black Dragon back with his own fire.

I had never felt this powerful. The Olive Grove, the birthplace of the Benandanti, was feeding me. It was like that Tudor house inside me had opened up and become the whole world. I raised my hand, staring in wonder at my white fingers. Jesus, I was magnificent.

An ungodly shriek made me turn. Nerina and Alessia had brought the Harpy down and had her on the ground. One of her wings tilted at an odd angle. I drifted away. They didn't need my help. Who did? I closed my eyes and sensed fear just to the right of me. Without even opening my eyes, I sent a blast of Pakistani magic. When I looked, I saw one of the Benandanti racing away toward the heart of the Grove.

I followed, drawn to the deep root of the power that surged through me, pulled by the fraught, electric thread that connected the Rabbit and me. That was where he was, I was sure of it. Glancing back at the battle, I saw that the Benandanti had the upper hand. Four of the *Concilio Argento* were still fighting, and the rest of the Malandanti Friuli Clan was nowhere to be seen.

Friuli Clan, follow me, I ordered. They were the only ones I needed for the spell to work, to reclaim the site. We fled through the trees, pounding the earth with our need to get to the center of this entire war, to the place where it had all begun. I felt that source of ancient magic flow up through the ground and into my veins. My breath slowed even though I was running. God, it was too powerful, it was taking me over. I couldn't contain it . . . I was going to break apart.

"Holy shit," I breathed, and then I was something else, something beyond me, something a hundred million times better than Bree.

The silvery bubble of the Malandanti's magic loomed around the site in front of us. My Clan fanned out around its perimeter, facing off against the two Malandanti who were inside, crouched at the base of the twisted trunk. I knew they wouldn't leave willingly; I was going to have to bring down the barrier in order for us to get inside. And there, through the murky gray magic, I spied the Rabbit. He was waiting for us. For me.

My lip curled. "Come and get me," I whispered.

I was standing on ancient ground, the roots of the

trees far deeper than grass and dirt. It ran into the soul of the earth. I could feel its power creep up from beneath my feet and twine itself into my bones. I was one with this magic. I *was* this magic.

From across the barrier, I saw the Rabbit raise his arms. The magic inside me reached out in all directions. I knew what he was going to do before he did it, maybe even before *he* knew he was going to do it. With one exhalation, I breathed his spell away. He threw spell after spell at me as I moved toward him, but each one I flicked off as though it were a fly I was shooing away.

Behind me, the rest of the Benandanti were fighting off the other Malandanti who had come to join their Clanmates inside the barrier. I rolled a wave of my power into them, surging their auras with a blast that sent the Malandanti reeling. Each spell I cast seemed to feed me, rather than drain me like it usually had. God, I felt like I could fly, like all I had to do was lift my arms to the sky and I would fly . . .

The Rabbit rushed at me, his feet stumbling over one another. And I realized the magic wasn't flowing through him like it was through me. For whatever reason—maybe because he was a total asshole—he couldn't access it like I could. My mouth broke into a full-on grin. Oh, yeah. I was going to make him my bitch and get the Malandanti the hell out of our Olive Grove.

I pushed my hand through the air, pushed my magic toward him, and with a loud pop, a little green halo appeared above his head. *Get on your knees,* I thought, and he obeyed. I didn't even need to speak; my power broke down any taboos that might have been left between the Malandanti and us. *Kiss the ground,* I told him, and he bent forward until his forehead touched the ground. *Stay there.*

With the Rabbit out of the way, I turned my focus to the barrier surrounding the Grove. Their magic was strong; I could feel its pulse deeper and deeper the closer I got. I reached out to touch the glowing silvery dome, and it shocked me even before my fingers met it.

Okay, so it wouldn't go down easy. But neither would I.

Snarls and growls and yelps filled the air as the two Friuli Clans battled each other, but I tuned it all out. I pulled out every strand of magic from each of the sites, weaving them together to create a weapon powerful enough to break through the barrier. The sounds of the battle around me grew louder and louder, sharpened to a point where I could no longer ignore it. A Benandante Wolf flashed past me, blood streaming down its mottled brown coat, a Malandante Cougar hot on its tail. If I didn't destroy their magic soon, we would lose.

I raised my arms, and the weapon I created lifted into the air, a multicolored arrow made of light. I drew it back, as though I had a bow to shoot it out of, but just as I was about to let go, something blasted me off my feet.

"You just don't get it, do you, you little bitch?" The Rabbit stalked toward me, magic pouring out of his hands. "You can take down Tibet, and you can even take down this site, but the Malandanti will always win. We have power you cannot even imagine."

Seriously? He thought knocking me on my ass was going to get him a win? Fuck this guy. I pulled myself back up to standing and stomped my foot. The earth beneath us shook, and cracks of light shot out in all directions. The Rabbit stumbled backward, his magic stunted. I came at him, my body lit from within. The power of the Olive Grove lifted me off the ground, bore me aloft on the invisible backs of all the Benandanti who had come before me. The Rabbit stared up at me as I hovered above him, his cloak of shadows gone, his weaselly little face pinched with shock. *You have no idea what true power is, you fool,* I thought.

The Rabbit pressed his hands over his ears; he'd heard me. There was no barrier I couldn't cross, no taboo I couldn't smash. I was beyond anything he'd ever encountered. I was so full of magic that my body felt like it had expanded all the way to Switzerland. But it was totally different from when I'd first felt it, that day in study hall when I'd made people bend to my will. There was so much goodness in this magic, so much strength. And I realized . . . the more good I did with this power, the more powerful I became. What the Rabbit did with the magic, wielding it for bad, weakened him.

I reached up and my fingers grazed the weapon I'd fashioned. *Get ready,* I told the Friuli Clan. My voice sounded like someone else's, the voice of someone maybe one day I'd become. I arched back and, with every ounce of my being, shot the arrow into the heart of the Malandanti's barrier.

The magic screamed in my ear as it went down. I watched it sizzle and fizz like a fire desperately trying to stay lit. One extra push of the Redwoods magic from me, and it went out with a last gasp.

The Benandanti rushed in to take down the last remaining Malandanti. I drifted back to earth. They didn't need me to retake the site; that spell belonged to the Clan alone. My feet hit the ground just as the sky illuminated into brilliant, beautiful Benandanti blue. It was done. The Olive Grove was ours again.

Breath found its way back into my body. The magic was still all around and inside me, yellow and green and red smoke flooding in and out of my pores like sweat. I heard dim cheers in my head . . . the Benandanti Clan and the *Concilio Celeste* celebrating . . . but the magic was so loud that it drowned everything else out.

"You think you're pretty clever, don't you?"

I blinked. The Rabbit stood over me, his cloak gone, just him and his stupid tweed jacket. *Actually, yeah, I think I am.*

Words were still beyond me, the magic still so strong. But the Rabbit's jaw tightened. He'd heard me; I was sure of it.

"How the hell are you doing that?"

How are you not?

"You little cu—"

You can't even access this magic, can you?

"Shut up!" And then he slammed his fist against my jaw.

So freaking typical, a guy resorting to violence when a woman uses words he doesn't want to hear. Problem was, being punched in the face really hurt. I fell back, pain ricocheting across my skull. The Rabbit reached down and grabbed my sweater, dragged me up, propelled his arm back for another blow . . .

A jet of fire shot right past his ear, so close I smelled singed hair. He dropped me. I scrambled backward as a huge shadow loomed over me. Dario lowered his wings around me, opened his jaws, and breathed another lick of flames at the Rabbit. And like his stupid code name, the Rabbit turned tail and ran, disappearing into the darkness beyond the Olive Grove.

Get on, Dario said, dropping low so that I could climb onto his back.

I could've handled him myself.

Oh, I know that. I was just worried you'd give him something worse than fire.

I held on to the little ridge at the base of Dario's neck and smiled. He lifted into the air, and it hit me: *I was riding a freaking dragon.* I wondered if I could put that under Special Skills on my future résumé.

You were magnificent back there, Bree. We could not have retaken this site without you.

A snippy retort formed in my mind, but I let it go. *Thanks.*

Dario winged back into the valley where we'd all met up before the battle. Below us, I spotted a dozen figures, their auras streaming around them like cloaks made of stars. I could feel Nerina and Alessia nearby. I could feel all of them: the Friuli Clan guarding the now-regained site, the rest of the *Concilio Celeste* racing back to safety, the Twin Willows Clan all the way back in Maine, the Redwoods, the Congo, Angel Falls, Pakistan, the Snow Leopards of Tibet. I felt them all inside me, my soul as expanded as it had been when I'd been working the magic. *There's something here,* I said to Dario. *Something more powerful than anything I've ever encountered.*

It's not the site, Bree. It's you.

What do you mean?

The hillside rose before us and Dario landed gently on its crest. The rest of the Benandanti gathered around us. I lay forward on his neck because I didn't want my Dragon ride to be over quite yet, but also because I didn't know if I had the strength to stand up by myself.

I wasn't sure I would see this in all my many lifetimes, Dario said. He'd opened his thoughts to everyone else, and I could feel them all listening with hushed attention. *I had almost given up hope.*

See what?

Dario raised his wings so they fanned around me. I was caught in the middle of his aura, surrounded by celestial light. I held my hand in front of my face. No. It wasn't his aura that enveloped me—it was my own. Somehow, even though I could not separate my soul from my body,

I had grown my own aura. *What's happening to me?*

Wind scattered over the hill. A faint line of gray appeared on the horizon. *You've crossed over. You've moved beyond the place of the mages to the place where the magic of all the sites joins. You have become . . .*

I held my breath.

. . . the Abbess.

CHAPTER TWENTY-FIVE
Fine, I Get It, Soft Doesn't Necessarily Mean Weak

Bree

"What the hell is the Abbess?"

I paced the length of the rug in Alessia's grandparents' living room. The Clan and the rest of the *Concilio* had scattered to safety while Nerina, Dario, and I had headed back to the house. It was the wee hours of the morning, but my body buzzed with energy and restlessness. Remnants of magic still curled around me, wisps of multicolored smoke rising off me like steam.

"The origins of the Benandanti are shrouded in mystery," Dario said from the tall, throne-like chair beside the couch. "But it's believed that the magic was discovered in the days of ancient Rome and that the goddess Diana created the Benandanti to protect the gods."

"Diana?" Alessia piped up from her seat on the couch next to Nerina. "Like, the goddess of the hunt?"

"But that's myth." I paused long enough to stare down at Dario. "I mean, the gods and goddesses were things that people made up to explain their world."

"Oh, ye of little faith." Dario smiled and stroked his trim little beard. It was hard to reconcile this neat, skinny guy with that massive Dragon. In human form, he looked like someone who spent his days taking notes in museums. "The gods and goddesses of ancient cultures were real. *Are* real."

"Come on. You can't tell me Diana is still hanging around Mount Olympus."

"The gods are as real as we choose to make them, Bree." He peered at me over the top of his round, owl-eye glasses. "Think about the magic. That's as real to you as anything, isn't it?"

"Yes, but—"

"And that magic had to come from somewhere." Dario's eyes crinkled, showing fine lines at the edges, the only outward sign of his age. "Why not from a powerful Roman goddess?"

The information was crowding into my brain like passengers onto a train during Tokyo rush hour. I pinched my forehead. "Okay, but you're still not telling me what the Abbess is."

"Eventually, the Benandanti turned away from Diana and to Christ." Dario rested his elbows on his knees, his chin in his hands. I knew he was like five centuries old, but he looked like he'd never lost his curiosity in all that time. He still had a childlike wonder at the world. How had he kept it all those long years, through everything he must have seen? And how had I lost it after only sixteen years? Oh, ye of little faith, indeed. "Diana retreated. But she dispersed her power amongst the seven sites. And only a mage who truly connects to each site's magic can awaken that power."

I locked eyes with him. "When I was in Tibet," I said, measuring my words, "the Rabbit had rigged some sort of brazier to pour out the spell to turn all those people into Malandanti." I hugged myself, shivering with the memory. "I stopped the spell by spilling whatever was inside that brazier out. But something . . . else happened."

Nerina sucked in a breath. "Why didn't you tell me this?"

I put my hand on my hip and looked at her. "Oh, like you've never kept anything from me?"

Red bloomed in her cheeks, and she sank into the couch cushions. I turned back to Dario. "So, did I awaken Diana's magic in Tibet?"

He shook his head. "No. But I believe that was the first step. The Tibetan magic is unique in that it is the source of our ability. I believe it wasn't until tonight—until you set foot in the Olive Grove, the magic that binds all the magic into one—that her power came alive inside you." He looked like a little elf who'd just played a clever trick and gotten away with it. "The Benandanti call the one who awakens Diana's power the Abbess. There hasn't been one since the generation before I was Called." He clapped his hands together. "And now we have one! The Malandanti have no idea what they're up against."

"Well . . ." I ran my hand through my hair. "I think

they kinda do. The Rabbit saw me with that power. He might be an asshole, but he's not an idiot. He's gonna figure it out."

"But he might not be able to figure out how to fight it," Dario said. "And any advantage we can gain, I'll take."

Twenty-four hours later, we were back in Twin Willows. It really wasn't fair. The only sightseeing I'd gotten to do was that dumb church Alessia had made us stop at. I'd been in the land of luxury goods, and the only shopping I'd done was for postcards at the airport. But Dario wanted us back in position in case Angel Falls was reclaimed. Angel Falls and the Waterfall were the two sites that remained under Malandanti control. No one could deny that things were coming to a head. I could feel it in my blood and bones. Then again, I felt everything in my blood and bones these days. The magic was awake in me all the time. It made me feel strong and powerful. It also made it really hard to sleep.

Which is why I found myself pacing the perimeter of Jenny's house in the middle of the night, reinforcing pieces of the protection spell that had become frayed. If Pratt found out this was where Alessia was, she was dead meat. We were all dead meat.

Cold starlight flickered down, reflecting on the few patches of snow that still remained. Most of Jenny's yard was brown grass and earth, but it still gave me hope that spring would someday, finally, come to this frozen corner of the planet. Yet another reason it would've been nice to stay in Italy a few extra days. It was *warm* there.

Behind me, a twig snapped and footsteps crunched on the hard ground. I turned, not surprised to see Cal. He'd been wearing his puppy dog face since we'd gotten back . . . actually since before that. Since we kissed in the kitchen. Which we hadn't really talked about. I'd let it happen, and then I pretended it hadn't.

"I thought you might want some company," he said. "And cocoa." He held out a tin cup with a few big fluffy marshmallows floating on top.

"I'm almost done." I started pacing again. Undeterred, he fell into step with me.

I took the cocoa from his hand but didn't look at him.

"So, uh, Nerina mentioned something about . . ."

"Ah." Now I did look at him, a wry smile twisting my lips. "You are looking at a bona fide Abbess here, mister."

Cal whistled low. "That's pretty . . . ah . . . okay, fine. What the hell is an Abbess?"

I laughed. Everyone else—Nerina, Heath, and Alessia, who I could tell was a little miffed I'd once again stolen her thunder—was acting like it was some great big honor, like something I'd actually nominated myself for. "I guess I unlocked some magic that's hard to unlock or something. No biggie."

"Well, it sounds like a biggie." Cal looked sideways at me and grinned. "It also sounds like you really want to stop talking about how biggie it is."

I took a sip of the cocoa and let my eyes dance at him over the rim of the cup. Exactly. Maybe I didn't give Cal enough credit. Maybe we *should* talk about that kitchen kiss.

"Tell me about Italy," he said before I could say anything. "Tell me about the Olive Grove."

"You probably got to see a lot more of Italy than I did when you were there," I said. "But the Olive Grove . . ." I trailed off. For once, I had no sarcastic quip. I couldn't deny that I'd been changed there . . . and that this new, deeper Bree was someone who maybe didn't have to bite and snarl so much. "The Olive Grove is amazing," I whispered. "It really is the source of all things. You can feel it inside you even before you get there."

Cal met my gaze, his eyes golden puddles of warmth that sparked my insides. His look was so soft, softer than any look a guy had given me for a long time. If ever. I wasn't really known for choosing guys who could be soft. "Bree . . ." he murmured, and he made my name sound like a prayer. He took one step toward me.

I took one step back and held up my hand. "You need to know something about me." How come I could pour out magic without any fear but I couldn't talk to this kind, good guy without my voice shaking? When had *I* been the one to go soft? "I'm not nice. And I don't stay. It used to just be my family who moved around. But now it's me. I get restless, and I move on."

"Bree," he said again, and I realized it wasn't that

I'd gone soft. It was that the magic hadn't just awakened power inside me. It had awakened possibility. Possibility in all things . . . like maybe it was possible that this time, I wouldn't run. "Why don't we just relax? I'm not asking you to marry me."

I stared at him and started to laugh. Of course he wasn't. When had I started taking things so seriously? I wasn't *Alessia*, for Chrissakes. I was still laughing when Cal took my face in his hands and kissed me, capturing my laughter on his tongue. The cold Maine night fell away, leaving me only with the heat of his mouth on mine and the fire that ignited in my belly.

Cal pulled away for a moment and searched my face. "I might not be asking you to marry me, but I still think you're the most incredible woman I've ever met. I doubt there are a lot of men out there who deserve you. All I hope is that I might be one of them."

Coming from any other guy, it would've been a line, but somehow I knew that from him, it wasn't. I dragged him back to me, tasting sweet and spice and cold on his tongue. We stumbled our way to the back porch, found a dry spot beneath the eaves, and made out hardcore for a long time. He was so comfortable to be with; he made it easy to forget all the crap that was going on all around us. It wasn't until sunlight began to streak the deck that we came up for air. "We should probably go back in," Cal said, snuggling me back against his chest.

"Probably," I agreed, but neither of us made a move

to get up. We watched the sun rise above the horizon, turning the sky pink and gold and blue. The colors were brighter than I'd ever seen them. Cal nuzzled my neck. I put my hand on the back of his head, my fingers tangling in his thick golden hair.

After several more minutes, he pulled away, his breath ragged. "Okay, now we really should go in. Before they send someone out to find us."

I sighed and stood up. "Yeah, you're right." We held hands all the way back around the house, only breaking apart as we walked through the front door. I skidded to a stop in the living room, where Nerina was with the entire Clan.

"There you two are," she said, and by the once-over she gave both of us, I could tell she knew *exactly* what we'd been up to.

I pressed my cold hands to my flushed cheeks. With forced nonchalance, I leaned against the couch. "I was just reinforcing the protection spell. What's going on?"

Nerina held up her phone. "I just got off the phone with Dario. Last night we regained Angel Falls."

Cheers erupted from everyone, excited questions about how it had happened, what was next. But I didn't need to ask what was next. I swallowed hard and searched the room until I found Alessia's gaze. She wasn't smiling or cheering either.

The war *was* coming to a head, and the final battle would be fought on our turf.

The Waterfall was the last stand.

CHAPTER TWENTY-SIX
The Legacy

Alessia

"Dario has sent out the word to all the Clans," Nerina continued when everyone had quieted down. "Whoever can be spared from each site will come here, along with the entire *Concilio*."

"Hang on," Bree said, "won't that leave the other sites exposed to a Malandanti takeover?"

"As long as one Benandante is inside the barrier, they cannot break through. Not without the Rabbit, who will surely be here." Nerina's gaze swept over each of us. "Everyone will be arriving sometime today. When they do, we will go in."

A heated conversation began about where everyone would stay, who we could trust to put them up, how we were going to hide an influx of "foreign tourists" into Twin Willows from the rest of the town's residents. I peeled myself up from the couch and ducked around the back of it. When I got to Bree, I tugged her into the kitchen.

"What is it?" she asked in a low voice.

"You need to get me to Jonah." It was the only thought in my head, the only thing I could focus on amongst all the swirling bits inside me.

Bree pressed her lips together. She searched my face for a minute. "Okay. But not now. We should wait until tonight."

I ran my hands through my hair. I wanted to go *now*, before anyone could give me a million things to do. But Bree was right. We needed the cover of night. "Thanks, Bree."

"Yeah, well, I'd like to see him too." She grinned at me. "But don't worry, I'll give you two plenty of alone time."

I tugged on my hair, like somehow I could tug all the thoughts out of my mind and stomp on them. *Alone time.* Maybe for the last time ever. Even if we both made it out of the battle alive, we would still be on opposite sides . . . no matter which side won. I dragged my hands from my head to my heart. Would the ache ever go away?

"Come on," Bree said. "They're going to notice we're gone."

"By the way," I said just before we reached the living room, "*I* noticed you and Cal gone this morning."

She grinned, but there was no mirth in it. "Yeah, our timing is *awesome*, isn't it?"

I touched her arm. "It might be the best timing ever. You never know."

There was a ton of activity in the living room. The whole household was up now. I headed for the stairs, but Heath blocked me. "Hey, I want to show you something," he said.

I followed him into the den, and it was only when we were inside that I realized Lidia was right behind me. She shut the door, blocking out the hustle and bustle from the rest of the house. "What's going on?" I asked, my nerves alight as I looked between them.

Heath went to the desk and pulled the chair out. "Sit." My gut flipped over. What had I done now? What kind of lecture were they double-teaming me for? But when I sat, Heath swiveled me toward the desk. On its surface lay the book I had pulled from our basement, the one that had given me away to Pratt. "We read it while you were in Italy." Heath's dark blue eyes were soft on my face. "You should read it, too."

I stared at the book. The moment I touched the pages, it began to glow with cerulean light, like it was lit from within.

I hadn't had any chance to look at the book before I'd been hustled off to Italy, and now I saw how truly ancient it was. The first several pages were made from animal hide and covered in pictures drawn in what looked like red chalk. "What is this?"

"It's from the most ancient civilization known to inhabit Maine," Heath said. "The Red Paint People."

Confused, I turned more pages. The pictures morphed into words and images, a strange language I still couldn't read.

"Algonquin," Heath said before I had to ask. "Spoken by the Passamaquoddy Indians."

Lidia put her hand on my shoulder and squeezed. "This book is a history of all the Benandanti of the Twin Willows Clan. Going back before Europeans ever settled here."

My breath caught. The letters and images on the pages swam before me. This was my history, my legacy. I turned each page like it was the most precious object on earth. The language moved from Algonquin to Spanish and French and finally to English. Names, dates, and short entries like this one:

August 26th, 1794
We were beset upon by the Malandanti when the Moon was directly overhead. I was forced to Call the Clan in its Entire. After a hard-fought Battle, we maintained Control of the site but at the Cost of our own Cougar. The Ritual was performed.

And:

October 21st, 1794
We have replaced the Cougar with the Fox, Ned Jacobs, who is of fine Character and Upbringing. In bocca al lupo.

With tears streaming down my cheeks, I touched the well-aged ink on the creamy parchment. *Ned Jacobs . . .* I looked up. Lidia nodded. "He was your five times great-grandfather."

"Oh," I breathed. "It really is a family tradition."

Lidia leaned over, hugging me tight. "I was such an

idiot," she whispered in my ear, "to think I could ever keep you out of it. It is in your blood." She straightened, cupping my cheek in her warm, calloused hand. "It is in your name."

"My name?"

"I knew from the moment you were born what you would be," Lidia said. Her brown eyes gleamed with tears. "And when I asked your father to name you, I knew that he knew, too."

"Why?"

"Your name, *cara*." She held my face in her hands. "It means 'defender.' You were born to defend the magic, and your father knew it. You have been a Benandante since long before you were even born."

I couldn't speak. Heat trapped itself in my throat, wrapped itself tight around me. I looked down at the book in my hands, worth more than diamonds, rubies, emeralds, or gold. I remembered all those weeks ago in the lair with Heath, flipping through the files we'd stolen from the Guild. *Where are the Benandanti files like this?* I'd asked him. He'd said the Benandanti had never had such files. But he was wrong. The Benandanti just didn't hide their records inside cold glass and steel like the Malandanti; they hid them in the basement of an ancient farmhouse, protected by generations of love.

I flipped to the last page. The last two entries were dated fifteen years ago.

We have lost the Waterfall. More than that, we have lost the Owl and the Hawk. The Ritual was performed. We are searching for their replacements. We are all in mourning. God willing, we will reclaim the Waterfall soon.

And then, one last entry, written in my father's unmistakable hand:

The Hawk has been replaced by the Stag. I know my best friend, Jeff Sands, will devote his life to the Benandanti the same way my father did. They are still searching for the Owl's replacement. If Alessia were old enough, it would be her. But I know someday she will be Called and she will make me—and every Jacobs who came before her—proud.

I have been entrusted with the safety of this book. For now I think it's best to hide it. May the Benandante who finds it continue its history.

I splayed my hand flat on the opposite page, which lay blank and empty. "There were a couple of loose documents tucked inside too," Heath said, "but we're still trying to decipher them."

I reached out and grabbed a tissue from the box at the edge of the desk, blew my nose, and wiped my eyes. "Pull up a chair, both of you." When they were both seated on either side of me, I picked up the fanciest fountain pen I could find in the desk drawer. "Let's pick up where he left off."

And as they told me the last fifteen years' worth of history of the Twin Willows Clan, I recorded it all, so that all the Benandanti who came after me would know our legacy.

Sneaking out of the house wound up not being a problem at all that night. Everyone else was off picking up the various Benandanti who were arriving on all sorts of planes, trains, and automobiles. Jenny was the only one left, and when she saw me and Bree leaving, she said, "I never saw you," and put on her headphones.

The problem turned out to be that because everyone was out, so were all the cars. Bree and I stood in the driveway, staring up its empty expanse. "Crap," I said. "Is there a bus that goes near there?"

"Look up 'the middle of nowhere' in the dictionary," Bree said. "There's a picture of that cabin." She grabbed my arm and directed me around the back of the house. "Come on."

We fought our way through the woods behind the house, coming out on the next street. . . which was the Wolfes' street. A few doors down from Bree's house, we crouched by the side of the road.

"Is your mom home?" I whispered.

"No. I told her to get out of town when we went to Italy. I don't know where; I told her not to tell me."

"Did she leave her car?"

Bree shook her head. A dark sedan rolled down the street, its headlights sweeping across the road. We shrank back into the shadows as it passed. Once it disappeared around the corner, Bree pulled me up. "We gotta hurry. It'll be back again soon."

"But if your mom took her car—" I jogged alongside her. As soon as we got to her driveway, I rounded on her. "Are you kidding? Your dad's car? They'll spot that from a mile away."

"Not if we get out of Twin Willows fast enough." Bree unlocked the front door to her house and rummaged inside in the dark for a minute. When she came out, she dangled a set of keys in front of my nose. "Haven't you ever wanted to ride in a Porsche?"

This had *bad idea* written all over it. But it was either Mr. Wolfe's sleek silver sports car or nothing. I muttered a prayer under my breath and ducked into the passenger seat.

Bree kept the headlights off as she drove the car slowly out of the driveway and down the road. Main Street was empty this time of night, but a rising full moon illuminated the pavement, slick as a mirror. We passed sleeping houses on our way out of town. Once the willow tree that marked the border was in the rearview mirror, Bree flicked on the headlights and gunned the engine.

Several miles up the highway, Bree turned off onto a lonely road that twisted through dark woods. "You sure you know where you're going?" I asked as she made a hairpin turn onto a desolate street with no sign.

"I made Jonah ride shotgun when Mr. Salter took us," she said. "That way, I could sit in the back and map the way with the GPS on my phone without him noticing."

We turned off the paved road and onto a narrow dirt lane. Barren trees rose on either side of us, curving inward so that it almost felt like we were traveling beneath a covered bridge. I could see nothing past the pool of light created by the car's high beams, but after a moment I felt us going down a hill. At last we emerged into a small clearing, in the middle of which sat a cozy log cabin.

The lights in the cabin were off. I jumped out of the car. "Jonah?" I called out. "It's us. It's me and Bree."

Somewhere close by, an owl hooted. Cold wind swept through the clearing, rattling the bare branches overhead. A moment later, the front door creaked open, and a thin beam of light shone out. "Alessia?"

The sound of his voice lit my insides. I ran across the clearing, didn't stop until I collided into him. I couldn't see his face in the dark, but I sensed him all around me, his warmth, spicy pine scent, and his heart, his whole alive heart, beating in time with mine.

Jonah dropped the flashlight he'd been holding and caught me tight in his arms. My feet left the ground. I buried my face into his neck. "Oh, God, Alessia," he muttered, his mouth pressed against my ear, "every night I dreamed you would come."

I half-sobbed, half-laughed. I didn't care how many Benandanti were arriving in Twin Willows at that very instant, how soon it would be before Jonah and I were fighting on opposite sides of the Waterfall's banks. Nothing mattered except him and this moment.

My lips found his, and I tasted winter and the promise of spring on his tongue. He held me to him, devouring me like I was the prey to his Panther. Still kissing me, he backed us up into the cabin. His hands slid up under my coat, his palms like firebrands against my skin. I buried my fingers in his hair, pulling him closer, closer . . .

"Ahem."

We broke apart, our breath heavy. Bree stood in the doorway, holding the flashlight that Jonah had dropped under her chin so that she looked like a campfire ghost. "What am I, chopped liver?"

Jonah cleared his throat. "Hi, Bree."

"'Hi, Bree'? That's all I get?" She shone the flashlight in his face.

He opened his arms, and she went to him and hugged him tight. It was always a jolt to see them together, the beautiful Wolfe twins, so fierce and lovely at the same time.

"How's life off the grid?" Bree said.

"You know, being a hermit isn't all it's cracked up to be." Jonah crossed to the mantel over the fireplace and lit a kerosene lamp, bathing the cabin in a soft yellow glow. Now I could see it was a lot like Heath's cabin, only a little bigger and with two deer heads mounted on opposite walls. Jonah lit another lamp on the table in the tiny kitchen and came back over to me. "It's a little *too* lonely."

He pulled me against him. "God, I missed you."

"Okay, you two are gross." Bree switched off the flashlight and tossed it onto a chair in front of the fireplace. "Let's get our business out of the way so you can be alone to . . . do whatever."

"What business?" Jonah lifted his head but kept his arm around my waist. "And how was Italy?"

"The Benandanti reclaimed the Olive Grove," I said, searching his face as I spoke. "And Angel Falls."

He touched my cheek. "That's good, isn't it?"

"Not for you," Bree said.

"Why not? If the Malandanti fail, I'm free, aren't I?"

I bit my lip. "I don't know. I don't know what happens if one side gains all the sites." I looked at Bree. "Do you?"

"No." She crossed her arms. "But I can't imagine it's good for the losing side." She raised her eyebrow at Jonah. "Have you been Called while you've been here?"

"Of course I have." Jonah's eyes darkened. "I couldn't stop myself from transforming. But I didn't go to the Waterfall. I kept my mind closed off and ran through the woods way north of here, so that if they sensed me it wouldn't lead them to the cabin."

"Well, expect to be Called again soon," Bree said. "The Waterfall is the last site under Malandanti control. Every Benandanti who can be spared is flying in to help reclaim it."

Jonah ran his hand through his hair. "I don't know how much longer I can go on ignoring them. Each time, the Call feels stronger, like I'm being pulled toward the Clan by some invisible force."

Bree's gaze flickered between me and Jonah, something not quite readable behind her green eyes. "You shouldn't ignore the Call this time. You should come to the Waterfall."

"Bree—he'll be killed. By his own side."

"They can't, remember? They can't attack him." She took a long shaky breath. "But if one of our side gets hurt . . . is . . ."

"Don't say it." I held my hand up. "I don't want to think about that."

"We have to, Alessia." Bree tightened her jaw. "It's a big battle. And you can bet your ass that we'll be outnumbered, because all the other Malandanti Clans don't need to be at their sites but at least one Benandante has to stay behind to protect them. You're stupid to think we're all going to get out of this alive."

Cold silence stretched between the three of us. I knew Bree was right, but when I let my mind go there, my body was flooded with an icy fear I couldn't control. Wasn't I allowed one night, one hour, to not think about it all?

That thought must've been clear on my face, because Bree broke the silence by digging into her jeans pocket for the car keys. "Anyway. Consider yourself warned."

"Where are you going?"

"Back to Jenny's." We followed her to the front door. "Alessia, call me when you're ready to be picked up. And . . . be careful."

I rolled my eyes at her. As she jogged back to the car, Jonah called after her, "By the way, don't think for a minute that the Porsche is yours, Bree. We're twins; we share everything."

She flashed him a grin and ducked into the car. A minute later, she disappeared back up the dirt lane and the rumble of the engine faded into the night.

Jonah and I shut the door and stared at each other.

We were alone.

Well and truly alone.

We closed the distance between us in one breath. He lifted me up and I wrapped my legs around his waist, my arms tight around his neck. He carried me to the bed and we tumbled onto it, our bodies connected so that it was hard to tell where he ended and I began. Time slowed down, became luxurious, capturing us inside a snow globe where minutes stretched longer than sixty seconds.

I knew we weren't going to make love; he would make some romantic protest about not deserving me. Besides, I doubted there was a condom anywhere within twenty-five miles. And somehow, the lack of that expectation softened us and sweetened those long minutes. There was only so far we were going to go, and that was fine. In the shadow-lit cabin, it was easy to pretend we would have another chance, more time, a future.

We slipped under the thick quilts and stretched out long. The warmth of him surrounded me like a protective bubble no one could break through. We spoke to each other in whispers, even though no one but the wind and the trees would hear us. Anything louder would break the bubble.

"I just want time to stop," Jonah murmured, his lips at the hollow of my throat. "Stay here forever."

I stroked my fingertips up and down his spine, feeling the goose bumps that rose on his skin. All the forces beyond the cabin that kept us apart dissolved into the warm darkness beneath the quilts. For as long as this moment went on, we were safe. There was nothing that could come between us here.

But there was one force, one thing that would always slam its way in, one thing we could not keep out.

I felt the Call inside him at the same moment I felt it in me. It shuddered through us both, tugging at our hearts. "Oh, God, no," Jonah whispered. He wrapped his arms around me, crushing me against him. I clung to his shoulder, my nails biting into his skin with the effort to keep from shifting. He kissed me hard. Our hearts beat frantically against one another. And in the same breath, we both let go.

I hovered near the ceiling, the Panther below me. And on the bed, our bodies lay silent as death, still entwined in a lovers' kiss.

CHAPTER TWENTY-SEVEN
The Longest Night

Alessia

I'm coming with you, Jonah said. *When you were in Italy, it was easy to ignore the Call. But I can't stay here while you're fighting at the Waterfall. I need to be there to watch out for you.*

I can handle myself, thanks very much.

Oh, I know. Jonah pawed at the doorknob, the door fell open, and we lit out into the night. *But I'm still a gentleman.*

Ha-ha. Somehow joking with him made it easier to wing my way toward the Waterfall, toward what might be our last night on earth.

Alessia! Where the hell are you? Heath's frantic voice broke into my thoughts.

I'm—

Never mind. Get to the farm, to Nerina's lair.

Why there?

Just get here now!

I shut my mind off to him and opened back up to Jonah. *I have to meet them at my farm. I can fly faster—*

—if you're not waiting for me, Jonah finished. *Go.*

I tore off through the trees, my heart still with him below. I watched his silver-haloed figure disappear into the woods. The main road soon appeared, and I followed it back to Twin Willows. I tried not to think about where Jonah was, or what would happen to him when he showed his face to the Malandanti, and veered over the roof of my farmhouse.

I pulled up short.

The hillside beneath me was bathed in blue, alive with light. Benandanti from every Clan swarmed the pasture and beyond, their celestial auras beaming out like the great hope I suddenly felt in my chest. It was the most beautiful thing I'd ever seen, so many strong, determined Benandanti in one place, come to fight the last battle in the long, good fight. I dove to join them, and five other winged Benandanti joined me in the air. Eagles, Hawks, another Falcon, and an Owl, the same shape my grandmother had taken.

Lions, Lynxes, Foxes, Wolves, more than one Stag, the Snow Leopards of Tibet that Bree had told me about, and the *Concilio.* The twin White Tigers, Sal and Gio, crowded in next to the Leopards. Adamo the Phoenix joined us in the air. And above us all, Dario, the enormous red-and-gold Dragon, his tail dripping blue light each time it swished.

I swerved through all the figures, searching for my Clan, for Bree. I found them at the front of the crowd, next to the stone wall, where Bree was opening the trap door that led down into Nerina's lair. *What are we doing here?* I asked Heath the moment I spotted him.

Finally! Where were you?

Does it really matter? What are we doing here? I repeated.

He twisted his neck to look up at me. *We deciphered those pages we found in the Twin Willows book. They were coded blueprints for the lair.*

So?

So one of them showed a secret passage. Your grandparents must've built it and then died before they told anyone. Heath pawed at the ground, his whole body tense. *A secret passage that leads directly from the lair to the Waterfall.*

I spun upward, my gaze fanned out over the Benandante-covered hill to the farmhouse beyond. It was my grandparents' last gift, like they'd known someday their granddaughter would be fighting the war for them. A secret passage, a surprise attack, an upper hand that we so desperately needed.

Bree disappeared down into the lair. Dario hovered above the stone wall and faced his army. *We'll head into the passage two by two. Just like Noah. I want the Twin Willows Clan at the front. They will not be surprised to see you . . . but hopefully what comes behind will surprise the hell out of them.*

Cora dropped in next to me, and together we fluttered into the lair. It had been untouched since that day Nerina had been taken, the chairs still overturned, the cushions still spilling their guts out, the fancy espresso machine in the kitchen still smashed. We followed Bree to the back of the lair and watched as she felt along the bottom edge of the wall.

"There," she breathed, and pushed hard.

Like she'd just said *Open Sesame*, the outline of a door appeared and began to creak slowly, painfully, open. Bree peered down the passageway, looked back at us, and shrugged. "I just hope there aren't any snakes," she said and headed into it.

We came right after her, keeping close to each other. The passage was narrow; we wouldn't have been able to come in any way *but* two by two. The walls and floor were earthen, and twisted tree roots sprung out on all sides. I glanced behind me. Heath and Cal were right on our tail, Jeff and Nerina just beyond them.

The ground began to rise up, up, up, the tree roots thinning out. We hit a dead end, but Bree climbed up three footholds in the dirt wall and pushed at a stone in the ceiling. A trapdoor opened and moonlight beamed down, bathing Bree in white light. "I think we're at the top of the stream," she whispered. "Someone with wings should go first, in case there's a Malandante close by."

I surged forward, Cora at my tail. A string of fear threaded through me—this was it!—but I wasn't going to let it slow me down. This *was* it, and it only seemed right that I was on the front line.

We soared out of the confines of the tunnel, just

above the rocks where I used to sit with my father. The air was so clear I could taste the stars. Inside the Malandanti barrier, the Raven rose, his wings beating with frantic, jerky movement. I barreled toward him, but stopped short of the mottled silver dome that surrounded the site. We stared at each other through the magic, my body rigid with the urge to strike, bite, claw . . . whatever I had to do to take him down.

But he could not leave the barrier and I could not go in. We were trapped there, each of us itching for revenge.

The rest of the Twin Willows Clan fanned out around the Waterfall. The Raven tore his beady gaze away from me and dove toward the water. An instant later, hordes of Malandanti poured out of the woods; that's where they'd been waiting for us, expecting us to come in through the birch trees. A mass of silver auras tumbled out of the brush; every Malandanti Clan had been Called to Maine to defend their last remaining holdout.

I could almost hear their laughter as they faced off against the six of us. I imagined the words flying through all their brains right now. *Stupid Benandanti thought that having right on their side was enough to overtake all of us.* Snarling and snapping, the Malandanti closed in.

The ground beneath the stream rattled and shook. As the Malandanti pounced, Dario burst out of the tunnel, spraying fire at the first line of Malandanti. Yowls and screeches echoed across the water as they fell back. The *Concilio Celeste* tumbled out behind the Dragon, the

Phoenix showering sparks, the White Tigers diving into the fray, the Pegasus lighting up the dark, and the She-Wolf leaping for the closest Malandante, her jaws gaping.

But the element of surprise lasted only so long. As the rest of the Benandanti flooded into the open, the Malandanti seemed to find their footing. From my high vantage point, I spotted those mangy Wild Dogs from the Congo, spreading out in their familiar circular pattern. *The Dogs are surrounding the site,* I said. *Watch out if you try to leave the perimeter.*

A black Malandante Hawk collided into me, knocking me sideways. I faced off against it, our auras crackling blue and silver as we circled each other. The Hawk struck out with its talons, catching me on my leg. I kicked out and snagged my claws across its back. Screaming, it surged at me, but I spiraled up. The Hawk climbed behind me, its beak snapping. When I reached the tree-tops, I dove, whizzing past the Hawk so fast it spun in the air. With a cry, it plunged after me. But nothing can catch a Falcon on a dive.

I pulled up fast, too fast for the Hawk, and it slammed into a Malandante Vulture. Thinking it was being attacked by the enemy, the Vulture knocked the Hawk away with one swish of its massive wing. The instant it realized its mistake, the Vulture craned its long neck and launched toward me. Its wingspan blotted out the moon as I dodged this way and that, trying to shake it off my tail.

Adamo appeared to my right, his fiery feathers a beacon in the dark. *On the count of three, we turn and fight,* he said. *The Vulture won't be expecting that. Bene?*

Bene, I answered.

Uno.

We veered around a barren oak tree. Was that a bud on one of its branches? Was spring dawning at last?

Due.

Over the tip of a pine, its needles brown and drooping from winter fatigue, the Vulture's wings beat so hard I could feel its gusts of wind. We dropped lower, and the Vulture followed.

Tre.

Like it was a dance we had choreographed, we spun at the same time and buffeted toward the Vulture. The enormous bird halted in midair, thrown sideways as Adamo went high and I went low. It didn't know which one of us to attack first . . . I latched my claws into its belly while Adamo fixed his beak on the back of its neck. Together we dragged the Vulture down, down. It twisted and screamed in our grasp, trying to free itself, but I pressed my claws in deeper.

The second before we hit the ground, I let go. The Vulture smashed into a fallen log. I pounced onto one of its wings, hard enough that I felt the bone snap. Adamo sliced his talon across the Vulture's back. We rose, and it did not follow. It just lay there on its side, its broken wing sticking up at an angle that made me cringe. I knew we

351

hadn't killed it, but it would have to return to its human body in order to survive.

With a *good job* nod, Adamo veered away. I plunged through the brush, keeping low so I could catch anyone who needed my help. As I rounded the birch trees, I spotted a telltale silver glow within their copse, but even before I reached him, I felt him in my mind. *Jonah?*

He jerked his head up. *Thank God. You okay?*

Yeah. What are you—?

A ball of silver crashed into me, saliva-dripping jaws snapping at me, huge paws swiping, grasping . . . Jonah was yelling in my head, but I couldn't take the time to answer as I scrambled out of the Lion's reach. I flew up, but the Lion gathered its back legs and sprang so high it might as well have had wings. Jonah raced out of the birch copse, streaking in front of the Lion, who swerved to avoid a collision. In that moment, I mounted the air, well out of the Lion's range.

I kept my eyes on the flash of silver that I knew was Jonah. He positioned himself between two Wild Dogs at the perimeter of the site. *Anyone needing to get outside the perimeter,* I told the Clans, *head for the northwest section. There's a Malandante Panther there who will let you through.*

How the hell do you know that? Sal shot back at me.

She's right, Heath said. *We can trust that Panther.*

I circled high above the Waterfall, picking out pieces of the battle below. Nerina and the Harpy fought in the center of the stream, their auras sizzling each time they clashed. Earth and sky were separated into two battle-fields, each element flooded with blue and silver light that flickered and charged the air with electricity. I saw two Benandanti head northwest out of the site. When they reached Jonah, he padded backward, bowing a little as they passed. *Who is that Panther?* one of them said, but they disappeared into the brush before I could answer.

Besides, I didn't think now was the right time to go into the details of my complicated love life.

The two Benandanti Jonah let pass reappeared from beneath bushes and low trees, and I saw now what they were doing: attacking the Wild Dogs from behind, while the Dogs were expecting all the Benandanti to come from the front. It was brilliant. I dropped low in the air and found Heath, fighting his way past a Malandante Cougar. Before the Cougar even knew I was there, I scratched it across the face. It yowled and fell back.

Some of the Benandanti are using Jonah's passageway to attack the Dogs from behind, I told him.

Let's go.

His sleek white form raced below me as we dashed to the northwest corner. Jonah moved aside as we came through, his jewel-green eyes wide when he saw me.

Thank you, I said. *For—*

Don't. It's the only thing I can do that doesn't make me hate myself. He reared up, his aura shimmering around him like a shiver. *Be careful.*

Smoky silver light leaked through the woods as we

approached the closest Dog from behind. It whirled just as Heath pounced and pinned it down. I went for its eyes, clawing at them while the Dog thrashed and yelped, making such a commotion that we didn't see the other three Dogs coming.

They were on us in less than the blink of an eye. Pain seared across me as sharp teeth ripped feathers out of my body, tore into my flesh beneath. I screamed, and the sound of my own fear hurt my ears. The stars blacked out above me. I fought wildly, striking out with everything I had, but the Dogs were too much, too many. Once they had their teeth sunk in, they wouldn't let go.

With a roar of effort, Heath shook one of the Dogs off and charged at the one holding me. Taken by surprise, the Dog lost hold of me. Breath flooded back into my body, and the pain ebbed away. I soared up, just out of reach, and gathered myself to dive back in to help Heath. After all, nothing was faster than a Falcon on a dive . . .

. . . Except three Wild Dogs intent on killing my Guide.

His brilliant white fur disappeared in a sea of yellow-and-black spots. I tried to fight my way in, but one of the Dogs struck me away at every attempt. They had their prey . . . they would not let go until he was destroyed. *Heath? Heath!*

The only answer was the sound of pain echoing across my mind.

Help! I cried out to all the Benandanti. *I need help, southwest corner!*

A breath later, Cora, Adamo, and the Snow Leopards of Tibet were by my side. *It's Heath. The Dogs have him.*

En masse, we plunged in. The Snow Leopards, so ethereal to look at, were fiercer than their beauty let on. Within seconds, they dragged the three Dogs off Heath. Adamo, Cora, and I separated to face each Dog, helping the Snow Leopards subdue them. When they lay still, I flew back to Heath and landed on the ground beside him with a heavy thud.

His fur was muddied red, smeared with so much blood that you couldn't tell it had once been white. Three long wounds gaped open from his throat to his belly. I pressed in close to his chest, listening, feeling. A heartbeat was there, so quiet and erratic that several times within one breath I thought it had stopped. *You're going to be all right,* I told him. Opening my mind outward, I shouted for Bree.

Half a second later, she appeared with a pop of magic and fell to her knees beside me. "Oh, Jesus," she breathed, her hands shaking as she hovered them above Heath's wounds.

You can save him, right? Like you saved me with the Redwood magic?

She swallowed hard. Her face was stained with dirt and grass, but her skin glowed with the power inside her. Yellow smoke seeped out from her fingers and swirled around Heath. After a moment, Bree looked at me. "I can't, Alessia. He's too far gone."

No! You can do it, I know you can. You're the Abbess— you can fix anything.

Her eyelashes dripped with tears. *Not this,* she said, as though using her mind instead of her voice would soften the blow. *There are limits even to my power.*

You have to.

It will . . . be . . . okay.

We jerked our heads down to look at Heath. His voice felt so far away in my mind, like he was already halfway to the world beyond this one.

We'll get you back to your body, I said. *And then Bree can heal you.*

It's too late. His words faded and then flared to life again. *I'll be . . . gone.*

God, it was the Lynx all over again, only a thousand times worse. I became aware of the Snow Leopards surrounding us, of Cora and Adamo fluttering just over my head. *No,* I said, refusing to accept what was right in front of my eyes. *No.*

And then, into that cavernous space of grief that was forming inside me, Heath spoke again.

Get . . . Jonah.

What?

Get Jonah. His voice strengthened, like there was still one last fight in him.

Bree jerked back and faced me, her eyes wide, her face pale beneath the streaks of dirt and mud and magic. "Get him. Now."

The truth of what they were asking dawned on me like a terrible sunrise. I leaned down low, spread my wings wide so that it was just me and Heath, like it had been in the beginning. *Are you sure this is what you want?*

His tone was stronger, with a note of pleading in it now. *Yes. Without a complete Clan, you cannot retake . . . the Waterfall. This is . . . the last gift I can give to the Benandanti . . . to you. Let me give it.*

Every minute of my life leading up to this one seemed to gather inside me. I hopped back, stuck between the past and the present, unable to move. "Hurry, Alessia," Bree whispered. "I might be able to keep him hanging on a little longer, but you need to hurry."

The two Dragons screamed overhead and flashed past, a reminder that we were still in the middle of a battle. *It's not safe here,* I said. *Can we move him?*

The Snow Leopards padded forward. *We'll move him to the birch trees and protect you while you do the spell.*

I need the entire Twin Willows Clan, Bree said. *Adamo—* Before she finished, he took off in a swirl of firelight.

I couldn't hesitate any longer. As the Snow Leopards hoisted Heath onto their backs, I took off, careening through the trees. I opened my mind to him before I saw him, calling his name over and over.

I'm here, I'm here. What's wrong?

You have to come. It's Heath. He—

I didn't need to say the words. Jonah read it all in my mind. *Why do you need—?*

The spell, I said, and then I saw him, his body tense

as I flew toward him, his ears pricked forward. *The spell to turn a Malandante into a Benandante. Is that truly what you want?* I halted right in front of him, my wings beating hard to keep me aloft.

Jonah rose slightly on his hind legs, high enough that his eyes locked onto mine, their emerald depths plumbing my own. *If Heath dies, it will leave your Clan incomplete. You won't be able to retake the Waterfall. You won't be able to win.*

Yes.

Then that is what I want, he said, *because I want to see the Malandanti destroyed.*

Come with me. I turned tail and flew back through the woods at breakneck speed, Jonah's strong, dark figure racing beneath me. We burst into the copse of birch trees with a crash and slammed to a halt.

The Twin Willows Clan huddled within the shimmery tree trunks. I could feel their grief in my mind, in every vein of my being. Heath lay in the center of them. His broken body, once so full of strength, looked small and frail. Nerina was curled beside him. Their heads bent together, a conversation in their minds that the rest of us could not—should not—hear.

I couldn't imagine what that was like, having only minutes left to tell the love of your life everything you wanted to say. My heart squeezed for Nerina. What if that were Jonah and I? What would I say to him? I spun to face him. *Jonah,* I cried, *I love you. I love you so much.*

He closed into me until our auras blended into a storm of blue and silver. Everything inside me was crying, a tangle of grief that was going to knot me up and strangle me into nothing. Somehow Jonah knew there was nothing he could say to make it all right, but the warmth of his silence was enough.

Nerina pushed herself up onto her legs, her head still bent low so that her cheek rested on Heath's. *It's time.*

I could hear the sounds of the battle raging beyond us, growls and crashes and yelps. I couldn't even comprehend how the rest of the Clan had pulled themselves away from that, but it didn't matter. We were all here now. The Snow Leopards circled the birches, their smoke-colored fur gleaming beneath their auras as they prowled the perimeter to keep us safe. And above the tips of the trees, Adamo swooped back and forth, ready to take on anyone who might fly near.

Bree came forward. Her face was paler than I'd ever seen it. What if this spell was beyond her? What if the whole thing backfired and Heath died for nothing? "Jonah," she said, "you lie down next to him, just there." Her hand shook as she pointed to the ground beside Heath.

Jonah obeyed his sister. He and Heath looked like the yin and the yang, the White Wolf curved around the ebony Panther, their auras crackling against one another's. Bree stood in the center of them, the blue and silver light snaking around her legs, enveloping her in their glow.

Bree looked at all of us. "The thing about this spell," she said, "is that it won't work if one of them is not completely willing to enter into it. But it also won't work if the Clan doesn't agree." She raised her eyebrow.

In answer, the rest of the Clan closed in tight around them. The Eagle and I perched atop the Stag's antlers. A tight anxiety gripped me. Was this really going to work? And what if the Malandanti broke through our defenses before we could finish it?

Bree closed her eyes and held her hands out, palms up. As I watched, red smoke poured out from her fingertips. It spilled into the two auras at her feet, and a whirlwind of blue, silver, and red spun up around all three of them. She knelt and touched Heath, turning his bright fur the color of blood. "Do you give yourself with your whole soul?" Bree's voice seemed to come from some other-worldly place; it was the Abbess speaking, not her. "Do you dedicate the end of your life so that this Malandante may continue his in your place?"

Yes, Heath answered. *With . . . all my . . . soul, yes.*

Bree laid her hand on Jonah. His black fur looked fiery in the red smoke's wake. "Do you accept the essence of this Benandante with your whole soul? And will you dedicate the rest of your life to the Benandanti and the *Concilio Celeste*?"

I sprang away from the Stag and swept down to Jonah. His eyes found mine as he answered. *Yes. With all my heart, body, and soul, yes.*

A screech rent the air, splitting the reverent hush that had fallen over the Clan. I twisted to look up, just in time to see the Harpy clash with Adamo. His fiery feathers gleamed against her steel-gray body, his talons locking onto her wing before she could break into our circle. As he dragged her up and away, Bree stood and pushed her palm toward the Harpy. She shrieked; Bree swished her arm, and the Harpy disappeared with an angry pop, blasted into another time and space by the Pakistani magic.

I tucked my wings in tight, my insides skittering like dead leaves. The Harpy had seen what we were doing. The Malandanti knew now they'd been betrayed by one of their own.

We had to move fast.

With one hand on Heath and the other on Jonah, Bree raised her gaze skyward. "By the magic of all seven sites, by the blessing of the *Concilio Celeste*, we accept this exchange. One soul here on earth, one soul to ascend." She brought her arms over her head, drawing the smoke high into the air where it puffed into a cloud just above all of us.

With a terrible knowledge, I backed away from Jonah and fluttered over to Heath. *I'm right here,* I told him. *I'm right here.*

The smoke shimmered with all the colors of the earth. It stretched and stretched, so much that wisps broke off and dappled down, no more substantial than pieces of a rainbow. I felt a warm body move in next to me; it was

Nerina. We pressed in close to Heath, keeping a vigil over his last moments on earth.

Keep fighting the . . . good fight, Heath said.

Always, I replied. *I promise.*

Nerina?

Sí, cara? she said. She brought her face to his, a remnant of their last kiss.

I can see you . . .

What do you see, cara?

Beautiful and blinding, the smoke cloud burst open, multicolored fractals of brilliant light showering us. I turned my face up to it, each fragment falling like a glorious, gentle rain. My heart lightened—maybe everything would be okay after all . . .

But when I looked back down, the heaviness dropped over me again.

It started at the tip of Heath's tail, his whole body dissolving into the air, becoming a beam of shining, glimmering light.

Cara! Nerina cried.

I can see you there . . . in the town square by the fountain . . .

Yes, yes, I remember. She scrambled to get closer, but the Wolf was slipping away, half his body gone. I pressed my face to his chest, trying to memorize everything I had ever known about him.

And you said . . .

I remember . . .

His front legs dissolved, floating up to join the gathering light. *And you said . . .*

"Finally, you have come," Nerina said, desperately trying to keep Heath's face against hers.

The white fur beneath my feathers disappeared. A sob filled me. I locked my eyes onto Heath's, those blue eyes that were the first Benandanti eyes I'd ever seen. His gaze shifted from me to Nerina.

Finally, I have come.

And then he was gone.

All that was left of my beloved Guide was a brilliant ball of sapphire light. Nerina collapsed onto the ground, her claws scrabbling at the empty space where Heath had lain. The world closed in tight. I couldn't breathe, couldn't understand why I was still there when Heath was gone.

Bree reached up and cupped the luminescence in her hand. In its glow, her whole body was alight with a certainty I hadn't seen since before she'd been tortured. If it was redemption she sought, at that moment she was holding it in her hands. "One soul ascended," she said softly, "and one here on earth." With a quick, nimble motion, she poured the radiance down like water onto Jonah, smothering him with Heath's aura. A long low moan filled my mind. Jonah twisted on the ground, his old silvery aura putting up a resistance against the new one.

I froze, wanting to go to him but knowing there was nothing I could do. He had to do this willingly, without my help. His silver aura blackened, fractured under the pressure of the light, and broke apart. The essence encircled him like a cloak made out of sky, lifted him off his feet and into the air. His body contorted, the powerful limbs lengthening, his face elongating, his black fur brightening . . .

In one final explosion, the Benandanti blue ripped away any last fragment of silver. The final wisps of red smoke blew away. Bree slumped forward, her forehead on her knees. Silence fell over the Clan. From the air, Jonah descended back to earth.

He was no longer a Panther.

He was a White Wolf.

I stared at him, at his new shape. He turned, and I saw the one difference between him and Heath. It was his own jewel-green eyes that shone out from the bright white fur, his own soul that now possessed the Wolf's form.

His fresh aura shimmered around him like the rings of a celestial planet. The Clan slowly moved in to surround him. And in the center of that circle, the White Wolf raised his head and howled, one lone note of stillness in the chaos of that long night.

CHAPTER TWENTY-EIGHT
The Blue Woods

Alessia

We can't hold them off much longer!

I shot up into the sky, out of the birches. Below, the Snow Leopards crashed body-to-body with rows of Malandanti, locked in deadly combat. I'd been so entwined with Jonah's transformation that I hadn't even noticed the birch copse had been under attack.

Out from behind their silvery trunks, Jonah leapt into their midst, his powerful form shiny with his fresh aura. He sank his jaws into the Malandante Coyote and dragged it off one of the Snow Leopards. The Coyote yowled, its eyes flashing with fury at this betrayal of one of its own Clan. Jonah slammed one paw into the Coyote's throat, holding him firm to the ground.

Twin Willows Clan, get to the Waterfall, Dario commanded. *All other Benandanti, your sole job is to hold the rest of the Malandanti off. We need to retake the site before we lose anyone else.*

I plummeted to the Coyote and delivered one long

scratch down the length of its back. Jonah let it go and followed me through the brush to the edge of the stream. There, in the middle of the water, the Rabbit stood with his arms raised. Behind him, the Raven zoomed in manic circles within the Malandanti barrier. I could sense his fury at Jonah's betrayal, but he must've been ordered to stay inside and hold the magic in place.

Showtime. Bree pushed past Jonah and splashed out into the stream. Magic poured out of her and lit her whole body up like a lantern. *He's not going to make it easy for me to bring down that barrier,* she told us. *So work on a way to get the Raven out.*

I dropped low just as Nerina and the Harpy barreled past me, their bodies a tangle of claws and wings and beaks as sharp as daggers. Their auras meshed and melded, then broke apart with each blow they delivered. Beyond them, the two Dragons breathed fire at one another, singeing the treetops. I climbed the air and surveyed the chaos. In the woods beyond the Waterfall, the Snow Leopards battled with the remaining Dogs. Everywhere there were pockets of fighting, blue against silver, the forest terrifyingly alive with the sound of combat.

At the base of the Waterfall, the two Twin Willows Clans faced off, Stag against Boar, Catamount against Coyote, Eagle against Bobcat. The Malandanti clearly knew they had lost Jonah and we had gained him. I could see the rage in their bodies, in every crackle of their auras. But they were outnumbered now. Surely we could overtake them. And still that damn Raven swished back and forth across the Waterfall, keeping the barrier in place.

Jonah. I fluttered down so that I was just above his ears. He raised his head and met my gaze. Even though he was the same White Wolf shape as Heath, he looked completely different. Because each soul was unique, and Jonah was nothing if not a unique soul. I brushed my wingtip across the top of his head. *I have an idea.*

I swooped low away from the stream, back into the dense bushes and trees. Jonah followed me down the slope of rocks and craggy ground. I could hear the Waterfall on the other side of the tangled underbrush. I never came this way to it; the birch trees were always my touchstone, my entry point to the magical site whose water flowed through my soul like blood. But the birch trees were tainted for me now. They would always be the place where Heath died.

Like he could hear the grief in my mind, Jonah tilted his face up toward me. *I'm so sorry about Heath, Alessia. I didn't want it to be like this.*

I can't, I said. *If I think about it now, I won't be able to fight. I'll think about it later.*

Jonah rose as I floated down to him. My wings brushed his face. *I promise I'll make this body proud.*

How does your new form feel?

He sprang up the rocky slope, his lithe legs stretching long. *Different but good. Less violent . . . more majestic.*

I flew ahead of him, and he sped up to catch me.

Despite the grief that had made it, I could see his joy in this new shape, the freedom in every arch and footfall. It was like Jonah had finally become the Wolf he'd always been meant to be.

We reached the top of the slope, separated from the Waterfall by a thicket of brush and bramble.

Now what? Jonah asked.

You stay here, I said. My wings beat against the air, ruffling his fur. *I'll tell you when to come out.*

What exactly are we doing?

Following a hunch. Without telling him more, I crashed through the bushes and emerged at the top of the Waterfall.

In the center of the stream, Bree and the Rabbit fought each other, the air around them smoky with magic. For as much as she contained the power of the Abbess, the Rabbit was holding his own, popping in and out of time, making her spin each time he reappeared. She threw a ball of green Congo magic at him, but he dodged it and sent back a jet of red smoke. I could hear her cursing out loud and in my brain. I shut her out. In order to do what was required, to help her and the rest of the Clan, my sole focus had to be the Raven.

I shot forward until I was right up against the barrier and hovered there. Like he sensed my presence, the Raven rose from the pool below until he was at my level. His beady black gaze fixed on me. I flew back and forth in front of him, my wings so close to the magic that kept him inside and me outside that I could feel its sizzle on my feathers. *You know who I am,* I thought, even though he couldn't hear me. *You know I'm the one he did it for.*

The Raven cawed a stark, lonely sound that rippled across the water. In a sick, twisted way, he was in mourning too. He'd lost his charge. He'd failed as a Guide.

I answered him with a call of my own, a cry of triumph. He flapped his wings and almost flew into the barrier—almost, but not quite. No, he wasn't quite there yet . . . not quite filled with the rage I needed.

And I knew the one thing that would get him there.

Now, Jonah!

Out from the tangle of leaves and branches, Jonah burst into the top of the Waterfall, water splashing out from beneath his white, blue-haloed body as he skidded to a halt beneath me. The Raven screamed in fury and sliced through the air, his wings quivering with uncontainable rage. I rose up, up, up, ready to dive, hoping with every last possible hope that he would do exactly what I wanted him to do.

Murderous eyes laser-focused on Jonah, the Raven flew out of the barrier.

Because I'd remembered what Nerina had said on the plane to Friuli. *She was my Guide,* she'd told me and Bree about the Harpy. *You cannot imagine her hatred.*

The silver bubble of protection fizzled into nothingness, tiny pinpricks of magic dancing in the air like raindrops. The Raven instantly realized his mistake and scrambled backward, but it was too late. The Malandanti had lost their claim of the site, and without a complete Clan they could not regain it.

Control of the Waterfall was now up for grabs, and I intended the Benandanti to snatch it.

Twin Willows Clan, into the Waterfall!

But that was easier said than done. The Raven had refocused on Jonah and slammed into him. Jonah struck out with both his front paws, knocking the Raven out of the air, but before Jonah could grab one of his wings, the Raven swerved upward, just out of Jonah's reach.

At the base of the Waterfall below, the Stag had locked his antlers onto the Boar's tusks. They tossed each other this way and that without one of them being able to break away. I plummeted down to help Cora with the Bobcat, who had caught one of her wings in its paws. Before it saw me coming, I ripped the top of its head with my talons. Blood poured over its forehead and into its eyes. With a roar, it let Cora go and staggered into the woods, yowling.

Working in unison, Cora and I landed on the Boar's back and dug our claws in. The Boar bucked, trying to throw us off, but we held fast until it tore its tusks away from the Stag's antlers. Jeff gathered his back legs and kicked the Boar hard in the face. I heard the crunch of bones breaking. One more kick, and the Boar was down for good.

Two down, two to go. Cal and the Malandante

Coyote had their jaws on each other's throats. Cora, Jeff, and I surrounded them, and in one breath we closed in. Jeff's antlers gored the Coyote's side as Cora's and my talons scratched down its back. The Coyote let go of Cal and stumbled away, its eyes glassy, its bleeding sides rising and falling rapidly with its heavy panting.

Where's Jonah? Jeff asked.

Top of the Waterfall.

We plunged into the pool of water, the rising mist from the Waterfall cold on my feathers. I mounted the air until I could see what was happening above. Jonah and the Raven circled each other, the black bird hovering just out of reach every time Jonah swiped his paws at him. Just beyond them, Bree and the Rabbit were deadlocked, their magic arcing between them.

And in the woods all around us, the Benandanti and the Malandanti clashed. Nerina and the Harpy still battled overhead, and the Dragons screamed fire at one another somewhere nearby.

It's time to end this, I said to Jonah, to Bree, to everyone. I flew down and rammed into the Raven, sent him tumbling.

Jonah leapt up with one powerful jump and caught the Raven in his mouth. *This is for my father,* he said, *and Alessia's.* He gave one hard toss of his head and threw the Raven into the air.

Bree shoved her magic at the Rabbit, who disappeared with a pop. As the Raven arced above her, she raised her hands. Red and silver smoke spiraled out from her palms, caught the Raven in their mist, and pulled him apart until he, too, disappeared with a loud, satisfying smack.

Come on, I called to Jonah, diving to meet the rest of the Clan. Behind me, Jonah gathered his hind legs and sprang up out of the Waterfall, his beautiful white fur glistening in the mist as he soared into the pool below. Jonah, who hated to swim, who was afraid of water because he'd almost drowned as a child. He broke the surface of the water, his green eyes sparkling with triumph.

We closed into one another. The Twin Willows Clan may have been different from when we started this battle, but we were still complete. Whole.

Above us, Bree splashed to the very edge of the Waterfall, the blessed water tumbling around her in glorious abandon. She brought her hands up high over her head. The glow started at her heart and radiated outward, out from her fingers and feet, from her eyes and the crown of her head, until she was made of light. She was an otherworldly being, the Abbess.

The magic streamed out from her and began to weave an intricate web of light over the entire Waterfall. All around the pool, Malandanti poured out from the woods, trying to get in, but it was too late. The web wove its way down into the earth, a million shimmering particles of Benandanti magic. I had seen this spell all those weeks ago when we had first retaken the Waterfall, but that was before Bree, before the Benandanti had the power of the

Abbess to wield it. She swished her hand in the air, and the beams of light tumbled outward, beyond the Waterfall, into the woods, until the whole forest had turned blue. Every leaf and branch, every bush and tree, lit up with a cerulean glow, dripped with sea-colored magic.

I blinked. We were all glowing too; not just our auras, but our feathers and fur, even our eyes. And I felt it within me, the magic of not just the Waterfall but all seven sites. We had bound them together, under Benandanti control, all seven sources of magic well and truly ours forever.

A scream of terror ripped across the Waterfall.

I looked up. The Harpy screamed again, a sound so filled with fear and pain and rage that I wanted to cover my ears. In the stream and sky above us, the rest of the *Concilio Argento* joined her, each of them shrieking and twisting and writhing. Nerina and Dario backed away, and even from my vantage point below I could see their eyes wide with horror.

On the banks of the Waterfall all around us, just outside the Benandanti's barrier, the remaining Malandanti collapsed to the ground, each of their cries as painful and terror-filled as their *Concilio's*.

What's happening to them? Jonah asked, his gaze fixed on his former Clanmates' trauma as if it were a car crash he couldn't look away from.

They are losing their magic, Dario answered.

What? Why? I asked.

It belongs to the Benandanti now.

One by one, the Malandanti on the shore disappeared. Their auras fractured and broke apart, the animal within vanishing into thin air. *They've lost the ability to separate their souls from their bodies,* Dario said. *They're going back to their human forms now, never to return as animals.*

I fluttered down to Jonah's side. He shrank against me, his eyes dark as the forest while he watched. *That was almost me,* he whispered for my mind only. *As much as I hate the Malandanti, I still love—*

—the power to transform, I finished for him. I knew that love, deep in my soul. That power was part of me. To lose it would be to spend the rest of my life feeling incomplete.

So without the magic . . . I began. But without finishing, I spun to look upward again. The rest of their Clans gone, the *Concilio Argento* were frozen but still there, still solidly in their transformed state. If they had lost the power to transform, why weren't they disappearing too?

But then they began to disintegrate, and I knew the terrible truth.

The *Concilio Argento* had not just lost their power to transform. They had lost their immortality. Hundreds of years old, they could not survive without that magic. The Harpy screamed again as her tail turned to dust, the years eating away at the rest of her body, inch by inch. They would not be returning to their human bodies like the rest of the Malandanti. They were all dying where they were, the last sight they would ever see the brilliant blue woods the Benandanti had created with their victory.

Nerina floated until she was right in front of the Harpy. Her powerful wings—so alive, so strong—beat up and down, taunting her old Guide. What was it like to stare down your enemy in triumph after so many hundreds of years of war? I could not imagine, and a warm gratitude spread through me that I would never have to.

Bit by bit, the *Concilio Argento* crumbled into dust, until there was nothing left but wind.

It was over.

We had won.

The true impact of that shot through me. I swooped out of the air and into the water, letting it wash over me like a baptism.

The seven most powerful sites of magic in the world finally belonged to the Benandanti and would be safe for generations to come.

I broke the surface and soared, water raining down from my feathers. And that meant . . .

I was free.

CHAPTER TWENTY-NINE

Family Comes in Many Shapes and Sizes

Bree

The magic coursing through me was stronger than anything I'd ever felt, stronger than the Olive Grove had been when I'd stood on that hallowed ground. All around me, the Benandanti celebrated, their cheers like champagne bottles popping open in my head. But I couldn't rest. Not yet.

Alessia. Jonah. Come on.

Her wings dripping with water, Alessia swooped over my head. *What? Where?*

There is no way in hell I'm letting the Rabbit and Pratt Webster get off scot-free. I clambered out of the stream, congratulating myself for choosing my over-the-knee boots for our let's-blow-the-Malandanti-off-the-face-of-the-earth battle. Somehow I'd sensed that I'd wind up in the water at some point, and boy did I call that one. *I'll bet good money they're going to hightail it out of here, and that's not happening on my watch.*

Jonah dashed up the rocks and met me on the bank

at the top of the Waterfall. *I know where that weasel lives,* he said. *Let's go.*

But before we could get one foot into the forest, Dario blocked our path, his scales flashing red and black in the blue light that dripped from the trees. *The magic will work beyond the sites,* he said. *It will find its way into the world. Justice will be done.*

Yeah, well, I don't have the patience to wait for that, I said, planting my hands on my hips. *Those two assholes killed my father.*

And mine, said Alessia, swooping low so that she was right in Dario's face.

It's too personal. We can't just hope that karma does its thing, I said. *So you can either get out of our way or help us get there faster by giving me a ride.*

The Dragon stared at us for a moment, then lowered his front legs so I could climb on his back. We rose high over the treetops and kept Jonah's sleek white form in sight as we raced back toward the town. Far ahead on the horizon, the pink light of dawn stretched over Maine. It had been the longest night of my life, but one that would live in me forever.

This way, Jonah said and swerved off Main Street, down a side street not far from the school. All of the houses were dark, their occupants still sleeping, the whole town oblivious to what had been happening just beyond its edges. And hopefully would stay that way for a really long time to come. But one house, at the end of the road, was lit up like a freaking jack-o'-lantern, its windows blazing with artificial light.

Dirt kicked up from beneath Jonah's paws as he ran down the driveway. Dario landed heavily, and I tumbled off his back. *I can't stay here,* he said. *Imagine what would happen if someone woke up and saw a dragon out his front window.*

I would actually pay good money to see that, but yeah, not exactly the reason we were here. *See you soon,* I said and chased after Jonah, Alessia winging overhead.

Jonah didn't even stop at the front door; he just crashed into it with such force that it blew off its hinges. He leapt over the fallen door and skidded to a halt in the foyer of the house. I climbed in after him and followed as he trotted straight to the back of the house. Frantic sounds of thuds and crashes, a machine whirring, and two people shouting at each other echoed out from the open door all the way at the end of the hall.

The moment we appeared in the doorway, all the noise stopped.

"You!" Pratt yelled and launched himself at Jonah.

Did he seriously think he could take on a massive wolf? Jonah had him pinned beneath his front paws in the blink of an eye.

I pushed past them, deeper into the room, my gaze fixed on the skinny, sweater-vested bastard behind him.

An industrial-sized shredder sat in the middle of the room, surrounded by towering boxes filled with all sorts of papers I was sure the FBI would love to get their hands on. So this was where all those documents had gone, the ones they'd smuggled out of the Guild, the absence of which was the only thing keeping Pratt out of prison. I stepped around the shredder and the boxes, and the Rabbit backed up against the wall. In my high-heeled boots, I was taller than him, and I could tell by the hungry look in his eyes that the magic still clung to me, still rose off my body in wisps. "Tell me," I said, my voice just above a whisper, "where is your power now?"

He straightened his shoulders, as if he had anything left that he could use against me. "You don't deserve the magic," he spat. Saliva landed on the toe of my black boot.

I curled my lip. "I think the fact that I have it and you don't would indicate that I do deserve it. More than you ever did."

There was a small commotion behind me. I glanced over my shoulder to see Pratt scrambling to crawl across the floor. Alessia dove and hooked her talons into his ankles. Pratt yelped in pain, his upper body thrashing.

The Rabbit reached for me, his fingers itching for my throat, but before he could touch me, I flung my hand out. In one swoosh, he flew up to the ceiling and hung there, suspended by the ropes of Angel Falls magic I wound around him. Keeping one hand high, holding him in place, I pulled my cell phone out of the back pocket of my jeans. My thumb poised to dial, I looked up into his face. I saw the fear there, the deep knowledge of what the rest of his life was going to look like dawning in his eyes.

The line rang and clicked into connection. "Federal Bureau of Investigation, how may I direct your call?"

It might've been the ass-crack of morning, but apparently the FBI didn't sleep. "I need the head of the investigation into the Guild. Tell them I have two key players in custody."

The operator put me on hold, and for a minute we were all forced to listen to a really bad Muzak version of "Don't Stop Believin'." Then the line clicked again and a clipped, all-business-no-play voice said, "This is Agent Amelia Rosen. You're calling in regard to the Guild investigation?"

"Yes," I said. "I'm standing here in a room with Pratt Webster, Head of Operations, and . . ." I trailed off and narrowed my eyes at the Rabbit. Covering my phone's microphone with my thumb, I said, "What the hell is your name, anyway?"

For an instant, he looked defiant, like he was in any position to refuse me. I twisted the red ropes tighter, and a tendril of smoke touched his bare skin. "Jeremy Bush," he gasped.

"Jeremy Bush," I said into my phone.

There was a deep intake of breath on the other end. "Bush? You—have him?"

"I'm staring right at him."

"Lady, I don't know who you are, but you're getting a medal." I could hear the rustle of paper and a pen scratching across its surface. "We've been looking for that guy for weeks. Every time we got close, he disappeared."

"Yeah, he used to be able to do that real well. Don't worry, his disappearing days are over." I twisted the ropes again, just for good measure. "Who is he, anyway?"

"We have no idea what his real title was," Agent Rosen said, "but whenever there was a mess to be cleaned up, he was the one to do it. Usually with a lot of casualties on the side. Listen, where are you now?"

"Twin Willows, Maine."

"Jesus, where the hell is that? Never mind. I'm chartering a plane as we speak. I can be there in a few hours. Can you secure them for that long?"

I looked back at Pratt. He'd resigned to his fate beneath Jonah and Alessia's grasp, his hands clutched to his head. I swung my gaze up to Jeremy Bush, the Rabbit no longer. He gave me one last glare and turned his face to the wall.

"Oh, yeah," I told Agent Rosen. "We're not going anywhere."

Three Weeks Later

"Bree? You ready to go?"

"In a minute!" I swiped lip gloss on and stepped back to survey myself in the mirror. A breath of wind gusted in from the open bathroom window, lifting my hair off my neck. I grinned and raced down the stairs to meet Mom.

"Is Cal meeting us over there?"

"Yeah." I grabbed my handbag from the counter in the kitchen and opened the front door for Mom, whose hands were laden with two canvas bags filled to the brim with Prosecco, orange juice, gourmet cheeses and meats from the fancy deli in Willow Heights. "He went over early this morning to help unload all the construction stuff." I closed the door behind her. "Like the do-gooder he is."

"You could do a lot worse."

"I *have* done a lot worse."

Mom laughed and kicked beneath the rear of the car to pop the truck. "How are things with you two anyway?"

A month ago, it would've been insane to talk to my mother about this. I don't think I'd ever told her about any boy in all the years I'd been dating them. But—and I felt like a total shit for thinking this—somehow in my dad's absence the three of us had gotten closer, banded together, and become a real family. It was like he'd pushed us together in a final act of love.

"Good, I guess," I said as I slid into the passenger seat. "We'll see what happens when he goes to Yale in the fall."

"Well, you have your whole life ahead of you," Mom said as she started the car. "You don't have to settle down with someone at the age of seventeen."

"True."

The snow had melted, and the trees along Main Street were covered in buds waiting to bloom. Spring had finally come to Twin Willows. I breathed onto the window and traced the outline of a wolf with my fingertip. I stared at it for a moment, then smeared it away with the heel of my hand.

Alessia's driveway was filled with cars and trucks. We parked up the street and each took a canvas bag from the trunk. Mom linked her arm through mine. Her red hair tumbled over her shoulders in loose waves and glinted in the morning sunshine. I leaned my head on her shoulder as we walked down the driveway. She was like a flower; Dad had blocked her from the light, and now that he was gone she was in full bloom. My heart twisted a little that this was his legacy.

But that was the choice he had made, and that wasn't my fault. I knew that now.

"Hey, they've made pretty good progress." Mom pointed past the farmhouse where the skeleton of a new barn was beginning to take shape. Carly's dad, who owned a construction company, stood in the middle of the rising framework, calling out directions. I spotted Jeff and Mr. Salter, the usual suspects, along with half the town. In the field next to the barn, a few long tables were set up, their checkered tablecloths fluttering in the breeze. Mom and I headed toward them.

"This is like a good old-fashioned barn raising," I said as we squeezed the bottles of wine and cheeses and meats in between the bowls of pasta and potato salad. "I feel like I should be flicking a fan and looking for a husband."

Mom laughed. Lidia crossed the field to us, a platter of bagels and cream cheese in her hands. "*Buon giorno,*"

Mom said, and they kissed once on each cheek. "You know I'm more of a Chinese take-out kind of cook, so I brought mimosas."

"It's five o'clock in the world somewhere," Lidia said. Her cheeks were rosy, her eyes sparkly in the sunlight. "Thank you for coming."

I leaned close to Lidia. "Our Italian friend hasn't left yet, has she?" Lidia shook her head. I nudged Mom. "I'll be back in a bit, okay?"

"Okay, sweetie." She and Lidia walked back toward the crowd of people in the field. I spotted Alessia and Jenny, lounging on a blanket, calling out joking instructions to the guys working on the barn.

As I headed toward the pasture, Cal caught my eye. He gave one final pound to the nail he was hammering and grinned at me. I gave him a long once-over, fully appreciating the warmer weather that allowed him to wear tight T-shirts without anything over them. I pointed to the woods. He nodded once and picked up another nail.

I walked over the crest of the hill and to the edge of the forest. It was probably the last time I'd make this trip. I pressed the special rock in the stone wall, and the trapdoor opened.

"It's me," I called out as I descended.

Nerina stood in the middle of the main room, her fleet of Louis Vuitton suitcases stacked beside her. The lair had been cleaned up since the Malandanti had destroyed it, the broken chairs replaced, the smashed espresso machine removed. Everything looked tidy. Too tidy.

I met Nerina's gaze. "You're never coming back here, are you?"

She shook her head and sank into the leather armchair, a sad smile on her face. "I hope I will never need to."

Where my mother had bloomed in my father's absence, Nerina had shriveled in the wake of Heath's death. She was a smaller, paler, thinner version of herself. Though her face was still unlined and youthful, I could see the years in her eyes catching up to her. Creeping in.

"But the sites still need to be protected."

"And that is why we have the Clans." Nerina folded her hands in her lap. Her whole being had quieted, like someone had put her on mute. "Without the threat of the Malandanti, the *Concilio* won't need to be as involved anymore."

I sat on the couch. "Are they *really* gone?" Part of me still didn't believe it. The part that still woke up in the middle of the night, cold and convinced that the Rabbit was hiding in my closet. But he wasn't. He and Pratt Webster were being held in a federal penitentiary without bail, considered dangerous flight risks. They were never getting out.

"Yes. For now." Nerina stroked her cheek with her finger. Her nails were bare and clipped shorter than I'd ever seen them. "But remember . . . the Malandanti were born from the Benandanti. From those who wanted the power for themselves. That threat will never go away."

"So we have to stay vigilant."

"*Sí.*"

I sighed and leaned back into the couch. "Is that what you're going to do? Return to Italy and stay vigilant?"

"Oh . . ." Nerina looked at her suitcases. "I thought I would travel for a bit. I've never been to Hawaii." She bit her lip. Tears gathered at the corner of her eyes and dropped onto her cheeks. "What am I going to do, Bree? How am I supposed to live forever without him?"

My throat closed tight. I got up from the couch and squeezed in next to her in the armchair. She bowed her forehead to my shoulder, her quiet sobbing very dignified and completely un-Italian. Which made it even sadder.

"I don't know, Nerina," I said, because I really didn't. I couldn't imagine such an empty eternity stretching out before me. "I think, maybe, you just take it one day at a time."

Nerina raised her head, her face streaked with tears. Somehow, she still looked like a Botticelli painting. I looked like a Picasso when I cried. "I have never lived one day at a time," she said. "I've always lived for years or decades, always thinking ahead to the next century. Perhaps it is time to change that." She squeezed my hand. "And there is something I want you to do for me."

"What?" Great. What was she going to rope me into *now*?

"I want you to come to Italy for the summer."

I pulled back a little. "Seriously?"

"*Sí*, yes, of course. You must come." She shook me gently. "You still have so much to learn about the magic."

"But with the Malandanti gone . . ."

"*You* still have your power. There is so much you can do with it, so much good you can bring to the world." She took both my hands in hers. "Come. Spend the summer with me and Dario and the *Concilio*. Cal can come too. And Alessia told me she and Lidia are planning a trip to visit her grandparents again." The dark irises of her eyes swam behind the tears that filled them. "It will give me something to look forward to. Something to live for."

"Well, okay. When you put it like that." A wide smile broke out across her face, and I answered her with one of my own. "I mean, I have to check with my mom, but I'm sure it will be okay."

"Bring her. And Jonah." She swallowed. "It would be good to be surrounded by family."

We *were* family, weren't we? Funny how that had happened . . . My mind flashed back to the day we'd come to Twin Willows. I'd been so sure that we wouldn't be here long, that we'd leave this town in the dust like we'd left all the others. And now . . . I had roots here that I never wanted to pull up. I hugged Nerina hard. "Thanks, Nerina. For everything."

Nerina kissed both my cheeks. "You have a great destiny ahead of you, Bree. I cannot wait to see what you do with it."

I breathed in deep. I wasn't going to settle for great. I was going to make my destiny nothing less than freaking awesome.

CHAPTER THIRTY
The Promise Fulfilled

Alessia

The sun crested over the treetops, dappling the hillside green and gold. I leaned back on my elbows and imagined summer, the pasture covered with grazing goats, the pigs in their newly built pen, the hens squawking once again in their trailers.

My eye caught the little cabin on the edge of the farm, lonely and dark. I breathed in deep to keep the lump from closing my throat. I missed him every day. But I also knew I was sitting here now, watching our new barn rise up out of the ashes of the old one, because of him. He'd given me so many gifts, and I was going to spend the rest of my life celebrating them instead of feeling sad about it.

"Enjoying the view?"

I looked up.

Jonah loomed over me, his green eyes dancing. He peeled off his hoodie, revealing a form-fitting T-shirt beneath that, in fact, did fit his form very nicely.

I grinned. "I am now."

He dropped onto the blanket I was sharing with Jenny and mopped his face with the discarded hoodie. The sunshine of recent days had colored his skin, deepening it from winter pale to a healthy spring tan. He grabbed the glass of lemonade nestled in the grass, downed it, and surveyed the four of us sitting there. "It doesn't really seem fair that the girls are all hanging out here while the boys are working our asses off."

Jenny wiggled her fingers. "I just got a manicure."

Carly held up her hands. "My parents told me to protect my precious piano-playing hands at all costs." Her lips curved. "Which means if I break a finger, I'll get out of lessons." She jumped up and bounced over to the barn, where Mr. Salter handed her a hammer.

Melissa tossed her hair. "Good. She can hold down the fort for a while. Or rather, hold up the barn," she added with a chuckle while we all groaned at the lame joke.

I reached out and brushed Jonah's hair off his forehead. "And I think I deserve a break, don't you?"

Jonah snaked his arm around my waist and pressed his face into my neck. "Yes, you do," he said, his voice muffled against my skin.

"Oh, God, you two, get a room." Bree flopped down next to Jenny. "At least *you* get to deal with them next week."

"Are you kidding? I am finding myself a hot Frenchman the minute we land, and I don't intend to come up for air the whole week." Jenny shimmied her shoulders.

"*Voulez vous coucher avec moi*, indeed."

I laughed so hard a crick ached up my side. "Poor Carly," I gasped out.

"Poor Carly?" Melissa pouted. "Poor *me*. I thought we were going to hang out all week together, Lessi."

I leaned back into Jonah, felt his chin rest on top of my head. "Well, take it up with my mom. She's the one who changed her mind about me going."

But it wasn't really Lidia. It was me, proving to her that I could live outside her shadow and take care of myself. Also me pointing out that after everything I'd been through, I deserved a trip to France.

Bree sat up and leaned across Jenny. "Hey, I'm around all week. We should do something."

Melissa raised her eyebrows. "Won't you be with Cal?"

"Not every minute of every day." Bree shrugged. "I do have my own life, you know."

"Just like Gloria Steinem—and my mother—tell us we should," Jenny said.

"Says the girl who's going to run off with a Frenchman," Jonah muttered in my ear.

I elbowed him in the gut.

"Well, that would be nice." Melissa rolled onto her stomach and kicked her feet up. "We could have a *Game of Thrones* marathon."

"Yeah, we can fast-forward all the parts that don't involve Jon Snow," Bree said as she twisted toward me and Jonah. "By the way," she added quietly so Melissa couldn't hear, "it looks like we're all going to Italy this summer. Nerina could use the company." She climbed over Jenny and settled next to Melissa so they could plan their spring break.

I nudged Jonah. "Hey, I'm going to pass out lemonade and then we should, you know, do the thing. Grab my backpack from the kitchen, will you?"

He nodded and unfolded himself to his feet, then reached down to help me up. I stood on my tiptoes to kiss him, as natural and easy as though we had never broken up, never been enemies on two sides of a deadly war. He was mine now, a Benandante for as long as he lived.

I gathered a tray of lemonade from the picnic table and passed it out around the barn. The framework was almost done, a strong set of bones that would stand on this farm for a long time to come. Even though they weren't here, I could feel Heath and my dad in every inch of it, their blessing hammered into the wood just like the nails. I handed Cal a cup of lemonade. "You know, it's okay to take a break and hang out with Bree for a while. You have my permission."

"I will in a minute." He ran his hand over the corner he'd just fitted together. "You know, it feels good to build something from scratch." He leveled his gaze at me. "Especially something for a good friend."

I patted his arm in answer, unable to voice just how deep my thanks were. I turned and wove my way through the workers, handing out drinks. I remembered what Heath had said, about how lucky I was to live here amongst people who loved me. This barn was a testament to that: it was filled with love that was seeping through the wood, spiraling up from its foundation like a vine.

There was one cup left on my tray. I held it out to Mr. Salter—Ed, as he now insisted I call him—who pushed his hard hat back off his sweaty forehead. "Thanks, Alessia." He looked out over the length of the barn's framework. "It's coming along, isn't it?"

"It really is. I bet it'll be done by the time I get back from France." I touched his arm. "Thank you." I knew it had been him who'd organized this, put the word out through the town, and gathered everyone here.

His eyes softened. "Well, you know I would do anything for your mom." We both looked across the lawn to where Lidia stood, chatting with Miriam Wolfe beneath the eaves of the house. She caught us watching her and waved at the same time she laughed at something Miriam said. Her laughter rang out over the yard, a soundtrack more joyous than the playlist blaring from the iPod dock on the picnic table.

She was happy.

I hugged Ed hard. "I know you would," I whispered. "And I'm glad."

Ed coughed and hid his red cheeks with his cup of lemonade.

I hopped off the raised floorboards and met Jonah just past the barn. I slid my hand into his, and we headed for the woods.

As we climbed over the stone wall, I thought about

Nerina beneath us, in her lair below the roots and rocks. It was going to be weird not having her here; I'd gotten used to her presence on my farm. But I knew that as much as the sight of Heath's cabin punched me in the gut every time I saw it, for Nerina it was a million times worse. She needed to go back to Italy to heal.

The trees closed over us the deeper we went into the forest, surrounding us with cool, calm quiet. Here and there, I saw remnants of the magic: a leaf lined with shimmering blue, a branch dripping with azure glitter. Jonah and I pointed them out to each other, our eyes seeing things the rest of the world could not.

Dario had been right: the magic had worked its way into the world long after the spell. Though the Malandanti had disappeared that night without us knowing who they were—a side effect that drove me crazy—over the next couple of weeks, there had been a few small-town scandals. My government teacher, Mr. Clemens, had been discovered laundering money in his basement. Josh Baker's mother was indicted in an insider trading deal gone south. And the mayor of Willow Heights was being recalled for improper use of government funds.

The Bobcat, the Coyote, and the Boar, reduced to nothing without their power.

"It feels so weird to walk here," Jonah said, "instead of running through these woods as a Panther." He paused. "Or a Wolf."

"I haven't walked here since . . ." I stopped. "Wow.

Since the day I spread my dad's ashes. The day I met you—in both your human and your Panther shape." I watched a bird circle down from the top of a towering pine tree. "It feels like a lifetime ago."

"For me it was."

I looked into Jonah's eyes, as green as the forest would be in the lushness of summer, not so long from now. It was impossible to look back on that day now and not see everything that lay between then and now, the long journey we'd had to this point. After a moment, Jonah looked away and gazed over the trees and the shifting sunlight through the branches. "These woods . . . It's not just the magic. It's what happened here—what Heath did for me—that makes them sacred."

I squeezed his fingers, my throat too tight to answer. After a moment, we continued on, climbing over fallen logs and passing beneath trees whose branches were just beginning to blossom. The copse of birch trees appeared in the scattered sunlight, their trunks glowing like moonlight. I stood in the middle of them and breathed in deep. Heath's spirit was here, but it wasn't tainted like I'd thought it would be. It was a place of grace, as much as a church or temple was.

Because it wasn't just the place where Heath had died. It was the place where Jonah had been born.

From here we could hear the Waterfall tumbling over rocks, rushing end over end. We came through the brush and climbed out onto the large, flat rock. "God, it really is beautiful, isn't it?" Jonah said. "I don't think I've ever just sat back and appreciated its beauty."

It had been a long time since I'd done that, too—not since before my dad died. And as I sat there now, my back nestled against Jonah's chest, I knew that was what he'd want me to do now: appreciate it . . . and savor the hard battle we'd won to protect this place.

A Benandante was not on guard now; we'd agreed to take turns checking it once a day, just to be sure it was safe. Enough to keep my toe dipped into the Benandanti world, but not so much that I was stuck here forever. The Waterfall sparkled with Benandanti magic, a celestial web of light arching over it like a spun-glass bubble. Magic touched every corner of the site, from the shining stream above to the willow trees whose low branches hung like prisms caught in the sun. I knew that the other sites were like this now too, and that someday I'd get to see them all. I could do anything now, go anywhere, be anything I wanted.

Even in death, Heath had kept his promise to me.

I reached for my bag and drew out the small box inside. There were four such boxes. One had gone with Shen to take back to the Tibetan Temple. One with Nerina to bring to the Olive Grove. And one would go with me to France, where I'd scatter its contents over the lavender fields of Provence.

But this box belonged to Twin Willows.

I opened it carefully and stood. I waited a long

moment, breathing in the scent of water and pine all around me. And then the wind shifted, carrying a breeze from another land. The tree behind us bent in its wake and the sun shone through, dappling the water with warmth and light. I turned the box over.

Heath's ashes caught on the wind, danced there for an instant, and floated down to the water. Beside me, Jonah's breath caught. I turned. He held his hand out to me and I took it, twining our fingers together. Together, we watched the ashes swirl on the surface of the water. The stream carried them to the Waterfall, and there they became part of the magic forever.

For just a moment, the world seemed hushed all around us. Even the Waterfall. I could feel Heath everywhere, in the trees and the sky and the sacrifice he'd made for the beautiful boy I loved. Jonah pulled me in tight against him and I knew he could feel it too. We stood in stillness until the world came alive again. I could feel it all thrumming inside me, the magic of all seven sites brimming in my soul.

I tilted my face up to Jonah's. "Once more for posterity?" I whispered.

He bent his mouth to mine. Before the kiss was over, we'd dropped to the rock, our arms locked around one another. But our souls were gone.

I rose up, up, up and then dove fast, the wind whistling through my feathers. This power would always be mine, would always keep me separate. But it was glorious to have someone else to share it with.

Jonah ran below me, his long legs stretching out over the ground, his fur glistening in the sunlight. He tilted his head up, and his emerald eyes flashed at me.

Race you to the ocean?

You're on.

And we soared through the forest, the world laid out before us, full of endless possibility.